MEKONG COVENANT

The Jonah Wynchester Series of Vietnam War Novels
in order of publication:

Jonah's Cathedral
Mekong Covenant

MEKONG COVENANT

A Novel of the Vietnam War

R. D. Wall

YAJDEK PRESS

Mekong Covenant
Copyright 2018 by R. D. Wall
All rights reserved.
ISBN: 978-0-9988374-2-0
Library of Congress Control Number: 2018902424

All rights reserved. No part of this book may be reproduced or transmitted in any form or by any means, electronic or mechanical, including photocopying, recording, or by any information storage and retrieval system without the written permission of the publisher, except where permitted by law.

This book is a work of fiction, and the novel's story and characters are fictitious. Names, characters, businesses, events and incidents are the products of the author's imagination or are used fictitiously. Any resemblance to actual events or persons, living or dead, events or locales is purely coincidental. Long-standing institutions, agencies and public offices may be mentioned, but the characters involved are wholly imaginary.

Cover Photograph by R. D. Wall
Cover Design by James MacGhil
Author Photograph by Ivory Fine Art Portraits
Formatting by Nowick Gray of Hyperedits.com

YAJDEK PRESS
Tallahassee, Florida
www.rdwallauthor.com
author@rdwallauthor.com

Dedicated
to those who served
on the Large Slow Targets.
Semper Fortis

TABLE OF CONTENTS

Ship Description i

Chapter 1   Atlantic 3

Chapter 2   The Butterfly 31

Chapter 3   The Movie 57

Chapter 4   Pearl Harbor 91

Chapter 5   Westpac 118

Chapter 6   Chu Lai 156

Chapter 7   Spiritus 194

Chapter 8   Onsen 227

Chapter 9   Sayonara 268

Chapter 10 Covenant 302

Chapter 11 Mekong 335

About R. D. Wall 357

SHIP DESCRIPTION

USS Winchester County
Landing Ship Tank - 542 Class
Commissioned: 1944
Length: 327'   Beam: 50'   Draft: 14' 6"
Complement: 100
Displacement (Fully Loaded): 4,080 tons
Tank Deck: 230' long x 30' wide x 12' high = 6,900 square feet.
Propulsion: 2 General Motors V12-567, 900 HP Diesel Engines.
2 Propellers;   1,700 Shaft Horsepower;   Max Speed: 12 knots; Range: 14,000 Nautical Miles at 9 knots.
Armament in 1966: Two Bofors 40mm Twin guns; Various .50 caliber and .30 caliber machine guns.

CHAPTER 1
ATLANTIC

February 1966
Lat: 36° 14' 39" N   Long: 74° 58' 14" W

The LST plowed into the swell, struggled up the face of the huge wave, shuddered, came down the back side and rolled heavily to port. In the wheelhouse, Seaman Poldolski stood at the helm with his knees flexed and his paint-spattered boots spread wide apart on the steel deck, his big hands holding the rim of the wheel in a death grip. He watched in amazement as the arrow-shaped pointer on the clinometer slowly moved across the face of the dial, swinging from 10 degrees to 15 to 20 to 25 to 30 degrees, until the ship miraculously steadied. Then it started rolling in the opposite direction when the bow rammed into another swell and sent a shock wave rumbling though the ship, subjecting each steel frame and stringer to a flexing, twisting motion. As the shock wave continued traveling aft it rippled through compartments, the decks and bulkheads bouncing and vibrating, and when it reached the stern it whiplashed the fantail where the two gunner's mates, Wynchester and Brickey, were standing in the #2 gun tub. The effect lifted them two inches straight off the deck.

"Damn, this is crazy," shouted Brickey, holding tight to one of the barrels of the 40mm gun. "*McMann* might'a been a corkscrew, but this thing's unbelievable!" He turned and looked toward Jonah whose eyes were shut tight; sweat beaded on the gunner's forehead and a green tint was spreading across his face.

"Oh, God," Jonah said. "I gott'a get out'a this gun tub and find a more stable spot."

"Not sure that's possible," Brickey said and he turned and looked at the Gulf Stream's 14-foot swells, the wave tops blowing off to leeward from the 40 knot gusts. "At least we're going downwind," he added. "But these swells are for ... look out, here we go again!" he cried looking forward and he watched the bow slam into another swell, the shock wave traveling aft along the main deck, working its way to the stern of the ship. Again, they bounced upward and came back down on their feet.

"How long will this go on?" Jonah said sliding down onto the deck. He leaned back against the inside of the gun tub with his knees up to his chest and his head down into his crossed arms.

"Hey, Brickey!" a voice yelled over the noise of the wind and breaking seas. Mills appeared above the rim of the tub. "Ain't this a blast, man? I'm loving this!" the bosun's mate shouted.

"You're crazy!"

"Yea, I know," Mills laughed.

"Does this thing always jump around like this?"

"Nah," Mills said. "This ain't bad at all. Wait 'till it gets rough!"

"Gee, thanks man. I'm really glad to know that," Brickey said.

"Yea. Hey, listen I'm looking for Wynchester. You seen him?"

Brickey pointed to the inside of the tub and Mills looked down.

"Oh, Wynchester!" Mills said.

"What?" Jonah replied, not bothering to lift his head from his crossed arms.

"Mister Sanders wants to see you."

"Oh, no."

"Yea."

"Oh, God, not now!" Jonah grabbed the edge of the tub and pulled himself upright.

"Sorry 'bout that."

"Where is he?"

"In his stateroom."

Jonah suddenly turned, a look of panic on his face, and he reached down for an empty bucket and puked up the remnants of eggs, bacon and potatoes. He wretched again, and wretched again. Brickey looked away not wanting to see Jonah's face or the flying puke. Mills shook his head with a disgusted look, turned away and climbed down from the gun tub.

Jonah lurched across the gun tub, arriving at the forward edge just as the ship took another plunge into another wave, the shock forcing him bodily into the steel enclosure and he puked into the bucket again. Somehow, he found the fortitude to climb over the lip of the tub and down the ladder when a blast of wind and the ship's roll knocked him off balance. He staggered forward toward the galley and then into officer country, passing the ship's office where he saw Underwood busily typing away. How can anyone use a typewriter on a day like this, he thought, and he continued forward until he came to Sander's stateroom.

"Mister Sanders? You wanted to see me, sir?" Jonah said, holding on to the side of the doorway, looking into the small stateroom where Lieutenant junior grade Sanders, the Gunnery

Officer, was sitting at his desk. Sanders looked up from a stack of papers and saw the green gilled gunner's mate with the pink eyes and pale lips standing outside the green curtained doorway.

"Wynchester! What's the matter with you?" Sanders asked.

"I'm doing okay sir, all things considered," Jonah said, his stomach churning. The smells coming down the passageway from the galley made him wince.

"You don't look too good."

"No, sir."

"You sure you're okay?"

"Yes, sir."

"Okay. Regardless, we've work to do."

"Yes, sir."

"I need an inventory of all the small arms ammo by 1600 today."

"Today, sir?" Jonah asked, thinking that the closeness of the companionway and the smells were beginning to make his head spin.

"Yes, today! What's wrong with today? Just because it's a little breezy?"

"Uh, nothing sir."

Sanders face transformed from an uninviting glare into a smirk. "Okay, then get to it," and he looked at his watch. "You've got six hours."

"Yes, sir. By 1600, sir."

"That's all," Sanders said, and he looked back to the papers on his desk.

"Yes, sir." Jonah turned and staggered through the rolling passageway, bracing his hands on the bulkhead to keep him upright. *That sonov'a'bitch is on my back, he's on my back again,* he thought as he passed the ship's office.

Underwood stuck his head out of the open Dutch door. "Hey, Jonah! Hold up a second," Underwood said.

Jonah rolled his eyes and turned half way around. "What?" he asked, his face and posture clearly signaling he didn't want to spend one more minute in the confined, nauseating green passageway.

"You want'a play some gin tonight?" Underwood asked, puffing on a cigarette.

The smell of the burning tobacco made Jonah blanch. *I gotta get out'a here*, he thought. *I gotta get some fresh air*. "No thanks," he said and hurriedly walked out to the main deck, reaching the railing just in time to puke over the side as a blast of wind hit him, spraying the bile right back onto his boots.

≈≈

Chief Cunningham watched the XO move the pencil along the edge of the parallel ruler, drawing the line on the chart to mark the ship's course. "Sir," Cunningham said, holding the phone. "It's Mister Wilson in the engine room."

Crane laid the pencil on the chart table and shook his head, thinking *this can't be good*. "XO," he said into the phone.

"Sir, we got a problem down here," Ed Wilson, the Engineering Officer said.

"A problem?"

"Yes, sir. Port engine's heating up. Temp's climbing. Not sure what's causing it. We gotta shut it down and find out."

"You kidding me?" Crane said, his eyes wide open, thinking *those sonov'a'bitch engines, old, worn out pieces of ...*"

"No sir. It's beginning to heat up pretty bad. Approaching the red line."

"Port engine?"

"Yes sir."

"Heating up?"

"Yes, sir."

"What the hell's wrong with it?" Crane said, and as the ship took another roll he grabbed the edge of the chart table and braced his feet.

"Don't know, sir. Chief Beckers thinks it might be lube oil filters getting clogged from all this rolling and pitching. We'll need to shut it down and find the problem."

"Dammit!" Crane said, and he closed his eyes, a painful expression spreading across his face. "How long will that take?"

"Could be an hour. Could be longer, sir."

"This is a hell of a lousy time to be shutting down a damn engine!" The ship took another long roll and a parallel ruler, and several pencils slid across the chart table in the other direction. "Okay. Standby. I'll call you right back." Crane looked up to the overhead, his face turning into a sour grimace, and he dialed the captain.

"Sorry to bother you, Captain," Crane said.

"What 'ya got, Charlie?" the captain asked.

"Well, sir, I just got a call from Ed Wilson in the engine room."

"Yea?"

"Yes, sir. They've, uh ... they've got a situation with the port engine."

"A situation?"

"Yes, sir. The port engine's heating up and they've got to shut it down, and ..."

"What?"

"Yes, sir. Beckers thinks it might be a lube oil problem. Possibly the filters getting clogged from all the junk in the lines ... breaking free from the rolling and pitching, and he wants to ..."

"Bloody hell!" the captain said. BLAAMM! Crane distinctly heard something heavy slamming down onto a hard surface, then there was a long pause on the circuit. Crane listened, waited for the captain to speak, to break the silence.

"Sir?" Crane said, wondering if the phone's circuit was still open.

"Charlie," the captain said.

"Yes, sir?"

"How long will it take?"

Crane was beginning to feel he was staring into the barrel of a large gun. He was afraid to answer. "Uh, sir, Ed says an hour, maybe longer, sir."

"Hell and damnation!"

There was another long pause.

"Sir?"

"Dammit! We're going to roll around like a rubber duck out here!"

"Yes, sir."

"Meet me in the engine room!"

"In the engine room, sir?"

"Yes, dammit! In the engine room!" and the line went dead.

Oh, man, Crane thought, here we go, and he let out a deep breath. It's always something, now it's the engine room. "Grief!" he said out loud.

"Sir?" Cunningham asked, surprised at the XO's comment.

"I'll be in the engine room, Chief," Crane said trying to control his emotions in front of Cunningham. "Call me there if you need me," and Crane left the bridge and went quickly down two decks to the escape trunk and then carefully and slowly descended straight down through the narrow, claustrophobic space two more decks to the engine room.

Crane stepped off the bottom rung of the escape trunk ladder and onto the engine room deck plates. He was sweating profusely, a pallor beginning to spread across his face. He gripped the ladder, unwilling to let go. He hated being in the engine room. He was overwhelmed by the heat and the noise of machinery and the stink of diesel fuel and lube oil; the oppressive reek floating out of the bilges filled his nostrils. He thought he was going to be sick. Oh, God get me out of here. He saw several people huddled around the port engine; Ed Wilson the engineering officer, Win Jones the assistant engineering officer, Chief Beckers, several enginemen, machinist mates, an electrician, and the captain. The captain's broad back, bald head and thick neck were clearly evident in the center of the group. Jones turned and looked at him. Does he know I hate being down here, he thought, does he know I despise this place? He held tight to the ladder.

"So, Chief, let me get this straight," the captain was saying to Beckers as Crane cautiously made his way toward them, the ship taking deep, violent rolls. The captain saw Crane, saw the sickly green face. He shook his head in disgust and turned back to Beckers. "Are you telling me, Chief, that the gunk in the lines is breaking free because the ship is rolling and pitching?"

"Yes, sir," Beckers said. Wilson stood alongside Beckers, looking very nervous. Jones stood next to them holding on to a stanchion, watching and listening.

"And now you've got to shut down this engine?" the captain said and pointed to the starboard engine.

Wilson pointed to the other engine. "The port engine, sir."

"Hell," the captain said. "The PORT engine!" and looking exasperated he shook his head and pointed to the port engine.

"Yes, sir," Wilson said and nodded, trying to appear calm.

"Okay," the captain said. "So, we have to find the problem, that you THINK is contaminating the lube oil?"

"Yes, sir."

"In the port engine," and again he pointed to the port engine.

"Yes, sir."

"And you THINK you'll know within 30 minutes, and you THINK it'll take you another 30 minutes to get it running again?"

"Yes, sir. At a minimum. Could be longer, sir."

"Damnation!" the captain said, and he yanked a cigar from his shirt pocket and peeled off the cellophane wrapping. With a hand on his forehead he started walking a tight circle in the cramped engine room, turning and turning as he struggled with the problem.

"Okay," he suddenly said, and he pulled the cigar out of his mouth and turned toward the XO. "Go ahead and shut it down. And, Charlie?"

"Yes, sir," Crane said, his eyes wide, sweat running down his cheeks.

"Tell the OD ... who's the OD?"

"Uh, Sam Browning, sir."

"Tell Sam what's going on. Tell him to ring down starboard engine stop."

"Port engine, sir," Wilson interrupted.

"The damn PORT engine!" the captain yelled, his eyes hidden behind the sunglasses.

"Yes, sir."

"And Ed," the captain said turning to Wilson. "Keep the XO informed every step of the way. Do NOT hesitate to let him know of anything. Anything. You got that?"

"Yes, sir."

"Get started!"

"Yes, sir."

"Charlie," the captain took Crane by the arm and guided him to a corner near the log table.

"Yes, sir?" Crane was feeling very sick. His stomach was churning, the bulkheads spinning.

"Charlie," the captain said in a hushed tone. "Make sure you're on top of this."

"Yes, sir," Crane thought he was about to puke.

"Monitor this situation constantly. Let me know what's going on. I want to know everything. Everything." The captain walked uphill against the ship's roll and pulled his ponderous bulk up the ladder through the escape trunk.

Crane tried to calm himself, tried to control the nausea. Easy does it, he thought. Take it easy. The ship rolled sharply, and he was caught off balance again. He sensed the bile rising and his esophageal sphincter about to open. He desperately looked around him, afraid of what he might do if he couldn't find what he was looking for. There must be one here somewhere. God, where is it? He looked and looked, started to panic, then spied one under a work bench. He quickly went over to it, knelt down onto the deck plates and vomited into the galvanized bucket.

※

The officer pulled the green curtain closed, shutting off the compact stateroom from the passageway. Except for a dim light from the desk lamp, the stateroom was dark, and he braced his feet wide apart to keep the chair from sliding across the deck. As the ship took another roll he started writing with the blue duofold pen:

Diary #103
16 February 1966
0130 Hours ... At sea ... somewhere southeast of Hatteras

He looked up at the overhead, and once again counted the 9 electrical cables running through the bulkheads, and the two asbestos clad pipes; one pipe was stenciled "Fresh Water" with an arrow pointing aft. The other showed "Sea Water" flowing forward. He moved his head from side to side, and continued writing.

It's now 16 hours since we departed Little Creek...and a sad bereavement it was. Sad faces on the pier, sad faces on the ship. Rain. Wind. Overcast. Cold. Ugly. No one was happy. Not the crew, not the dependents, not the girlfriends, and certainly not the bars or liquor stores. Or the whores. Not anybody. And now we've been struggling through the Atlantic under one engine for what seems a lifetime...but in reality, it's only been an hour. The rumor mill is going non-stop. One theory says it's contaminated lube oil. Another that the filters are WWII vintage and have disintegrated. But the one that is receiving the most notoriety is that someone in the engine room sabotaged the system, so we'll have to go back to Norfolk. Makes sense to me.

Pushing this barge through a seaway as bad as this with both engines is the most masochistic experience I can imagine. Trying to do it on only one engine comes close to self-flagellation. Whoever designed the LST should be found certifiable, for their crazed mind was obviously unable to perceive normal cognitive behavior.

I hear we're averaging just over four knots, and that's downwind! Slightly more than a good walking pace. God forbid we should turn around or the wind should shift into the south! We'd be in a heap of trouble. We wallow around in the swells, the proverbial hog in the pigsty, grunting, snorting, plowing our way through, making headway one yard at a time, with the most uncomfortable ride imaginable. Roll, plunge, shudder, blamm, bang, stutter, and roll again. The number of seasick crew is appalling. Harvey Hobson, our new ensign extraordinaire, is flat prone on the deck in his stateroom. The XO's visage is very offensive, and the rank eau de cologne wafting through the passageway from the galley is enough to make the strongest cast iron stomach blanch.

The horse named "Chaos" is coming around the club house turn.

De nauta illa admirabilis vitae.

※

"I hear we're lost," Davant said inserting a fork full of string beans into his mouth with one hand as he held his coffee cup with the other, his feet braced far out from his chair against the roll of the ship.

"More than usual?" Browning asked, and then looking down to the end of the wardroom table as the ship started rolling back the other way he said, "Excuse me, Harvey? Would you mind passing the potatoes?"

Harvey Hobson, his face an odd shade of green, reached for the bowl of potatoes sliding across the tablecloth.

"Scuttlebutt says..." Davant swallowed, "...that the Loran is acting up. It's on strike, not wanting to navigate us to the canal, or contribute in any way to finding our position. Soon the XO will be relying entirely on the sextant."

"Must be retribution," Browning said. The 1st Lieutenant sliced the potatoes into small pieces. "For all our past sins."

"Possibly future sins as well," Davant said, looking around the table at Browning and Hobson. Johnston, the Operations Officer, sat near the end of the table eating with his usual abandon, concentrating deep into another manual, his left hand keeping his plate from sliding.

"I'm late," Sanders said as he came into the wardroom. "Mendoza? Coffee, ASAP."

"Your absence was noted, and demerits have been issued," Davant said, holding up his fork with a potato stabbed onto the tines.

"That damn gunner," Sanders took his seat, shaking his head.

"The gunner?" Davant asked.

"Yea, Wynchester. That guy's sicker than some drunk who just staggered out of a saloon. He's about as worthless as Dorsey's meatloaf."

"What's going on?" Browning asked.

"This morning, right after quarters, I asked him for an inventory," Sanders spooned beans onto his plate. "Inventory of all the small arms ammo. Asked for it by the end of the day. And now..." and he looked at his watch. "...it's after 1700. No report. No nothing. The guy's worthless."

"Maybe he'll feel better tomorrow., Browning said. "After all, it's eight days before we reach the canal, why not give him a break? "

"Who the hell are you telling me what to do?" Sanders snapped back with an ugly sneer, a knife in one hand, a fork in the other, and he glared back at Browning. Everyone in the wardroom stopped what they were doing and looked at Sanders. Even the focused Johnston was interrupted from his reading and looked up, his mouth wide open. The stewards stood silently in the corner, averting their eyes. Ensign Hobson with a look of shock, sat frozen in his chair. Browning returned a lethal stare back at Sanders.

"Ahem," Davant mumbled and the captain entered the wardroom. Chairs scraped across the deck as everyone stood.

"Please, gentlemen, please," the captain said, sweeping his hands magnanimously, and he sat down in his chair at the head of the table. "The XO is busy trying to get the Loran working again, so he won't be joining us. Thank you, Mendoza," he said as the steward placed a cup of coffee in front of him. "And just how is everyone today?" he asked adding cream and sugar. "Are you getting settled, Harvey?" the captain looked at Hobson. The ensign quickly sat bolt upright, his spine straight as an arrow, aligned with the back of his chair, his eyes bulging in the captain's direction, his hands hidden under the table.

"Uh, yes, sir, fine, sir," he said, his eyes glued on the heavy man in the sunglasses sitting at the opposite end of the table.

"Excellent, excellent," the captain said. "Uh, Mendoza?"

"Yes, sir?" Mendoza said.

"What bread do you have?"

"Bread, sir?"

"Yes. What kind of bread."

"Uh, white bread, sir."

"White?"

"Yes, sir."

"Any cheese?"

"Yes, sir."

"What kind'a cheese?"

"Uh, American, sir."

"Excellent. Could you fix me a grilled cheese sandwich?"

"Yes, sir."

"Excellent."

"With two slices of cheese, please?"

"Yes, sir."

"And burn the toast."

"Yes, sir."

"Excellent."

"Well, Len," the captain said, looking at Davant. "I'll bet you're glad to finally get your 1st class storekeeper."

"Yes, sir. Glad indeed," Davant said, laying his fork down and wiping his chin. "I think he'll be a great addition to the supply department."

"Excellent. What's his name?"

"O'Toole, sir. Came from a tin can."

"O'Toole. Excellent," the captain said. "And, Harvey?" the captain said looking at Hobson at the end of the table. "How's your new damage controlman?"

"Uh, yes sir, I think, I think he'll be an excellent controlman, sir," Hobson said, licking his lips and blinking his eyes, moving his head in short, rapid twitches, as a chicken would look for corn. The captain frowned, and his eyebrows dropped to a severe angle above the sunglasses. Everyone at the table carefully watched the captain and Hobson. Johnston had a hand covering his mouth. Sanders stared across the table at the new ensign. Davant glanced at Browning who caught his knowing look, eyebrows up, a thin smile on his lips.

"Hmmm," the captain said. "Ah, Mendoza, more coffee if you please."

"Yes, sir," Mendoza said.

"Well, I'm sorry," the captain said, and he took a big bite of the cheese sandwich. "Shory I wasn't abl ta be at the par'y." Everyone sat silent. Sanders chewed his food as he looked at the captain out of the corner of his eye. Hobson was beginning to look very sick. Browning pushed his plate aside and slid his coffee cup in front of him. Davant appeared as if he was going to say something but quickly suppressed the urge. "Sounds as if it was a good one, hmm?" the captain added.

"Yes, sir," Browning said. "A very good party," and he looked at Davant who had to force himself from smiling.

"Excuse me," Wilson said entering the wardroom, his shirt and pants stained with oil, his steamer cap smudged with grease.

"Ed, what's the news?" the captain asked.

"Starboard engine is operable again, sir," he said taking his seat to the Captain's left.

"Excellent. What was it?"

"Several things, sir. Bad batch of filters, junk in the line, and a valve that wouldn't open all the way. But now it's working smooth as silk. Shouldn't cause us any further problems. We'll be ready to answer all bells in 15 minutes max." He slowly slumped into his chair and exhaled.

"Excellent, Ed. Excellent."

"All the credit should go to Chief Beckers and the snipes," Wilson continued, as he wiped the sweat from his face with a handkerchief. "They worked their tails off," and he laid a clean napkin on his oily trousers and then spooned salad onto his plate.

"Excellent," the captain said.

"And, Win Jones is the one who solved the big mystery."

"Oh?"

"Yes, sir. After we got the filters replaced, the gunk out of the line, and still had flow problems, it was Jones who figured out the problem with the valve. The guy's a genius."

"Excellent. That's great news. Great news, indeed."

"I'm sure glad he was there today," Wilson added. "We probably would'a found the problem eventually, but he zeroed in on it faster than a bird dog sniffing quail in the brush."

"Excellent," the captain said, and he stood up. The other officers stood. "Please," he said, lifting his plate from the table. "Please go ahead and enjoy your meal. I find I have some paperwork waiting for me so I'll finish my sandwich in my cabin. Again, good job, Ed. Good job."

"Thank you, sir," Wilson said.

"Uh, Mendoza?" the captain said.

"Yes, sir?"

"Bring a small pot of coffee to my cabin, please. Good night gentlemen," and he walked out of the wardroom.

No sooner had the captain departed, when there was a knock, and everyone turned and looked at a tall, thin, grimy, young fireman apprentice standing in the doorway, his dirty ball cap in his hands. "Excuse me, sir, Mister Wilson?"

"What is it, Lithgow?" Wilson said.

"Uh, s-s-sir," the sailor stuttered. "Mister Jones, uh, sent me to report, sir, uh," and he stood paralyzed in fear, completely motionless.

"Go on ..." Wilson said.

"Yes, sir, to report, uh ..." He paused again and then he took a breath and rapidly belted out the message, "... that both bells are answering ready to stand by all engines. Sir."

Wilson shook his head and looked around the table with an embarrassed, exasperated expression. "Thank you, Lithgow. I got it. Tell Mister Jones I got the message."

※

"I can't hear you!" Mills yelled over the noise of the air hammers, his right hand cupping his ear as he bent his head to listen to the Seaman Apprentice.

"Biagotti wants you!" the SA yelled back. "He's in the paint locker!"

Mills nodded his head, raised his hand in acknowledgment and walked aft through the tank deck thinking this painting business was going on forever. He sidestepped sailors busting rust and painting red lead, while others spread a light green paint across the bulkheads.

"This is never going to end!" he said, and he walked into the paint locker where Biagotti was handing a gallon can of haze gray paint to Jonah.

"Wha? Waz not gonna end?" Biagotti asked, holding a clipboard in one hand and pencil in the other, a very disagreeable look on his face. Jonah stepped back to allow some space between the two bosun's mates.

"This fucken painting business," Mills answered.

"What do you mean this fucken painting business?"

"When's it going to end?"

"What you mean when's it going 'ta end?"

"When are we going to be able to stop all this painting?"

"Well, Mills," Biagotti removed the stubby cigar from his teeth. "What you expect? This here's a navy ship! And you'z a navy bosun's mate! And the purpose of navy bosun's mates is to splash fucken paint on fucken navy ships! So, stop complaining for shit's sake! Otherwise, go become a cook or something!" Jonah took another step back, not wanting to get in the direct line of the fire breathing Biagotti.

"Well, excuse me!" Mills said with an indignant look. "I didn't know you were affected by the full moon?"

"Mills!" Biagotti said, his face turning red as the big 1st class bosun glared at the smaller 2nd class bosun. "One more shitty remark from you'z," and he pointed his cigar straight at Mills' face. "And you'z going on report! Report!" he repeated. "You'z got that?"

Mills stood in the doorway, his arms folded, a wicked, angry look on his face. He glanced at Jonah and then looked back to Biagotti and he said nothing.

"Got that?" Biagotti said, and Mills nodded his head.

"Okay," Biagotti said. "The reason you'z here is 'cause the 1st Lieutenant wants to make sure we make some progress on the starboard side of the tank deck bulkheads before we reach the canal. That's four days from now. Four days. And you'z and me gonna make that happen, or my name's not Angelo Fiore Biagotti. Got it?" And Mills silently nodded again.

"Hey, thanks for the paint," Jonah said, and he quickly left the two bosuns standing in the locker.

"Okay," Biagotti said and he unfolded a sheet of paper and laid it across the top of a 5 gallon pail of paint.

"What's this?" Mills asked, his eye squinting as he looked down at the paper with circles and lines and arrows.

"Dis here is the master plan," Biagotti said, holding up his chin, a know-it-all look on his face. "Now, pay attention," and he pointed his huge hand at the paper. "We now paint'n up here, near frame 22. Like 'dis," and he moved his hand from side to side and then down the paper. "In order to meet Mister Browning's deadline, we gotta get all 'dis painted, all the way to frame 40 before the canal. And then after the canal up to 'dis frame by next Tuesday, 'dis here by Wednesday, and finish up by the end of Thursday. And then we start on the port side."

"Pheew!" Mills said through his pursed lips, scratching his head through his ball cap. "That's a mighty big job!"

"Yea, no shit!" Biagotti said. "But we can do it. We got the whole deck force on the job. Every boot, every seaman, plus you and Ross. Except for 'doz people on watch."

"And what about you?" Mills said, looking sideways at Biagotti as a dubious dog would look at a treacherous cat. "What about you? Are you gonna be painting too?"

"Don't you'z worry 'bout me," Biagotti said, his lips curled. "You'z just worry 'bout you'z."

Mills nodded with an exasperated expression. "Okay, Mister Big," he said. "You're the boss. We paint up to frame 40 before the canal," and he gave Biagotti a left-handed salute and walked out of the paint locker.

"Yea," Mills mumbled to himself as he went forward through the tank deck. "Yea, no need to worry about me. You just you worry about you, Angelo-big-ass-Biagotti!"

∽∾

"Man, I'm loving this, we got the best seat in the house," Mills said, standing in the forward gun tub as he looked down at the Panama Canal pilot boat coming alongside.

"The Canal is sure a long way from Little Creek," Jonah said.

"And getting hot!"

"Feels good," Jonah said. "After all that cold and wind and gray skies and rolling my guts out. This sun is nice, real nice."

"And as soon as that sun gets higher it's gonna be warmer than the inside of one of Dorsey's soup pots. Feel that humidity?"

"Looks like a lot of people are skipping breakfast this morning."

"There's your buddy," Mills said looking aft at some of the crew standing at the railings, and Jonah turned around.

"Mister Zero," Jonah said.

"Zero? Is that what you call O'Toole?" Mills asked with a wide-eyed expression.

"Yea, Zero. And there's Smitty."

"Smitty? Who's he?"

"Postal clerk. One of O'Toole's gangsters."

"He doesn't look like much."

"Don't let that fool you. He may look innocent, but he's devious as hell."

"That little dough boy? What's his deal?"

"He keeps the books for O'Toole's slush fund."

"No shit?"

"Yep."

"He came from your other ship?"

"Yep."

"Did he have a big operation?"

"Monstrous."

"A lot of cash?"

"Must'a been."

"O'Toole trusts him?"

"Absolutely," Jonah said, lighting a cigarette.

"How come?"

"He and O'Toole are cousins."

"No shit?"

"Yep. His little fat cousin."

"YAJDEK," Mills said shaking his head.

"Say, what's the word on Hobson?" Jonah asked as they watched Ensign Hobson escort the canal pilot along the main deck.

"Homer says he's a bumbling idiot," Mills answered. "Can't find his way around the ship, gets lost, seasick most of the way south. Pretty wet behind the ears I guess."

"I can sympathize with the seasick part," Jonah said.

They looked out at the muddy tan colored water and toward the town warming in the rising sun.

"So how long will it take us to go through the canal?"

"Biagotti says about eight hours," Mills said. "We should be in Rodman around 1500."

"Liberty, here I come," Brickey said as he climbed into the gun tub.

"You better keep an eye on that guy," Mills said looking at Brickey with a devilish smile.

"You got that right," Jonah said. "The virgin gunner of Winchester Cathedral."

"What?" Mills asked, astonished. "Brickey, is that true?"

"I'm 'fraid so," Brickey said with a sheepish grin "But not for long!"

"Damn. I didn't know there was such a thing!"

"Another miracle of Navy life," Jonah said laughing.

"Hey," Mills said. "I gotta go. It's gonna get busy going through these locks. I'll see ya later." They watched Mills climb down out of the gun tub and walk aft along the main deck.

"I heard he kept Rat in his place when you and O'Toole were going at it outside the Cesspool," Brickey said.

"Yea, he and Poldolski had Rat boxed in. But I didn't see 'em. I was kind'a busy."

"Damn! I never, never thought I'd see O'Toole again," Brickey said with a disgusted look. "I thought those guys were history."

"Me too." Jonah had a faraway look in his eyes.

"So, what are you gonna do about them?"

Brickey's question put Jonah into deep thought. After a long pause he finally said, "Well, for one thing, I ain't gonna play poker with 'em, that's for sure. Don't get me wrong. I like poker, the strategy, the mental part of the game. But not with O'Toole. Playing with those guys is the closest thing to playing with the devil himself. And secondly, I'm gonna keep as far away from 'em as possible."

"Won't that be hard to do, on the ship I mean?"

"Maybe, but I figure they'll be busy doing their jobs and we won't have any interaction. Besides they won't risk doing anything on the ship; too many khaki uniforms around. O'Toole won't risk that."

"What about on the beach?"

"That's a different story. I'll have to take that as it comes. But I can tell 'ya one thing. I've lost too much on account of those guys. I lost my 1st class stripes and I lost the best girl I ever had. And that ain't never gonna happen again."

The ship moved slowly through Limon Bay, toward the Gatun Locks. Those crew who weren't on watch lined the rails, looking out on the brilliant green of the Panamanian rain forest and the village of Colon. Fishing boats went out the bay, pilot boats went from ship to ship, and something they hadn't seen before cruised by; a boat with its guns bristling.

"Look at that," Brickey said pointing to the Navy Swift Boat. "First time I've seen one of those."

"Yea, they look all business," Jonah said. "Must be here to protect the canal."

"Or to get a sun tan," a voice said, and they both turned and watched Underwood's face appear above the rim of the gun tub.

"I thought you were on the conn with the phones." Jonah said.

"Fugit has this morning's watch. I go on at noon," Underwood explained as he climbed over the rim of the tub. "This is Holt, The Volt," Underwood said introducing a 2nd class petty officer with a Nikon camera hanging from a strap around his neck. "We were on a DE together, before *McMann*," Underwood explained and turned and pointed at the two gunners. "Wynchester and Brickey."

"The Volt?" Jonah said surprised at the name.

"Radioman," Underwood explained.

"Oh, right," and Jonah nodded in recognition. "Yea, right. I got it. The Volt. A radioman. That's a good one."

"Thanks. It's my moniker, but not of my design," The Volt said and Jonah's face screwed up into a question mark. "So you're the famous Wynchester," Volt asked taking off his glasses and wiping them on his shirt sleeve. "I've seen you working on the 40s."

"Yep, that's me," Jonah said, and he looked at Underwood with a sly grin.

"When Dorsey told me..." Volt said, putting his glasses back on. "...that somebody by the name of Wynchester had come aboard the Winchester Cathedral I almost choked on my coffee."

"Didn't know I had such a powerful effect on people," Jonah said. "How long you been here?"

"Six months and 14 days," and Volt looked as his watch, and 12 hours."

Jonah's eyes widened. "How's Mister Johnston to work for?"

"Easy going. Knows his stuff. I like him," Volt said matter of factly. "And you and Sanders?"

"Hmm. That's another story," Jonah said frowning, looking back and forth between Volt and Underwood. Brickey stood at the rim of the tub watching the scenery.

"Yes, I figured that would be the case," Volt said.

"Here we go," Brickey said and they all turned and looked forward as the ship started entering the Gatun approach canal, heading for the first lock.

"Have you been through the canal before?" Volt asked as he moved to the forward rail of the tub.

"Never," Jonah said. "You?"

"Yes, just over a year ago. Round trip. It's a fascinating piece of engineering. A Frenchman, name of de Lesseps, started to build it in the late 1880s, but he gave up...obviously not up to the task."

"Sounds like the French," Underwood said.

"Then," Volt continued as he looked to starboard. "Teddy Roosevelt took over in 1904 and finished it 10 years later. They moved a lot of dirt and poured a lot of concrete. And here we are going through it 52 years later," and he quickly lifted his camera and focused the long 300mm lens on something on the green shore, waited a moment, watching carefully, and then pressed the shutter. The motor drive engaged, snapping off 1, 2, 3, 4 shots in quick succession. Brickey's face lit up and his eyes grew wide as he looked at the camera. The Volt saw Brickey's astonished look and said, "It's a motor drive. Advances the film ten times faster than you can do it manually."

"What did you just take a picture of?" Brickey asked, puzzled, his head cocked to one side, looking out to the shoreline and then back to the camera.

"A quinquenervis."

"A what?"

"A quinquenervis."

"What's that?"

"A species of orchid."

"Orchid?" Brickey said with an incredulous look.

"Yes, I like orchids."

"No kidding?"

"It might be of the genus gongora."

"The who?"

"Genus gongora. They're common in some parts of Central America, but somewhat rare in Panama. I got some really nice shots of one last time I went through the canal."

Brickey's face contorted into astonishment, with the look of someone who's just learned an impossible to believe fact. Jonah appeared confused. Underwood just stood there, his arms crossed, a knowing smile on his face

"So," Volt continued without missing a beat, pointing forward as if he was a tour guide. "Gatun Lock, up there, is the first of three sets of locks. From the Caribbean side, the Gatun Locks will raise us up 85 feet to the level of Gatun Lake," and he waved his arms from seaward toward the land, and then down and up again as if he was conducting the rising water in the locks. "Then we'll travel through the lake and then through the Culebra Cut," his arms now moving from left to right. "That was a huge earth moving project. Then we go through two more locks, Pedro Miguel and Miraflores, where we'll drop down to the level of the Pacific," and he bent his knees slightly as he lowered his arms. "And then we're at Rodman."

Jonah and Brickey looked at Volt with their mouths open, trying to understand just who this guy was. Underwood nodded and chuckled.

"Woody," Jonah said looking at Underwood and then Volt."What duty section are you guys in?"

"Starboard," Underwood said, and The Volt nodded in agreement.

"Perfect. Let's hit the beach together."

"I don't know about The Volt, but I've got a shit load of registered mail coming aboard at Rodman, I'll check with the XO," Underwood said.

"Great, and how 'bout you, Volt?" Jonah said looking at the radioman. "Since you've been here before, you know all the best places."

"Sounds good to me," Volt said. "The *Mariposa* is probably the best, and not many sailors know about it because it's out of the way."

"The what?"

"*La Mariposa*. The Butterfly."

"Good place?"

"The best."

"Good look'n girls?"

"Affirmative."

"Can we get one for Brickey?"

"Hablare con la mamacita," Volt said. "Ella lo encontrara la mejor chica."

"What?"

"I'll speak to the mamacita," Volt translated. "She'll fix him up."

"Damn," Jonah said. "He speaks Spanish!" he said looking at Underwood. "You're okay, Volt."

"You're welcome," Volt said as he looked through the camera's viewfinder again.

"And this is gonna be Brickey's big initiation night," Jonah said.

The Volt lowered the camera and turned around to look at Jonah. "Big initiation?"

"Yup," Jonah said. "He's gonna lose his cherry."

"Really?" The Volt asked. "A virgin?"

"Yep, he's a virgin. And all the drinks are on me."

"You're kidding?"

"Nope."

"Well, then, definitely count me in. I can't ask for a better deal than that. A virgin, huh?"

"And Homer is gonna join us," Jonah said.

"Perfect. Homer is always good to have along on liberty," Volt said.

"Okay then. So, we'll meet you on the quarterdeck at 1900?"

"Roger that," Volt said, and he turned back to look at the passing shore through the camera's viewfinder. He focused the long lens once again and snapped off another six shots, the motor drive wheezing and clicking in rapid succession. Brickey stood behind him, squinting in the sun's hot glare, looking out along the direction The Volt was aiming the lens, trying to catch a glimpse of the rare, elusive quinquenervis as the ship slowly moved into the first of the Gatun locks.

CHAPTER 2

THE BUTTERFLY

"Cuanto para La Mariposa?" The Volt said to the taxi driver, asking how much to take them to the The Butterfly.

The driver smiled back, his crooked teeth covered in tobacco stains, and he turned and looked at the other sailors. "Veinte dolares, senor," he said with a big grin.

Volt frowned, shook his head, thinking 20 dollars was outlandish. "Diez," he said, offering 10.

The driver's smile quickly disappeared and was replaced with the look of someone who just encountered an adversary. "No senor," the driver said in a sing song voice, his hands turned up, indicating he couldn't do that. "No puedo hacer eso," he said shaking his head. "Quince," he countered.

Volt shook his head, mumbling, "Fifteen dollars?" He peered into the cab, looking closely at the dirty floor and the ripped seats. "Robo! Y sus asientos estan rotas," Volt complained about the condition of the cab and countered with 12 dollars. "Doce."

The driver peered up at The Volt with a belligerent look, shook his head and frowned.

"Okay, if that's what you think," Volt said and then he turned toward the others sitting in the back seat. "Hey, you guys, start gett'n out of the cab, but real slow. Real slow." Homer looked at Jonah and Brickey in the back seat, and Underwood up front, and motioned for them to slowly follow him out of the cab.

"Okay, senor," Volt said, and he put his hands up in mock surrender. "Pondremos otro taxi." Volt straightened himself up and waved to the next taxi waiting in the line, motioning for him to drive over.

"No, no!" the driver suddenly cried. "Doce," he said. "Por favor, senor. Doce."

"Doce dolares?" Volt asked.

"Si, senor. Doce! Doce dolares!"

"Okay. Que bueno. Doce." Volt said, and he looked over at Underwood, Jonah, Homer and Brickey who were now standing outside the cab, not understanding the Spanish that was flying back and forth. "Okay, guys. Get back in. We're going in this one."

"What the hell was that all about?" Underwood asked as the cab drove down the pier and crossed the huge steel arch Bridge of the Americas spanning the canal entrance.

"A little exercise in Panamanian bargaining," Volt said. "It's one of my favorite games," and he took off his glasses and wiped them on the sleeve of his white jumper, then looked over to Brickey. "It'll be about a 10-minute ride, Brickey," and he put the glasses back on. "So, you better start girding your loins."

"Hey, Brickey," Jonah said. "You got your equipment?"

"Yea," Brickey said, looking embarrassed. "Doc gave me five. You think that'll be enough?"

"Five?" Homer laughed. "Shit! If that ain't enough, I don't know what is! If you use five, you'll tie the record."

"The record?" Underwood asked.

"Yea," Homer said. "The only guy I know who went through five in one night was a sawed off, pee-wee Puerto Rican cook we had on that AK. We called him the Spanish Flea."

"Spanish Flea! That's funny," Volt laughed.

"Yea." Homer continued. "And when he went back the second night and the girls seen him coming in the front door, they all run out the back door."

The cab wound its way up and up and around and down and Volt described various places of interest along the route, the others looking completely lost and bewildered. Jonah was beginning to get car sick and was about to ask the driver to pull over when they drove into a small, narrow street and came to a stop against the curb. Thank God, Jonah thought, a greenish tint on his neck.

"Ok, guys," The Volt said as he paid the driver the 12 bucks plus a two-dollar tip. The driver's face lit up as bright as a neon sign. "Hey, you guys! Listen up. Here's the deal," Volt said. "Since we're here for a night of liberty, and most importantly for Brickey's initiation, if you want, I'll do the translating."

"You're in charge." Jonah said, and the others nodded in approval.

"But first, let's walk around the old town and try out a few bars," Volt suggested, striking a match and lighting a cigarette.

"Good idea," Homer piped in. "I'm thirsty as hell in all this heat." They started walking down the narrow street lined with 2 story buildings and overhanging balconies with wrought iron railings. They stepped over gutters flowing with greasy water and unidentified objects, the fetid smell filling their nostrils, and as they passed by various store fronts they looked through open doorways into noisy courtyards and the busy interiors of barber shops, bars and small restaurants. And everywhere they went in their white uniforms they were propositioned by the girls in short shorts, high heels, low cut blouses and copious makeup.

"What you name, sailor boy?" a dark-skinned redhead said through bright red lips.

"Who me?" Homer asked, stopping in his tracks, looking back at the girl.

"Si, you," she said.

"Well, honey, I'm called Big Balls."

"Que?"

"Big Balls," Homer repeated.

"Beeg Bulls?"

"Ha ha. Beeg Bulls!" Jonah said. "That's a good one, Homer. Beeg Bulls!"

"Hey, Homer," The Volt interrupted. "This way. There's better ones at The Butterfly. Come on, let's get a drink in here first," and Volt led them into a bar. "Hey, listen up," Volt said. "Let's have a couple of drinks here, then we'll walk over to The Butterfly and find Mamacita. Besides the drinks are cheaper here."

"Sounds like a plan," Jonah said. "What ya think Brickey, you okay with that? How 'bout you, Beeg Bulls?"

"Yea. I'm good," Brickey answered.

"The first round is on me," Homer said laughing and taking a seat at a table and motioning to the waitress. "What you having Brickey, rum and coke? How bout you Volt?"

"Un seco con vaca, por favor," Volt said looking up at the mahogany colored waitress standing next to the table in her shorts, tank top and flip flops.

"What did you say?" Jonah asked.

"A seco con vaca. Strong white rum distilled from sugar cane. Poured over coconut milk, on the rocks."

"Damn, man, I gotta try one of those!" and Jonah wrung his hands together.

"You can count me in," Homer said looking around the bustling bar full of people of every stripe; orientals, whites, black, various shades of coffee colors.

"How bout you Woody?" Volt asked.

"Perfect."

"Brickey?"

"Uh, I'd better stick to plain 'old rum. After that last adventure in Naples, I don't want'a mix my octanes."

"Good idea," Jonah agreed. "Besides, you'll need all your energy if you're gonna make it through the night."

"Boy, it's hot and humid, ain't it?" Homer asked of no one in particular. "I thought Norfolk could get hot, but it ain't noth'n compared to this," and he wiped his face and neck with a paper napkin, then held his head up to the ceiling fan blowing hot air across the room.

"I guess it would take a while to adjust to this," Jonah said. "But it sure is better than some of that freezing cold shit we had in Little Creek."

"Speak for yourself," Homer chimed in. "Hey, Volt, give us the skinny on Mamacita and The Butterfly."

"Well, everybody has their favorites, but The Butterfly is definitely on the top of my list. Small place, nice girls, reasonable prices, and if you get too shit faced, well, they've got rooms where you can sleep it off. And they'll always see to it that you get back to the ship in time."

"So, what's it gonna cost?" Brickey asked.

"For you, Brickey?" Jonah said. "They probably won't charge you too much since you're a beginner."

"The girls always like beginners," Underwood said with a sly grin, and he polished his glasses.

"Yea, Brickey," Homer Said. "You virgins don't last too long, so the girl gets less bang for her buck."

"Ha, that's funny," Jonah said. "Less bang for her buck. Ha ha."

Brickey's freckled face started to turn red.

"Uh, oh. Here we go," Homer said as the waitress approached them with a tray of drinks.

"Man, that looks good," Jonah sniffed into the frosted glass of milky liquid, a curl of icy vapor floating off the surface.

"Here's to the Virgin Brickey," Underwood said holding up his icy glass.

"Yea, to the Virgin Brickey," they all clinked glasses.

"Hmmm. That's powerful," Jonah licked his lips.

"Damn," Homer said after taking a mouth full. "I think I can feel my brain dissolving."

"Better take it slow, Homer. You're drinking 70-proof," Volt said, lighting up a cigarette.

"Seventy?" Jonah said in surprise. "You kidding?"

"Nope. Seventy."

"Thanks for the warning," Homer took a very small sip and put the glass back on the table. "No need to get plastered with the first drink. Right?"

"Hey, look at that," Brickey whispered, motioning toward the rear of the bar.

"Well I'll be damned," Homer said quietly and they all turned toward the far corner of the bar to see Mister Browning sitting alone at a table, sipping from a glass of amber liquid, his cigarette burning in an ashtray.

"Man," Jonah said in a hushed tone. "I never expected to see him in here."

"He's been known to get into his booze," Volt explained. "You should'a seen him down in San Juan. Man oh, man, he tied one on almost every night. The captain put him in hack for a week."

"I didn't know he was a boozer," Jonah said.

"Oh, yea," The Volt said. "He likes his rum, that's for sure."

"Hey, you seen that crack in the main deck?" Homer said, changing the subject.

"A crack in the main deck? Where?" Jonah said with a look of disbelief.

"Yea," Homer continued. "I didn't believe it myself. Remember that day we were getting our butts kicked off Hatteras, when we were under one engine? You remember?"

"How could I forget," Jonah said.

"Well, it was Biagotti I guess, had noticed it from below, down in the tank deck, and sent a messenger to the OD. And then Mister Wilson had me go take a look at it. I went down to the tank deck and found Biagotti. He was looking up at the underside of the main deck and water was streaming through from several places, aft of the deck ramp."

"Man! How come we didn't hear about this?" Jonah asked.

"Shit if I know, but yuz hearing 'bout it now. So, I'm standing there, you see, under this shower of water with Biagotti and Mister Wilson and we're all looking up at this thing and every time the ship hits a wave this crack closes and the water stops. And then when the ship passes over the wave I guess it bends the ship the other way and the damn crack opens up again and the water starts squirting through again. We're all standing there, you know, like a bunch of dumb asses just look'n up at this thing, cause, you know, it's sort of memorizing."

"You mean mesmerizing," Underwood said.

"Yea, mesma ... or whatever. Anyway, I didn't like the looks of it cause I'm think'n that if that crack is doing that in this seaway, what the hell would it do if it really got shit stinking rough, ya know? And I can see Mister Wilson looking at it and he don't look too good, you know, he looks kinda worried sorta and then I looks at Biagotti and he looks like's he's gonna have kittens, you know sort'a like he wants to find somewhere else to be other than standing under this thing. So, Mister Wilson looks at me and says to me, he says, Homer, and I says, yes sir? And he says Homer can you weld that together? And I look at Mister Wilson, and then I look at the crack opening and closing and opening and closing and the water coming through the crack and I'm thinking how the hell am I gonna weld that shut if the damn thing keeps moving around like that?"

"So, what did you say?" Jonah asked.

"Well," and Homer paused and took a sip of his drink. "I was kind'a think'n, you know, embarrassed to say exactly what I was think'n. So's Mister Wilson asks the same question again and I have to find a way to explain all that to him," and Homer took another sip of the seco con vaca.

"And then what?" Volt asked.

"And then I guess I figured I had nut'n to lose so I just opened my big mouth and said that I couldn't do it. At least until the ship stopped bouncing around."

"Shit, how come we didn't know anything about this," Jonah asked, looking back and forth between Homer and the Volt. "I mean, come on, the ship is breaking in two and we don't know? God Almighty."

"Probably best that we didn't know at the time," Volt said. "So that's what you were doing up there when we finally got out of the bad weather?"

"Exactly," Homer continued. "We had kept our eye on it. Me and two other guys took turns watching it. One hour on, two hours off. Looking and looking. Never took our eyes off it. Good thing for us it didn't get no worse. Once things calmed down we welded it back together with some big angles underneath."

"So, how's it now?" Underwood asked.

"Well, hell," Homer said with a look of superiority across his face, his chest inflating. "The damn thing's better now than it was when the tub was built 23 years ago, cause now it's got more steel under it!"

"Jeezum," Jonah said. "I sure hope so."

"Uh, oh," the Volt said and they all turned to watch Mister Browning get up from his table and start walking toward the bar, asking the waitress something. Browning came closer and closer and then walked through a doorway with a sign overhead; "Bano".

"He didn't even notice us," Underwood said.

"He don't look so good," Homer added.

"Poor guy, he's really messed up," Jonah said.

"Let's get out'a here and get to The Butterfly," and the Volt stood up. He mashed his cigarette into the ashtray and lifted the glass to his mouth, downing the last of the smoking milky liquid.

⁂

"Damn, this place is something else," Homer said looking left and right as they opened the tall wrought iron gate leading through a courtyard and into the spacious foyer of *La Mariposa* with its red stucco walls, subdued lighting and Spanish tile floor. A plump, heavy-set woman with a coffee colored face of leathered wrinkles approached them from the bar, her downturned mouth and discerning eyes giving the sailors a serious looking over.

"Mamacita!" the Volt said with his arms out, beckoning to the old woman. Her eyes opened wide and her dark sour face suddenly turned into bright sunshine, her white capped teeth flashing.

"El Voltio!" she cried, her smile growing with each step. "El Voltio ha vuelto a casa!" Her low, growling voice could have come from a gunnery sergeant. She grasped the Volt within her huge arms, her floor length red flowered gown completely engulfing him, except for his eyes poking out from under her armpit. Jonah thought she was going to crush him.

"El Voltio!" Mamacita yelled again and finally she let Volt go. He staggered, gasping for breath.

Gaining his balance, he pointed to the four sailors standing behind him. "Mamacita," he said. "Mis amigos."

Mamacita took a step toward Jonah. He started backing up when all of a sudden Homer pushed him forward into her arms and she engulfed him as she had done to Volt. Then she turned her attention on Homer and Underwood who both hugged her back with abandon.

"Y Brickey," Volt said, holding Brickey's shoulder. "Que esta aqui en su primera noche. Una Virgen," the Volt added, explaining who Brickey was.

Mamacita stared at Brickey's freckled face. Her eyes grew wide, her mouth opened into a big smile and she grabbed Brickey's shoulders and held him at arms-length looking closely at him. "Una Virgen? Verdad?" she asked. "Una Virgen?"

"Si," Volt answered for Brickey. "Una Virgen."

"Cuantos anos?" Mamacita asked.

"How old are you, Brickey?" Volt said.

"Seventeen."

"Diecisiete," Volt said to Mamacita.

"Increible," she gasped, and turning toward the back of the room where three girls were watching, she waved them over. "Una Virgen!" she cried pointing at Brickey. "Diecisiete!" she said, explaining his age as the girls approached.

The three girls hovered around Brickey, fascinated with El Virgen. One, an oriental girl in her mid-twenties with pale skin and dyed rust-colored hair, ran her fingers through his crew cut as if she was squeezing grapes, testing for ripeness. Another, the oldest of the three, possibly in her late twenties, grabbed his arm muscles through his uniform, a smile growing over her face. The third girl, petite and not much older than Brickey, was dressed in a blue bustier with a gardenia in her raven hair. She circled around him, licking her lips as if she was trying to decide whether to have desert; the conclusion was evident, she must have desert.

"Bonito," the gardenia girl said nodding her head, her mouth slightly open. "Delicioso," she added.

"Que chica es la mejor para Brickey?" Volt asked Mamacita which girl would be best for Brickey.

"Debe elegir," Mamacita said shaking her head with her arms crossed.

"Brickey, she says you have to choose," Volt said.

"Me?"

"Affirmative. It's up to you to choose your girl."

"Gosh. I don't know. They're all so ... so beautiful."

"Que habla el mejor Inglés?" the Volt asked which of the three girls spoke the best English.

"Maybe me," the petite gardenia girl answered in English with a light, musical Spanish accent, and she stepped forward and extended her hand toward Brickey, the gold bracelet on her wrist vibrating and flashing. "My name is Gardenia," she said coyly. Brickey took her hand and his face lit up, the excitement from her touch evident in his eyes.

"Would you like to buy me a drink?" she asked smiling, her almond shaped black eyes staring intently into his.

"Uh, yea," Brickey answered wide eyed.

"Come," she said holding his hand, leading him toward the bar as a horse to a trough, her raven hair flowing over her bare shoulders, her skintight black pedal pushers accentuating her curves above red high heels.

"Well, that's settled," the Volt said nodding his head with an approving look as he watched Brickey and the Gardenia girl walk away. "Come on guys, we need a drink," and he started walking to the bar.

"I think I'm gonna have another one of those wicked Seca things," Jonah said leaning against the bar.

"Yea, sounds good to me," Homer said.

"I'm in," Underwood said.

"Quatro seco con vaca," the Volt said to the bartender. "You know," he continued as he peeled open a fresh pack of cigarettes. "I don't know what you guys think, but this WESTPAC deployment could be a good thing for us."

"How d'ya mean?" Jonah asked.

"Well, first, as far as I know there's only three guys in the ship who've ever been over there," and he paused lighting a cigarette with a book of bar matches. "Chief Cunningham, Chief Beckers, and Doc Slaughter. And, second, I've talked to all three of them, and from what they say the liberty in Subic is okay, in Kaoshung it's good, but in Sasebo it's definitely four-oh."

"Better than this?" Homer asked sipping his Seca.

"A helluva lot better! Especially Sasebo."

"Where's Sasebo?" Jonah asked.

"Japan," Underwood answered. "Doc says we'll probably get there several times because that's where *Ajax* is."

"What's *Ajax*?" Homer asked.

"A repair ship," Volt answered.

"Oh, yea," Jonah chimed in. "Yea. I remember that name. She's a sister ship to the tender I was on in Key West."

"And Sasebo's also got a shipyard for the big repairs," Volt added.

"How far is that from Vietnam?" Homer asked as he looked around the room at a few more girls sauntering in.

"I checked it out, and depending on where we are in Vietnam, at the speed *The Cathedral* makes, it's about five days to Sasebo. And Subic is only about two days away."

"Hot damn!" Homer said. "I'm ready. Let's get to WESTPAC!"

"But you better get through tonight first," Jonah took a sip of the Seca.

"Yea," Homer looked toward the rear of the room. "And I think I just saw how I'm gonna do that." He stood up from the bar stool and approached a large girl in a black and gold flowered muumuu dress.

"I didn't know Homer liked big girls," Underwood said watching Homer and the girl at the other end of the room.

"She looks about twice his size," Volt said. "That's a hell of a lot more than I could handle."

"Maybe he has a death wish," Jonah said.

"More like masochistic," Underwood said.

"What?" Jonah asked over the lively Latin music floating through the room.

"Masochistic," Underwood shouted. "Someone who likes pain."

"Yea, I'm familiar with pain."

"Homer's a guy who loves to get in trouble," Volt said.

"Well, that girl's definitely trouble, fer sure."

"Uh oh," Volt pointed toward the other end of the bar.

Jonah turned and saw Brickey and Gardenia talking to the bartender. "What's going on?" Jonah asked.

"Bet you five bucks," Volt said watching the pair. "They'll disappear in less than five minutes."

"Hmm," Jonah thought about that for a moment, then held his hand out toward the Volt. "Okay, I'll take that bet," and he checked the time on his watch.

The gardenia girl said something to the bartender, her hands waving around, her tight pants showing more curves than Jonah thought was possible.

"What are they saying?" Jonah asked, not understanding the Spanish.

"She's telling the bartender that Brickey wants to stay the night," the Volt answered. "And they're discussing the details."

Gardenia then spoke into Brickey's ear. He reached down into his socks, pulled out some cash, counted out some money and laid the bills onto the bar. She smiled at him, Brickey smiled back at her, and the bartender scooped up the cash.

"He's paying the bartender?" Jonah asked.

"Yea. That's how they do it here. The bartender is sort'a the banker. You pay him, then you take your girl upstairs."

Brickey and Gardenia continued talking and laughing. The bartender placed two more drinks in front of Brickey and then Gardenia started pulling him away from the bar.

"Uh, oh, here we go," Volt said.

They watched intently. The girl kept pulling, and Brickey laughed and laughed then chug-a-lugged one of his drinks, laid the empty glass on the bar, wiped a paper napkin across his lips and followed Gardenia up the stars.

"Damn," Jonah said examining his watch. "That only took three minutes!"

Volt grinned and held his hand out toward Jonah. "Five bucks," he said.

The gardenia girl switched on the single light and the tiny room was bathed in a soft sultry red glow reflecting off the magenta walls. Brickey looked around him, at the narrow bed, the assortment of different pillows, the rusting porcelain sink in the corner, a small table covered with bottles and jars filled with mysterious contents, and a window open to the steamy sounds of the street below. A thin calico curtain waved in the breeze from the ceiling fan and a slight scent of stale moldy dampness suffused the air.

Gardenia slithered out of her tight pedal pushers revealing a tiny pair of electric blue panties, the same blue as the bustier. Then she unzipped the bustier exposing her small buoyant breasts, and a mole between them. She stepped up to Brickey and lifted his neckerchief over his head, her breasts vibrating as she moved.

"Take off your clothes," she commanded.

Brickey had been unconsciously holding his breath, and suddenly he involuntarily gasped.

"Is it true you are virgin?" she asked while soaping up a washcloth at the sink. Brickey nodded, his body inflating with aroused expectation. "Gardenia never had first time sailor," she said walking toward the now naked Brickey. "But she will give you best first time."

"I'm here for the whole night," he said with concern, wanting to make sure she understood.

"Si," she confirmed, reaching down to him with the washcloth in her hand. "The whole night," and she looked up at him with an amused, knowing expression.

Brickey's instantaneous spasm was followed by embarrassment and self-conscious awkwardness, eventually nursed back to vitality by Gardenia's slow, patient acceptance. Soon he was ready and willing again, and with her assistance he climbed to astonishing heights, something completely unknown in any of his previous 17 years. Approaching one of his apogees he heard a couple in the adjacent room, the sounds from the squeaking bed and their laughter penetrating through the thin plywood wall.

The whole night was a paroxysm of emotional and physical convulsions followed by short cycles of sleep and then more turbulent passion. The scene repeated itself over and over and when a pair of hands shook him awake he didn't know where he was.

"Es el momento," the female voice whispered that it was time, her hands motioning for him to get up. "Rapido," her hands turned faster. "Ahora!" Her whisper was becoming louder. He sat up on one elbow, his eyes trying to adjust to the vision of Mamacita silhouetted against the red wall. He blinked, tasted the stale aftermath of rum in his dry mouth, and squinted at his watch; 0500. "El taxi esta esperando," Mamacita said pointing downward to where the taxi was waiting out in the street. "El taxi," she repeated.

"Okay. Okay," he whispered back, swinging his legs over the side of the bed, noticing that half of the mattress was skewed off the box springs. He felt his head swimming around and around, and his stomach churned. "Okay," he said again and started dressing as Mamacita quietly tip toed through the open doorway and left the room. Sitting on the edge of the bed tying his shoes he looked at the naked Gardenia lying next to him. She was on her side, her back toward him, and her olive skin glowed in the red light; the glint of every curve, the shadow of every recess were stark from the light. Even with the ceiling fan turning, the perspiration on her skin glistened. Her raven colored hair was draped across her shoulder and her left hand lay across the bed with long red fingernails gleaming. Lying there unmoving, Brickey thought she seemed much different than she first appeared in the bustier just hours ago.

"Gardenia," he whispered. "Gardenia," he said louder. She stirred, rolled onto her back, one knee bent, her eyes still shut, her breathing barely audible. She gave out a faint moan and didn't move further. Brickey examined her sleeping face, wondering how she would appear without the heavy makeup or the long fake eyelashes, without the argent colored eyeshadow below the thick black brows. Her breasts were rising and lowering with each breath, and her compact triangle formed an erotic ornament on her guileless torso. He felt exhausted and clammy with sweat, and a pain of sadness filled his chest. He turned slowly, gently closed the door behind him and went soundlessly down the dark stairwell.

The foyer of the Butterfly was uninhabited, the atmosphere hushed, imparting the sensation of desolation; nothing stirred except the flicker of shadows from the slow spinning ceiling fans. Opening the ornate wrought iron gate and stepping onto the wet street he inhaled the cool fresh breeze coming off the Pacific and looked up to the eastern sky aglow in the yellow and red of dawn.

≈≈

Diary #104
25 February 1966
1630 Hours ... In the Pacific ... one day out of Panama.

I must admit, and some of my brothers in arms will razz me endlessly for saying this, but I thought the transit through the canal was fascinating. For someone who doesn't get too excited about things, the canal was an amazing experience, filled with history and feats of engineering prowess beyond full comprehension. And to think they did that back in the early 1900s. I was extremely impressed. And, after two nights of liberty in the bars and joy houses of Panama, we now find ourselves steaming westward on our way to Pearl Harbor. The alcohol saturated faces and rheumy eyes of the crew (and a few of the officers, I might add) appear stark against the Pacific's intense blue. Fortunately, these blue skies and pleasant breezes should help the drunks return to sobriety soon enough. This humble scribe, however, did not partake in the frivolity for two very good reasons. One, I was overwhelmed with work trying to process a mountain of replacement parts that were waiting for us on the Rodman pier, and, Two, I didn't have any damn money! Between the big bite my allotment takes out of my feeble pay, and, trying to save a few bucks for a good time in Hawaii, I couldn't afford to spend anything in Panama. However, rumor has it that a few of my brother officers spent more than their fair share and easily made up for my miserly ways. *Ex victoribus in praedam.*

Charley Crane has let it be known that over the next 20 days of steaming toward Pearl we will go through drill after drill, and splash on paint and more paint. According to Charley, the captain vows our fine LST will enter Pearl Harbor with newly applied fresh paint covering every square inch of topside space. He has decreed that not one iota of rust will be visible. Charley must have an inside track with the weather gods... neither rain, nor waves, nor spray, nor dark of night will keep us from our appointed painting. If I remember correctly, we loaded several pallets of paint before departing Little Creek, and now Biagotti says we've got only part of one remaining. Where in the hell does it all go? Let's see now, here's an idea: if we paint everything on the starboard half of the ship, maybe we can fool half of Pearl Harbor half of the time.

My God! What is that awful smell coming out of the galley? Mendoza tells me we're having roast beef, potatoes and cabbages for supper. Fortunately, the stuff is relatively fresh, having just been brought aboard in Panama. But woe betide the cooks after all the fresh food is consumed over the next few days. Oh yes, and, let us not forget the captain's material inspection tomorrow morning! Everyone is *overwhelmed with joy about that. After prolonged and careful thought, I will be submitting a new motto for consideration by the SOUSA board of directors: "Disarray and Disruption; our Guiding Light."*

The ship and crew seemed to breathe a collective sigh of relief as the sultry heat and oppressive humidity of Panama was finally left behind. It was good to be at sea again, Jonah thought, although he would never admit that to anyone. He couldn't quite put his finger on it, but there was something putrid and rotting about Panama. Now this fresh breeze and blue horizon were acting as a cleansing to his soul, washing away his memories of Panama's gutters, decaying buildings and brown water. Maybe the next 20 days at sea will be just what everybody needs, a time to get into the cycle of watches and work and some pleasant time steaming through gentle seas with enormous clouds above and an unlimited horizon ahead.

"Well," Underwood said, climbing into the gun tub. "In 20 more days we'll be entertaining hula girls and drinking rum out of a coconut on Waikiki Beach."

"Yea, and a lot of drills before we get there."

"You think Sanders will let you shoot a few rounds out of these 40s before that?"

"We'd better. God only knows when they were fired last. They need some exercise."

"You got gun crews all assigned?"

"I gave Sanders a list of names, and he's working on it now with Browning. He'll let me know. And then we'll need to have a lot of dummy practice before we can shoot. Don't want anybody to lose a finger, or a hand."

"Hey guys, you see this sunset?" Brickey asked as he climbed into the gun tub.

"Well, if it isn't Mister Romeo," Underwood said leaning against the side of the tub as the wind whipped across the ship. "How'd you make out with the Gardenia girl?"

Brickey turned a pale shade of embarrassed red.

"I think he did all right." Jonah said. "Poldolski said he came back to the ship at 0530."

"No shit. Brickey? Is that true?" Underwood asked.

"Yea, I guess it is," Brickey said looking self-conscious.

"Well, my boy," Underwood continued. "Everybody has to start sometime. How was it?"

"Best time I ever had." Brickey smiled ear to ear.

"The Volt made a good choice," Jonah said. "The Butterfly was first rate."

"I agree," Underwood said. "But some of us got a little too drunk," and he arched his eyebrows as he looked at Jonah.

"Yea, I guess that's true," Jonah replied. "Pattie was on my mind. I just sat there, drinking secos, one after the other after the other, and shooing the bar girls away and thinking about Pattie and remembering the good times we had together. I was sorta feeling sorry for myself. Before I knew it, I felt as if somebody had hit me in the head with a sledge hammer. God, I must'a really gotten shit faced. I remember you, Volt and Homer dragging me into a cab, and that's it. I have no recollection of the cab ride or getting aboard the ship."

"Homer got you aboard in a fireman's carry," Underwood said.

Jonah shook his head. "I'm telling 'ya, those secos are wicked," he added. "Damn, I was hung over. Never thought I'd make it through the next day."

"How do you think you did on the material inspection this morning?" Underwood asked.

"Not great. We had several gigs, but most of 'em are just some minor things that need painting," Jonah said. "I saw you scribbling like crazy on that clipboard, writing down all the old man's remarks. But, I'll tell 'ya, the best part was when Sanders hit his head on that low hatch coming out of the forward magazine."

"Yea. I didn't see it happen. I had my back turned, but I sure heard the noise. It sounded like a church bell ringing!"

"It was all I could do to keep from laughing," Jonah said.

"A lot of people and a lot of compartments did much worse than you," Underwood added. "Much worse. Dorsey got gigged pretty hard for stuff in the galley. And I thought Homer was going into conniptions with all the gigs the captain was giving the shipfitter's shop ... paint those, clean this, straighten that. Ensign Hobson was standing there biting his lip. I thought he was gonna have a stroke. He was scared to death having both the captain and the XO in front of him. I watched his face turn from caution to terror in less than 60 seconds. He's got Homer in the shop now trying to get all the discrepancies taken care of."

"Ha, I can't wait to hear Homer's version of what happened. It'll be another tall tale, that's for sure. By the way, just who the hell is that?" Jonah asked, looking down, pointing toward a big, stocky sailor with a pug nose face.

"Oh, you mean Pike?"

"Pike? Is that his name?"

"You mean that guy right down there with the strange face?"

"Yea. The guy with the face that ran into a building."

"Yea, Pike. First Class Signalman. What about him?" Underwood said.

"I've seen him around. He came through the aft berthing compartment yesterday morning, immediately after reveille, as if he was looking for a fight, growling and pushing people aside. What's his deal?"

"Did you say anything to him?"

"I guess I was in his way and he shoved me aside. I asked him what the hell he was doing, and he just snarled back. He reminded me of a junkyard dog."

"Keep your distance from him."

"Why?"

"He's our new Master at Arms."

"Are you shit'n me?"

"Nope."

"A cop? How long has he been here?"

"Came aboard just before we left Little Creek."

"Damn, I hate people like that. Throwing their weight around, acting like God's gift to mankind. So, he's the XO's toady?"

"You might say that."

"He gave me a hard time about my towel," Brickey chimed in.

"What you mean?" Jonah asked.

"The morning we were about to go through the canal I had just gotten out of the shower and he told me I couldn't hang my towel from the bottom of my rack. He said I had to fold it and lay it on my blanket."

"A wet towel?"

"Yea."

"Well that's stupid," Jonah said. "Lay a wet towel on a clean blanket? That'll sure dry out real nice. God! Woody, where do these idiots come from, anyhow?"

"Look at that," Brickey said, and Jonah and Underwood turned to follow Brickey's pointing finger.

"Oh, man!" Jonah said as he watched Pike and O'Toole walking together along the port side of the main deck. "Those two are in cahoots? What the shit?"

"Looks like they're buddies," Underwood observed. "I wonder what gives with them?"

"Was Pike ever on *McMann*?" Jonah asked.

"Not during my time aboard," Underwood answered

"They're definitely disagreeable characters," Underwood added.

"Yea," Jonah said. "They remind me of two scupper trout."

Underwood leaned over the edge of the gun tub and called out. "Hey, Volt! Volt!" The Volt turned and climbed up the ladder toward them.

"Good evening. To what do I owe this privilege?" Volt said.

"Hey," Underwood said. "What were you doing on the LCU this morning?"

"What do you mean?"

"I saw you climb up on that thing and then disappear inside it."

"Oh, you did?"

"Yea. What gives?"

"Ah, I was just picking up some cumshaw."

"What cumshaw?"

"Well, you know we're carrying that thing half way around the world, right?" The Volt said. "Well, it has one fine radio set on it. A very fine radio set. In fact, it's got some tubes in that radio set that we could really use in our radio set. We put a chit in for those same tubes through supply weeks ago, even before we left Little Creek, and so far, nothing. Absolutely nothing. We even put a high priority on it. Still nothing, and we can't just wait until we get to Pearl, we need them now. So I figured we'd just borrow some tubes from that LCU radio and then replace them when ours finally come in."

"What else did you find interesting enough to borrow?" Underwood asked, glancing a look at Jonah.

"Oh, nothing much. A few things here and a few things there. Nothing much of interest."

"Maybe a canned heat stove or something like that?"

"A canned heat stove?"

"Yea, you know, one of those little jellied alcohol stoves? I've seen those things on LCUs before"

"Well, on second thought, yea, there might have been one of those in that tiny galley. Hmm, yea. I think there was."

"Homer could sure use one of those," Underwood said, raising his eyebrows and looking furtively between Jonah and The Volt."

"Homer?" Volt asked confused.

"Yea, he's been building up a little apparatus in the shipfitter shop. You know, for experimentation purposes?"

"Apparatus?"

"Yea. But just for experimentation purposes, you understand."

"Really?"

"Yup."

"You know, come to think of it," Volt said looking off into space, then looking back at Underwood. "Our second day in Panama...you know I saw Homer carrying several gallon cans of raisins. Yea, they were definitely gallon cans. He must'a had four of those raisin cans!"

"That sounds about right," Underwood confirmed, nodding, his eyebrows rising.

"Yea, okay. I see what you're saying," Volt said obviously in deep thought. "Well, yea, maybe I can get Homer in there, so he can take a look at it," Volt volunteered.

"That would be a good idea. When are you on radio watch next?"

"I've got the mid watch."

"Okay. I'll get him to meet you on the LCU. How about at 2200? How's that?"

"Perfect."

"Okay then."

"Right."

"And I'm sure that Homer would allow you to have some of the fruits of his labor," Underwood said smiling. "That is if you like raisins."

"Oh, man, are you kidding?" Volt said. "Definitely count me in. I'm into raisins."

"That makes three of us. Listen, I've got things to do, see you guys later," Jonah said, and he went down to the aft berthing compartment where the faint odor of sweat, body odor and sour sheets made him pinch his nose. This is a long way from the fresh air on deck, he thought, and he spied Brickey sitting on his rack holding a small bottle up to the overhead light, looking intently at the contents.

"What you got there?" Jonah asked walking over to him.

Brickey looked up with a sheepish grin. "Just some sand I picked up in Panama."

"Sand? Let me see."

"I'm collecting sand from wherever we go," Brickey said handing the bottle to Jonah. "I thought it would make an interest'n collection. Ya know, sort of a souvenir of our travels."

"Sand? Hm, well, I suppose that's certainly different," Jonah said examining the bottle, reading the label where Brickey had written *'Panama, Feb 1966.'*

"I've got plenty of bottles. Look..." Brickey opened his locker and showed Jonah a cardboard box full of the small glass bottles with their metal caps."

"You think that'll be enough? I mean, it looks like you've only got maybe 20 or 30 in there?"

"Thirty-five to be exact."

"Hmm, yea, I guess you do have enough."

"You think?"

"Well, you're the expert on sand, Brickey, not me. But just be careful with all this extra weight, will ya? You don't want the ship to list too far over to starboard."

CHAPTER 3

THE MOVIE

"Remind me not to eat so many of Dorsey's crummy potatoes next time," Underwood said in disgust as he threw his cigarette over the edge of the gun tub and watched it disappear into the ship's wake.

"I heard that was the last of the steaks," Jonah said.

"Yea, and tomorrow morning it's powdered eggs."

"I hate powdered eggs."

"And Pearl's still another 11 days away," Underwood said. "Eleven days before we see fresh food again, and we don't have any UNREP capability. Zero. Zilch. Zippo. Talk about a horse and buggy operation!"

"Homer will probably start selling rat meat again."

"Oh, man, don't even say that!"

"YAJDEK."

"No way."

"Have you ever seen such clouds before?" Jonah said changing the subject, looking around him and toward the sun hovering just above the western horizon.

"I have not," Underwood said turning. "In fact, I've never seen anything quite like the Pacific before; the color of the water, these clouds, the pleasant breezes. Now I understand what those Hawaiian cruise ship brochures were always raving about."

"You ever want to take a cruise?" Jonah asked.

"Hell no! Why would I ever go on a cruise? We're on our own cruise! Think about it; we've got plenty of activities, nightly entertainment, four squares a day, decent accommodations. Even free clothing. And they pay us."

"Don't forget the friendly ship's crew," Jonah said.

"Ha! Friendly crew? Now you're being a smart ass." and Underwood shook his head. "And once you retire from the Navy you'll go to work on a cruise ship."

"No way. Never happen."

"You could be the gunner's mate on the SS Aloha."

"I don't think so," Jonah said.

"Come to think about it..." Underwood said. "...the only thing we don't have is happy hour."

"Yea, well, Homer's gonna fix that. After The Volt got him into the LCU, he's been cooking raisin Jack almost every night since we left Panama."

"I've smelled it," Underwood said.

"When's it gonna be ready?"

"Any day now I guess. Homer says you can't rush a good recipe."

"What's he putting in besides raisins?"

"Don't know. I asked him, but he's tight lipped. Says great chefs don't reveal their secrets."

"You going to the movie?" Jonah asked.

"Yea, but I'm gonna take a shower first," Underwood said.

"It starts at 1930."

"Right. So, save me a place," and Underwood climbed out of the gun tub.

Jonah watched the last of the sun's rays streaming through thin bands of low stratus clouds, then he turned and looked over the transom where the ship's screws were churning the Pacific into a seething white furrow. As he watched the clouds turning and swirling, their tremendous shapes undulating and transforming, his thoughts drifted and his mind started replaying memories of the Idaho farm, and how his father would stagger through the barnyard, drunk as could be, searching for the 12 year-old Jonah, the only son remaining out of three. He remembered the old man's huge hands, the hands as large as dinner plates, heavily calloused with dirty, broken fingernails reaching out for him as he cowered in a dark corner of the barn. The hands would grab his arm and pull him into the light in the center of the barn where the big man's brass buckled leather belt could do its work. Jonah's mouth was turned down and he took a deep breath. His thoughts changed and then he remembered *McMann*, serenely anchored in the Bay of Naples with the beautiful sea, sky and landscape, and then he remembered the chaos of the fight in the *Blu Focena* and the defeat and abandonment he felt after the captain's mast. He thought about the fire on the carrier and his panic when the two ships came alongside each other. And then he envisioned Pattie's face. He stared into the clouds and in his mind's eye saw her sensual mouth and smile and remembered her contagious laugh and the way she walked with her hips swaying in that distinctive rhythmic tempo. You really screwed that relationship up, he thought, yea, you really did. That was the best thing you ever had. The very best. Emotion surged up from deep in his gut, plunging him into further depths of sadness, and that song started playing through his mind again, that song he couldn't get rid of: *A time to weep and a time to laugh, a time to mourn and a time to dance.* As his eyes began to swell he pulled the bill of his cap down, almost over his eyes, and watched the surging wake receding behind the ship, receding further back and back, until the white crease gradually became less distinct, eventually disappearing into a massive cluster of cumulonimbus clouds on the eastern horizon.

༄༅

The LST continued steaming into the twilight, slowly moving westward through the gentle cross sea, rolling in time to an invisible pendulum as the balmy breeze infiltrated the ship's many compartments with its fresh calming clarity. Steaming into an area where the California current swept down from the northern latitudes, thousands of flying fish began leaping and gliding over the water's surface, their aerodynamic shape and winged fins whisking them along at a remarkable speed, easily exceeding The Cathedral's plodding pace. The fish darted out of the face of waves, their tails propelling them and their wings rapidly beating the air. They flew quickly forward and then disappeared back into the water. Instantly more fish darted out of more waves and the spectacle repeated itself over and over.

In the midst of this exceptional weather Chief Cunningham, the Quartermaster, watched Charlie Crane lean over the chart table and painstakingly pencil a small "X" on the thick paper. Then Crane looked at his watch and added the time and the date. The position on the chart was determined from their evening sights and the orthogonal time-distance chains of the Loran fix, and according to their calculations they were now at the halfway point between Panama and Pearl.

"This is amazing, Chief," Crane said. "How those four thin Lines of Position came together so effortlessly."

"Yes, sir, that happens sometimes," the chief said.

Crane never had a four LOP fix before. Feeling very pleased with himself, he reached across the chart table and patted the green glass covering the Loran's cathode ray screen. Life just couldn't get better than this, he thought, and Cunningham watched him walk away, through the wheel house, and out to the open 01 level.

Three decks below and 220 feet forward of where Charlie Crane was standing, Underwood walked through the Ops Division berthing compartment; a few of the crew were already sacked out in their racks, their sleeping bodies resembling shapeless, blanket-covered mummies. Underwood didn't take notice of the dungaree trousers and shirts hanging from the bunks, or the shoes and boots scattered in corners, but he did see The Volt in his skivvies, sitting on his bottom rack looking through a cardboard box of LP records.

"Hey, Volt, what's going on?" Underwood asked.

The Volt looked up, his mouth and eyes in some distress.

"You okay?" Underwood said.

"Yea, sort of," Volt answered.

"You going to the movie tonight?

"Nah, I'm beat. Really beat." The radidoman's face was drawn, his eyes bloodshot.

"What's the matter?" Underwood asked.

"These fucken double watches are killing me!" Volt put his hand on his forehead.

"What are you gonna do?"

"Well, I'm telling you, if that new 3rd class radioman we got coming, whatever the hell his name is, isn't waiting for us on the damn pier when we get to Pearl ... well, then I'm gonna turn into a real mean sonov'a'bitch and might have to punch somebody. That's what I'm gonna do."

"Sorry 'bout that," Underwood said. He had never seen The Volt in such a state before.

"So, I'm gonna crash," Volt said.

"It's supposed to be a good flick."

"Yea, I know. But we only picked up seven movies in Panama. They're gonna have to show it at least one more time before we get to Pearl. I'll see it later," and Volt pulled an album from the box.

"You sure?"

"Yea, I'm sure," and he looked up, the exhaustion clearly evident on his face.

"Okay then, see ya in the morning," and Underwood walked forward through the open watertight doorway and climbed up the doghouse ladder into the fresh breeze coming across the main deck.

The Volt reached under his rack and pulled the turntable out, sliding it along the deck, making sure the dime was securely taped to the end of the stylus. He gently pulled the record from the album and read the label: Bellini's opera, *"I Puritani,"* the 1954 recording with Colombo and Rossi. He carefully placed the record on the turntable, pushed the start button and moved the tone arm into position at the third track, the beginning of Act 1, Scene 3; the *"A Te O Cara."* Crawling into his rack, he hung his glasses from the lashings of the rack above him, placed the large, bulky headphones on his head, and adjusted the amplifier hanging from wire coat hangers on the bulkhead next to him. Ops Division berthing was on the port side, the most forward compartment in the ship, and Volt thought the syncopated reverberations pulsating through the deck and bulkheads this far forward blended beautifully into the calming music. The aria's orchestral melody began with the lilting, soft introduction, then Lord Arturo, the tenor, entered bearing presents for Elvira. *"Te, o cara, amor talora; Mi quido furtivo e in pianto..."*

The compartment's sounds and rattles from the locker doors were shut out by Volt's headphones, and as the opera transported him into a state of semi-consciousness his eyes closed, and his breathing slowed. As he drifted off he started to experience a sort of dreaminess. He saw The Butterfly with the glasses of seco con vaca and the lithe Chinese girl, then his body temperature started dropping, his heart rate slowed, and he sensed a cocoon of comfort enveloping him. Soon he fell deep into sleep, his brain's reticular circuits activating, and he dreamed of the canal and Panama, and saw himself on a bus riding along the rain-soaked streets. It was a carnival colored painted bus and it twisted and turned and floated above the cobblestones, and somehow in that freakish sleight of hand that dreams seem to create, he was transported into The Butterfly's great room, watching the red walls growing and stretching. The top of the varnished bar overflowed with thousands of booze bottles, some of them floating in the air as the ceiling fans revolved above him. The music from the Bellini opera filled his dream and he saw himself dancing in a slow motion across the barroom floor with an extraordinarily graceful woman. Together they glided around the tables and over the chairs and up to the ceiling with the fans pushing them to the other side, and then he looked at the woman's face for the first time and saw who it was; it was a refrigerator sized Mamacita, her tiny feet hovering above the wet, red ochre Spanish tiles.

Three decks below and 170 feet aft from where Volt was dancing through his dream, Ensign Jones and Chief Beckers were standing in the main engine room.

"Oh, yes, sir," the tall, thin Beckers said as he sucked on a lollipop, the stick protruding from his lips. "Liberty in Panama is always fine, very fine."

"How many times have you been to Panama, Chief?" Jones asked.

"Hmm. I guess four times before this one. Maybe five. They seem to run together after all these years."

"You didn't spend all your money, did you?"

"Oh, hell, no, sir. Just had a couple of beers at a local kroeg ... that's a Dutch word for pub."

"And then?" Jones asked.

"Then I came back to the ship and slept the sleep of babes. My days of debauchery are far behind me, sir. My old Dutch father, he used to say, that when the drunken man goes to the kroeg, only the bartender comes out ahead. He knew what he was talking about."

"You going to the movie?"

"Oh, yes, sir. Wouldn't miss it for the world. Movies always put everything in perspective."

"How do you mean?"

Well, unlike this ship, no matter how bad things get, the hero in the movie always comes out on top of his situation," and Beckers' broad smile lit up his thin chiseled face with its bold, cleft chin.

Jones nodded, thinking about the chief's sage philosophy. "So, who's relieving you?"

"Russel, sir," and Beckers looked at his watch. "Should be here any minute."

"And who's in the generator room?"

"Nowak and Tate, sir."

"How's Tate doing?"

"He's learning, sir. He's young, still a little wild, but an excellent mechanic. He's a good kid. And since we're only running two generators in there right now," and Beckers pointed toward the bulkhead just forward of where they were standing. "They won't have any trouble."

"Then I'll see you at the movie," Jones said, and he climbed up the 30-foot vertical ladder, up through the narrow, claustrophobic escape trunk and out the 25-inch diameter scuttle to the main deck.

Forward of the main engine room and on the other side of the bulkhead from where Beckers was writing in a log book, Electrician Third Class G.D. Nowak and Engineman Albert Tate were standing their watch inside the auxiliary engine room. It was a noisy, tightly packed bird's nest of engines, generators, high voltage cables, switches and valves. In one corner of the compartment Nowak lounged in a chair drinking coffee and reading a comic book as Tate sorted through a bucket of tools. Two of the three gray painted 250 horsepower, 6-71 Detroit Diesel engines were on line, running at 1800 RPM, each cranking out close to 100 kilowatts and 480 volts of 3 phase electricity; enough power to operate all the necessary electrical equipment in the ship. Behind the engines, and along the aft bulkhead were five black electrical panels, six feet high, covered with gauges, reverse current trip and hold switches, field rheostats, ammeters, power feeder circuits, voltmeters, and dozens of fused knife switches. It was an electrician's paradise, or nightmare, depending on the circumstances. Along the forward bulkhead was the complex network of pumps, valves, switches and gauges controlling the ship's 17 ballast tanks.

As the 18-year old Tate walked aft toward the control panel with a heavy 24-inch screwdriver in one hand and the tool bucket in the other, he spied what he was looking for and knelt down on the deck plates. He reached into the bucket, drew out a flathead one-inch stainless machine screw, hand started it into a hole in the deck plate, and finished driving it flush with the big screwdriver. Tate knew all about tools and engines, having grown to adolescent maturity on a farm in the Smoky Mountains. He had also been his home town's delinquent hot rodder and loved nothing better than to work on his 1932 lowboy deuce coupe. The car's motor was first rate, he thought, but the jalopy wasn't much to look at. If he had been able to earn some extra cash working in the local garage he might have been able to fix the car up. He had plans to chop it and drop it, that is until the local sheriff gave him a free night in the county jail after pinching a pack of beer from the local country store. At court the next day the judge sat behind his stately bench, slowly and silently reading through the numerous pages of the boy's rap sheet containing his considerably disreputable past and current shenanigans. After what seemed an eternity of raised eyebrows and pursed lips, the judge finally looked down at Albert and gave him two choices: Albert could either be carted off to the state reform school in Concord, or join the Navy. Albert didn't think twice. Surprisingly, the Navy turned out to be a much better place than where he had come from; he had never before experienced having his own bed, or been able to eat so much food at every meal, and besides, he thought, working around all these engines was the neatest thing in the world, next to hot rods.

"Tate!" Nowak yelled over the noise. "Tate!"

Tate turned, saw Nowak motioning to him, and walked over as he stuffed the large screwdriver into his back pocket and removed a wad of toilet paper from his left ear.

"Go up to the galley," Nowak yelled. "Tell Dorsey to give you a can of fresh coffee. We're out and this stuff tastes like shit," he pointed to the black tar substance inside the pot which was heating on the single burner.

"All rah't," Tate said in his Smoky Mountain accent and he scampered up the port escape trunk. When he got to the height of the port wing he decided to take a shortcut. He opened that watertight door, latched it back and went aft to the galley, allowing the distant thrumming sounds and smells of the generator room to waft up the trunk and into the port wing.

Up on the 01 level, almost 40 feet above the deck plates of the auxiliary engine room, the stewards were carrying chairs from the wardroom and setting them in front of the movie screen to form the first row reserved for the officers. Other chairs, brought from recesses of the ship by crew who had chairs available, formed second and subsequent rows. Those who didn't have chairs sat wherever they could find a spot; on the deck, on top of ready ammo boxes, or standing against the railings. Underwood brought his chair up from the ship's office, and Jonah carried his old chair up from the armory. Brickey arrived carrying an empty 30-gallon galvanized trash can and a life jacket. He placed the can upside down on the deck next to Underwood, then arranged the life jacket over the can's bottom and sat down on his custom perch. Pike, with his Master-At-Arms badge shining in the lights, stood squarely in front of the white movie screen, his huge arms folded across his powerful chest, his fleshy jowls and mouth drooping, his hostile pug face and squinting eyes scanning the crew assembling in front of him.

"Pike looks real happy tonight, don't you think?" Jonah said slouching in his chair.

"Shit! To me he looks like he always does," Underwood said with a smirk. "Ugly and disagreeable."

"Do you think he gets those looks from smoking flag halyards or something?" Jonah asked.

"Hell, no, he gets his looks from all the dog food he eats."

"Dorsey's dog food?"

"Nah, his own private stash."

"Yea, that could be," Jonah chuckled.

"He is one ugly fucker."

"Yea, but his mama loves him."

Underwood laughed. "Not likely," he said and reached into his pocket for his cigarettes.

"Hey, I got a question for you," Jonah said.

"Yea?"

"What's his first name?"

"Who?"

"Pike."

"Pike?"

"Yea, what's his first name?"

"I'm not supposed to reveal stuff from personnel files."

"Oh, come on; somebody on the ship probably knows his first name. Probably O'Toole. It can't be a secret."

Underwood looked left and right and then behind him, leaned toward Jonah and whispered. "You can't let this out."

"What?" Jonah whispered back.

"That I told you his name."

"What's wrong with his name?"

"I'll tell 'ya, but you can't let it out. Understand?"

"Yea, okay," Jonah said impatiently, still whispering. "Yea, I understand."

"Okay?"

"Yea, okay."

Underwood took another look around. "Keep it to yourself?"

"Yea. Yea."

"Percy."

"What?" Jonah said in astonishment.

"Shhh."

"Really?"

"Yup."

"You shitting me?"

"Nope."

"Percy?"

"Shhh."

"Percy Pike? Are you kidding?"

"Shhh."

"That's unbelievable!"

"Yup," Underwood said.

"Ha ha ha," Jonah laughed, squirming in his chair. "Just unbelievable."

"Shhh," Underwood said, moving his hands in front of him.

"Oh, man, you really hit my funny bone with that one."

"You're welcome."

"You're not shitting me, right?"

"Nope."

"That's really his first name?"

"Yup."

"Oh, you just made my day," Jonah said, still laughing. "Ha. I can't get my breath. Oh, God, that's funny," and Jonah shook his head, grinning ear to ear.

"Remember," Underwood said in a serious voice, pointing a finger straight at Jonah.

"Yea, yea. I won't let it out," Jonah promised, shaking his head. "Unbelievable."

"Attention on deck!" Pike shouted, and the crew rose and stood at an easy attitude of attention as the captain entered the open-air theater with the XO tight on his tail, taking their seats front and center. Jonah and Underwood glanced at each other.

"Well, I'll be damned," Jonah whispered to Underwood as they sat back in their chairs. "That's the first time I've seen the old man out here for a movie."

"You know what Homer said a couple of days ago?" Underwood said in a hushed tone.

"What's that?"

"A name."

"A name?"

"Yea. Homer said that the old man reminded him of something, you know with those aviator sunglasses he's always wearing?" Underwood took a sip from his can of soda.

"Reminded him of what?"

"A bat."

"A bat? Oh, man! That's good," Jonah said laughing. "The bat."

An electrician's mate flipped a switch and the area lights went off, the projector lamp shot a beam straight at the screen, the reels started turning and the film's title and credits marched across the screen, the theme music blaring from the speakers.

"Hey, save my chair, will 'ya?" Jonah said. "I gotta go to the head."

"But the movie's just starting!"

"Yea, I'll be quick," and Jonah worked his way through the audience and went down the ladder to the main deck where he found Ensign Jones admiring the sunset.

"Beautiful night, Mister Jones," Jonah said, and the ensign turned around.

"Yes, it is. Very beautiful. You been in the Pacific before, Wynchester?"

"No sir, this is a first for me. Well, I have seen it from a beach in Oregon, but this is the first time I've been in the middle of it. And those flying fish we saw today are something to watch, that's for sure."

"Indeed they are. You're not at the movie?"

"Oh, I've seen it before, sir. I'm in no rush. By the way, what do you suppose gives those fish such an ability to fly like that?"

"Don't know for sure, but it's obviously the survival of the fittest; you know, Darwin's theory of evolution? They've adapted a mechanism to allow them to flee their predators. They fly. Otherwise they wouldn't survive."

Down in the generator room, three decks below, Nowak was still reading his comic book when Tate came back down the escape trunk with a gallon can of coffee.

"Dorsey say'd you owe him," Tate yelled, inserting the toilet paper back in his ears, trying to reduce the high-pitched resonating noise from superchargers, pistons, valves, pushrods, cams, connecting rods and shafts spinning generators and armatures at enormous speed. It was a screaming sound, and alchemizing with the smells of diesel fuel, lubricating oil, bilge water and hot electrical equipment, the environment was known to make some people nauseous.

"Owe him what?" Nowak yelled with a disagreeable face as he looked up from the comic book.

"Hell, I don't know! He just say'd you owe him!"

"Ha, we'll see about that."

In the Main Engine Room, on the other side of the bulkhead from Nowak and Tate, Chief Beckers finished bringing his relief up to date on engine orders, RPMs and fuel flow, and climbed up through the escape trunk. As he stepped from rung to rung, carefully gripping the side rails, he wondered if he was getting too old for this; too old to be climbing these damn ladders or standing long watches in noisy engine rooms. He automatically took in every detail around him; he looked at the power cables running through the trunk, made sure doors were closed and dogged, checked the lights mounted along the sides, and when he reached the top and opened the scuttle to the main deck, he gratefully inhaled the fresh air. It was a far cry from the stink below him, he thought as he wiggled his tall, thin frame out of the small opening and onto the deck where Jones and Wynchester were admiring the view.

"Nice evening," Beckers said, wiping his hands on a rag.

"It certainly is," Jones observed. "It's the nicest we've had in a long time."

"We should have great weather from here all the way to Pearl," Beckers said. "And after that, it'll start to get hot and humid again. When we reach the Philippines and then Vietnam, well, then we'll be in a real sauna."

"When do we get to the Philippines?" Jonah asked.

"We'll only be in Pearl for a few days," Jones answered. "Then it'll take us another 23 days or so to get to Subic."

Jonah thought about Jones' comment, that they'd only be in Pearl Harbor for a short time and then spend another 23 days at sea. He lamented that circumstances couldn't make it the other way around.

Four levels below in the Auxiliary Engine Room, Tate walked over to the coffee pot next to where Nowak was sitting.

"It's might'a air'ish outside," Tate said in his nasal twang as he removed the lid of the coffee maker.

"Huh?" Nowak said, looking up from the comic book, holding a cupped hand behind one ear.

"You know, air'ish? Temp'a'ture's get'n kind'a cool?"

"Oh, yea," Nowak nodded.

"And we miss'n the movie," Tate said, and he started cleaning out the coffee basket. "Damn, this thang is sure gaum'd up," and he dropped the burnt, blackened remains of the previous brew into a dented galvanized garbage can, the red painted stencil proclaiming "Aux Eng Rm."

"Yea, but there's other movies," Nowak yawned, stretching his arms above his head with the comic book in one hand.

"I sure would like 'ta seen this'a one," Tate said, and he reached his oily hand into the new can of coffee and pulled out a fist full of fresh grounds.

"Tomorrow's a western, I think," Nowak said.

"I ain't partial to westerns," and Tate dropped the grounds into the coffee basket. "But I suppose if that's the movie ... oh shit!" he cried.

"What?" Nowak asked in alarm.

"I plumb left the damn wing door open!"

"You left the wing door open?"

"Yea," Tate said, clearly embarrassed with his mistake.

"You went out the wing door?"

"Yea. I guess I was try'n a shortcut."

"Through the wing door?"

"Yea."

"The wing door is supposed to stay secured underway, you idiot!" Nowak yelled, clearly angry at Tate and his stupidity.

"Aw'right, dammit!" the frustrated Tate yelled back. "I'll close the fucken thing r'aht now!" and he started fast walking toward the escape trunk. He angrily yanked the ball cap out of his rear pocket and the 24-inch screwdriver came out with it. It flew through the air, cartwheeling in a long arc, its long steel shank revolving around its axis faster than the eye could follow. It spun up and up and then down and down toward the base of the #2 engine, landing hard with a loud BLAANG! The flat head wedged into the connection terminal of the battery cable and the steel shaft struck the edge of the steel drip pan.

A glowing white, hot spark of electricity shot into the drip pan igniting the accumulated diesel fumes and fuel under the engine.

SSZAAP!

A flash of light lit up the entire compartment as a fireball erupted from under the hot engine.

BLHAUUM!

Up on the main deck, Beckers and Jonah abruptly turned away from the twilight and looked down at the deck. Jonah noticed Beckers' quick movement and they looked at each other, their eyes wide open. Beckers cocked his head toward the source of the sound.

"What the hell?" Beckers said.

"Did you hear that?" Jonah said, looking left and right. It was some type of strange disturbance, a sound and vibration that he instinctively knew signaled something out of the ordinary. His years of shipboard experience had tuned his sensory faculties to a very sharp pitch, and having been aboard The Cathedral for several weeks he had become familiar with her quirky shakes, jerks, rattles and noises. But what he had just felt was completely outside his library of sounds and vibrations. He instinctively knew something was wrong.

"Come on!" Beckers shouted and he and Jonah started running.

Jonah's mind was racing as they dashed inside the deck house. Where did that noise come from, he asked himself? Was that in the engine room? Or in the generator room? The tank deck? The wing deck? They flew down the ladder.

"It must be the auxiliary engine room!" Beckers shouted. "The quickest way down is through the wing deck!" Jonah ran right on the chief's heels, and Jones followed several paces behind.

When the fireball erupted from under the #2 diesel, Tate's eardrums were compressed as if they had been slugged by a gigantic hand. Nowak was knocked off his chair; his head slammed into a stanchion and his body slumped down onto the deck plates with his arms and legs resembling a rag doll. Tate was thrown to his knees, and as the compartment started filling with smoke he crawled to the OBAs, the Oxygen Breathing Apparatus masks hanging on the bulkhead. He put one on and and dragged another to the unconscious Nowak.

In the port wing Beckers and Jonah ran forward, breathing hard, running through compartments, jumping over shin knockers one after the other. God Almighty, Jonah thought, take it easy chief, you don't want to have a heart attack! Ahead, Jonah saw a glow of light coming through the open wing door leading straight down to the generator room, a door that was not supposed to be open. Then he saw the door was held securely back with its steel hook. As they stood looking at the door, gasping for breath, perplexed as to why it would be open, the glow of light in the doorway started wavering and a cloud of smoke rose up the escape trunk, as smoke would float up a chimney. Now Jonah understood what he and Beckers had sensed. The open door had allowed the strange noise and vibration to easily reach the main deck. Beckers stepped to the lip of the opening and peered down the vertical escape trunk into the thickening smoke.

"Anybody there?" Beckers shouted, his eyes squinting through the smoke. "Is anybody there?" he shouted louder. "Nowak! Tate! Can you hear me?" He yelled.

Ensign Jones arrived behind them, breathing hard, unable to speak.

Beckers turned to Jones. "Sound General Quarters!" Beckers yelled, a severe look on his now grim face. "Fire in the Auxillary Engine Room! NOW!" he commanded, and at that moment the traditional distinction and hierarchy between enlisted Chief and commissioned Ensign was instantly superseded by experience over the unseasoned. Without questioning Beckers' authority, Jones ran aft to a phone in the next compartment.

"Wynchester," Beckers yelled. "Get five OBAs!" the chief pointed forward and Jonah ran to the next compartment.

Further forward in the Ops berthing compartment The Volt floated inside his Butterfly dream. He saw himself sitting alone at the bar gathering up several bottles of booze and mixing his own drink. It was a unique cocktail, he thought; a little rum, some vermouth, a dash of vodka, more rum. The dream was incredibly vivid. He could even smell the acrid smoke rising from the candles on the bar tables as it wafted through the red walled room, the smoke snaking into corners and floating under his bar stool. Volt thought the smoke was getting thicker and thicker. He coughed and gagged for breath. Instantly he opened his eyes and saw the compartment's red night lights bathed in a swirling opaque fog. Was he still dreaming? Was this an illusion? No, it wasn't an illusion.

"SMOKE!" Volt screamed. "SMOKE! Everybody out! Everybody out! SMOKE!"

Six compartments aft from where Volt was screaming, Jonah pulled five OBAs off the rack and ran back to the open wing door where Beckers and Jones were buttoning their shirt sleeves and stuffing the cuffs of their trousers into their socks.

"Get those OBAs on!" Beckers yelled.

Jonah froze. Realization hit him. A flash of fear ran through him. He stared at Beckers in disbelief. Beckers was expecting him to climb down into the escape trunk, into the smoke, into the fire! Oh, no, he thought. Oh, no! He didn't want to do that. No! He didn't want to go down there. He definitely didn't want to go down into that smoke. Never! He wanted to run. But, but he couldn't run. Oh, God, help me! The fear started bubbling up inside him. He was horrified with the thought of going down the escape trunk. He couldn't go down there. But he couldn't show how afraid he was. Beckers was expecting him to go down there. There was no question about him going down there. Oh, Dear God! No!

Jonah started shaking as he tried to put the Oxygen Breathing Apparatus over his head, fumbling with the straps, struggling to adjust them, trying desperately to remember what he had been taught to do; to follow the procedure he had trained for countless times. Oh Lord, help me!

"Wynchester!" Beckers yelled, startling Jonah out of his terrifyingly real nightmare. "Hurry up, dammit! Let's go!"

Jonah turned toward the chief who was standing at the precipice of the open door leading down into the smoke. The grotesque OBA mask completely covered Beckers' face, but Jonah could see his eyes. He could clearly see the chief's piercing eyes looking back at him. The blue eyes had the look of unhesitating determination, and they were serious, deadly serious.

"C'mon!" Beckers shouted. "Check your damn mask!"

Jonah had been holding his breath and he suddenly sucked in a big gulp of air. He looked around him. The smoke was now pouring out of the open doorway. Beckers had his OBA on, standing at the edge of the escape trunk, and Ensign Jones was making a final adjustment of his mask. Jonah stared at them.

"Wynchester! Move!" Becker yelled.

Jonah checked the tightness of his mask; he pinched the breathing tubes and inhaled. Then he charged the OBA by depressing the starter valve and inhaling, then releasing the valve and exhaling. His breathing was coming faster. He counted as he did this, 15 times; inhaling, exhaling, inhaling, exhaling, inflating the breathing bag and starting the chemical reaction in the canister.

"You ready yet?" Beckers shouted again, impatient with the slow moving, fumbling gunner's mate.

Jonah nodded and he slung the two spare OBAs over one shoulder and cautiously followed Beckers down the vertical ladder into the smoke-filled trunk.

In the thick smoke Jonah could see the ladder rung directly in front of him. He could see Ensign Jones' boots coming down directly above him; and he could see the next rung below his eye level. But he couldn't see the rungs further down where he was trying to place his feet. This is bad, he thought, real bad. He moved one foot down, feeling for the rung, then moved the other foot down, feeling for the rung, then the other. The process was painfully slow, and he was becoming overwhelmed with fear, the fear of trying to go down without falling, and the fear of what he was going to encounter when he got to the bottom of the ladder.

"AAhh!" Jonah screamed inside his mask as Jones' steel-toed boot came crushing down onto his right hand, the boot's hard rubber lugs compressing his fingers onto the steel ladder rung. Without thinking, Jonah instinctively reacted; he wrenched his hand free, tearing off skin and flesh. Looking upward, his voice muffled through the OBA, he yelled. "Take it easy up there dammit! Slow down!"

Jonah's respiration was increasing. His pulse was climbing. He started to feel claustrophobic inside the OBA mask. He had the sensation that he might puke. He was beginning to think that, yes, he was going to puke. Oh, God, no! Please, no! Don't let me puke inside this mask! Easy there! Calm down! Get ahold of yourself. Take it easy. Get to the deck plates in one piece. Go slowly. Go down slowly. Slowly is better than falling quickly. With every step down the ladder he came closer to the heat and the flames. He could feel the temperature in the trunk rising, rising with each step. His chest was heaving. His heart felt as if it was about to jump into his throat, but somehow he continued down, down into the black smoke-filled vertical escape trunk toward hell.

Up on the 01 level, the credits were still scrolling across the movie screen when Underwood turned to Brickey and asked, "Have you seen this flick before?"

"Yea," Brickey answered. "I saw it in Norfolk. The girls are something else."

"You know," Underwood said. "That French actress in this movie? Damn, I can't remember her name, but she's got the greatest pair of ...," and the 1MC blared out with the shrill call of a bosun's pipe.

"Now hear this, now hear this!" the anxious voice said over the 1MC loudspeaker.

Underwood's face turned angry, angry that some stupid announcement would interrupt his movie. He looked up at the 1MC on the bulkhead, scowled and muttered. "Fuck off!"

"General Quarters! General Quarters!" a panic-filled voice yelled from the loudspeaker.

Underwood's mouth opened and he stared at the 1MC in disbelief. Some of the sailors were frozen in place, others stood, silhouetted against the bright screen.

The frightened voice on the 1MC continued. "Fire in the Auxiliary Engine Room! Fire in the Auxiliary Engine Room!"

Now the entire audience was on their feet and running, running into people and knocking over chairs. Brickey's trash can was bowled over and went spinning downhill with the roll of the ship.

"All firefighting parties report to your stations!" the voice on the 1MC said. "All firefighting parties to your stations! Fire in the Auxiliary Engine Room. Set Condition Zebra through the ship. This is NOT a drill! This is NOT a drill! General Quarters! General Quarters!" and the ear-piercing GQ alarm of a blaring horn and ringing gong filled the ship. As the movie continued running across the screen, someone tripped over the projector's power cord, sending the projector through the air. It hit the steel deck making a tremendous crashing noise of metal and glass, but no one heard it over the blare of the GQ alarm. The projector's reels, lenses, focus knobs, lamps, levers and controls scattered across the deck, with the film coming to rest in a jumbled heap against Underwood's vacant chair.

Down below in the escape trunk, Jonah continued down the ladder, slowly, carefully placing each foot securely on a rung, then moving one hand down, then the next. Go slow, he thought. Go slow. He didn't pay any attention to the GQ announcement, he didn't even hear the alarm, he just kept going and going. Finally, his feet felt the hard, flat surface of the deck plates and he saw red and orange flames shooting out through the dense smoke. He froze. It was impossible to tell what was what in the thick environment of carbon particles and heat. Beckers grabbed a battle lantern off the bulkhead, aimed it through the smoke and walked carefully around the engines to the control board; the chief pushed the stop button and closed all the power switches to the #2 engine.

"Wynchester!" Beckers yelled. "Get an extinguisher on that fire! NOW!"

Jonah was startled out of his paralysis. He looked left and right through the smoke in the unfamiliar generator room and found a red fire extinguisher hanging from the bulkhead right next to him.

"Mister Jones!" the chief yelled. "Get on the phone and tell Damage Control we need help down here!"

Up on the conn, 60 feet above the generator room, Len Davant, the Officer of the Deck, quickly moved aside to make room for the captain who was rushing into the confined space.

"What the hell's going on, Len?" the captain yelled, breathing hard.

"Mister Jones called up, sir!" Davant said. "Fire in the Auxiliary Engine Room!"

The captain turned to Underwood who had the sound powered phone. "Get a status report from Damage Control!"

"Yes, sir," and Underwood repeated the order through the phones. "Damage Control reports Mister Jones, Chief Beckers and GM2 Wynchester are in the generator room now sir, and fire teams are on the way."

"XO!" the captain said, turning quickly toward Charlie Crane who was coming up the ladder, clearly out of breath. "I want you to go down into the Auxiliary Engine Room. Find out what's going on. Oversee what's happening! Put everybody you need on that fire! Get control of the situation, Charlie, and report back immediately!"

Crane froze in horror and his face turned pale. Everyone on the conn watched him as he walked backwards. The captain stepped out of the conn and grabbed the XO by the arm, forcing him toward the starboard signal lamp. Pike and another signalman moved out of the way.

The captain turned, looked at Crane, their faces inches apart, and he spoke in a low, hushed voice. "Charlie! What's wrong with you?"

"Sir," Crane sputtered. "Uh, sir. Don't you think ...," and he gulped.

"Think what?" the captain asked quietly, his mouth turned down into a severe scowl. "Think what Charlie?"

"Sir, don't you think that, uh, Hobson, sir, should be able to handle that?"

"Hobson?" the captain asked in disbelief, his voice becoming louder. "Hobson?" he asked again, louder.

"Yes, sir, he's uh ... he's the Damage Control Officer."

The captain's neck turned red, his forehead wrinkled, the sunglasses looked straight into Crane's face and in a seething voice through his clenched teeth he hissed. "Hobson couldn't extinguish a flame on a damn candle!" Crane's head jerked backward. "You, get the hell down there, Charlie!" the captain yelled. "You get into that damn generator room. You take over that situation. You see that the fire is under control, and you report back to me! NOW!"

"Yes, sir," Crane said, and he ran down the ladder. "Holy God!" he muttered under his breath, his pulse racing and his adrenalin beginning to overwhelm him.

Down in the smoke-filled generator room, Jonah lifted the 30-pound fire extinguisher off the bulkhead, pulled the pin and started fogging the fire through the now almost impenetrable smoke, his fearful mind beginning to approach the breaking point. You can do this, he thought, you can do this, just keep concentrating, aim the nozzle at the base of the fire, not at the top, aim at the base, keep concentrating, keep fogging. Concentrate! Think of what you're doing. Oh, God help me!

In the smoke, out of sight from Jonah, Tate was kneeling on the deck plates and Beckers stumbled over him. Tate's red eyes looked up and saw the chief's ghostly face behind the OBA mask.

"Mister Jones!" Beckers yelled. "Over here!" and he pointed at Tate. "Help him!"

Jones quickly checked the mask on the boy's face. "Breathe!" Jones yelled. "Breathe!" he yelled again, and Tate gulped in the filtered air as fast as he could. "Can you get up the ladder?" Jones yelled.

Tate nodded. "I think so," he mumbled through the face mask.

"You sure?" Jones asked. Tate nodded once more, stood up, started swaying and then collapsed. Jones caught him just before he hit the deck.

As Jonah continued aiming the extinguisher on the fire he saw Rat Reader and Homer appear from the opposite escape trunk, OBAs on their faces, helmets on their heads, trousers tucked into socks. They skillfully connected a fire hose to a four-foot gooseneck applicator and opened the valve on the nozzle. The fine misting fog of water engulfed the fire, the black smoke quickly turning white just as Jonah's extinguisher sputtered empty.

"Keep it up, keep it up!" Beckers shouted to Rat as the fog started to take effect on the flames.

"Wynchester!" Beckers yelled. "Wynchester! Call Damage Control on that phone," and the chief pointed to a phone on the bulkhead. "Get Doc Slaughter and some Stokes stretchers down here! ASAP!"

Beckers got down on his hands and knees and crawled toward Jones who looked up at him with pink eyes as he held Tate's head. "Is he okay?" the chief shouted. Jones nodded. Beckers continued crawling along the deck plates to the #2 engine, searching for what he knew he would find. He aimed the battle lantern and carefully examined the pipes and fittings on the hot engine. He continued crawling over the deck plates, searching the engine's recesses and fittings as the fog of water poured down on him. He examined the fuel and lube oil piping, he pointed the beam of the lantern at the cooling hoses running alongside the engine. He crawled around to the opposite side and did the same, looking everywhere on the engine. Everything looked normal, nothing out of the ordinary. Then he lowered his head down onto the deck plates, looked under the engine, and that's when he saw the large screw driver resting on the drip pan and a stream of fuel squirting out of a cracked fitting. He methodically crawled around the engine turning off valves and the fire quickly diminished and went out. "Keep spraying!" he called over to Rat and Homer. "Cool it down!" and then he turned toward Jones. "Mister Jones!" he shouted. Get the ventilators on high speed and get this damn smoke out'a here!"

Soaking wet, Beckers pulled himself up from the deck plates, stretched his back with a painful grimace and walked around the compartment wiping his head and mask with a rag as he inspected the electrical panels, switches and engines. Satisfied that all was secure, he signaled Reader to stop spraying the engine, then picked up the sound powered phone and pushed the talk button.

"Damage Control ..." he called into the phone. "Auxiliary Engine Room," he said identifying the name of the compartment he was calling from. "Auxiliary Engine Room fire is out ... at ..." and Beckers paused and looked at his watch. "... at time, 1950 hours." He hung up the phone, shook his head and took a deep breath through his OBA.

As the smoke was being sucked up through the ventilators Doc Slaughter came down the ladder followed by Mills and Poldolski lowering two Stokes stretchers. Then Charley Crane's face behind an OBA mask appeared through the open trunk door. The XO took one step into the compartment and stopped cold. He looked around wide eyed, at the smoke receding, at Reader and Homer standing by with the fire hose, at the water dripping from the #2 engine, at Jonah and Slaughter kneeling alongside Tate and Nowak, and Beckers and Ensign Jones at the control panel.

"Fire's out, Mister Crane," Beckers said removing his OBA and wiping oily water off his face as he walked toward the XO. "It was a cracked fuel fitting on the #2 engine ... filled up the drip pan and then ignited ... not sure how, but it did. Maybe Nowak and Tate can tell us more later."

Crane stood without moving, staring at the engine.

"Sir!" Beckers said, trying to get the XO's attention. "Sir! The fire's out! Did you hear me?"

Crane didn't move. He was staring at some far distant point in the center of the compartment, seeing but not seeing.

"Sir? Are you alright?" Beckers asked with concern, looking into the XO's vacant eyes.

Crane turned and noticed the chief for the first time. "Yes," he gulped, his voice muffled inside the OBA. "I'm ... a ...," and he choked. He choked again. He pulled off the OBA and spit out particles of vomit onto the deck. He suddenly turned around and rapidly climbed up the ladder. Beckers shook his head as he watched the XO go up the escape trunk.

Slaughter had Nowak and Tate sitting up on the deck plates, examining their faces through the masks. "We'll get Nowak up first," Slaughter said. "Leave their OBAs on for now."

They strapped Nowak into one of the stretchers and Beckers leaned down and looked at him through the mask "Hey, Nowak. How' ya feeling?" Nowak nodded and grinned as a tackle was lowered down from the wing deck. They secured the tackle to the stretcher and began hoisting Nowak up through the escape trunk, with Mills climbing just behind to make sure the stretcher went up smoothly.

Beckers watched Nowak being hoisted up the trunk, then went over to Tate sitting against a stanchion waiting his turn. The chief knelt down on the deck in front of the boy, wiped the wet, oily soot off the young sailor's OBA mask, and closely examined his face through the plastic. "Tate?" Beckers said. "You need anything? Anything I can do for you?"

Tate smiled back and started coughing, his chest rapidly rising and falling. "I sure could use ... a ... a ... nice cold beer right 'bout now," he said in a rasping voice through the mask.

Beckers laughed. "I'll tell 'ya what Tate," he said with a conspiratorial grin. "If you can wait 'till we get to Pearl, then I'll buy you and Nowak all the beer you'd like."

"That's a deal," Tate said, still coughing.

"Okay, Tate," Slaughter said, walking toward him. "You're next."

Slaughter and Jonah took Tate's arms and helped him into the Stokes. They buckled the straps tightly around his chest, his waist and his legs. Jonah looked up the trunk, saw Biagotti's face peering down at him, and waved his arm. "Take him up!" he called. The stretcher was carefully raised to the vertical and rose upward with Slaughter and Jonah climbing after it.

Tate saw the blur of the escape trunk's walls pass by, inch by inch, foot by foot, level by level, and when he came to the wing deck several hands pulled the stretcher through the open door into the bright lights. Lying in the stretcher and looking up through his foggy OBA, he could see faces looking down at him, recognizing the captain and Mister Wilson and several others. He noticed the fire hoses laid along the deck, and Brickey's fire team standing by with their pants stuffed into their socks, some of the team still wearing helmets and their OBAs. They all curiously watched Tate as Slaughter knelt alongside the stretcher and gently pulled the mask off the boy's face.

"Just relax, Tate," Doc said looking down at Tate's bloodshot eyes, singed hair and face covered in black oily water. "Just relax. We're going to take you for a short ride," and Slaughter turned and nodded at Jonah who was standing alongside the stretcher.

"Ready?" Jonah asked, looking at the three other sailors bending down and gripping the rails of the stretcher. "Lift," he ordered and four pairs of hands raised the Stokes smartly from the deck. "Alright, step easy now," Jonah said, and they started off, carrying Tate over the shin knockers and through the open watertight doors, going aft, through one compartment after another toward the sickbay. Tate watched the overhead and the tops of the doors glide by above him, and then he closed his eyes and breathed, then breathed some more, noticing for the first time in his life just how delicious cool, fresh air really tasted.

Brickey sat at a corner seat in the empty mess deck, scratching along the surface of a new pad of paper with a black ballpoint. There was just enough light from the red night lights for him to see what he was writing.

10 March 1966
Dear Mary Jo:

Hope this letter finds you doing well, and that your folks, and the dogs, and your job at the Sundae Shop are all ok.

I have not had a good chance to write since we left Little Creek 'cause we've been pretty busy gettn things done here on the ship and goin thru the Panama Canal. That was quite a experience I have to tell you. So I hope you don't think I forgot you cause I ain't. In fact I think of you often except for the time spent in Panama seeing the sights and experiencing the history and meetn some of the people of the town.

I'm on the same ship as Jonah Wynchester again. You remember me talkn bout him when I was home on leave? And there are other new people also, some good some not so good. Underwood, the yeoman from McMann is here, which is good. But O'Toole and his gang are also here, which is about as crummy a deal as you can imagine. Mister Beaufort was also transferred here but we don't see much of him cause we ain't in his division. Instead we are in Mister Sanders division and he is one snake in the grass, if you get my meaning. If you put your mind to it, he's sort of the same as old man McGuffy down at the village grocery. You might call him "snappish." Anyhow, Jonah and me have not taken a liken to him, so he ain't on our favorites list.

After three days in Panama we are now headn for Pearl Harbor which I am really excited about seeing. Not many guys on the ship have been there before, except for Chief Beckers and Cunningham, and Doc Slaughter. It will be a new experience for the rest of us and everybody is really lookn forward to seeing Hawaii. Scuttlebutt says we will be there for only a few days to refuel, replenish, pick up spare parts, and practice some beachings. That should be different, running a ship onto a beach instead of trying to keep away from the beach. I'll be sure to tell you all about it afterward. I also have to tell you about our gunnery exercise, but before I do that we had some excitement of a couple days ago.

Seems as if they had some type of problem down in the auxillary engine room with one of the diesels. You had a thought that it was the end of the world with all the commotion. It all started just as the evening movie was beginn up on the O1 level. Anyway, they sounded General Quarters and everybody ran to their firefighting stations. Me, I was in the Port Firefighting Team, and we all assembled on the wing deck just aft of the Aux Gen Room door. Anyway, Chief Beckers and Mister Jones, they are engineers, and Jonah, all went down there and took control of the situation, along with some guys from the Starboard Fire Team. I have to tell you I was pretty scared that I would have to go down there too but fortunately they put the fire out before that had to happen. A couple of the snipes down there was overcome with some smoke and spent the next couple days on easy duty. That must a been nice for them, the easy duty I mean, but I'm just glad it weren't me.

Now for the gunnery exercise. You see, the captain and the XO, Mister Crane that is, have been itching to shoot the 40mm guns ever since we left Little Creek, and yesterday was the first chance we had. You have to know that we had to make sure we were in a part of the ocean where there were no other ships around cause we didnt want to be shooting at other ships. So we waited until we got to this empty part of the ocean. The guys in radar made sure there was no other ships on the screen, and then we started the live fire drill. It was somethin else as you will soon come to understand.

Well, first we had already assigned the gun crews since we need a bunch for both 40mm guns. There's the gun captain, that is either Jonah on the aft gun or me on the forward gun. Each gun has a trainer and pointer, and the 1st loader on the left gun and the 1st loader on the right-hand gun. Then each loader has a 2nd loader working with him, passing the 40mm clips up to the 1st loader. Then each 2nd loader has an ammo *passer who passes the clips to them. Then they have other guys who bring the ammo up from the magazines. So, each gun, the one on the bow and the one on the stern, you know the one on the bow is the front and the stern is the back? Well, each gun has 11 guys in each gun crew. So that means we needed 22 guys in all to work both 40mm guns. Then there's Mister Sanders the gunnery officer who is in charge of the whole shooting match so to speak. After the gun crews were chosen we spent a couple of days dry firing and going through the motions, practicing so everybody would know their job. We didn't want nobody losing any fingers or hands when loading the 40mm ammo. Then this morning when the guys in the radar shack told us the coast was clear, we commenced firing. My gun crew did real good, but Jonah had some problems.*

First we painted a 55-gallon drum with red lead and lowered that over the side...that was the target. Then the ship moved away to about 200 yards away. When all was ready, the captain gave the command and my crew commenced firing our forward gun. We only fired on full manual, and only one round at a time. Poldolski was the trainer on our gun and he did mighty fine keeping the target sighted considering the ship was rolling pretty good, moving at such a slow speed and with that fat LCU lashed high up on the main deck. Anyway, we rolled and fired and rolled and fired and we were pretty close to the target. Mister Sanders then told us to go to full clips and to fire off a full clip. And would you believe that every round of that full clip hit that can? Wham! Wham! Wham! Wham! Boy, were we ever excited about that. I started jump'n up and down and Poldolski was yelling like a wild man. Mister Sanders told us to cut that out right off, but he sure could not keep the grins off everybodys faces. We shot several more full clips until that can sunk plumb out of sight. Then it was Jonah's turn on the aft gun.

Well, he didn't do so good. That aft gun me and him had worked on quite a bit, but I guess we didn't do as good a job as could be expected. Anyway, after they put another can over the side and the ship moved away about 200 yards, Jonah started shooting. He could not hit a dang thing. Over and over they tried, but they would miss and miss. Not by much, but they still missed. Boy, I just knew that musta been awful frustratn for Jonah. I saw Mister Sanders, and, well, he was not a happy person. Not at all. You should'a heard him hollering. He threw a hissey and gave Jonah what for right in the gun tub, in front of everybody. I ain't never seen Jonah so whupped, that is since he was busted for that fight in Naples. Poor guy. He sure did look like that old hound dog of yours.

Well, I got the mid watch coming up soon, so I better finish this letter now. Enclosed is a couple of post cards from Panama, one showing the canal and the other card showing part of the old town which I found interest'n. I'm also enclosing some pictures I took goin through the canal. The one with me also shows Jonah, he's the guy with the scar on his face, and Underwood, he's the tall one with the thick glasses. The big guy on the left is Biagotti, our bosun's mate. And the short tough looking guy on the right is Homer our shipfitter (that's a welder.) We are about 10 days from Pearl Harbor so this letter won't get mailed till then.

Please give my hello to your folks and I hope you can write soon.

Sincerely yours,

Billy

PS: just to remind you, my address is:
   GMSN - William D. Brickey, USN
   USS WINCHESTER COUNTY
   Fleet Post Office
   San Francisco, California 96601

CHAPTER 4
PEARL HARBOR

The purple-gray silhouette floating above the horizon resembled a reclining woman, with her long hair flowing back and disappearing into the low clouds. Most of the island was hidden in the Kona fog, but the heady scent of humid earth, hibiscus and tropical vegetation wafted across the water leaving no doubt where they were.

"Waikiki," Davant said, his pipe clenched firmly in his teeth, and he pointed toward the hotel lights winking through the thinning clouds five miles in the distance. "And Diamond Head over there ..." his pointing hand shifted to the right. "Did you know that crater is half-a-million years old?" he added, standing next to Browning as they watched the light of early dawn beginning to infuse the clouds with an orange glow. "Doesn't this make you feel as if you're approaching paradise?"

"I don't know about paradise," Browning said, rubbing the back of his hand across the bristles on his face. "But what I am feeling is the aftermath of the mugging Crane gave me last night."

"What do you mean, mugging?" Davant asked, relighting his pipe.

"What do I mean? Hell! How could I know we were gonna run out of haze gray paint?" and Browning turned and looked at the bulkheads pockmarked with red lead. "What did I do in a former life to deserve this?"

"Sometimes, Sam..." Davant said, taking the pipe from his teeth. "...life just throws a curve ball at us and there's just not much we can do about it."

"Well, that's easy for you to say, Len. You weren't the one the XO ripped up one side and down the other."

"That is true, my friend," Davant said. "But I feel your pain. Hey, it's not just you; the entire ship will receive the astonished stares of the Pearl Harbor beautification committee when we putt-putt through the channel later this morning. None of us will escape their sharp, glaring eyes, nor the low marks they'll give us on our score cards."

"Aw, hell! Do you have to be so damn sarcastic about everything? Can't you just empathize for a change? For crying out loud!" Browning's black dog mood matched his black eyes. "I'm gonna get cleaned up," he said in disgust. "I'll see 'ya at breakfast," and he turned and walked through the open door of the deck house into officer country.

No one aboard The Cathedral was immune from the unpleasant certainty that all of Pearl Harbor was watching them as they entered the channel two hours later. The ship's diesel exhaust-smudged sides, rusting bluff bow, the hulking LCU on the main deck and the splotches of red lead paint scattered across the bulkheads gave her the appearance of some toxic floating disease. While every member of the crew visible on the weather decks were now dressed in their whites, they were acutely aware that clean uniforms were not disguising their ugly shanty town as they entered the holiest of all places in the annals of the U.S. Navy.

They slowly passed Waipio Point off the port side and saw Ford Island coming into view ahead, and when the ship turned 90 degrees to starboard they watched large gantry cranes crawling along the numerous piers where dozens of ships were moored. They looked in amazement at the lush green mountains, the sleek destroyers and powerful cruisers dazzling in the calm water, and the freshly manicured lawns surrounding the immaculate whitewashed buildings. The Cathedrals had never seen anything so neat, so perfect, so Real Navy in all their experiences. And as they entered the Southeast Lock with its submarine base and tall training tower, the ship approached a concrete quay to starboard, and there, standing on the quay, neatly lined up in two rows with their crisp white uniforms displaying perfect knife edged creases, their spit-shined shoes and polished instruments glinting from the bright Hawaiian sun, stood a Navy band playing *Hello Dolly!*

"I ain't never seen the likes of 'dis before," Biagotti said as the ship approached the quay. "Just look at 'dis!" and he waved his hand out towards the band and the buildings beyond. "Have you ever had a band welcome your ship before?"

"Come to think of it," Mills answered. "No, I ain't. I ain't never been to Pearl Harbor before neither. But I'm loving this."

"Well," Jonah said. "Either they knew Biagotti was arriving," and he glanced at Mills. "Or, they had noth'n better to do this morning."

"Of course 'dey knew Biagotti was arriving!" Biagotti laughed, a comical grin across his face. "Why else would 'dey go to all 'dat trouble of shining 'der shoes? Ha, ha."

"All right, Biagotti, let's get this damn brow over," Browning ordered, his freshly shaved face and clean uniform unable to conceal his dark mood.

"Yes, sir," the big bosun said, and he turned toward Mills who was standing right next to him. "Mills, you heard what the 1st Lieutenant just said! Get the damn brow over!"

Mills rolled his eyes and shook his head as the hierarchy of cascading orders eventually fell upon his shoulders. He released his frustration by yelling at several of the deck gang. "Get this damn brow moved, you lazy bunch of no good ..." Six sailors manhandled the big, heavy brow and slid it across the deck. Smitty stood a few paces away with a large, bulky leather mail bag slung over one shoulder, fidgeting and shifting from one foot to the other, anxious to go ashore and get to the post office.

Davant was also waiting for the brow, holding a thick file of requisitions in his hand.

"You ready to be turned down again, like when you invited that girl on your first dance?" Browning asked

"Well," Davant answered. "I figure they have to honor most of these requisitions. Over half of 'em are priority; we've got a pile of equipment that needs replacement parts. Plus, our wonderful laundry machine crapped out again last night, and God knows we've got to get that fixed before we leave Pearl."

"Yea, good luck with that," Browning added

"Don't worry, we'll get it fixed before you know it."

"Maybe, but if not, you won't find any laundry trucks waiting for us in the middle of the Western Pacific. And if it doesn't get fixed, all hell's gonna break loose. You know, Len, I'm glad you have such a mighty positive outlook towards the supply miracles of Pearl Harbor," Browning said. "Just make sure my pallets of haze gray paint are included, okay?"

"The req's are all right here in the file," and Davant patted the large folder he was holding.

"That's good. Requisitions are good. But paint is better. When do you think it'll be here?"

"Should be today. We radioed the list to them two days ago."

"It damn well better," Browning said, watching Mills lowering the brow down to the quay. "Cause if I don't get that paint, well then, I won't be the only one having to answer the XO," and Browning leaned forward and looked straight at Davant.

"All set, Mister Browning," Biagotti called over when the brow was across.

Davant saluted the quarterdeck then the ensign, and went quickly down the brow with Smitty following, as a large, rotund chief petty officer waited on the quay. As soon as the brow was clear the chief chugged his way up against gravity, huffing and puffing, saluted Homer, the petty officer of the watch, and stepped onto the main deck. "Where can I find a Mister Sanders?" the chief asked in a scratchy baritone voice.

Jonah noticed the exchange between the chief and Homer, and he saw Poldolski lead the stranger into the deck house. Oh, shit, I know what that's about, Jonah thought and turned and walked back to the armory. A few minutes later Mendoza stuck his head into the confined space. "Hey Wynchester!" Mendoza said.

"Yea?"

"Mister Sanders wants you."

"Where?" Jonah asked.

"Stateroom."

"What kind'a mood is he in?"

Mendoza frowned, rolled his eyes and shook his head.

"Okay, 'Doza. Thanks for the warning," and Jonah locked the armory door and walked to the deck house and into officer country, thinking, oh, God, here we go!

"You wanted to see me, sir?" Jonah asked, standing just outside Sanders' stateroom.

"This is Chief Erikson," Sanders said, pointing at the rotund chief whose shirt buttons were clearly straining against his very large belly.

"Morning, Chief," Jonah nodded in the chief's direction.

"The chief's here to help us with our 40s," Sanders said as he looked at Jonah out of the corner of his eye. "As you remember, I requested help after your poor performance during our gunnery practice eleven days ago."

"Yes, sir." Jonah felt the heat rising in his neck with Sanders' use of the words *your poor performance*. He knew Sanders was mocking him. The chief's stoic face, looking between Jonah and Sanders, didn't reveal a thing.

"The chief's going to see to it that the sights on our 40s are properly aligned."

"Yes, sir," Jonah said, his hands behind his back bending and twisting his ball cap.

"The sight test target will be set up on the quay," Sanders continued. "And the chief will help you align the sights on both guns."

"Yes, sir," Jonah nodded.

"My crew is setting up the test target now, sir," Erikson said. "We can get started as soon as Wynchester is ready," he added looking at Jonah.

"He's ready now, aren't you Wynchester?" Sanders asked, more of a command than a question.

"Yes, sir."

"And Wynchester?"

"Sir?"

"We're only going to be in Pearl a few days. Tomorrow morning we go around the island to Kaneohe Bay for beaching practice. So, this sight alignment has to be started now and completed by 1600 today. You got that?"

"Yes, sir."

"Okay," and Sanders looked at his watch. "You've got seven hours."

⊷⊶

"Come, on!" Dorsey shouted to a work party of a dozen sailors who were unloading boxes of cans, frozen meats and crates of fruit from a truck on the pier. Jonah and the chief stood aside on the main deck, allowing the work party to climb up the brow.

"Come on people!" Dorsey continued shouting. "What'ch wait'n fer, get 'em up'a here! What'ch doing with 'dat? Can't you carry noth'n? Hey, you, where'd you git 'yo muscles, from, 'yo mama, or did 'yo answer some advertisement from 'dat muscled Carl Hatless guy? Come on man, move it, we ain't got all day! You want those steaks to melt on dis here concrete, or do you want 'em to melt in 'yo mouth at lunch today? Wat'sa matter w'you? Well, dats what you gonna have for lunch, so hurry up. Hey, you, I don't know 'yo name, but you be one lazy boot. Oh, no! No!" he yelled as a sailor dropped a crate of oranges on the pier. "Oh, no man! No!" The crate's thin wooden slats burst open and oranges went in every direction with the sailor chasing the fruit in an ever-expanding circle.

"God, Almighty, dis here bunch'a boots ain't worth noth'n," Dorsey said as he came up the brow with an armload of oranges. "And if this ain't The Cathedral Circus, well I don't know what is!" and he looked at Jonah with a sly, conspiratorial grin. "But..." he said in a low voice, "...we be having steaks for lunch today, Wynchester, so yo better bring 'yo appetite."

"Don't worry, Dorsey, I'll be there. Maybe the chief can join us too?"

"Well, sure man," Dorsey said, looking at the chief's belly. "The chief looks like he could handle another steak."

Jonah and Erikson went down the brow and started walking across the quay when Jonah suddenly yanked the chief's arm, pulling him out of the way of a speeding truck.

"Holy Shit!" the shocked Erikson said. "That sonov'a'bitch! That guy could'a retired me on the spot!" and he looked at Jonah wide eyed. "Thanks, Wynchester. That was close. That was too close." He brought his hand up to his forehead.

"Yea, no problem, Chief. I'm glad I saw him coming."

"Man, oh, man. You ain't the only one."

"We need to be a little more careful out here. Those guys aren't paying no attention."

"You got that right!"

They cautiously continued to the other side of the broad quay where two other gunner's mates were bolting a 5-foot long horizontal aluminum bar to the top of a 5-foot high aluminum tripod. The horizontal piece had four round targets bolted to it; two of the targets were near the ends of the bar, the other two targets were near the center.

"Hey, Leonard, you almost done with that target?" the chief asked the tall gunner.

"Yup, be ready in 5-minutes, Chief," Leonard answered.

"Did you level it with the bubble?"

"Yup, sure did, Chief. Leveled right on the money."

"Did you measure off the distance?" the chief asked.

"Yup, 150-feet. Ain't that right Lovatt?"

"Sure is, 150 feet." the short gunner answered.

"Okay, then," the chief said. "Now, I want you to make sure no damn car or truck parks between the target and the ship."

"Right, Chief. No damn cars or trucks. Don't worry, Chief. Lovatt and I will keep the target clear. Not even a laundry truck will interrupt us."

"Especially no laundry truck. And be careful out here with all these crazy drivers."

"Right, Chief."

"So, Wynchester, we understand the #2 gun gave you the most trouble?"

"Right, the aft gun."

"That's what we were told. We'll start with that one first."

"I've already got our tools and the boresight up there now."

"Okay, then. Hey, Leonard, like we talked about, we're gonna do the aft gun first."

"Right, Chief. Just like we talked about, the aft gun first," the tall gunner replied, tightening the last of the bolts on the target.

"So, get lined up and make sure your bubble is level," Erikson said.

"Lined up and level for the aft gun. Will do, Chief."

"Wynchester, what boresight you got?" the chief asked as they cautiously walked back across the quay to the ship, carefully looking left and right, and left and right again.

"A Wollensak. The Mark 1."

"That'll work," Erikson said, climbing back up the brow, gasping and out of breath.

"Chief, this is Brickey, gunner striker," Jonah pointed to Brickey as they stepped into the aft gun tub. "He's gonna help us today."

"Okay, Brickey" the chief said. "Get the breech open, and then get in the trainer seat. Wynchester, hand me that sight."

Jonah handed the heavy brass "L" shaped boresight to the chief.

"This thing's hardly been used!" the chief said, surprised at the almost brand-new boresight as he spread a thin film of oil around the large end. He held it up to the light and made sure the oil was evenly spread around the bore end, then leaned over with a grunt and gently inserted it into the breech of the right-hand barrel, with the sight's eye-piece sticking out at a 45-degree angle.

"Wynchester, go ahead and get that muzzle sight in the right-hand barrel," the chief ordered. Jonah lightly oiled the other sight, and using a long brass rod slowly inserted it through the right-hand flash hider and six inches into the muzzle end of the barrel.

"Okay, Chief, we're good."

"Wynchester, you get in the pointer seat and aim your sight," Erikson said. "Brickey, you're going to train the gun toward the target. Both of you, let me know when your sight is lined up. You ready? Go slowly, now."

Brickey and Jonah slowly turned the control wheels; Brickey training the gun around to the left, Jonah pointing the gun down, their collective controls aiming the gun towards the target across the quay.

"My sight's on," Brickey called out.

"Elevation is good," Jonah said, and the chief, with his big belly getting in the way, bent over the breech of the gun and looked through the eye-piece of the boresight.

"*Jaevla! Chick-chick-chick.*" Erikson shook his head and clicked his tongue behind his teeth. Jonah glanced at the chief. "This thing is some uff-da!" the chief said in his Minnesota accent. "Really uff-da."

"What?" Jonah asked. "Uff-da?"

"Snakker du Norsk?" Erikson replied.

"Huh?"

"You speak Norwegian?"

"Uh, no," Jonah answered.

"Well, glem det," the chief said. "Never mind, but, man, these sights are really pickled. Hey, Brickey, come left an inch, real slow. A little more. More. Stop. Hold that." The chief took off his cap, wiped his eyes, and looked through the eye piece again.

"Wynchester, come up two inches, real slow, more. Stop."

"Okay," Erikson said. "Let me look through your sight, Brickey." The chief moved over and crouched behind Brickey, looking through the pointer sight. "Damn! This is brutal. I don't think you could hit a barn with this gun. Wynchester, did you make any hits with this gun?"

"Not really, Chief. All misses with a couple of close ones."

The chief thought about that, his silence deafening. Brickey and Jonah exchanged glances.

"Doesn't surprise me," the chief finally said, shaking his head. "All right, now let me check your pointer sight," and the chief moved into a position behind Jonah and looked through his pointer sight. "Man! We got our work cut out for us on this thing. Okay. Brickey, get your wrenches and let's start by adjusting your sight first."

A minute later Sanders climbed up to the tub and stood watching as the three gunners went through their paces. Jonah and Brickey trained and pointed the gun as the chief called out directions. They sighted the bores directly on the target, and then adjusted the sights degree by degree. During the sighting process two different trucks attempted to park between the ship and the target, the drivers not realizing they were interfering with an operation of significant importance, and Leonard and Lovatt quickly shooed them away, clearing the visual path of the bore sighting gunner's mates. After a few minutes of this repetitive series of adjustments, an apathetic Sanders climbed down out of the tub and walked away.

Erikson leaned over the breech and peered into the sight. "Well, dammit to hell!" he yelled.

Jonah turned in his seat and stared at the chief. "What?"

"Some damn jeep just parked in front of my target!"

Jonah sat upright and turned. Erikson was looking across the quay with a steely-eyed glare. He leaned out over the edge of the gun tub and shouted to Leonard across the quay. "Get that jeep out'a there!"

The driver, an ensign, stepped out of the jeep and started to walk away. Leonard chased after the officer, and using subtle expressions and groveling body language, tried to convince the ensign to move the jeep.

"Sir! Sir!" Leonard cried, running after the officer. "You can't park there, sir," he said waving his hand.

The young ensign stopped and turned around. "Why not?" he asked, clearly feeling his oats and the superiority of his rank over Leonard's 3rd class stripe.

"Sir, we're bore-sighting in some guns, sir," and Leonard pointed to the stern 40mm gun on the LST across the quay. "From the guns on that LST to this target here, sir," and then he pointed to the target on the tripod. "The one your jeep is parked in front of." The ensign turned and looked at the ship. He saw three men standing in the gun tub, watching, with their hands on their hips, frustration apparent on their faces.

"Well, that's stupid," the ensign said. "Are you trying to make me believe that this ridiculous contraption is gonna help you aim that gun?"

"Yes, sir. We set it up early this morning and the chief up there ordered me not to let nobody park in front of it."

The three gunners on the ship, at a standstill with the jeep blocking the target, watched the pantomime unfold as the ensign argued with Leonard, the words impossible to hear over the distance. Leonard's hands and arms waved and pointed from the ship to the target and back to the ship.

The ensign looked toward the ship again and saw the chief frantically waving his arms. The glare in the chief's eyes appeared as if he was trying to move the jeep through telekinesis. "Well, I'm only gonna to be a minute," the ensign said, turning back to Leonard. "So, you'll just have to wait. Besides what's in this envelope..." and he tapped a large manila envelope he was holding. "What's in this envelope is a lot more important than your stupid gun," and he walked away.

Leonard threw his hands up in a gesture of defeat as he looked back toward Erikson with a pleading expression on his face.

"Well, damn, that's a kick in the pants," Erikson said. "That pint-sized wet behind the ears pimple-faced butterbar of an ensign is screwing up my entire alignment!" and he began waving to Leonard, waving for him to come over to the ship. Leonard ran across the quay, avoiding a speeding truck, and stopped at the water's edge opposite the gun tub.

"Push it forward a length or two," the chief yelled down to Leonard. Leonard looked up cupping his hands to his ears. "Put the jeep in neutral...!" the chief yelled louder over the noise of trucks and cranes moving along the quay. "Put the jeep in neutral and push the damn thing out'a the way!" Leonard raised a hand in acknowledgment and ran back across the quay to the jeep. In a matter of seconds he and Lovatt had the problem solved. A minute after Leonard put the jeep's hand brake on, the ensign returned, got in and drove away. "Don't that beat all."

The loosening, adjusting and tightening of the front and rear sights on the trainer and pointer sight assemblies went on and on, over and over, and back and forth. Two hours later, to Erikson's satisfaction and Jonah's relief, they had zeroed in both sights of the gun to the target across the quay.

"Well," Erickson said, wiping his sweaty face and arms with a handkerchief. "That was a hell of a lot more time consuming than I ever thought possible. It don't appear as if that thing had been sighted in years."

"I never imagined it could be out," Jonah said with a guilty look. "Certainly not that far out."

"Ah, don't worry, Wynchester. You found out ten days ago and now it'll shoot straighter than Route 71."

"Route 71?"

"Yea, 71. That's a road that goes between Big Falls and Mizpah, back near my hometown in Minnesota. It's about 25 miles of the straightest damn road you ever saw. People driving on it get transfixed. They fall asleep and go right into the ditches. But man, it sure is straight. Okey dokey, one gun down, and one gun to go," Erikson said looking at his watch and rubbing his big belly. "Say, did that cook of yours say you were having steaks for lunch today?"

"Yep, sure did," Jonah replied.

"Hey, Brickey!" the chief said. "Go down there," and Erikson pointed. "And relieve Leonard and Lovatt for chow. I'll have them back in under 20 minutes, then you can go eat. And don't let nobody get near that damn target! Come on, Wynchester, let's go see what kind'a smorgasbord that cook of yours has whipped up today."

❧

"Well, this has turned out to be a good day after all," Erikson said, and he belched as he and Jonah stood in the forward gun tub. "Not only was that steak the best I've had in a long time, but we also found out your forward gun is sighted spot on. So, now you've got accurate shoot'n guns on both ends of this LST. What could be better than that? By the way, Wynchester, tell me, do you guys eat that good all the time?"

Jonah, dumbfounded, turned and looked at the chief in disbelief. "Ha, that's funny, Chief," he said laughing and shaking his head. "We ran out of fresh food almost two weeks ago ... when we were somewhere near half ways across from Panama. Until that steak you just had, we've been eat'n food that came from tin cans and boxes."

"Oh," the chief said. "Sorry, I didn't realize. Yea, that makes sense. But, damn that sure was a good steak. Don't 'ya think?"

"Well, pretty good; maybe not the best I've ever had, but pretty good," Jonah said, thinking about the steady diet of fresh steaks on the ranch. "Back on the ranch we ate cow every day, breakfast, dinner and supper."

"A ranch?"

"I grew up on a cattle ranch. In Idaho."

"So that's where the cowboy drawl comes from. I thought you were just making that up."

"Nope. Sorry to disappoint."

"Well I'll be damn. Idaho, huh? Amazing. You know, you being from Idaho and me being from Minnesota, well, ya just can't get much further from salt water than those two states, can ya?"

"Yea, I suppose not."

"So, you're going to WESTPAC?" Erikson asked.

"Yep, next stop is Subic Bay, and then Vietnam."

"Subic? Oh, brother. Ha. Subic!" Erikson's face turned sour as if he'd just sucked on a lemon. "Well, I'll tell 'ya my friend, if you go on liberty in Subic, in that piss pot, you better hang tight to your wallet."

"That bad?"

"It ain't Hawaii, that's for sure. Listen, liberty on this island is wonderful. Beautiful. Four-oh in every category. And I sure hope you get a chance to experience some of it while you're here. But, Subic? Hmm, maybe you'll luck out and not be there very long. Let me tell ya, once you blow all your money in Olongapo, well, there ain't noth'n else to do there. You better hope you leave about as soon as you arrive."

"What's Olongapo?"

"A shitty town across a shitty river where everybody goes to get shit-faced. If you cross the bridge into Olongapo, well, just make sure you don't bring all your money with you. Leave some back on the ship. Those bar girls and pickpockets will fleece you faster than a greased fart. And make sure you get back to the base before they lock the gate at midnight!"

"Thanks, I'll remember that."

"Don't mention it. Remember, midnight."

"Right, midnight. Thanks."

"So, how long you been on this fine look'n LST?" Erikson asked looking around at the old ship, the rust, the LCU chained to the main deck, and he inserted a toothpick between his molars and started digging.

"Reported aboard New Year's Day ... the coldest damn day I'd experienced since I left Idaho."

"Cold in Little Creek?"

"Yea. Snow. Ice. It was miserable. Big snowstorm came through the day before."

"Damn. I never knew it snowed in Little Creek! I always thought that was just a hot and humid swamp?"

"Well, not when I was there," Jonah said with a look of disgust.

"Huh. I'll be damn. Guess I'll have to file that away in my encyclopedia. So, tell me, you like it here? On this LST?"

"Well, it's sure a whole lot different from what I was on before."

"What was that?"

"A tin can."

"Out of where?"

"Norfolk."

"Hmm."

"Yea, an old Fletcher."

"Which one?"

"McMann."

"*McMann?*" The chief's eyes lit up and a big smile spread across his face. "Well I'll be. Hah, *McMann!*"

"You know *McMann?*"

"Yea. I've got a good friend who's on *McMann.* Or at least he was the last time I heard from him. Did you know a chief gunner's mate by the name of Roland Foster?"

Jonah stared at Erikson in shock. He knows Foster, Jonah thought. He knows Foster. But apparently he doesn't know what happened. He doesn't know about the fire on the carrier, or about *McMann.* He has no idea. Good God. "Yea," Jonah said cautiously, looking at the chief sideways. "I did know him."

"You knew him? Well I'll be. Ain't this a small world? Absolutely amazing. Did he finally get off that old ship? Did he retire?"

"Uh ..." and Jonah looked away, diverting his eyes away from Erikson. "No, he didn't."

"What?" Erikson asked with an almost unperceived look of caution.

"Well, he, uh ..." and Jonah paused again, asking himself if there was any good way of saying this. Do I tell him? Do I just say that I knew him? That maybe I was transferred off *McMann* before I knew any details?

"What?" the chief asked again.

"He, uh..."

"He what?"

"He ... died."

There was silence, a long silence that enveloped them as they both looked at each other; Erikson in confused disbelief, and Jonah in a regretful, painful awkwardness, not knowing what he should say next.

"He died?"

Jonah slowly nodded.

"How?"

"He...uh...he had a heart attack."

"Oh, no! Oh, Dear God!" and Erikson looked down to the base of the gun tub, shaking his head "Oh, no!" he said again. " Wha ...?" he looked up. "Were... Were you there?"

Jonah nodded, an awkward, pained expression on his face.

"What happened?"

Jonah, reflexively inhaled, and thought I've got to be careful how I explain this. God forbid he has a heart attack too. "Well, we were fighting a fire," he finally said. "Fighting a fire alongside a carrier. The *Gloucester*. You might'a heard about it."

Erikson nodded. From the look on his face it was apparent the chief was beginning to understand. His eyes indicated that, yes, he had heard about the fire on *Gloucester*.

"Yea, I did hear about that," Erikson said in a soft voice. "About *Gloucester*...but I had no idea...no idea that *McMann* was with her...I had no idea about Foster..."

Jonah watched him. He could see the chief was struggling, trying to come to grips with this awful news.

"Tell me," Erikson said. "How did it happen?"

Jonah paused before speaking, thinking of Foster, trying to form the right words to explain this. Then he began to recount the day; how he heard the explosions when *McMann* was a mile away, and how he wasn't sure what it was. And then the ship went to general quarters. He used his hands, moving them in front of him, palms down, to show the relative positions of the ships and how *McMann* approached the carrier and came alongside her port quarter. And then he described the explosions and fire and smoke on the flight deck, and how the day was filled with hours of non-stop, semi-controlled panic; the heat and the fire, the firefighting teams trying to get water across the deadly space between the two ships. And then the explosion. The sudden explosion. And then described how he found Foster lying on the deck. Jonah could see Erikson was following his description of the fire and the position of the ships, he was nodding at each part of the story. It was obvious to Jonah that the chief was picturing everything, saw the ships, the flames and the smoke, and the chaos of an aircraft carrier on fire. Erikson was visualizing all of this with a far-away look in his eyes as he nodded, as if he too had been on *McMann*. There was a long breathing space, and the sounds around them from the work parties on The Cathedral and from the trucks driving by on the quay filled the void between them.

"Roland was an old friend," Erickson finally said breaking the silence, his face desolate. "My oldest friend. He and I grew up in the same town. Back in Minnesota. We...we went to the same school, went fish'n in the same creeks, enlisted on the same day. Went through boot camp together, at Great Lakes." Erikson forced himself to breathe and shook his head. "Then we went to Class A school together," he continued. "We didn't see too much of each other after that. But...but we always kept in touch, always exchanged letters, always got together whenever we could. Always had a good time getting caught up." Then the chief was quiet for a moment, lost in thought. He looked up. "I was the best man at his wedding," and he put a hand up to his head. His eyes lost their focus, seemingly looking into the past. "Oh, his wife, Mabel. She must be devastated."

Jonah watched him, saw the despair and the pain from the shocking news. "I'm sorry," Jonah said, thinking he would give anything not to be in this spot at this moment, not to be the one telling all this to Erikson. "I didn't know," and Jonah immediately regretted his comment, thinking this isn't getting any easier, there isn't any better way of breaking this terrible news.

Erikson inhaled and looked up. His eyes stared but he didn't see what was around him. He didn't see the brilliant green hills or the white buildings or the ships alongside the piers. Jonah watched the chief and thought the world must have suddenly stopped for him.

"It's all right," Erikson finally said, staring at nothing. "You had no way of knowing. But you said you were there," and he turned toward Jonah. "You worked with him? You got to know him?"

"I did. He was one heck of a great guy. Our crew thought he was too. And they were all devastated. There were a lot of casualties on *Gloucester*, a lot. But Foster was the only fatality on *McMann*. We had some injuries from the explosion, but he was the only fatality."

"The only one," Erikson said in amazement. "The only one."

"You know, he was a strong personality, knowledgeable in so many things. Everybody liked him. From the snipes in the shaft alleys, all the way up to the old man. They all liked him, respected him a lot. And he was probably the best chief I ever worked with. The very best."

Erikson nodded, understanding what Jonah was trying with difficulty to say. "Yea, that he was," Erikson said quietly. "Yea, he was the very best." Erikson was lost in his thoughts, and then he looked at Jonah. "Was he wounded from the blast? Was he hurt?"

Jonah shook his head. "Our corpsman said he hardly had a scratch on him, that the explosion must'a triggered the heart attack."

Erikson's face was sorrowful and vacant. "Had he been sick? Did he have any signs? Any signs of being sick?"

"He was slowing down. Looking back on it, I guess he was going up ladders kind'a slow. But I don't think anybody knew he might'a had a problem. I don't even know if he knew he had a problem. The Doc had him in sickbay a time before when he complained of heartburn. But I don't know if there were any other signs."

Erikson stood up and moved to the edge of the gun tub, and his eyes seemed to focus, seemed to be comprehending once again what was going on around him. He turned and looked at Jonah. "Thanks," he said. "Thanks for being the one to tell me. I'm ... I'm glad I found this out from you, and not from some obituary in a newspaper. Not from some newspaper that was printed three months ago," and he steadied himself, holding tight to the barrel of the 40mm gun. "I appreciate you telling me."

Jonah nodded, thinking there was nothing else he could say.

Erikson looked up to the sky, the blue sky with the cumulus clouds speeding by in the breeze, his face blank without expression. "Well," and he shook his head. "I guess we're done here." Erikson wiped his hands on a rag and he turned toward Jonah. "I think it's time we probably go see your Mister Sanders. We should report on what we've done."

"You want to do that?" Jonah asked, wondering if Erikson was emotionally ready to talk to Sanders. "Are you up for that?"

"Yea, I think so. Let's get it over with," Erikson replied. Jonah could see the chief was trying to gather up his fortitude, to get control of himself. "Yea, let's do it."

The two gunner's mates walked in silence along the main deck, and Jonah glanced at the big chief and looked at his face. Erikson's mouth was set firm and his eyes seemed to have sunk back in his head. They turned into officer country and found Sanders in his stateroom.

"We're all done, Mister Sanders," the chief reported, holding his cap under his arm as he and Jonah stood in the passageway just outside the doorway.

"All done? So, every thing's perfect for a change?" Sanders said, turning toward Jonah with a look that said he really didn't believe what he was hearing.

"Yes, sir. All perfect again," Erikson said. "Those sights on the number two gun were way off. Must'a been that way for a long time, a real long time ... from the looks of the amount of paint on the bolts. There was no way anybody could hit anything with those sights. Nobody. No-how. I'm surprised that Wynchester got as close to your target as he did during your gunnery exercise. As far as I'm concerned, that's darn good shoot'n. Now he won't miss a thing. That's gun's dead-on now."

"And the forward gun?" Sanders asked.

"Spot on sir, nothing wrong with that one. All our time was taken up with the aft gun. So, if I may say so, you're back in business. And Wynchester and Brickey did a 4.0 job assisting me. Thanks to them, we got it done sooner than expected."

Jonah saw the look on Sanders' face, a face that wasn't liking what the chief was telling him.

"Well," Sanders said dismissively. "Wynchester should have known about the sights needing aligning way before this."

Jonah's eyes opened slightly, but he held himself in check and didn't move. He could feel his neck getting warm.

"With all due respect, sir," Erikson said. "I understand Wynchester only came aboard in January, and the ship departed Little Creek just a few weeks later. Sounds like he had a lot to do in that time. And no one would have thought the sights were out. No one. And you sure wouldn't bet they were out that much. Even I couldn't have dreamed they were that far off. Sights on 40s don't get misaligned just sitting there. Those sights must'a somehow been knocked off center, maybe from getting hit by something. Whatever it was, they should have been aligned a long time ago. A very long time ago. And Wynchester couldn't align them once you were at sea. If you hadn't had your live fire exercise, well, you wouldn't have known. Now your problem's solved. Now they're perfect."

Jonah watched Sanders, sitting there with his eyes squinting, teeth clenched, hands tightly gripping the arms of the chair. He's not liking this, Jonah thought. He's not liking the chief telling him this at all.

"All right, Chief," Sanders said, his scowl slowly turning into a faked, timid smile. "Well done," and he stood up and shook the chief's hand. "Thanks for all your help. We couldn't have done it without you. Nope, certainly not with our people," and he glanced at Jonah.

The left side of Jonah's jaw started pulsing.

"Glad to be of help," Erikson said. "Well, sir, since we're finished here, I'll just be getting my gear packed up."

"And if you're through with me, sir," Jonah said. "I'll get the guns cleaned up and secured."

"Before you go, Wynchester, you should know about this message we just received."

"Sir?"

"It's about the present you're going to receive tomorrow."

"Present, sir?"

"Yes, after we return from our beaching practice at Kaneohe. It's quite a big present, as a matter of fact," and Sanders turned to the papers on his desk and rifled through them.

Jonah's eyes narrowed as he watched Sanders pick up the message.

"Looks like you're going to be busy, Wynchester."

"How's that, sir?"

"We're going to get six new .50s and four new .30s tomorrow?"

"Six .50s, sir?"

"And 24,000 rounds of ammo." Sanders handed the message to Jonah.

With his mouth open, Jonah read the message, the Navy jargon, the cryptic wording, saw the *From* and the *To* with the *Copies* going to several different names; the order for six new .50 caliber and four .30 caliber machine guns, and 24,000 rounds of ammunition, all to be delivered to *USS Winchester County* on Friday, 25 March 1966.

"Holy..." Jonah said, not finishing his comment.

"And, Wynchester," Sanders continued. "You better get busy, 'cause you'll need to find a place to put it all," he said with a contemptuous smile.

"Yes, sir," Jonah mumbled, and he handed the message back to Sanders.

"Oh, one more thing," Sanders continued. "Let me know by quarters tomorrow morning how you plan to accomplish all that." Sanders reached out and shook Erikson's hand again. "Thanks again, Chief," and Sanders reached up to the green curtain and yanked it closed.

Jonah and Erikson stood in the passageway, staring at the closed green curtain, and then looked at each other in disbelief. The chief jerked his head for Jonah to follow him.

"Don't worry about him," Erikson said as he and Jonah walked forward along the main deck. "He's just an ornery kind'a guy. What we call *fractious* where I come from. The more you leave those kind'a people alone, the far less they'll bother you. Just do your job, keep your nose clean, and he'll be less of a problem for you."

"Thanks Chief, I appreciate what you said to him, back in his stateroom. That went a long way."

"No problem. You need any help cleaning up?"

Jonah shook his head. "You've already done more than enough," he said as they stopped near the quarterdeck shack where Mills, the Petty Officer of the Watch, was busily writing in a log book. "And, anyway," Jonah continued. "Brickey's probably got the job almost finished by now."

"Well, then, in that case," Erikson said looking at his watch. "I think I better be getting back to the barracks and do some thinking," and he took a deep breath and looked around him. "Yea, I need to do some thinking. I need to do some thinking about Foster. And I need to get a note written to Mabel, his wife." He turned and looked square at Jonah. "So, I guess I'll be seeing 'ya," and he shook Jonah's hand. "Good luck to you over there. And God bless 'ya." Erikson said, and he turned and saluted the quarterdeck, then the ensign, and went down the brow, making his way cautiously across the quay where Leonard was waiting for him in a jeep, the engine idling and the canvas top shaking.

Jonah watched them drive off, and the heat that had been building in his neck got hotter and hotter and he pulled his ball cap off and smacked it violently into the side of the quarterdeck shack. "Sonov'a'bitch," he mumbled loudly under his breath.

Mills turned from writing in the log book and glared at Jonah. "Hey! What the hell's wrong with you, Wynchester?"

"Ah! None of your damn business!" and he walked aft, burning inside, lost in thought as he headed toward the armory. New guns and 24,000 rounds of ammo? This is crazy, he thought. Two-hundred and forty cans of ammo? Who's gonna carry it all? Dammit, we're gonna need a hell'uv'a work party to get all this stuff aboard. A big work party! He was getting hotter. And where in the hell are we gonna put all this shit? Does Biagotti have any empty compartments? Jonah visualized carrying the 83-pound .50 caliber machine guns in their wooden crates, and the 35-pound ammo cans, plus the .30 caliber guns, up the steep brow, across the main deck, down to the tank deck, and then storing them in a compartment. Maybe two compartments! This is gonna take hours! We'll probably need a bunch of people! At least 10 people! Maybe more! Sonov'a'bitch. It never fails. It's always something, and he stepped over the shin knocker into the armory.

"Boy, that Chief Erikson was sure a funny guy, wasn't he?" Brickey said, his smile suddenly turning serious as he noticed the angry dark cloud across Jonah's face.

"That sonov'a'bitch just told me we got some damn stuff coming aboard tomorrow!"

"The chief?"

"No, Sanders!"

"What stuff tomorrow?"

"More guns."

"What guns?"

"New .50 calibers."

".50s?"

"Yea, and .30s. And ammo!"

"Ammo?"

"Yea, a shit load ... 24,000 rounds!"

"Holy cow!"

"Yea, holy cow. You got that right! Shit!" and Jonah looked around him, at the open boxes of tools spread around the deck, a pile of oily rags in the corner. "Hey, get these damn tools put away! What the hell 'ya been doing all afternoon?" and Jonah turned and started walking out of the armory. "And get this damn place cleaned up! It looks like a shit storm came through here!"

"What, mess?" Brickey said, suddenly turning angry. "I've been working on it, ain't I? Give me a break, Jonah! I'll get it done! For crying out loud!"

"Aw, hell! I gotta find Biagotti!"

CHAPTER 5

WESTPAC

Underwood thought the short, thick robusto cigar firmly clenched in the captain's teeth was very much the same as the man smoking it: bulky, hulking, with a short, hot fuse. And as the tall yeoman watched the acidic, meaty smoke blowing away in the powerful northeast trade wind he realized he knew very little about Lieutenant H.I. Kell, USNA Class of 1959. He knew the captain had come from a destroyer squadron desk job, that he was married, had lived somewhere around Norfolk, and was 27 years old. What Underwood didn't know was that Kell had once been a second string defensive tackle on the Navy team, until on a fateful day in '58 during the final minutes of the annual slug fest against Army, his right knee was forced into an unnatural position, tearing most of the ligaments. As trainers carried Midshipman Kell off the field that day, with his dreams of fame and glory sinking fast, he experienced a sudden premonition that he might have witnessed his apogee, that things could be much worse than Navy's 22-6 defeat. He was correct. Eventually graduating 790 out of a class of 800, Kell found himself on a steep downhill treadmill, assigned to a series of old ships and backwater desk jobs, until he was unexpectedly selected as the Commanding Officer of *USS Winchester County*. Some of his former classmates, however, recognized the assignment for what it was, knowingly whispering to each other that a second string defensive tackle with a gammy knee and ranking near the bottom of his class, was not going to be awarded any of the juicier plumb assignments. Instead, Kell received orders no one else wanted; to a dilapidated LST considered too old, ugly and slow for the higher achievers.

Although the stubby cigar was only the third the captain had smoked since the ship departed Pearl four hours ago, it was clearly evident from the bulge in his shirt pocket that he was carrying an ample reserve supply. As he sucked on the cigar, he paced back and forth from one wing of the conn to the other, growling and grimacing, repeatedly pausing to peer through his aviator sunglasses and into his high-powered binoculars, searching for the elusive sea buoy somewhere ahead marking the entrance to Kaneohe Bay.

"Charlie!" the captain yelled over the loud drumming of the signal flags above their heads. "You got the bearing on that tower yet?"

There was no answer from Charlie Crane. He was frantically attempting to take a bearing on the captain's favorite tower as the ship rolled and plunged in the deep swells and strong breeze. The captain watched the XO sighting through the eyepiece of the pelorus, struggling to balance himself against the ship's gyrations, and tired of waiting, he decided to ask someone else. He swung around and looked at Cunningham, the Chief Quartermaster.

"Chief, you got it?" the captain asked as Cunningham tried to take the bearing among the numerous buildings, church steeples and radio towers cluttering the Kaneohe peninsula and beyond.

"Yes, Sir," Cunningham answered. "Two-seven-zero to the tower. Another three miles to the sea buoy."

"Very well," the captain acknowledged, shaking his head. "Just keep on it, will you?" he added with a frustrated look. "Charlie! I wanna get into the bay in one piece! Okay?"

"Yes, Sir," Crane said, the strain of coastal navigation clearly showing on the XO's haggard face.

The morning had started off on the wrong foot for the Cathedrals; the 0430 reveille, to the crew's consternation and grumbling, was immediately followed by one of Dorsey's indigestible breakfasts, and then the Special Sea & Anchor Detail was set at 0600, all this early preparation so the ship could depart Pearl Harbor at 0630. They were now cautiously making their way along Oahu's sunny east coast, searching for the invisible channel that would take them to the beaching area of the Kaneohe Bay Marine base.

The tension on the conn was palpable. In addition to the Captain, the XO and Chief Cunningham, there were six others: Davant as Officer of the Deck, and two lookouts, plus Pike, O'Toole and Underwood ... a total of nine people moving in and out of the conn and along the wings.

Underwood, standing just inside the conn, adjusting the straps on his sound-powered phone, wondered how many times he had done this before; maybe 200? Or 300? Four ships over five years? Yea, 300 is probably about right, he reflected. But today is gonna be a first, he thought; the first time I'll be on a ship that will intentionally run into a beach! This'll be interesting. Definitely interesting. He depressed the button on the phone's transmitter. "All stations, Conn," he said into the microphone. "Phone check."

As Underwood waited for the other stations to reply, he moved the tight-fitting earphone off his left ear and up to the side of his head, the better to hear what was being said by those around him.

And he watched the surf rolling into the windward side of the coastline, the huge waves smashing against the ragged volcanic rocks and throwing exploding jets of water high into the air.

"Bow anchor, aye." Poldolski's voice came loud and clear through Underwood's right earphone, acknowledging the request for a phone check. Underwood looked forward the 250 feet to the bow and saw Poldolski standing next to Browning, both of them looking toward the shore and the sprawling Marine base on the peninsula guarding Kaneohe Bay.

"Stern anchor, aye," another voice crackled through Underwood's right earphone, this one from Ross on the stern of the ship acknowledging the request for a circuit check.

"Conn, aye," Underwood repeated into the mouthpiece. "Ross," he said. "Check your plug, you've got a helluva lot of static."

Underwood turned and looked around him, at the people on the conn, including O'Toole adjusting his phone connecting him to the engine room. With the need for the captain to communicate to multiple parts of the ship during the beaching exercise, two telephone talkers were on the conn this morning; Underwood's phone, connected to the bow and stern anchors, and O'Toole connected to the engine room. Underwood clearly understood the importance of the multiple phones, and since he had done this hundreds of times before, it was nothing new for him. But looking at O'Toole, it was apparent the big storekeeper was not at all happy about being on the conn or having to stand so close to the captain. The eyebrows on O'Toole's owl shaped face came together as he scowled and fidgeted with the earphones, fighting a losing battle trying to make the bulky WWII device more comfortable. The long, twisted and knotted cable connecting his phone to the bulkhead jack was also giving him trouble, preventing him from moving out of the confined space. O'Toole impatiently yanked the cord's plug out of the jack box and stormed out of the conn, aggressively flipping and straightening the cable, untying the multitude of knots as he mumbled and cursed under his breath.

Go ahead, Underwood thought. Go ahead O'Toole, make an ass of yourself.

The ship slowly made its turn into the channel, heading for the beaching area, its bow doors now opened wide and the ramp lowering down to a 45-degree angle. The moderate gale pushed the ship sideways across the channel, crabbing the ungainly hull toward the left side. The captain nervously paced from one wing to the other, forcing people out of his way as if they were bowling pins, everyone moving aside in a confused jumble. Underwood retreated from the fast walking captain, allowing his phone cable to unwind as he walked backward, then coiling it up again as he went the other direction. He suppressed a rising, barely controllable laugh, watching the others going through a series of awkward dance steps, all perched on a confined space 40-feet above the water.

The captain looked forward through his aviator sunglasses, judging the distances in the channel, his cigar jutting from his mouth seemingly pointing in the direction he wished to take the ship. He looked aft, and then from port to starboard, the cigar always preceding him by several inches.

"Right 10 degrees rudder," the captain ordered, and Davant repeated the command through the voice tube leading down to the helmsman in the pilot house two levels below.

"Right 10 degrees rudder," Davant said, and the helmsman repeated the order back to Davant. "Very well," Davant acknowledged.

"Stand by the stern anchor," the captain ordered.

"Stand by the stern anchor," Underwood repeated the command through his sound-powered phone connecting him to Ross at the stern anchor winch.

"Both engines ahead one-third," the captain ordered, and O'Toole repeated the command into his phone.

"Engine room answers both engines ahead one-third," O'Toole said.

"Rudder amidships," the captain ordered.

The strong wind came across the bay and pushed against the high slab side of the ship, the LCU on the main deck adding even more sail area, and the LST continued crabbing to the left.

"Right 10 degrees rudder," the captain ordered, attempting to compensate for the ship's leeway.

"Right 10 degrees rudder," Davant repeated through the voice tube.

The ship continued crabbing toward the left side of the channel.

"Port engine ahead two thirds!" the captain shouted over the noise of the wind.

"Port engine ahead two thirds, "O'Toole repeated through his phones. "Engine room answers port engine ahead two thirds." O'Toole, unaccustomed to handling a sound powered phone in the stressful atmosphere on the conn, was not happy. He had a frustrated, confused look, and he fidgeted with the cord with one hand and tightly gripped the phone's transmitter with the other.

The captain rushed to the port wing, looked forward, turned and looked aft, watching the wake to see if the course change was having any effect over the wind. The ship's course was steadying up, the rudder and engine changes having overcome the leeway, and now they approached the 90-degree turn to the left.

"Port engine ahead one third," the captain ordered.

Davant repeated the order down to the wheel house, and O'Toole did the same through his phones to the engine room.

"Engine room answers port engine ahead one third," O'Toole said, perspiration now beginning to spread across his forehead.

"Left standard rudder," the captain ordered.

"Left standard rudder," Davant acknowledged.

The ship was now making its turn, the wind shrieking above their heads and pushing the ship faster. The captain rushed to the port wing and leaned far over the rail, looking aft, attempting to gauge the effect the wind was having. "Sonov'a'bitch," he said under his breath. "Rudder amidships," he ordered, and Davant repeated the order. "Rudder's amidships, Sir."

"Charlie? What's the distance to our beach?" the captain yelled over the noise of the wind tearing through the signal flags.

"Uh..." Crane stammered sighting through the pelorus on the port wing.

"Come on, Charlie!" the captain shouted.

"Uh..."

"Charlie?"

Cunningham watched the XO attempting to determine the distance, and in a hoarse whisper said, "Twelve hundred yards!"

"Uh ... twelve hundred yards, Sir!" Crane said, and he nodded his head toward Cunningham.

"How many?"

"Twelve hundred yards, Sir!" Crane shouted.

"What's the bearing?"

"Zero-nine-zero, Sir!" Crane shouted.

"Chief? What's the wind speed?"

"Twenty-five knots, Sir! With gusts to 30!"

The captain shook his head. "Well, this is a real kick in the butt," he said to no one in particular, and several faces turned in his direction. "This sure as hell isn't the best day to be doing this! What's the bearing now, Charlie?"

"Zero-seven-zero, Sir!"

"Shit."

"Gusts hitting 35 knots now, Sir!" Cunningham said, and the ship continued crabbing toward the right of their designated beach.

"Come left to course zero-seven-zero!" the captain ordered, and Davant repeated the course change to the wheel house.

The ship continued crabbing.

"Port engine stop!" the captain yelled.

"Port engine stop!" O'Toole quickly repeated the order through his phone.

Underwood could clearly see how the wind was pushing the ship to the right. Every minute it was becoming more difficult to maintain a perpendicular course to the beach, and the captain's engine orders were coming fast and furious. O'Toole was barely keeping up.

"Port engine back one third," the captain ordered.

"Port engine back one third," O'Toole repeated through his phone to the engine room.

"Engine room answers port engine back one third," O'Toole reported.

As the ship's course adjusted from the engine changes, the captain called out another order.

"Port engine ahead one third!"

"Port engine ahead one third," O'Toole repeated. "Engine room answers port engine ahead one third."

And a moment later another command. "Port engine stop."

"Port engine stop."

The engines and engineers in the engine room were getting a good work out with the continuous engine order changes; Chief Beckers was constantly and rapidly shifting reduction gears and fine-tuning engine RPMs.

Suddenly O'Toole's eyes grew wide open, and he blurted out, "Engine room reports....WHAT?"

The captain turned and stared at O'Toole.

"Engine room, Conn...say again?" O'Toole yelled.

"What is it?" the captain shouted.

"Sir!" O'Toole stammered.

"What?" the captain yelled.

"Engine room reports ..."

"Reports what?"

"The starboard reduction gear...!"

"What about it?" the captain spun around 180 degrees.

"Engine room reports they've experienced...!" O'Toole said, alarm clearly showing across his broad face. He closed his eyes as he concentrated on the message being transmitted through his earphones.

"A casualty... w-with..." O'Toole stuttered.

"What casualty?" the captain shouted.

"With ... with the starboard reduction gear, Sir!"

"Are you kidding me?" The captain yelled in disbelief and he rushed toward O'Toole, his large, broad shoulder knocking Charlie Crane into the railing.

"What did you say?" the captain yelled at O'Toole.

"S-Sir...!" O'Toole stuttered again.

"Tell them to repeat that message!" the captain yelled.

"Engine room, Conn. Repeat your last!" O'Toole said. "Uh, yes, S...Sir. Engine room repeats; starboard reduction gear is jammed!"

"Give me that damn phone!" the captain yelled, and he yanked the phone transmitter from O'Toole's chest, the straps around the big storekeeper's neck pulling him off balance. "This is the captain!" he yelled into the phone, inches from O'Toole's face. "What the hell's going on down there?"

"Sir," Crane was trying to get the captain's attention.

"What?"

"Sir!" Crane called out. "We're beginning to swing. The wind is continuing to push us into the beach at an angle!"

The captain turned, holding O'Toole's phone as he would hold the collar of a big dog, and he looked forward. His his jaw dropped. The ship was heading for the beach 20 degrees off course at a speed of almost 5 knots. Everyone on the conn was now wide eyed, looking from the beach to the captain and back to the beach again. They could see the effect the wind and the non-operating starboard engine were having on their course. Underwood watched the bow slowly turning toward the left as the stern swung to the right, the ship drifting to the right of their beaching area; it reminded him of being in his old car, skidding sideways on an icy road. The captain ran back to the starboard wing, and Crane, Underwood and O'Toole quickly darted out of his way.

"Port engine ahead full!" the captain yelled.

"Port engine ahead full!" O'Toole yelled into the phone, panic on his face.

"Right full rudder!" the captain ordered.

"Engine room reports port engine ahead full!"

"Right full rudder!" Davant immediately called down through the voice tube.

Underwood looked forward to the bow. He could see Browning and Biagotti with a group of sailors standing by the windlass, ready to drop the anchor if ordered. Poldolski stood next to them looking up toward the conn, one hand on his phone's transmitter, the other pressing the earphone to his head. Underwood then turned and looking aft toward the fantail saw Mills at the stern anchor winch, ready to lower that huge anchor as the ship moved toward the beach.

'Let go the stern anchor!" the captain shouted, and Underwood repeated the order into his sound powered phone.

"Let go the stern anchor!"

Underwood looked aft and watched Mills backing off the circular hand wheel, turning the wheel to release the brake on the anchor windlass. Mills turned the wheel and turned the wheel and nothing happened. The cable reel was not moving. Mills spun the brake wheel faster and faster. Underwood could see the look on Mills face, it was the look of someone who was attempting the impossible; if he was to succeed, no one would notice, if he failed there would be hell to pay. Suddenly the huge cable reel started turning, slowly at first, then faster and faster, and the 3,000-pound Danforth anchor lowered into the bay on its 3 inch diameter cable. The ship continued toward the beach.

"Conn aye," Underwood said into the transmitter. "Stern anchor is down!" he shouted over the wind.

"Sir!" Davant tried to get the captain's attention as the ship continued heading toward the beach at an angle.

"What?" the captain yelled.

"Sir! Shouldn't we brace for beaching?"

"What?"

"Brace for beaching, Sir? We need to announce brace for beaching over the 1MC!"

The captain turned and looked forward, saw the beach approaching faster and faster, the single port engine and right full rudder still unable to counter the effect of the strong wind blasting against the ship.

Davant held up the microphone, as if he was pleading to make the announcement.

"Yes!" the captain yelled back. "Yes! Brace for beaching!"

"Now hear this, now hear this!" Davant shouted into the microphone. "Brace for beaching, brace for beaching!" Davant's shaking voice, amplified through the speakers, rumbled throughout the compartments of the ship and boomed across the waters of the bay, echoing off the volcanic cliffs and reverberating between the buildings and aircraft hangers on the Marine base. *"Brace for beaching, brace for beaching."*

Everyone on the ship grabbed the first thing they could get their hands on. Those deep in the engine room, unable to see what was happening on the conn or gauge how rapidly the ship was approaching the shore, clung to stanchions and spread their feet wide apart. Ensign Jones held tightly to the sides of the log desk as he looked up to the pipes and cables hanging from the overhead. Chief Beckers, gripping the housing of the inoperative reduction gear, rapidly chewed his lollipop, the juice running down one corner of his mouth. Those on the conn grasped the railings, watching the beach grow closer and closer. In the forward gun tub, jutting over the bow of the ship, Jonah braced himself against the inner rail and watched the beach seemingly coming at him quicker than he thought was possible.

The LST continued forward, the beach coming closer and faster and closer and faster, and as the bow was thrust into the dense, unyielding, white coral sand the ship's 4,000,000 pounds of momentum relentlessly propelled it up the slope. Jonah felt the shockingly unexpected overpowering force of the ship hitting the beach and then rapidly decelerating; he was physically thrust forward into the inside rim of the gun tub. The effect was that of a gigantic, invisible hand, shoving him, forcing him, pushing him hard into the rim for 1, 2, 3, 4, 5 seconds; until the ship finally came to a sudden, unyielding, abrupt stop.

Jonah didn't think it was possible, but The Cathedral's second entry into Pearl Harbor was even more painful than the day before. Thirty-six hours ago the ship had arrived under her own power, welcomed by the gleaming brass of a Navy band. This afternoon she arrived hanging on the towline of a tugboat. She may have had power on one engine, but no one could trust her to maneuver through the channel's twists and turns all by herself. The tug had taken her out of Kaneohe Bay, escorted her down the coast, and now the ship was ignobly returning as a dog with its tail between its legs. Watching the shoreline go by from inside the aft gun tub, Jonah imagined several pairs of eyes at Pacific Fleet headquarters looking down from their lofty domain, peering through strong binoculars, shaking their heads and clicking their tongues at the sickly, unwelcome LST.

With the ship once again safely moored to the quay, the captain, Crane and Ed Wilson were locked in the captain's cabin discussing the growing list of engineering casualties. The loud exclamations emanating from that regal space amazed everyone who happened to pass by, including Mendoza who was balancing a tray of coffee cups. As he reached up to knock on the door to the captain's cabin he paused. He didn't have to strain his ears, for the sounds coming through the gaps in the door easily carried out to the passageway; he couldn't understand all of what was being said but the tone of the conversation was unmistakable ... loud, angry and threatening. He thought about retreating back to the pantry, but the captain had explicitly ordered the coffee ASAP, so he knocked. The sounds from inside the cabin immediately stopped and the door opened. He quickly laid the tray on the captain's desk and fled as fast as his legs could take him.

Underwood, who was walking aimlessly about with a stack of papers in his hand, followed Mendoza to the pantry. "Hey, Mendoza," he said, jutting his head inside the small space. "Have you seen Mister Crane? I've got some important papers he needs to sign."

Not one to hold forth with more words than necessary, Mendoza nodded in the direction of the adjacent captain's cabin, frowned and rolled his eyes; "It's bad," was all he said. The message that came across to Underwood was loud and clear: the XO was with the captain, and if you value your life, don't disturb them.

Underwood shook his head and mumbled to himself, walking down the passageway to the ship's office. "We need this ASAP, Underwood. Drop everything, Underwood. It's got to be done now, Underwood."

⁂

"Man, you should'a heard what I heard today," Homer said with a mouthful of string beans, waving his fork in front of Jonah, Mills and The Volt, all sitting together at the same mess deck table. "I'm tell'n 'ya. I was walking down the pier, 'ya know, just mind'n my own business, sort'a lost in thought, look'n around at all this beautiful sky and green mountains and the fresh cut grass around all these white buildings, just wondering how in the world do they keep this place looking so squared away, when this guy comes walking down the pier in the other direction holding a radio," and Homer paused to insert a fork full of potatoes in his mouth, giving Mills the opening he was waiting for.

"Well, of course this place is squared away," Mills said, sponging up the last of his gravy with a slice of bread. "With this being CINCPAC headquarters, and all the people they've got here, you don't think they'd have some ugly, run down look'n place, do you?" and he took a bite out of the bread, the gravy oozing down between his fingers.

"Makes sense to me," Jonah said. "But what was it you heard today, Homer?"

"I'm glad you asked," Homer said, and he gave Mills a dirty look. "Cause I'm gonna tell 'ya right now."

"Oh, boy," Mills said. "Here we go."

"That's right, Mills," and Homer ignored Mills and gave all his attention to Jonah and The Volt. "Cause as I was say'n...here I am, walking down the pier, just minding my own business, and this other squid is coming toward me, and he's holding one of those small portable radios to his ear, well it was actually bigger than small, but it was still kind'a small, anyway, he's sort'a holding it on his shoulder next to his ear, and he's just walking along, sort'a doing a little dance, you know, when you're walking kind'a happy? So, he's walking along and I hear this music, and I say to myself, Homer I said, what is that music? And as he gets closer and closer I then figure out it's coming from his little radio, and the music, the music had this sort'a hypotizzing melody...."

"Hypotizzing?" Volt said with a bewildered look

"He means hypnotizing," Mills interrupted.

"If you interrupt me again, Mills," Homer said, "I'm gonna hypotizz your face!"

Mills grinned and started shaking with silent laughter. "Go ahead, Homer," he said. "I can't wait for you to hypotizz me."

"Yea, Mills," Homer said. "You better wait. Anyway, before I was interrupted; so this music is coming from this guy's little radio and as we get near each other, the music gets louder and louder, and then as he goes by it gets quieter...."

"The Doppler effect," Volt interjected.

"The who?" Homer asked.

"The Doppler effect," Volt said again, lighting a cigarette. "It's the increase or decrease in the frequency of sound waves. For example, as the source of the sound or the observer move toward or away from each other, the sound waves increase or decrease. It's really quite simple."

Homer's mouth opened. Jonah and Mills glanced at each other. Homer's face had the look of someone who just tasted something disagreeable. "Is there anything you don't know?" he said with an ugly look, staring at The Volt. "Is there?"

"I don't think so," The Volt answered innocently, his eyes open wide, looking between Jonah and Mills.

"Please continue," Mills said.

"Yea, Homer," Jonah echoed.

Homer looked at the three sailors sitting at the table, his face contorted with frustration. "So, as I was say'n," and he shook his shoulders. "As I was say'n, we walk by each other," and he pauses and stares at Mills. "We walk by each other and the music on the radio just stops me cold. I ain't never heard nothing like that before, all the harmony and stuff, and I turn around and start chasing after the guy, and I call out, hey, wait up man, and he turns around, and I say, what is that you're listening to on that radio? And as we're both standing there look'n at each other, the song is continuing, and he says it's the Moms and Pops."

"The what?" Jonah asked.

"Yea, he says it's the Moms and Pops, and I ask him to repeat that, and he does, and then I ask him if he knew the name of the song, and he said it was called 'Monday Sunday' or something like that."

"He means the Mamas and the Papas," Volt said, blowing smoke rings toward the overhead. "They just released that record. It's a 45 single, called Monday Monday. I heard it over the shortwave a week ago."

"Yea, exactly," Homer said. "The Mamas and the Papas. And you know what? You know what, Mills?"

"What's that?"

"I'm going up to the PX after work knocks off this afternoon and get me a copy," and he pulled out a wad of cash from his pocket and started counting through it. "Yea, I got enough. I'm gonna get me a genuine, brand new, original record with that song."

"Man, that's nice," Jonah said. "But how you going to play it?"

Homer, his eyes squinting, peered at Jonah and then to The Volt with a conspiratorial look. "I was hoping, that maybe, maybe, The Volt would let me play it on his turntable?"

"Uh, oh!" Mills said with a comical look of astonishment.

"Volt, what you think?" Jonah asked. "Would you let Homer use your precious turntable?"

They could see Volt was thinking about that.

"I can hear the gears going 'round inside Volt's head," Mills said grinning.

"Well, Homer," The Volt said. "You were pretty good in sharing your raisin Jack after we left Panama. And you might even have some more to share again in the future. I guess we could work something out. Yea, we could do something to listen to that record."

"Hot damn," Homer said, slapping his knee. "Thanks, Volt, you're okay."

"Hey, Jonah." It was Brickey approaching their table.

"What?"

"It's time," Brickey said. "We only got half an hour before that truck arrives."

"Holy shit," Jonah said looking at his watch, and he stood up from the table. "I need to go. Hey, Mills, remember, you gotta have your guys on the pier by 1700 to help unload that ammo truck."

"You know," Mills said with a sarcastic look. "My deck gang just loves to carry your shit, Jonah, your crates of guns and cans of ammo, and whatever else you have for us to carry, you know, up the brow and down into the tank deck. It's just one of our most favorite things to do. Why, hell, we even enjoy that more than going on liberty tonight."

"I'll tell you what," Jonah said in his best poker face, looking straight at Mills.

"Whats that?"

"Since we're in such an agreeable mood here today," Jonah continued. "Horse trading raisin Jack for turntable time and everything, I think you and me might trade for something."

"Yea?"

"Yea. Since we're gonna be in Pearl a few more days, more than we expected, and since we're gonna eat into some of your liberty time tonight unloading that truck, maybe if your gang gets their butts moving and everything stowed away quickly, then I'll just assign you and some of your deck apes to man those new .50s when we're at General Quarters in the future. How'd you like that?"

Mills' sour looking mouth lit up and a smile went across his face. "Well, that's one hell of a good idea!" he said. "In fact, that's a great idea. I like that. I especially like shooting 50s." and he held out his hand. "You got a deal!"

"Hey, what about me?" Homer piped up. "What about me on one of those 50s? I like shoot'n 50s too, ya know."

"Oh, Lord,' Jonah said. "Now Homer wants in on the act."

"It's getting crowded around here," Mills said.

"Well, Homer," Jonah said. "Maybe we can do something about you too. What 'you got to trade?"

"Me? Trade?" Homer said. "Damn, I don't know. I don't know, but...but I'll sure as hell think of some'n."

"I bet you will," Jonah said. "But before you wear yourself out trying to think of something, I bet you'll be on the pier in..." and

Jonah looked at his watch. "In 15 minutes to help us carry all that ammo."

❧❦

The young waitress in the turquoise flowered sarong and black bandeau placed two mai tais on the table, her brown Hawaiian eyes surreptitiously examining Jones who was deep into a newspaper.

"Thank you," Beaufort said with a look of longing, noticing her sun-bronzed face and bare midriff; her thick hair was accentuated with a red hibiscus. The girl smiled and walked away. "Incredible" he said watching her skirt flowing in the breeze. His right eyebrow twitched.

"Huh?" Jones said still reading the newspaper.

"Nothing," and Beaufort shuddered.

Jones reached for the mai tai without looking up and took a sip. "Oh, that's good, really good!" and he ran his tongue across his lips.

"You know, I could sit here all day watching this." Beaufort said, and Jones looked up from the newspaper for the first time in several minutes. "I mean, look at this place. Here we are on this beautiful Waikiki hotel veranda, with Diamond Head over there," and he pointed to the left. "And this beach, the surf, the palm trees, this pleasant breeze, these gorgeous girls. Have you ever seen anything so beautiful?"

"I have not," Jones said taking another sip of the iced drink, the tiny paper parasol poking him in the eye.

"You know," Beaufort continued. "If it wasn't for our ingenuity, we wouldn't be here now."

"What do you mean?" Jones said, beginning to notice the scene around him for the first time.

"Well, think about it. If you and Wilson hadn't come up with all those extra engineering casualty reports requiring more spare parts and assistance from the yard, we'd be long gone."

"Yea, I suppose so. But they were needed you know. It wasn't something we just pulled out of a hat."

Beaufort gave Jones a sidelong glance with a bemused smirk on his face. "Right. Of course you didn't. And Johnston didn't dream up all that radar work? And Davant didn't make up the need to repair the galley stove? And Browning didn't walk up to the stern anchor and jam a crowbar into it?"

"Did he really jam a crowbar in it?"

"Hell, I don't know. For all I know he did. But who's to say?"

"Well, you're right, you're right. We are where we are and we're not going anywhere for at least another few days."

"Man, take a look at that!"

"What?"

"That!" and Beaufort pointed to where a girl in a bikini was surfing along the face of a large curling wave. "Wouldn't you just like to spend a couple of weeks here?"

"I was thinking more of a tour of duty."

"Oh, yea, a tour of duty...in Hawaii; wouldn't that be perfect?" Beaufort said with a wistful longing look.

"Everything after that would be downhill."

"Yea, sorta like this mai tai," Beaufort said looking at his almost empty glass. "So, tell me what's going on in the world," and he pointed to the newspaper Jones had been reading.

"Things are getting hotter."

"Vietnam?"

"Yea. Lots of heavy stuff going on there."

"We might see some of it soon."

"Probably. Listen to this. According to this issue of Stars and Stripes, which was..." and Jones looked up to the date at the top of the page."Last week; there was some big battle at a place called Suoi Bong Trang."

"Man, they have strange names, don't they?'

"Apparently our guys and the Australians were fighting the Viet Cong..."

"Australians? I didn't know the Australians were in this."

"Yea. They were fighting the VC to protect some of our army engineers who were building some important road near Tan Binh, wherever that is," and Jones ran his finger down the page. "And then there was a battle at a place called Shau; apparently there were a lot of casualties. The article doesn't say what the outcome of that was, but reading between the lines here it doesn't look good for us."

"You mean we lost? How could we do that?"

"Well, it doesn't come right out and say we lost, but if we had won, then this article might have said so. Maybe they're keeping that one quiet."

"Hmm," Beaufort said taking the pineapple wedge from his drink and chewing on it.

"And this other story is about our ambassador, Henry Cabot Lodge, and the South Vietnamese Premier, Nguyen Cao Ky, not sure how that's pronounced, relieving some general in the city of Hue because of some Buddhist uprising. I don't get the significance of that, but apparently it was a big deal."

"I don't understand."

"Don't understand what?"

"What we're doing."

"What do you mean?"

"What we're doing in Vietnam? This is the most confusing war I ever heard of. I mean, here we are, the most powerful country in the world, with a huge number of our troops and equipment and planes and ships, half way around the world, helping some foreigners fight some other foreigners. What is it to us?"

"Well, in my opinion it's all about stopping the spread of communism. You do want to stop communism, don't you?"

"Of course."

"Well, you remember hearing about the domino theory. Right?"

"Uh, no."

"For crying out loud, JB!" and Jones looked stupefied by Beaufort's answer. "The domino theory is when one country goes communist," and Jones stabbed his finger onto the table. "Then the next one will go communist," and he stabbed his finger again. "And the next one. We're trying to help prevent that from happening."

"Okay. Yea I see what you're saying. Falling dominoes; one after the other. Yea, I remember now."

"Exactly. And here's another article, this one from a place called Da Nang where there was another Buddhist uprising, and our general, General Westmoreland, a four-star general no less, seems to have gotten pretty upset about it," and Jones turned the page.

Beaufort shook his head. "Hell, I don't know about Buddhists. But what I do know is that I need another one of these," and raising the empty glass he got the attention of the girl in the turquoise flowered sarong.

"And look at this," Jones said holding up the page showing another article, this one with a photograph.

"Well, I'll be damn. An LST on the beach? What's the caption say?"

"ARVN Rangers and South Vietnamese Marines debark from USS Washatow County at DaNang to help quell the Buddhist uprising."

"That looks serious," Beaufort said. "When was the last time we carried troops on the old Cathedral?"

"Beats me, we've only been aboard since January. But from what Wilson told me, maybe early last year when they went to the Dominican Republic?"

Beaufort shook his head with a look of confusion. "Hell, I don't know. But for the moment I don't care as long as we have an unlimited supply of these," and he carefully watched the lithe waitress placing two more mai tais on the table.

"Which?" Jones asked Beaufort as he watched the waitress walk away. "The mai tais or the flowered skirt?"

"Yea, exactly."

༺༻

Diary #105
26 March 1966
0430 Hours ... Pearl Harbor, Hawaii
Elysium abandoned.

These volcanic mountains and crystal beaches, the exotic food and mai-tais, the blue skies and balmy breezes, will all be history in less than four hours; we're about to get underway for the Western Pacific.

Nothing in my vocabulary can completely or definitively describe our stay here in Pearl Harbor or Oahu. The abridged version might be subtitled: "A whirlwind of work and liberty." Or... "The frantic pace of repairs and overabundance of alcohol has done us in."

What was supposed to be only a 60-hour stopover for fuel, stores and spare parts, has turned into a glorious seven days of sightseeing, exotic food, strong drink, beautiful beaches and extraordinary bikinis. Thanks to the breakdown of our primitive reduction gear, we've been stuck in this paradise an extra four days...not able to go anywhere until repairs were made. And on top of that, our devious, clever ingenuity to embellish, dramatize, and overstate dozens of other not-quite-so-critical needed repairs was getting us even more days ... that is until the Admiral finally got wise to our mischief and decided he was tired of looking at our squalid ark cluttering up his beautiful harbor. He has banished us. Go West Young Man, he has commanded. Now we are departing, not only with reduction gears operating at optimum efficiency, but with new parts installed in dozens of other pieces of equipment; including two items of critical importance: the ice-maker and our washing machine. Woe betide anyone who gets between me and my iced tea and clean uniforms!

Lest anyone believe our stay here has been all work and no amusement, one should know that a new incident has provided sufficient entertainment to last a lifetime.... someone has defiled our "Approaching Zero" sign. Whoever this individual is, they're clever. They skulked into officer country during the night, entered Sanders' stateroom while he was on watch, and using a grease pencil, scribbled a limerick upon the sacred holy grail:

>   *"We have a JG named Sanders,*
>   *whose brain always meanders.*
>   *Angry on the conn,*
>   *and pissed off in the john,*
>   *he's given up seeing his transfers."*

The graffiti was discovered the following morning by Mendoza when he entered the stateroom to ostensibly swab the deck. Minutes later, standing underneath the plaque, Sanders looked up and was brought into a near state of hyper apoplexy. His raving, spleen-busting outburst of temper reached proportions heretofore unseen. I must admit it was hilarious to watch. So far the unknown perpetrator remains at large. The word is now out and the crew have christened the culprit "Zero," a take-off on the famous Zorro. One can only imagine the black-cloaked character hiding in the shadows, behind watertight doors, ready to pounce out of escape trunks to commit another deed of derring-do. Everyone anxiously awaits the daredevil's next move.

On another note, it was on a bright, breezy morning that we departed Pearl for the Marine Base at Kaneohe Bay, entered the channel under a moderate gale of wind, found ourselves drifting off course through the many dog leg turns, and then at the critical moment our reduction gear decided it had taken enough abuse; it packed itself up and stopped working. Ed Wilson, Win Jones and Chief Beckers were unable to bring it back to life, and the captain's frantic, rapid-fire engine orders and rudder changes were unable to overcome the power of the wind. So we crabbed into the beach as a drunken sailor would exit a bar; staggering off course and landing with a bang.

Ah, but the day was not complete. There we were, stuck on the beach with a non-operating reduction gear; and did I also mention a stern anchor winch that wouldn't cooperate? Fortunately, Holt in the radio room was able send a priority message, requesting a tug to help us limp back to Pearl without further incident. But, woe is me, the anguished looks and embarrassed faces of those on our conn as we were being towed into Pearl Harbor cannot be thoroughly appreciated. If anyone thought we looked ridiculous when we first arrived here days ago, they should have seen us lumbering along behind that tug. It was pitiful. And not only that, there must have been 1,000 pairs of eyeballs watching us. I can only imagine some of the comments at CINCPACFLT: "Ensign Newby!" the Admiral probably commanded, "... send that LST an immediate message: *GO AWAY!*"

The Western Pacific days melded one into the other. The perfect sunrises were followed by a routine that had become so much a part of the crew's daily life, no one realized they had left the last of civilization behind. Reveille, quarters, sweeping, swabbing, painting, repairing, meals, the call of bosun's pipes over the 1MC, general quarters drills, live firing of the 40s and .50s, changing of the watch; all the small trivial details of a ship at sea filled each day as the Cathedral steamed onward, relentlessly onward toward something, something no one knew what. There was a psychic change among the crew. Weeks on the calendar had drifted by. Family and friends were just memories, and the constant flawless weather had everyone under a spell...a spell of routine but with a twist; the twist of knowing that they didn't know what was next. The LCU was still chained to the main deck, and the haze gray painting went on and on, but there was an underlying feeling that they were coming closer, each day coming closer to what fate held in store for them.

Seven days out from Pearl Harbor the last of the fresh food was consumed, forcing Dorsey and his mess cooks to open cans and cartons of mystery ingredients. And when the ship crossed the international date line we not only lost an entire day on the calendar, we also lost the use of the recently repaired ice maker and laundry machine, both dying with sudden unexpectedness within hours of each other; many of the crew whispered about this being a dangerous omen. Chief Beckers and two electricians took the machines apart, piece by piece, examined them minutely, but couldn't find the cause of the casualty. The dead machines were dejectedly left firmly welded to their spots on the deck, causing considerable contemptuous ridicule from all those who passed by. Some unknown comedian drew a cartoon on the ice maker; the universal symbol of a bald-headed character with a long nose peering over the rim of the world, his hands gripping the edge of the globe. The words customarily found on the famous cartoon were slightly modified to "Killjoy was here!"

With the loss of the washing machine the crew was then forced to scrub shirts, trousers, skivvies, socks and towels in sinks and buckets, that is until the day the evaporator clogged up and the ship lost the capability to make fresh water. A complete ban on fresh water consumption, except for drinking, cooking and Navy showers, then became the order of the day. In desperation some of the crew resorted to lacing trousers and shirts on a stout line, as pearls to a string, and dragged them thrashing and twisting in the ship's wake to allow the seawater to wash some of the filth out of the filth.

Sailors could be stoic as monks in an abbey when it comes to their routine, able to withstand a great deal of work and suffering in their monastic conditions, but change that daily pattern and they would become cruel, insensitive, unpleasant people. As a result, tempers grew short as the days remaining to the Philippines grew shorter still; the irritation, ill humor and agitation of the crew escalated exponentially. In the ship's office, Underwood and Fugete's tenuous armistice, with their respective territories divided by the XO's desk as the de facto demilitarized zone, saw an upswing in the number of daily incidents of disparaging comments; Fugete, being only a 3rd class petty officer, never won an argument in the smoldering battle against the more powerful intellect and bigger guns of the 2nd class Underwood. In the tank deck, Mills and Homer continued their repetitive, tiresome battle of hostile distaste and conflicting egos, and once again fell into a heated debate, this time over the number of years required to be eligible for a hash mark delineating length of service; the coveted stripe worn on the left sleeve of an enlisted uniform. Homer's analysis took the position that both reserve and active service combined would count toward entitlement. Mills resisted that argument by counter-proposing an alternative policy that only regular, active duty years qualified. Homer disagreed with that premise and said they should take a walk to the ship's office and call upon Underwood and his library of Navy Regulations to settle the dispute. Mills shifted his strategy and decided to bypass the debate rules completely, calling the burly shipfitter a stupid idiot. Homer disagreed with Mill's logic, and countered with a lightning punch to Mills' face. There followed a rapid exchange of more punches, until they were separated by Poldolski who threw himself between them. In the wardroom, within that insular, small community, the long-standing simmering disdain between Browning and Sanders steadily grew into openly hostile glares and snide remarks. The other officers kept their distance and took a neutral position, especially when Sanders approached several of them, pleading for support. And O'Toole, once a big fish in the larger supply department of his previous ship, was now on his own; a solo act without the assistance from disbursing clerks or other storekeepers he would have normally bossed around. His exasperating days were filled with dozens of impossible to fill requisitions, endless inventories, complex payday disbursements, and constant wisecracks from Davant, the line officer who didn't have the training of a bona fide supply officer. In the midst of this frustrating environment of immeasurable tasks, the old O'Toole who once had plenty of time on his hands, was now working seven days a week with not a moment to devote to his previous secret intrigues of poker games, slush funds, and other odious activities. His usual bad temper rose to even greater heights, prompting even Rat Reeder and Smitty to keep their distance from the volatile first class petty officer.

And, so it was within this miasma of putrid uniforms, tasteless food and short tempers, the ship steamed relentlessly forward into a seemingly endless western horizon of enormous cumulus clouds, brief but strikingly intense rain showers, and brilliant red ocher and cadmium yellow sunsets. During this time one highly improbable development did come about: the small group of old, long time Cathedrals and the greater numbers of more recently arrived novitiates had found a common bond; a bond established in rebuilding their ship and cleaning up its stinking, rusting, squalid condition before meeting the mortal enemy they were likely to find in Vietnam. They all knew the whereabouts of their eventual destination, and the closer they came to it, the more the real purpose of their being became clear; from Subic they would steam across the South China Sea into harm's way. The only question was, exactly where? And when?

❧❧

Underwood pulled the small envelopes from his shirt pocket and carefully examined the stamps and their 'Norfolk' cancellations. Choosing the one with the oldest date, he removed the thin, flimsy, translucent papers and once again read the small, delicate handwriting. A smile spread across his face as he visualized Alison writing the letter, possibly throwing her head to the side as she often did to fling that constant errant wisp of hair out of her eyes, and maybe even holding the top of the pen against her lips as she thought of the next phrase. He repositioned himself against the inside of the gun tub and turned the onion skin to the second page. She wrote reminiscing about how they met the first time, that night in The Cesspool with Jonah and Pattie, the same night she invited him back to her apartment. And she wrote about how the next morning he was shocked awake by a deafening, blaring, mind-stabbing noise coming from across the room. She had laughed at his reaction, and remembered telling him that the loud alarm clock was the only thing that would get her out of bed in the morning. He had said it reminded him of one of those klaxon horns used on submarines. Having set the alarm for a half-hour early, she said they needed to take advantage of the extra 30 minutes, and then she snuggled up to him and entwined her legs into his. Whispering in his ear she told him she would miss him terribly, more than he could know, and that she would write and hoped he would do the same. He put the paper down and with a sudden, uncontrolled emotion, he laughed out loud thinking about it all, how crazy this was, falling for a girl after only one night. He laughed again.

"What's so funny," a voice said, and Underwood looked up to see Jonah climbing over the edge of the gun tub.

"Letters from home," he said smiling, inserting the paper back in the envelope.

"Letters?" Jonah asked.

Underwood nodded.

"Did you get those in Pearl?"

Underwood nodded again.

"You're lucky. Some people get all the letters. Some don't get any."

"Yea, I suppose that's true sometimes," Underwood said, and still smiling he stuffed the envelopes into his pocket.

"From your folks?" Jonah asked.

"Nah, just a friend."

"Girlfriend?"

"Maybe."

"Hmm. Didn't know you had a girlfriend, Woody."

"Well, she's a friend. I don't know if she's more than that. Yet."

Jonah nodded and looked into the sunset. "You know what I was thinking?"

"That you wished you were back in Norfolk?"

"I hadn't thought of that, but that's a good idea. No, what I was thinking of is where are we? Where are we going? What are we going to do when we get there? And whether I'm going to ship-over for another four years or just walk down the brow one last time and go back to the ranch in Idaho?"

Underwood stared out toward the horizon, watching the colors in the western sky. "I never thought I'd be in the navy this long," he said lighting up a short, non-filtered cigarette. "When I decided to get out of Bayonne, it was 1962. None of this Vietnam stuff had really heated up yet. I mean, yea, stuff was going on in Vietnam, you know, but it really wasn't on the front pages yet. Anyway, the navy looked like a great way to get out of a town I didn't want to be in anymore. Besides, who would want to be drafted into the army? Not me," and he shook his head with the look of someone who was examining their own mental and emotional machinery. "I mean Bayonne used to be a nice place to live, but then it turned into something awful. I grew up there. But it slowly just ran downhill, especially when work at the shipyards dried up." He looked down to the base of the tub and took a deep breath. "The old neighborhoods just fell apart. I started to feel as if I was in a foreign country. It was time to leave."

"You just walked into the recruiter's office?" Jonah asked.

"I'd almost finished college. But inside my head I was just aimlessly wandering about, trying to find something, something I really wanted to do. I was drinking too much, carousing too much. And one night I got slapped in jail."

"Jail?" Jonah said wide eyed.

Underwood shook his head. "My old man was furious. He came to the jail the next day. God that place was awful; filthy, stunk like piss, disgusting people lying on the floor. You know, one of the worst smells in the world is the smell of a drunk's breath?" He shook his head, his face looked as if he had just smelled an open sewer. "But, you know what? He didn't bail me out. That's right, my old man didn't bail me out. Instead he looked straight at me. His eyes looked straight into mine. I remember that like it was yesterday. He looked straight at me and he said, I'll never forget this, he said, 'You've got to pay for what you did here. I can't be the one to dig you out of this mess. You're almost 23 years old! You did this to yourself, and you've got to get yourself out of it.' He let me stew in that jail. And the next day he let me go through the agony and embarrassment of a perp walk. Christ, he was there! I saw him in the crowd. He had the balls to come down and watch me go through the perp walk. And then, when I went before the judge, I never felt so awful in my life. All I could think of was what were my friends going to say, and how was I ever going to be the same after that?"

"What the hell happened? What did you do to get arrested?"

"Oh, man, it was something else. The court had a whole lineup of drunks to deal with, and I was just one of them. I mean, I was a mess, dirty, hadn't shaved in a couple of days, looked like hell from lack of sleep. But the judge knew my father, and he took a moment with me, a special moment, and he told me that I was stupid, stupid for getting drunk, stupid for driving when I was drunk, and stupid for losing control of my car and driving it through the plate glass window of that tire store on Broadway."

"You crashed into a tire store?"

"And more than that, I was stupid enough to put the life of my date in jeopardy."

"You had a girl in the car?"

Underwood nodded and threw the cigarette over the side. "It was about 11 o'clock at night. The car went out of control. Shit...I was the one who was out of control. I guess I was drunker than a skunk. That car went around that slight, gentle curve, just as if it was gliding on ice; I remember it clear as day. There I was holding on to the wheel, fascinated with the whole scene moving by in front of me. Then the car jumped the curb and headed for the tire store. Watching that store come at me in slow motion was the strangest thing. Then we went through that floor to ceiling plate glass window. It exploded! But the car's windshield didn't shatter then; it shattered when we hit that big concrete post in the middle of the store. That's when we came to a stop. That scene of that car and the store and the broken glass and all the tires scattered around the floor was incredible. You would have thought a bomb had gone off. Somehow, and you're gonna love this, somehow one of those tires, you know the tires that they put on display?...the ones that are stacked on top of one another? Well one of those tires had rolled out of the hole we had made coming in, and it was sitting in the middle of the street! That tire was sitting there, in the middle of the street! Anyway, only a couple of minutes later there were cops, ambulances, fire trucks. Man, that was some mess. But two days later, to be in that courtroom, standing in front of that judge, that was even worse than the wreck."

"Were you hurt? What about your date?"

"Jonah, I'm tell'n you, God was watching over me that night. Neither of us was hurt. Just some minor cuts from the windshield glass. That's all."

Underwood paused and looked toward the sky with its streaks of gold and orange between the clouds.

"What did the judge do?" Jonah said, breaking the silence.

"He gave me two choices. First, he said I needed to pay for the damages. I thought how in the hell am I gonna pay for the damages working part time as a waiter in an Italian restaurant? He also said I needed to either finish college, or get out of town, or both, before I was arrested again for another stupid stunt. I decided I needed a change of scenery. So, I worked full time at the restaurant for a year, paid off the damages, finished college and joined the navy."

Jonah watched the tall yeoman struggling with his past and thought how fate seemed to put people into situations where they paid for their transgressions. "Eventually we all seem to pay the piper," he said.

Underwood nodded with his head down, his eyes closed, and he came up for air and breathed deep, looking at the darkening sky, only a faint hint of the sunset remaining. "Yea, we do eventually."

"After you graduated from college, why didn't you go to OCS?"

"I thought about that. And yea, I had wanted to. But I was told that idiots who demolish tire stores and are arrested for drunk driving are disqualified. Later on, after I was already on active duty, I found out that wasn't quite correct."

"What happened to the girl?"

"Well, that's an interesting thing. When I came home on my first leave I saw her in town. We went into a little cafe and ordered coffee and some fresh baked apple pie and talked about everything: school, friends, her job as a nurse, me in the navy, we talked about everything, everything except the accident. Do you know that the Army told her that if she joined up, with her degree and RN license, they'd make her a captain?"

"Really?"

"Yea. Anyway, it was just as if nothing had ever happened. We finished our coffee, I paid the check, we walked out of the cafe, said goodbye, and that was the last I saw her."

"Amazing."

Underwood nodded. "Yea I know. I've thought about that countless times. I was lucky. Real lucky."

"What about now? What happens at the end of your current enlistment? You've got, what, another year to go?"

"Eleven months. I don't know. I don't know what I'm gonna do. I guess this ship has me pretty sour on the navy right now; going from a series of really decent ships to this junk yard. That was a real let down the day I reported aboard. You know that! Hell, you remember how angry I was that first day. And now we're going into ... I don't know where we're going. Into what?" Underwood paused. Jonah could see him thinking, thinking about the future. They both were lost in their thoughts, looking at the sunset, when Jonah broke the silence.

"I heard The Volt had a little problem when we were in Pearl," Jonah said.

"Yea, he got sort'a beat up," Underwood aid. "Have you seen him?" Jonah shook his head. "He's walking around with a busted face and some bruised ribs. He's not doing so well."

"What happened?"

"Apparently he rented a car and drove out to the north end of the island looking for orchids. You know he likes orchids?"

"Yea, I remember from Panama."

"I guess somebody told him there was an area somewhere, some sort of jungle, with lots of orchids just growing in the wild. From what he told me he was walking through this place with thick growth, taking lots of pictures of orchids, some of them apparently very rare. One in particular, I think he called it a *Planta Holo* or something like that, he found just before he stumbled across a hippie compound; some weird shacks built up in the trees. And some hippies came out and told him they didn't want any military assholes around there. He said he was dressed in civvies, but they must have figured he was military, maybe from his haircut or the navy issued glasses, or the anchor tattoo on his forearm. Anyway, they started arguing about who had the right to be there. He said it was a free country. They said it was their commune. He asked them if they owned the land. They told him to mind his own business. He told them they were a bunch of squatters living in trees like apes. And then they started throwing rocks at him and told him to leave. But he wouldn't leave. I never knew The Volt could be so bull-headed. Anyway, they got into a fight. The biggest hippie in the group jumped him and started beating him up. There were a lot more of them, and only one of him. They busted his face and broke his camera!"

"Sonov'a'bitch!"

"Yea! And they broke his glasses! The big guy deliberately stomped on his glasses. Crushing them into the dirt."

Jonah sat there shaking his head.

"Then he got lost trying to get back to where he left his rental car. I guess he stumbled around in the brush for over an hour. He can't see shit without his glasses. Anyway, he finally found his car and then somehow, blind as a bat that he is, drove back to Pearl, bleeding all over himself."

"Unbelievable."

"Doc cleaned up the cuts and bruises, iced his shiner and then walked him over to the hospital ER where they put four stitches in his lip and told him to stay out of jungles. And because Slaughter had to report the injury to the XO, well, then all hell broke loose. Crane reported it to the captain. Then the captain told Crane to report it to the shore patrol, who reported it to the Honolulu police, who reported it to the county police. I just finished typing up all the paperwork. You wouldn't believe how much paperwork a black eye and four stitches can create. Anyway, Volt said he had always thought hippies were peaceful and into free love and all that kind'a bullshit; but for now on he says he's never gonna look at a damn hippie the same way again."

"I don't blame him."

"He says they're just a bunch of filthy, antagonistic, no good communists.

"Yea, no kidding."

"Just unbelievable."

They watched the horizon and the light scattering through the multi layers of clouds.

"Your live firing exercise on the 40s went really well yesterday," Underwood said.

Jonah was still shaking his head, thinking about Volt getting beat up. "Yea," he finally said. "Getting those sights aligned in Pearl was the key. After that, everything else fell into place. And the two gun crews pretty much know what they're doing now."

"Brickey and the forward crew seem to be well oiled."

"Yea, he's doing alright. Much better than I'd thought possible at this stage in the game."

"And the .50 caliber crews are hot on the targets?"

"Getting Mills and Homer and some of those other guys on those .50s was the right thing to do. And Homer has turned out to be the best. I can't believe how he..."

"Hey, Underwood!" a disagreeable voice called up from below the gun tub.

"What?" Underwood leaned over the rim of the tub and looked down at the grumpy Fugete standing on the main deck, looking up with his hands on his hips. "What do you want?"

"Mister Crane wants to see you!"

"What about?"

"Hell. How should I know. You're the big dog; he always asks for you when something important needs to be done."

"Yea, right," and Underwood climbed down the ladder to the main deck. "What's it about?"

"Something about Liberty Guidelines for Subic."

"Oh, terrific! Where is he?"

"In his stateroom."

Underwood looked up toward Jonah who was looking down from the gun tub. "Hey, Jonah!"

"Yea?"

"If you see Brickey or Homer or Mills or any of those guys you better tell them to check their wallets!"

"Huh?"

"And cash in all their IOUs with anybody that owes them money."

"Why's that?"

"Because I gotta type up some Liberty Guidelines for Subic, and I think once the word gets out, the supply of cash on this ship is gonna disappear faster than a bad check."

CHAPTER 6

CHU LAI

"I expect to see everyone in your divisions thoroughly familiarized with this information," Crane said as he passed a stack of papers across the wardroom table. "Ed, take some of these..." he said to Wilson, "...and pass the rest on. Make doubly sure your chiefs and leading petty officers are up with all these Subic Bay regs regarding liberty, gate closing times, and the Shore Patrol." Wilson took a portion of the stack and passed it to Davant sitting to his left. "There's zero leeway in Subic," Crane said with a severe look on his face. "These regulations are administered with an iron hand, and the Subic Shore Patrol is a force to be reckoned with." He looked at the officers sitting around the table. "And if anyone in your division is detained by the Shore Patrol for any reason, and I repeat, for any reason, the captain has promised me that the guilty will receive full measures at mast."

Jones sipped his coffee, looking around the table, watching the others examining the papers. He particularly noticed Sanders, with his squinting eyes, carefully studying the regulations.

"And," Crane continued. "I want you to also take notice of the information regarding venereal disease. Doc tells me the problem is rampant in Olongapo, and that the figures have been sky high lately. Make sure your people are familiar with the causes and preventions. The captain will not tolerate any cases of VD by anyone on the ship. None, whatsoever."

Jones began to think about liberty in general and Olongapo in particular. Why bother, he thought. If it's that bad in Olongapo, why bother allowing liberty at all? If we know all these things, why subject anyone to them?

"And, lastly," Crane said, interrupting Jones' train of thought. "The gate closes at midnight. I repeat, midnight. And it does not open again until 0500." Crane looked around at the assembled group of officers. Except for the captain, they were all there: Browning, smoking a cigarette; Davant, carefully reading the regulations; Wilson, underlining certain sections; Sanders, bent over the table reading as if he was using an invisible magnifying glass; Jones and Beaufort, sitting next to each other, exchanging comments; Johnston, looking into space, and Hobson, fidgeting and jerking. "Anyone caught on the Olongapo side of the gate after midnight..." Crane continued. "...will not, I repeat, will not for any reason be able to re-enter the base until 0500."

Jones scanned the faces around the table again, particularly noticing Ensign Hobson looking very apprehensive, as if the regulations were designed specifically for him.

"Yes, Len?" Crane said to Davant who appeared to have a question.

"Yes, sir. A question," Davant said, looking down at one of the papers on the table in front of him. "It says here, uh, on page 2, line number 5-Alfa..." and he paused as everyone at the table immediately started leafing through the papers to page 2, line 5-Alfa. "It says on line 5-Alfa," Davant continued with his index finger on the printed line. "That after a command has been notified of any personnel being detained by the Shore Patrol at SP headquarters in Olongapo, said individual must be picked up by their appropriate division officer or leading petty officer without delay..."

"Yea?" Crane said. "So....?"

"So, sir, if the Shore Patrol detains them, and if an appropriate ship's division officer or leading petty officer picks them up, and if they should be picked up at, let's say at 2355 hours for example, but for some reason aren't able to complete the paperwork and get back through the gate before midnight..."

Jones watched Davant proposing the question and Crane standing in front of them with his arms crossed thinking about a plausible answer. Good question, Jones thought.

"Then," Davant continued. "Are both the sailor being detained by the Shore Patrol and the ship's division officer or leading petty officer, are they then all stuck behind the gate until 0500 the next morning? I mean, sir, what are they gonna do between midnight and 0500?"

Crane wore a look of irritated confusion and he shook his head as if he was trying to wake up from a bad dream. "Listen, Len," he said waving his hand, looking at Davant. "No one is going to be able to develop a solution for every possible preordained scenario you come up with."

"Yes, sir, I understand that, but if..."

"No, Len," Crane interrupted. "No ifs, ands or buts. None. If you find yourself on the wrong side of the gate after it closes, for whatever reason, you'll just have to deal with it. All the more reason to make sure your people toe the line and stay out of trouble."

"But, sir..." Davant persisted.

"The Shore Patrol will not bend the rules. The captain will not bend the rules. And Charlie Crane will not bend the rules. Got it?" All those around the table nodded and mumbled.

"Alright," Crane said. "Now, new subject. Tomorrow. Tomorrow, which is Wednesday, the Sea & Anchor Detail will be set at 0730. We'll be picking up the Subic pilot at 0800. Our ETA at the pier will be approximately 0900. Uniform for entering port will be undress whites for all those on the weather decks. The rails will be manned. I emphasize, the rails will be manned by all off duty personnel." Crane turned to Browning. "And, Sam...?"

"Yes, sir?"

"As soon as we're at the pier, there will be two barges coming alongside, with yard cranes. They'll be picking up the Mike boat and then the LCU."

"Yes, sir." Browning said.

"You'll need to be ready for that."

"Yes, sir," Browning said. "Offloading the Mike boat and the LCU."

"Right. Then, Sam..." Crane continued, looking at Browning. "The following morning, that's Thursday morning, we're going to get a full main deck and tank deck load of cargo; palletized Portland cement. Each pallet will contain thirty 94-pound bags. We'll load 410 pallets," and Crane looked at the papers on a clipboard. "For a total of 578 tons of cargo." Then Crane turned toward Beaufort. "J.B.," Crane said to Beaufort. "Give Sam a copy of that cargo loading order," and Beaufort reached across the table and handed the message to Browning. "Sam, you'll need to make sure the main deck and tank deck are ready to receive the cargo no later than tomorrow night. Wednesday night. They'll start loading the cargo first thing the next morning, That's Thursday morning. The stevedores will build a wooden cribbing around the main deck pallets and cover those with tarpaulins. Got that?"

"Yes, sir; we'll get ready Wednesday night for delivery of 410 pallets Thursday morning."

"Correct. And make sure all the pallets are secured by the end of the day." Crane looked around the men at the table. "Okay. Now, Ed?" Crane said, turning from Browning to Wilson.

"Sir?" Ed Wilson answered.

"We'll be receiving a lot of spare parts tomorrow. A lot of boxes. Most of them for engineering. There will be a truck waiting for us on the quay. Your people should be ready to receive them. You'll need a work party standing by. Don't waste any time. And see Len for a list. "

"Yes, sir."

"And, Len...we'll also be receiving six-dozen flak vests. You'll need to get them distributed to Sam and Billie for use by the 40mm and machine gun crews, and the personnel on the conn. Get ahold of Pike to find a place to store the ones for the conn."

"Yes, sir," Davant answered, busily scribbling notes on a pad of paper.

"And, Sam, after we get to Subic there will be a dump truck waiting for you on the quay."

"Sir? A dump truck?"

"A dump truck with a load of sand."

"Sand?"

"Yes, sand. About four cubic yards. They'll have to dump that sand in the tank deck, so figure out the best place for it. You might want to build a wooden enclosure to contain it. And you'll also be getting about 500 burlap bags. You'll need to get a work party together to fill the sand into the bags. Store the sandbags in the tank deck; half of them forward, the other half aft."

"Yes, sir; four cubic yards of sand and 500 sandbags." Browning said shaking his head in disbelief.

"They'll be used to protect the wings on the conn and around the .50 caliber mounts," Crane added. "And wherever else we might need them."

There was an awkward silence in the wardroom as everyone digested that unexpected information. Then Sanders broke the tension.

"XO?" Sanders said holding his ballpoint pen in the air.

"Billie?"

"When do we leave, sir? When do we leave Subic?"

"We leave Subic on Friday morning."

"For where, sir? Where are we headed with the cement?"

Everyone looked from Sanders to the XO.

"We're going west, Billie," Crane said. They all instinctively knew...they instinctively knew where 'going west' would bring them.

Jones looked around the table, thinking that they sure as hell wouldn't be taking the cement back to Norfolk! He noticed Wilson had the look of cautious expectation; Browning's face wore an expression of severe resolve. The others appeared disturbingly apprehensive. "And next Tuesday morning," Crane continued. "We beach at Chu Lai."

There was an enveloping silence throughout the room; the only sound coming from the small oscillating fan in the corner, humming and turning, humming and turning.

Jones stood up from the table and walked to a National Geographic map of Vietnam that someone had tacked to the wood paneling on the port bulkhead. He cocked his head as he started looking near the bottom of the map, south of the Mekong Delta, at a village called Dat Mui, and then he worked his way north, up the coast, past the other strange names, past a place called Vinh Chau and then Vung Tau. And he looked further north to Phan Rang then Nha Trang, and Qui Nhon, eventually stopping about

60 miles south of the Demilitarized Zone where he placed his finger on the map and noiselessly mouthed the name; "Chu Lai."

❧❧

The stewards had of course overheard what the XO said in the wardroom, and sixty seconds after the meeting ended, Mendoza was speaking with Dorsey in the galley and told him some of the details. Dorsey, inflated with the importance of knowing something no one else knew, couldn't contain himself; he told one of his mess cooks, who then spoke with an electrician, who told two of his shipmates. The word traveled through the ship faster than lightning. Brickey was standing in the chow line listening to Homer tell him all about the latest skinny; when they would be arriving in Subic, when the LCU would be offloaded, that a load of cement was coming aboard, about the sandbags, and that several dozen flak vests would be issued to topside personnel.

"Flak vests?" Brickey said. "We're gonna wear flak vests?"

"If you want'a keep your Florida cracker belly button from gett'n blown off, yea, you'll wear a flak vest!" Homer said. "Hell, I'm gonna wear one! That's for sure. You're not gonna find me out there bare-assed."

"I think he's pulling your leg," Poldolski said.

"Maybe," Brickey said. "But I was sure listening carefully to Mister Sanders at quarters this morning, especially the part about how to prevent VD."

"Did that get your attention?" Homer asked.

"Yea, it sure did. Man, I'm telling you, I'm lucky I got to the Doc early, while he still had a good supply."

"How many you get?" Poldolski said.

"Enough."

"You got any extra?"

"I don't know."

"Want'a sell some?"

"Not sure."

"Well, each duty section is only getting one night of liberty," Poldolski explained. "And ya gotta get back through the gate before they lock it up at midnight. So's you ain't gonna have much time. So how many you got?"

"Come on, you skaters!" Pike yelled, suddenly appearing out of nowhere. "Move it up, move your butts up!" The big master at arms pushed his way through the chow line, forcing people to move aside. "Come'on. Get your food. Move along. Stop wasting time. This ain't no fucken line for the double feature ya know."

"Yes, sir, Mister Pike, sir," Homer said in a sarcastic sort of way, rolling his eyes as Pike moved past him.

"Wha'd you say?" Pike said spinning around and glaring at Homer.

"Just being polite, Mister Pike. Just being polite here on this lovely day at this delicious chow line."

Pike stared at Homer for a moment, a muscle pulsating under his eye, and then looked at the others in the line before walking away.

"I'd like to move this right up his big fat..." Poldolski whispered, holding his fist up in front of him.

"Ah, don't pay no attention to him," Homer said. "He's just a dumb signalman. He don't know noth'n."

"Well, he sure ain't intelligent like you are, Homer," Poldolski said with his eyebrows arched and a smirk on his mouth.

"Uh, oh, here comes trouble," Homer said and they all turned and looked in the same direction, toward Ensign Hobson approaching the chow line, his head bobbing left and right as if he was looking for someone.

"Ah, Homer!" the damage control officer said spying Homer in the line. "There you are."

"Yes, sir, Mister Hobson. Here I am."

"We got to check the items on that list...those parts we ordered. We got to get ready to find places to store them. They'll probably be coming aboard tomorrow."

"Yes, sir. We can do that right after chow, Mister Hobson. Would you like to join us for chow? We could talk about it then. Or we could meet in my office afterward?"

"Office?" Hobson was perplexed. "You have an office?"

"Just kidd'n sir. I mean the shipfitter's shop. You want to meet there, or in the DC locker, or in your stateroom?"

"Uh, we...uh, better meet in my stateroom."

"Yes, Sir. How about 1300?"

"Uh, 1300?" Hobson said, looking at his watch as he moved his finger around the dial, suddenly coming to the realization what 1300 was. "Yes, one o'clock is good. And find Reeder and tell him," and he walked away.

The three sailors inched forward in the line as they watched Hobson disappear through the doorway into officer country.

"That guy is sure one nervous wound-up wet behind the ears know-nothing butter bar," Poldolski said, spooning canned peaches onto his tray, and then he leaned forward and closely examined an odd colored pudding sitting in a stainless pan behind the serving line, attempting to decide whether to try any of that mysterious substance.

"What you look'n at?" Dorsey suddenly cried out from behind the serving line. "You got a problem 'wit 'dat pudding?"

"No, Dorsey, not at all," Poldolski said. "Just wanted to thoroughly enjoy the looks of 'dat fine desert before somebody else started digging into it."

Dorsey stared back with a suspicious look

"Yea, as I was say'n," Homer said. "But you know what? It's up to us, us fine specimens of naval knowledge, to keep young ensigns in line. To teach them their trade. To help them along on the haze gray road to success. Don't you think?"

Poldolski looked up from the pudding and stared at Homer with an expression of disbelief. "Yea, Homer; you're definitely a fine specimen of knowledge."

※

Browning and The Volt stood alongside the quarterdeck shack looking at their watches.

"What time you got, Holt?" Browning asked.

"I've got exactly..." the Volt said holding his wrist up to his glasses. "Uh...1657 hours, sir...checked it on the radio just before coming on watch."

"Well, I guess we can't be too rigid about this. My watch says 1700," Browning said. "So, let's get started. But, remember; we're to check for spit-shined shoes, creases in trousers, clean jumpers, squared-away neckerchiefs, haircuts, clean hat, freshly shaved faces, ribbons and ship's rocker patch. You got that?"

"Affirmative, Sir."

"Al right, you people, step forward," Browning called out and the line began inching its way towards the quarterdeck where Browning and Volt inspected each sailor as they came forward. "Okay, next," Browning called, and the ritual went on and on, each sailor getting a close looking over before they were allowed to go down the brow for a few hours of freedom, booze, souvenirs and girls, and not necessarily in that order.

"Hot damn," Homer said as he, Jonah and Underwood stood on the quay waiting for Brickey to go through Browning's gauntlet. "I've been waiting for this for a long time, and man am I ever thirsty. I never thought we'd get here. Finally, liberty in the Philippines. What a night this is gonna be!"

"Yea, but remember," Underwood said looking up toward the line of sailors inching along the main deck. "Remember what they said about the bar girls and the gate closing at midnight."

"Yea, but that's the guy that needs to remember," Homer said pointing, and they turned to watch Brickey bounding down the long wooden brow."

"Okay guys, I'm ready!" Brickey said. "Where to?"

"According to this map..." Underwood said unfolding a piece of paper. "...we walk one block to the west," and he held the map up and pointed left. "And then one block north..." he pointed to the right, still examining the map. "...we come to the bridge."

"The famous bridge over the shit river," Homer said.

"Exactly, and that's where the the gate is, and the shore patrol office."

"Well come on, then," Jonah said, and they started walking along the route.

"Hell, we don't need no map," Homer said. "All we gotta do is follow that line of white hats and we'll get to where we want'a be going. Just look at that," and Homer pointed. They followed the long line of white uniforms ahead of them, snaking along the sidewalk, moving steadily past the buildings of the Subic base, and within a matter of minutes they walked through the gate and came to the small bridge leading to the trinket shops, bars and flesh pots of Olongapo.

"Man, will you look at that?" Brickey said leaning over the rail of the bridge and looking down into the black stagnant water.

"That's disgusting," Underwood said standing next to Brickey, looking at the thousands of greasy objects floating under the bridge.

"Shoes, pieces of plastic, beer bottles," Homer said. "And there's a white hat, not white anymore. And a... God Almighty, what is that?"

"Let's get off this thing. It stinks!" Underwood said, and they crossed the bridge and started walking aimlessly up the street.

"Hey, let's stop here a minute," Jonah said looking up at a sign hanging from an open-air shop with a corrugated roof. "LIGHTER LEON, that's a funny name," he said walking under the sign and up to a glass display case containing hundreds of different types and sizes of cigarette lighters.

The Filipino shopkeeper behind the counter bobbed his head, smiling, his white teeth shining in vivid contrast with his dark brown skin "I see you from *Winchester County*," he said examining the ship's rocker patch on the shoulder of Underwood's white jumper. Underwood's eyes narrowed with a look of suspicion that someone would recognize the significance of the patch. "I custom engrave for you here while you wait," Leon said. "You pick lighter, I engrave what you want. Look," and he held up a stainless lighter with a ship's plaque and the name *John Smith* engraved below. "And also these." He placed several lighters with different styles of engraving on the counter, his hands barely emerging out of the overly long sleeves of his white shirt.

"How long will it take?" Jonah asked holding the sample lighter, turning it over, flipping the lid and rolling the striker wheel. It gave off a spark and ignited a flame, the scent of the lighter fluid and the burning wick filled his nostrils.

"I do it for you in two minutes, you wait."

"Hey guys, I gotta get one of these. Can you wait two minutes?"

"Sure, go ahead," Homer said, and Jonah started looking through the glass case at the lighters.

"Which one you like?" Leon asked.

Jonah scanned the lighters on the glass shelves, his eyes going from one to the other. "I'll take that one," he finally said pointing. "That brushed chrome lighter in the blue box."

"Very good choice, very good choice," Leon said, his wide smile showing a broken upper incisor. "You write what you want," and he slid a pencil and paper across the top of the display case and reached into the case and pulled out the lighter.

Jonah thought for a moment and then wrote:

Jonah Wynchester

GM2 USN

Subic Bay 1966

"Man, this sure is a busy place," Brickey said as he stood watching the crowd of sailors pouring over the bridge. "Look at all these guys!"

Homer turned and saw what Brickey was looking at. "Yea, more sailors going the same direction than I ever seen before."

"Where's the best place for cold beer and pretty girls?" Jonah asked Leon.

"You go to Red Grotto," Leon said without looking up as he placed the lighter in a small hand-held vice, the jaws covered with hard rubber. He tightened the vice and then carefully drew Jonah's chosen script onto the case with a fine-point pencil. "That look good?" he asked, holding the lighter up to Jonah.

"Perfect," Jonah said examining the beautiful script.

Leon smiled and rifled through an ancient looking bamboo box, chose a sharp, flat steel graver with a short radius heel and expertly began pushing the point of the graver into the surface of the lighter's case. Rotating the vice with his left hand, and continually moving the graver onto the case with his right, he methodically and swiftly completed the entire engraving in a matter of minutes. "You like?" he said handing the lighter to Jonah.

"Beautiful," was the only word Jonah could think of, turning the lighter up toward the light, the sparkling brass showing through the freshly engraved cover.

"Good," Leon said with his big smile and he looked up at the other three sailors. "Who next?"

The three others shook their heads.

"Sorry, Leon," Underwood said. "Got one in Naples last year," and he held a lighter in the palm of his hand.

Leon looked carefully at the Italian engraving. His eyes widened. "Maganda!" was all he said.

"Where do we find this Red Grotto place?" Jonah asked.

"Ah," Leon reached into a drawer, pulled out a business card and laid it on the counter.

RED GROTTO

Conditioned Air

Pleasant Decoration Style

Appealing Girls - Living Music

Good Services - Bar - Food

Cheap & Much Enjoyment

Magsaysay Street - Olongapo City

Jonah read the card with a look of disbelief. "Is this place really any good?"

"Oh, yes. The very best, good drinks, plenty girls, nice music, soft lights. The very best," Leon repeated, smiling broadly. "Map on back."

Jonah turned the card over and looked at the map.

"You tell them Lighter Leon sent you," and he pulled a rubber stamp from a drawer and pressed it onto the card. "You see, Lighter Leon?" and he pointed to the red stamping. "Show them card. You get discount. Ask for Ligaya. My sister."

"Thanks," Jonah said flipping the card between his fingers. "Ligaya, your sister?"

"Yes, Ligaya, it means happiness. She the very best. She work there."

With a sly grin on his face, Jonah glanced at Underwood. "Leon's sister, Ligaya, works there."

Underwood nodded with a knowing look.

"You go one block straight," Leon pointed. "Then turn right," and both of his hands pointed east. "Red Grotto on left. You don't miss it. Big sign. Many lights."

"Okay, thanks," Jonah said, counting out dollar bills and placing them on the counter "The Red Grotto it is. You guys ready?"

"Let's do it!" Homer said.

"By the way, Leon?" Jonah said.

"Yes?"

"What's your sister look like?"

"She the pretty one."

Jonah nodded and chuckled to himself.

"Thank you Jonah Wynchester, USN," Leon called out as they started walking away. "You come back! I be here every day!"

Jonah was still looking at the map on the card as Underwood, Homer and Brickey gawked in amazement at all the bright lights and the bars on either side of the street.

"Damn, there's got to be dozens and dozens of places here!" Homer said. "You ever seen so many bars in one place in all your life?"

"Can't say that I have," Underwood said, staring at the multitude of neon signs lighting up the street, the different signs hanging so close together it was difficult to distinguish one from the other.

"This even beats San Juan!" Homer said in amazement.

"There it is!" Brickey pointed up the street at a huge light box suspended over the sidewalk, the sign's bright red neon lights blinking off and on and off and on; Red Grotto.

"Holy shit, this is unbelievable!" Homer said as they walked into the Grotto's cavernous space, the walls and ceiling resembling the interior of a cave with hundreds of small red lights set in recesses, bathing the large room in a diffused red glow. A band played rock and roll on a stage in the far corner opposite the bar which wrapped around one complete side of the cave. The four sailors were immediately accosted by Filipina bar girls.

"Oh, look," one of the girls, in high heels, mini skirt and tight blouse, shouted, grabbing hold of Brickey's arm and reading the rocker patch on his shoulder. "Hello *Winchester County*. Who you name?"

"Where's the boss?" Jonah said, taking command of the situation.

"There," one of the girls pointed to a short man with slick black hair washing beer glasses behind the bar.

Jonah walked away from the group, side stepping between tables, chairs, bar girls and waitresses.

"Lighter Leon sent us," he said handing the business card to the man.

"Oh, good, yes, good, very good," the man said wide eyed, examining the card.

"We want your best table."

"Oh, yes, yes. Best table

"And we want Ligaya."

"Ligaya? Oh, yes, yes, Ligaya." The slick-haired man immediately turned to the hostess, clapped his hands and shouted in his Tagalog language so he could be heard over the loud music.

"You come this way," the hostess said smiling. She walked Jonah across the room and through a bamboo curtain to a discrete alcove, the red opaque lights and low ceiling giving the space the sensation of close intimacy.

"Hey Woody, over here!" Jonah shouted through the bamboo curtain.

Underwood turned at the sound of his name and pointed toward Jonah whose head was poking through the thin strips of bamboo. Homer and Brickey, each with a girl on their arm, laughed and walked toward the alcove.

"Where's the famous Ligaya?" Woody said.

"I don't know, but she better hurry, cause I'm thirsty," Homer said.

"And hungry," Brickey added.

Jonah, who was sitting with his back to the wall with an unobstructed view of the great room, had his attention diverted by something on the other side of the bamboo curtain; an unusually tall, sinuous girl with long, thick black hair, wearing a form-fitting carmine and ultramarine jumpsuit. He watched her every move through the bamboo, her wide-set oriental eyes, high cheekbones, and the red high heel sandals in which she walked with a very long, flowing stride. But what really captured his attention was when she turned at the next table and headed straight for him. That was when he saw the front of her jumpsuit; it was completely unbuttoned, all the way from her neck down to her waist, exposing a tantalizing view of her ample and obviously very firm assets. Underwood, Homer and Brickey, startled by the appearance of this shockingly beautiful woman coming through the bamboo curtain, all jerked sideways in unison when she sat down next to Jonah. Ignoring the three other sailors, she laid her fingers on Jonah's leg, well above the knee, and closely examined the scar on his face. "Hello, *Winchester County*..." she whispered. "...you buy Ligaya a drink?"

❧❦

"Mister Browning...Sir...Sir...Mister Browning!" Poldolski said in his hoarse voice, shaking Browning's left foot. "Mister Browning! Sir, wake up!"

"Huh?"

"You got a phone call, sir!"

"Wha...?"

"You got a phone call on the quarterdeck!"

"Go away."

"Mister Browning, you're the Command Duty Officer! We got a phone call from the gate! Some chief is asking for the CDO! That's you!"

Browning raised himself up on one elbow and rubbed his face with his free hand. "What time is it?"

"Uh, it's 0430, sir. You gotta get up and take this phone call, sir."

"For crying out loud, Poldolski! Okay. I'll get up. I'll get up. Just leave me alone. Go away, for crissake."

"Yes, sir. It's a chief from the Olongapo gate. He's on the phone... on the quarterdeck."

"Okay, I'm coming, I'm coming."

"On the quarterdeck, sir," and Poldolski, thinking that Browning was sufficiently awake, quickly left the stateroom.

"Did you get him up?" Mills asked standing inside the quarterdeck shack holding the phone.

"Yea, yea, but man he sure is a deep sleeper. It took me forever to get him moving. He should be here in a minute."

"What the hell's going on, Mills?" Browning asked in a deep croaking voice. He was bareheaded, dressed in a pair of flip flops, wrinkled khaki trousers and a T shirt. He pressed his eyes tightly closed and blinked several times, trying to focus. His tousled black hair, red eyes and the dark bags under them were clear clues that he had been imbibing sometime in the past few hours.

"Some chief at the Olongapo gate, sir," Mills said, holding the phone out toward Browning. "Says they've got some guy who claims he's from our ship. Wants to talk to the CDO. That's you, sir."

Browning shook his head and pinched the bridge of his nose. "Arrhh. Give me the damn phone." Mills handed him the phone and Browning just stood there, holding the phone on his chest as he rubbed his face with his free hand. Taking a deep breath, he cleared his throat.

"This is..." he forced himself to swallow. "This is Lieutenant Browning," he said into the phone.

"Sir, this is Chief Dunaway, at the Olongapo gate."

Mills and Poldolski stood nearby, listening to the one end of the conversation and the scattering of semi-unintelligible words squeaking from the ear piece.

"Yea?" Browning asked, shaking his head, trying to wake up.

"Sir, we got a man over here who says he's from your ship."

Browning looked at his watch: it was 0435

"Yea? What man?"

"Sir, he says he's an ensign from *Winchester County*. That's your ship."

"An ensign?"

"Yes, Sir, an ensign. Says his name is Hobson."

When Browning heard the name Hobson, an alarm went off in his head, and he put one hand over the phone's mouthpiece. "Mills...you and Poldolski, move aside," he said. "This is classified. Move over there," and he pointed with his other hand.

"Chief, who did you say?"

"Says his name's Hobson, sir."

"Hobson?"

"Yes, sir."

"Hobson, you sure?"

"Yes, sir, says he's Ensign Harvey Hobson."

"What?"

"Yes, sir."

Browning stood with the phone to his ear, his other hand gripping the desk, his eyes were closed, his mouth shut tight. He was unconsciously gritting his teeth.

"Chief, you say you got a man there, who says he's an ensign? Harvey Hobson?"

"Yes sir."

"What do mean? He says his name is Hobson? Haven't you checked his ID?"

"No sir, he aint' got no ID."

"Whaddya mean he aint got no ID?"

"Well, sir, he's missing his wallet."

Browning shook his head. "Well what's he look like?"

"Well, sir, he's sorta average height, maybe five-ten, on the heavy side, round face, brown eyes, thin brown hair, pale skin. Sorta reminds me of a marshmallow. You know? Kinda wimpy looking?"

"Well, can't you see he's an ensign from his uniform?"

"Sir, he ain't wearing no uniform!"

"What ya mean, no uniform?"

175

"No, sir. No uniform."

"Not wearing a uniform?"

"No, sir!"

"Well, what is he wearing?"

"A shower curtain."

"What?"

"Yes, sir, he's wearing a shower curtain."

"Chief, I don't understand." Browning was now finally and fully awake, his eyes wide open, a look of bewildered astonishment on his face.

"Sir, apparently he got rolled somewhere in Olongapo. Whoever knocked him out, also took his uniform. And his cap. And his wallet. And his shoes. All's he's got left are his skivvies, and this plastic shower curtain with pink flowers on it. He's got it draped around him now, as if he was going to a toga party."

"Put him on the phone," Browning ordered.

"Hello?" A squeaky, tenuous voice came over the phone. Browning recognized it instantly.

"Harvey, is that you?"

"Sam?"

"Is that you Harvey?'

"Yea, Sam, it's me. Harvey."

"What the hell's going on?"

"Well, Sam...they rolled me."

"Who rolled you?"

"Some guys. I was a...I was with this girl, in her room, and something knocked me out. I don't know what happened. And when I came to...well...I didn't have...I didn't have any clothes...and they took my wallet, my money...and my ID...and my shoes...and..."

Browning could hear the emotion in Hobson's voice, the emotion of someone who was about to have a nervous breakdown. "Oh, for crissake!" Browning said, looking up to the sky where a faint streak of light was beginning to show behind the eastern clouds. "Put the chief back on the damn line!"

"Sir?" the chief said.

"Chief?"

"Yes, sir?"

"That's Hobson."

"He's who he says he is, sir?"

"Correct. Can you get him back here?"

"Yes, sir. But not until the gate opens."

"When will that be?"

"In, uh, twelve minutes, sir.

"Okay. But you can get him back here? Is that correct?"

"Yes, sir. I can drive him over to you in twelve minutes. In my jeep, no problem."

"Twelve minutes?"

"Yes, sir."

"Okay. I'll be waiting for you at the top of the brow. You know where we are?"

"Oh, yes sir, I sure do. I'll be there in twelve minutes."

Browning hung up the phone. He stood on the quarterdeck, stock still, looking up but not seeing the pale morning light that was low in the eastern sky, thinking, thinking. "Mills!" he said suddenly.

"Yes, sir?" Mills said, walking back to the quarterdeck shack.

"We've got an emergency here."

"Sir?"

"A very important, high priority, emergency."

Mills looked at Browning, wide eyed, his mouth open.

"I want you and Poldolski to take a break."

"Take a break, sir?"

"Yea. Take a coffee break. Go to the galley. Get yourselves a cup of coffee, and don't come back here. Don't come back until..." Browning looked at this watch. "Until 0520. You got that?"

"Yes sir. Me and Poldolski take a coffee break and be back here on the quarterdeck at 0520."

"Right."

"You sure you don't need us, sir?"

"No! Go. Go."

As Mills and Poldolski went aft to the deck house, Browning ran to his stateroom and frantically put on a shirt and a pair of shoes, grabbed his cap and rushed back to the quarterdeck just as a narrow pair of headlights came up the quay. A jeep stopped at the foot of the brow and a chief got out of the driver's side. A formless mass of something draped in plastic got out of the passenger side. The plastic object walked up the brow with the chief following close behind, and Harvey Hobson's head poked out above the top of the pink flowered shower curtain.

Browning stood at the top of the brow in disbelief.

"Mister Browning?' the chief saluted.

"That's me chief," Browning said returning the salute.

"Is this him?"

"Yea, it sure is."

"Alright, then, I'll leave him with you, sir."

"Thanks chief."

"No problem, sir. But I gotta tell 'ya," the chief said with a wide grin. "In all my time here in Subic," and he took off his cap and wiped his bald head with a handkerchief. "In all my time here in Subic this has got to be just about the craziest thing I ever did see. I'm just glad he weren't some new secret weapon the Russians were trying to sneak onto the base." The chief laughed, put his cap back on, saluted and went down the brow still laughing, got in the jeep and drove away.

"Sam, I'm sorry," Hobson said with an embarrassed, depressed, miserable look. "I'm really sorry. I should'a been more...."

"Aw, shut up Harvey!" Browning interrupted in angry frustration. "Just get the hell out'a my sight. Get inside and get cleaned up!"

"I'll never forget this, Sam...I owe you..." Hobson said and he turned and started walking along the main deck. "I owe you big time, Sam."

"What a circus..." Browning mumbled to himself, shaking his head, watching the pink shower curtain shuffle away, a pair of hairy legs poking out from under the plastic and two pigeon-toed bare feet rapidly skittering along the deck. "...an absolutely insane cathedral circus!"

"It sure is that," a voice said. Browning, startled, turned rapidly around to see a dark shape walking toward him from the inky recesses of the main deck. "What the hell you doing out here, Sam?" the apparition said lighting a pipe, the flame from the lighter revealing Davant's face.

"Jesus, Len!" Browning said. "You scared the shit out'a me!"

"Sorry 'bout that. I couldn't sleep...I decided to take a stroll. What's going on with that jeep?"

Browning, shocked that Davant saw the jeep and possibly also saw who got out of the jeep, stood frozen on the quarterdeck trying to find the right words. "Aw, just some drunk that the shore patrol brought back. I sent him below."

"Hmm. I guess there are some kind-hearted souls among the shore patrol after all." And Davant turned and looked around him. "Where's the quarterdeck watch?"

"Uh, I sent them to get a cup of coffee. Mills and Poldolski. Those guys rarely get a break, and I was already up. That was the least I could do."

"Another kind soul? Miracles will never cease. So, tell me, my esteemed 1st Lieutenant, I was wondering, where are you going to have that dump truck deposit your sand this morning? In the captain's cabin, or the XO's stateroom?"

"Not funny, Len. Not funny. No, I've got Biagotti building a wooden enclosure, a pig sty as he calls it, in the tank deck, aft near the winch. It'll be out of the way there."

"Save me one of those burlap bags, will ya?" Davant said. "Before you fill it that is. I'd like to have a souvenir of this historic event...a truck dumping beach sand inside an LST. Ha, ha. No one would believe that. So, tell me, you going on liberty tonight? You going to experience the delights of Olongapo?"

"Probably not. I think I'll just make a visit to the O Club. That might be a safer place. Safer than Olongapo anyway."

"I understand that not everyone who goes across that bridge into Olongapo survives to tell the tale," Davant said, his head cocked to one side and his eyebrows arched. "Is that true?"

"Could be," Browning said, wondering what Davant was getting at.

"And I understand some people come back to the ship with less than they started out with?"

"Hmm, sometimes." A warning light went off inside Browning's head, detecting a degree of concealed perception behind Davant's sarcasm.

"Any way," Davant continued. "I wonder if Harvey Hobson, our revered junior ensign, survived last night's soiree...you know, with the flesh pots, bar girls and alcohol dispensing establishments of Magsaysay Street? He's pretty green behind the ears, you know." Davant's face, lit from the pipe's glow, had the look of amused suspicion written all over it.

"Yea." Browning tried his best not to reveal anything.

"I'm looking forward to Mendoza's gourmet breakfasts this morning," Davant said and Browning was thankful for Davant's shift in subjects. "I'll need the extra calories today as we continue to process the thousands of spare parts coming aboard our ancient Cathedral."

"Including a new washing machine?" Browning asked, relieved with the new topic.

"Ah, yes indeed...a new washing machine. The dead machine has been uprooted from its welds, and is being donated to the Subic Bay trash pile. We are holding a ceremony today at 1000 hours, if you care to attend."

"No thanks, Len. I think I'm gonna be busy."

"Very well," and Davant yawned and stretched his arms. "Ah, here comes your relief," he said watching Mills and Poldolski walking forward with coffee mugs in their hands.

"Everything go okay with your emergency, Mister Browning?" Mills asked taking a sip of coffee.

Davant removed the pipe from his mouth and looked wide eyed at Browning and then Mills.

"Yea fine." Browning said, glancing at Davant, wondering just how much more complicated this charade was going to get.

"That's good, sir. And thanks for the coffee break."

"No problem."

"You don't need to stand any more quarterdeck watches this morning, do you Sam?" Davant asked, his eyebrows turned up.

"No." Browning shook his head.

"Well, then," Davant said. "You certainly don't need my professional assistance any longer, so I think I'll be getting a shave and a shower. See you at breakfast."

Browning watched Davant walk away, heading for the deck house. "Hey, Len," Browning called out, walking quickly to catch up. "Wait up, one minute..." Davant's eyes were wide open. "Listen, Len, I don't know what you saw this morning. And I don't know what you didn't see. But whatever you saw, keep it to yourself, okay? There's no need to be broadcasting this around the ship. Anyone can get themselves in a bind...even greenhorn ensigns. So, whatever you saw, it's just between you and me. You understand? You understand that?"

Davant nodded, his pipe tight in his teeth, the smoke wafting up from the glowing bowl. "I know what you're saying, Sam," Davant took the pipe out of his mouth. "I know you're just a soft-hearted guy underneath all that tough Texas drawl and discourse. Don't worry, Sam. I'm on your side. I understand what you did. And I'm damn glad you did it. It's a lot better than having that crazy Charlie Crane beating up on our junior ensign. Whatever I saw, you can count on me to keep it quiet."

"Thanks, Len. That's good of you."

"But what I really want to know is how could he be so stupid? How could Hobson get so shitfaced, lose his clothes and have to return to the ship in a shower curtain?"

"I guess it was his choice."

"Yea. Hobson's choice." Davant suddenly realized what he had just said. "Ha ha, that's funny," and he stuck the pipe back in his mouth "See 'ya at breakfast?"

"I'll be there."

"Good...I understand Mendoza's serving your favorite this morning," Davant said over his shoulder as he walked away.

"Yea? What's that?"

"Undercooked eggs, greasy bacon, and burnt potatoes."

Browning shook his head and walked slowly forward along the main deck, breathing in Subic Bay's hot, oppressive, humid, water-saturated atmosphere, asking himself the same old question: why did he have to wind up on a ship of fools? He unexpectedly felt a very powerful longing; a wistful craving for the dry, cool mornings back home in Texas. He closed his eyes and visualized the flat grassy plains and the golden cups of the prickly pear, the purple-pink flowers of the lace cactus, and the huge yuccas with their immense, floating, ghost-shaped bundles of creamy white blooms.

ೞಲ

It was an hour before reveille, and sleep had been impossible. Turning over, fighting with the blankets, lying there with his eyes open, Jonah was exhausted. The work of the last 48 hours had been unceasing; checking and re-checking the 40mm guns on the bow and stern, the .50 and .30 caliber machine guns, the M-1 Carbines, and once again going through the ammunition inventories and making the lists; the lists of personnel and ammunition to be assigned to each gun. And today had finally arrived. Today was to be their first beaching in Vietnam; a beaching where no one could predict the outcome. His apprehension had now reached the point where anxiety and tension were completely enveloping him, weighing him down with an enormous pressure, a pressure he was unable to control. Now he was lying in a sweat. One moment he was hot and the next moment cold. The red night lights transformed everything in the compartment into the pervading atmosphere of a macabre spook house; he visualized the racks as coffins, the people phantoms, the pipes and cables on the overhead slithered and writhed as snakes. He had never felt this way before; it was as if a tornado had started heading straight for him on Monday, was still coming at him on Tuesday, and then it got even closer on Wednesday. The anticipation was overwhelming. He felt as if there was a vibrating pressure cooker inside him that was about to explode and he jerked upright in the rack. The growing tension coming across his shoulders had now reached into his neck. The nerves in his legs were on fire. He held his hands out and they were trembling as he thought about the mysterious, potentially deadly place no one had been to: Chu Lai.

⋙⋘

"Radar dome bears two-five-five," Cunningham called out as he looked through the eyepiece of the pelorus. The distinctly prominent white radar dome he was sighting on was three miles in the distance, sitting atop the tallest hill above the marine base at Chu Lai. Foliage and trees once living on the hill and down its slopes were now long gone; chopped down, chewed up and bulldozed away to create a clear line of fire, a completely open killing-zone, protecting the valuable radar from a potential Viet Cong attack. Now the exposed red dirt hillside and the dry roads leading from the beach were covered in thick red dust, swirling, circulating and blowing downwind as fully loaded 10-wheel deuce-and-a-half trucks trudged their loads from the LST ramp uphill to their inland destinations.

"Ban-Than bears zero-four-zero," Cunningham said, this time sighting the pelorus on the jutting peninsula off the starboard bow.

"Four thousand yards to the sea buoy," Beaufort called out from inside the conn, his head quickly disappearing back into the black rubber hood of the radar repeater.

An hour-ago Underwood had climbed the ladder to the conn and was astonished by what he saw. The wings were crowded, not just with people, but with sandbags; sandbags stacked along the forward rails, sandbags along the aft rails, and more sandbags around the pelorus mounts, hundreds of sandbags creating a lumpy, burlap-colored, confined environment. He thought he had walked into a set for a World War I movie. Looking closely at the sandbags, he saw many of them had minute holes and tears, and sand was trickling continuously down onto the deck. The wing deck, normally subjected to a twice daily ritual of sweeping and swabbing, was now sacrilegiously covered with fine Subic sand, constantly being scuffed and blown from one side to the other. He looked around him, at the Captain, the XO, Beaufort, Cunningham, Pike, O'Toole, a quartermaster striker, another signalman and two lookouts; a total of 10 people crammed into the tight space, all wearing helmets and flak vests, with the cuffs of their trousers tucked into their socks and their shirt sleeves buttoned to their wrists.

"Both engines ahead one-third," the captain ordered through his cigar-clenched teeth and he picked up his binoculars and scanned the beach.

"Both engines ahead one-third," Beaufort repeated through the voice tube down to the pilot house. O'Toole repeated the order through his sound powered phone connecting him to the engine room.

"Engine room answers both engines ahead one-third," O'Toole reported, his owl shaped eyes looking at the orange-red dust rising from the hill in the distance.

Underwood adjusted the sound-powered phone connecting him to the bow and stern anchors, and the gun mounts, and he leaned over the railing and looked aft. There was Jonah and his eight-man gun crew in helmets and flak vests, all crouched down behind the 40mm gun tub's steel enclosure, a few pairs of eyes bravely peering over the top of the rim. Underwood could see the gun tub's ammo racks, filled to capacity with hundreds of four-round clips of 40mm shells, the bright brass of the 17-inch long rounds glinting in the sunlight. There must be at least 500 rounds in that gun tub, he thought, and thousands more in the magazine below. Then he looked along the port side of the main deck where a .50 caliber machine gun mount had been constructed of steel angles and curved 3/8-inch plate, and more sandbags were stacked on the forward and aft edges of that mount. Underwood could see Homer, and another sailor with a sound powered phone, both standing within the enclosure; Homer's large left hand rested on the gray gun's steel receiver, the fingers of his right hand nervously and repeatedly tapping out a drumming rhythm on the gun's handle grip. Looking further forward Underwood saw another .50-caliber gun amidships and another further forward near the dog house. In addition there was a .30-caliber machine gun mounted on the bow and stern gun tubs, and one each on the LCVPs, the 36-foot, 18,000-pound landing craft hanging from the Welin davits up high port and starboard. All tolled there were two Bofors 40mm twin-barreled guns, six .50 caliber machine guns, and four .30 caliber machine guns; all manned, all ready, and all with plenty of ammunition within easy reach. That's a lot of fire power, he thought. A lot of fire power.

    The ship had been at general quarters for over an hour, and the bright hot morning sun had now reached an altitude where it was blazing intensely down onto the steel decks. Those topside wearing helmets and flak vests were feeling the scorching heat; the heat from the sun, the heat inside the steel brain buckets on their heads, and the heat percolating under the heavy vests. Watertight doors, hatches and scuttles were closed and dogged throughout the ship. Down in the main engine room, Wilson and Beckers along with several enginemen, machinist mates and electricians were anxiously monitoring the V-12 diesels and the cantankerous reduction gears. Tempting fate, someone with a perverted sense of humor had painted a cartoon on the housing of the port reduction gear depicting a grinning jackrabbit, the animal's overly-large feet racing at blinding speed across the surface of a choppy blue sea; the speech bubble read: *Ain't stopping for noth'n*. Beckers, with his usual lollipop in his mouth, nervously patted the gear and gazed upward toward the overhead, appearing to be looking for divine intervention. Further aft in the auxiliary engine room, Jones and his crew had all three of the 6-71 Detroit diesels on line and running at 1800 RPM, generating the power necessary for all the many electrical needs of an LST about to make a combat beaching on an unknown shore. Doc Slaughter had everything he needed ready and waiting in the sick bay, and the stewards, under Slaughter's close supervision, had removed all but a few of the chairs from the wardroom, turning that compartment with its big table into a large first-aid station. The bow doors were now open, the ramp down and waiting at a 45-degree angle, and Browning, Biagotti and some of the deck gang in helmets and flak vests were on the bow, crouched down alongside the anchor windlass, intently watching Chu Lai coming closer and closer. The ship was at Condition Zebra, the maximum degree of readiness and watertight integrity, buttoned up as tight as it could be, and the crew was on the alert; tense, apprehensive and wondering what they were going to encounter. Biagotti was nervously tapping a screw driver on the railing; the noise of the slow metal to metal clink-clink-clink reminded Browning of Chinese water torture.

"Biagotti!" Browning said, glaring at the bosun. "Do you mind?"

Biagotti turned and looked at the 1st Lieutenant. "Sorry, sir," he said.

Back aft in the 40mm gun tub Jonah wiped the sweat from his face and pulled the bulky flak jacket away from his chest for a moment, seeking relief from the sticky heat. "Damn hot today," he said, looking over the lip of the enclosure.

"Could be even hotter on the beach," Mills replied with a knowing look, his hand resting on one of the 40mm shells. Jonah understood the message Mills was sending; they could soon be in a much hotter situation.

"Let's hope not," Jonah said.

"YAJDEK!" Mills said, his eyes wide open.

Jonah took a deep breath and shook his head.

"Two-thousand yards to the sea buoy," Beaufort announced from inside the conn, his head momentarily emerging from the radar hood.

The captain lifted his binoculars and looked forward, focusing the 7x50 powered glasses on the sea buoy. Then he shifted his attention to the sandbar jutting out toward the left side of the channel, and then to the very large radar dome on the bare hill beyond. Although the smoking lamp had been out for several hours he was still sucking on his unlit cigar, rolling it from one side of his mouth to the other as he repeatedly lifted the binoculars to his sunglass-covered eyes. He glanced at his watch. "Where's the pilot boat?" he shouted to Crane who was standing on the opposite wing.

"Sir, it's supposed to meet us at the sea buoy."

"Hell! I know that! Where is it?" The captain lowered the binoculars. "JB?" he yelled toward Beaufort. "What's the distance to the sea buoy now?"

Beaufort heard the exchange between the captain and the XO and was ready for the question. He answered immediately. "Nine hundred yards, sir!"

"Stupid, dumb, idiots! Where the hell are they?" the captain grumbled

"Sir!" Pike called out, looking through his binoculars. "There's a boat coming out!" and his hand pointed off the port bow. Six pairs of eyes all swung simultaneously to port, looking through binoculars in the same direction. The captain, with the cigar firmly in his teeth, leaned far forward over the railing, peering intently through the binoculars.

Those at the .50 caliber gun mounts along the main deck also saw the boat, and Underwood noticed Homer leaning over his gun and looking toward the single strange boat with the small cloud of blue exhaust smoke flowing behind it.

The captain rubbed his eyes and anxiously lifted his binoculars again, focusing on the boat with its disfigured bow pushing a large wave of white water in front of it.

"Distance to the sea buoy now?" the captain shouted.

"Seven-hundred yards, sir!"

"All engines stop!"

"All engines stop!" O'Toole immediately repeated through his phone.

Underwood looked at O'Toole and saw the large phone-talker helmet pressing down on the big storekeeper's head, and the small flak vest squeezing his huge torso. His shirt at the armpits was saturated with sweat. Underwood thought he resembled a fat two-legged turtle.

"Engine room answers all engines stopped," O'Toole said, and he wiped the sweat off his face with his shirt sleeve.

As the ship slowed, now making only a few knots of forward speed, the strange boat continued coming toward them, and all those on the conn were nervously focusing their binoculars directly at it. The captain, the XO, Beaufort, Cunningham, Pike and the lookouts watched it intently. Underwood and O'Toole, without binoculars, could only squint and stare.

The captain quickly turned toward Underwood. "Stand-by all guns!" the captain shouted; he was clearly in a very high state of nervous agitation.

For a brief second Underwood was startled by the order; an order he never imagined receiving, then he shouted into the transmitter. "Stand-by all guns!" The captain's nervous, agitated alarm was spreading.

Those who heard the captain's order and Underwood's transmission over the phone circuit were stunned. Crane lowered his binoculars and stared at the captain's back. Cunningham's mouth was wide open. Beaufort heard the order and his head abruptly emerged from the radar hood, a look of shock on his face.

Underwood saw the gun crew in the forward 40mm tub suddenly stand up from crouching behind the rim and quickly move into their assigned positions; Poldolski jumped into the trainer seat and placed his feet on the foot pedals and his hands on the control wheel.

"Conn, aye," Underwood said as he received the multiple reports from the various stations. "All guns report standing by, sir!"

Everyone on the conn was now on edge. Underwood sensed the tension, thinking it felt electric, as if a high voltage current was flowing all around them, and the smallest mistake, the most minimal spark could easily set off an huge explosion.

SLAAP! Everyone jumped at the noise. The captain turned around and glared at Pike, the CO's aviator sunglasses aiming directly at the big signalman. An embarrassed Pike reached down to pick up a dropped clipboard and the loose papers blowing around the deck.

Underwood watched Homer pull the bolt back on the .50 caliber, chambering a round. The burly shipfitter swiveled the gun toward the strange boat and looked along the sights.

"What is that boat?" the captain yelled.

Everyone with binoculars focused on the boat. No one knew the answer to the captain's question. No one spoke.

"Doesn't anybody know what that boat is?" the captain repeated, focusing his binoculars, leaning forward against the railing, desperate to find the answer to his question.

"Sir, it's a..." Charlie Crane sputtered as he looked through his binoculars. "It's a....I don't know sir!"

"JB," the captain shouted to Beaufort and pointed toward the boat. "Contact that boat on the TBS! Find out who they are!"

"Yes, Sir," and Beaufort pulled the Talk Between Ships radio phone out of its cradle. He keyed the mike and spoke into it; the line-of-sight signal transmitting across the water. "Unidentified boat off our port bow, this is the United States Ship LST *Winchester County*, identify yourself, over!" There was no answer. Beaufort repeated the transmission. "Unidentified boat off our port bow, this is United States LST *Winchester County*, identify yourself, identify yourself, over!" He repeated the transmission again. Still no answer.

"What the hell...?" the captain said looking through his binoculars.

"Sir?" Crane muttered.

The captain spun around and looked directly at Underwood. "All guns, stand by to concentrate fire on that boat off the port bow!" the captain shouted, spittle shooting from his mouth.

Underwood suddenly jumped. Catching his breath he repeated the command through his phone. "All guns, stand by to concentrate fire on the boat off the port bow!" he shouted into the phone. His face had a severe grimace. He was trying to control himself, but he was unconsciously squeezing the phone's transmitter, his fingers turning red from the pressure.

The courses of the two vessels were converging and the distance between them was rapidly closing.

Underwood heard the anxious replies coming through his earphones; he thought the voices seemed to be under tremendous strain. "All guns report standing by!" Underwood shouted. He could see the crews on the .50 caliber guns, they were clearly aiming at the target. Brickey, in the forward 40mm gun tub, was pointing his hand off the port bow and shouting something to Poldolski sitting in the gun's trainer seat. The 40mm gun slowly trained to port, the gun's big twin flared barrels aiming directly at the approaching boat. The 40mm gun in the aft tub also trained around. Underwood saw Jonah leaning out over the rim of the tub, looking forward, watching the target. Underwood felt a cold chill flash up his neck.

"What the hell...?" the captain yelled.

The range between the ship and the boat diminished faster with each second.

"What the hell kind of flag is that?" the captain shouted, continuing to peer through his binoculars.

Pike was fixated on the boat, staring through his binoculars, straining to see the....

"Pike, what is that blue flag?" the captain yelled.

Pike was clearly confused. The big signalman couldn't identify the flag, and he stuttered. "I...I don't...I don't know sir!"

"Well, hell, you're the signalman! You're supposed to know. Idiot!"

Underwood watched the boat, but without binoculars he couldn't see what the others were seeing. But when he looked down to the main deck he could clearly see Homer at the .50 caliber machine gun, standing with his feet wide apart, his eyes peering along the gun's sights, both of his hands tightly gripping the gun's handles; his thumbs were floating just above the wishbone shaped trigger, waiting for the order to fire...the order where there would be no turning back.

Everyone was waiting for the order. Underwood knew it was going to come any second. Crane's right foot was bouncing rapidly on the deck. Cunningham looked wide eyed from the boat to the captain and back to the boat again. Beaufort had abandoned the radar altogether and was intently watching the forward 40mm as its crew kept training the gun, and training the gun, aiming at the speeding boat.

"They're..." the captain said.

The boat was coming closer now, close enough to see with the naked eye, and everyone on the conn stood wide-eyed, mouths open, with looks of disbelief on their faces as the boat made a 180 degree turn and ranged up 100-feet off the port side of the ship.

Underwood could now see what the others had been looking at with their high-powered binoculars. There were three men in the battered, dirty, rusting outboard powered boat, all three men dressed more or less the same; in combat boots, short pants, and with .45s slung on their hips. Two of the men had on white T shirts and baseball caps; the third, the one everyone was now staring at, wore a pith helmet and a bright blue, unbuttoned, Hawaiian shirt that was flowing in the breeze. All three were waving and smiling, and the one in the Hawaiian shirt was holding up a megaphone.

"Welcome to Chu Lai!" he yelled in a high-pitched southern drawl, his words booming clear across the water. "Welcome to Chu Lai, y'all, courtesy of U.S. Navy Seabee Construction Battalion Ten! Follow us to the beach!" and he lowered the megaphone and smiled, a big wide grin across his face, his white teeth in sharp contrast against his dark tan. The blue Hawaiian shirt resembled a flag waving in the breeze as the boat accelerated ahead of the ship.

CHAPTER 7
SPIRITUS

"That was the closest I've ever come to a disaster," Jonah said as he and Underwood stood on the red dirt a safe distance from where the green giant was unloading pallets of cement through the bow doors. "Now I know how friendly fire happens!"

Poldolski walked by with a .30 caliber M1 Carbine slung over one shoulder and an ammo belt hanging around his waist. Jonah thought he looked very serious about his job. "Hey, Poldolski..." he shouted.
"Make sure no VC sneak into the tank deck now, ya hear?"
Poldolski turned and grinned.

"I was watching Homer," Underwood said as Mills drove past them on the big green fork truck, going back into the ship, its empty forks up high to keep from hitting the hump just aft of the bow ramp. "I was watching Homer as we moved slowly forward, with that boat coming closer and closer. He was training that .50 on that boat, training it inch by inch as the bearing changed. Hell, I could see his fingers doing a little dance on those grips. I thought, oh no, something bad is gonna happen here! This is definitely going to be bad!"

"At first I couldn't see anything from where I was," Jonah said. "But then I leaned out over the railing of the gun tub and looked forward." Jonah paused and looked up to the forward gun tub to make sure the crew manning the .30 caliber Browning machine gun was awake. "And that's when I saw Homer on the .50. And that boat was coming our way. And when I heard the order to stand by to fire...I thought, oh, God, here we go!"

"Well," Underwood said. "I'm telling you, I was beginning to feel myself shake inside. I could see the captain was nervous! Real nervous! He was walking between the wings like a caged lion. Crane, he was frozen in place; the poor guy was just standing at the port side pelorus, hanging on with both hands. And Beaufort, well...at least he had enough sense to stay inside the conn behind some cover. But hell, even with all those sandbags, we were about as exposed up there as the go-go dancer in that bar in Subic. I'm telling you it was tense. Real tense."

The green giant re-emerged through the bow doors with another pallet of cement and bounced its way from the ramp onto the beach, its huge shock absorbers compressing with each lurch and lunge across the uneven ground. A big cloud of red dust flew up in the air and Jonah closed his eyes and put his hand over his nose.

"God, this is an awful place," Underwood said looking around him, at the ship with its bow on the beach, and two other LSTs off their starboard side, all unloading their cargo. A line of Marine and Navy trucks, loaded with crates and pallets, were going from the beach up the red dirt road to the base, and empty trucks were coming back down for more loads. Large clouds of red dust swirled and rose into the air.

"When are we getting out'a here?" Jonah asked.

"I think as soon as this cement is offloaded," Underwood said blowing his nose. He looked at the handkerchief; it was covered in red snot. "And it can't be soon enough for me. Kinda makes you wonder if the rest of the country is any better, doesn't it?"

"Yea."

"Look at that!" Underwood said, pointing to where a group of Vietnamese wearing black and dark green pajama clothes and conical hats were walking down the road toward the water. They all walked into the brown water, dropped their pants and squatted. "Sonov'a'bitch! Look! Look at that! They're all taking a crap...old people, young people, kids, dogs! Do you believe that? Look! Look at those people! They're all taking a crap! For crying out loud! Man, I'm telling you, I can't wait to get out'a here. This place is disgusting. And we're here to help them fight a war? For what? So they can take a crap? The hell with this! I'm going back to the office. At least that hell hole is cleaner than this beach. See ya later."

"Hey, Wynchester!" Biagotti yelled. "Don't get too close! We might have to give you a broom so's you'z can help us sweep all 'dis cement dust out'a 'da tank deck. What ya think?"

"No thanks, Biagotti," Jonah replied. "I've got to take inventory of all the souvenirs I picked up in Subic. I'm sure you understand."

"Ha, ha. That's funny, Wynchester. Very funny. Inventorying your souvenirs. You're too much."

"Jonah!" Brickey called out, running out of the tank deck and down the bow ramp. He stood aside as Mills drove through with the green giant. "Hey, Jonah!"

"What's up?"

"Mister Sanders told me to find you," Brickey said out of breath. "Says he wants to see you in his stateroom, ASAP!"

"Oh, fucken great!" Jonah said and threw his ball cap into the red dirt. "And just what the hell does Prince Charming want from me this time?" and he glared at Brickey.

"Hey, Jonah! Chill out! I don't know what he wants! He just said find you! You don't have to get all riled up with me! I'm just the messenger! When you see him, why don't you smile and nod. Maybe he'll be in a better mood if you just smile and nod."

Jonah took a deep breath and walked in a circle. "Alright, I'll find him. In his stateroom you said?"

"Yea."

"Okay," and Jonah picked up his hat and started walking toward the bow ramp. He stopped in mid stride and turned around. "Brickey?"

"Yea?"

"Sorry 'bout that," Jonah said.

Brickey nodded, looking sideways at Jonah. Hearing the roar of the green giant behind him, Jonah quickly stepped aside as Mills beeped the horn and sped by. Jonah followed the machine's big tire tracks back into the tank deck where the pale overhead lights barely penetrated through the opaque cloud of white cement dust whirling and falling as if it was snow blanketing everything in sight.

※

Beaufort stepped into the stateroom and pulled the curtain closed behind him. "What's going on?" he asked.

"Oh, just the usual," Jones said looking through the papers on his desk. "More notices to mariners and other boring stuff: an abandoned barely afloat 40-foot fishing boat adrift, sighted somewhere out that'away," and he pointed east. "Some stuff about ancient Japanese mines floating around. Warnings about Vietnamese fishing boats without running lights....can you believe people would be out in fishing boats at night without running lights? Anyway, it's all the usual routine baloney."

"Well, I've got something that's not routine baloney."

"What's that?" Jones said looking up from the papers.

"Orders!" Beaufort whispered wide eyed, the smile of a canary-swallowing cat on his face.

"Orders?" Jones asked in a hushed tone, his mouth open. "What orders?"

"Japan," Beaufort said, his big grin growing bigger.

"What?"

"Yes! We've just received orders to Sasebo."

"Japan?"

"We're to proceed to Sasebo today, for resupply and repairs; alongside the tender."

"Are you pulling my leg?"

Beaufort shook his head. "And guess for how long?"

"Tell me."

"Ten days!"

"Ten days? God Almighty! I don't believe it! Ten days? This is incredible! Ten days in Japan? Are you sure?"

"The message just came in, and the XO is calling for a meeting of all officers in the wardroom. Now! Come on! Get moving.!"

"Damn. This is too much. I'm coming, I'm coming!"

Charlie Crane stood at the head of the wardroom table, papers in his hand, looking down at the officers sitting around the table.

"We've just received orders. As soon as we've offloaded all the cement, probably by this afternoon, we'll be leaving Chu Lai, and heading for Sasebo, Japan. ETA next Tuesday morning."

There was a collective deep sucking sound as everyone took a breath. Davant turned toward Browning with the look of someone who had just stolen a cookie from the jar.

"We'll be there for 10 days." More sounds and mumbled exclamations followed that announcement. "The primary focus will be to correct the ship's major deficiencies." Several heads nodded in approval. "Not R& R," Crane continued, and Davant slumped down in his chair. Jones' face, full of building excitement just a moment ago, now started to deflate. "Our priority will be repairing and replacing necessary equipment and bringing supplies aboard. There may be time for liberty, but it will be limited; no extended liberty, no leave, no one will be allowed farther than 50 kilometers from the base."

Beaufort wrote 'How far is 50 kilometers?' on his note pad with a big question mark next to it.

"And, visitations from family or friends is strongly discouraged; there will be no time. None whatsoever," Crane emphasized.

Wilson's mouth turned down at that announcement. Crane looked around the table, his stern face defying anyone from asking a question.

Davant, apparently not getting the message, raised his hand. "Sir, will 10 days be enough? Will 10 days be enough to accomplish all the work we need to get done. Won't we need more time?"

"Len, you are always trying to expand the envelope. We've been given 10 days and only 10 days and we will accomplish everything we need to get done in 10 days. There are 24 hours in a day, Len. That's 240 hours. Got it?"

"Yes, Sir." Davant looked down at the table.

"Each of you will determine your department's repair and supply needs. You will turn your requests in to me by 0800 tomorrow. That's 0800, tomorrow morning. You've got all night to work on it. The captain and I will review the requests and determine which ones have priority. Those requests will then be sent to Commander Service Group Three for appropriate scheduling. COMSERVGRU3 is embarked aboard *Ajax*, AR6, the tender in Sasebo. The highest priority items will be attended to first, the lowest priority will be last. Everything you may request may not be fulfilled. The work schedule of the tender and the yard will have a lot to do with that. Just because you may think you need something done doesn't mean it will be done. So organize your priorities carefully."

There was a subdued murmuring around the room and several heads nodded as notes were quickly being written down.

"Also, Sasebo is not Subic Bay. Sasebo is a much different port, and our relationship with the Japanese is on a very high plane. Liberty will be granted to the crew, but anyone who gets into any type of trouble will be immediately confined to the ship for the duration of the stay. The captain will not allow the ship to be perceived as a floating home for wayward delinquents."

Davant's eyebrows shot up. Browning turned slightly and for a brief moment stared at Hobson sitting stiffly at the end of the table. Hobson saw Browning looking at him and was unable to bear the 1st Lieutenant's steely gaze. He turned away.

"We will probably be alongside the tender, and the tender is the admiral's flagship. Therefore, strict compliance with all procedures will be in effect; especially the quarterdeck. There will be no skylarking, no soda cans, no sloppy uniforms, no dirty guard belts, no unshaved faces on the quarterdeck. We will be in Sasebo, not Chu Lai. The quarterdeck watch and the Command Duty Officer will be in clean, pressed uniforms of the day, ready to properly receive any COMSERVGRU personnel, or anyone else for that matter, at any time, day or night.

Beaufort raised his hand.

"JB?" Crane said.

"Sir, with the admiral alongside, should we anticipate a visit or inspection?"

"Probably not. But don't assume. We all know what happens when we assume. No, I don't think the admiral will want to bother us with an inspection. He'll know what our condition is and how many things we've got on our to do list. But he may come aboard. That's very possible. Therefore, all the more reason to maintain high standards on the quarterdeck. We don't want to look like a junk yard dog."

Davant put his hand up to his mouth, trying to hide his spontaneous, uncontrolled smirk at the XO's mention of 'junk yard.'

"Ed?" Crane said as Ed Wilson looked up with a question.

"XO, our reduction gears are among our biggest headaches. Does the yard have the capability of refurbishing, lapping and balancing those old gears?"

"The short answer is, yes. The Sasebo yard is one of the best in Japan. It can certainly handle your reduction gears. Plan on it. Give them priority."

Wilson nodded his head in satisfaction as Crane looked at the other faces around the table.

"Any more questions?"

"Sir," Joe Johnston said. "The radio shack has been waiting to receive replacements for a bunch of tubes...we put in a priority request weeks ago. I'm hoping those shipments will catch up with us in Sasebo. But if they don't, we'll want to request them from their local supply."

"Go ahead and put in another request now just in case. That way you'll be covered either way." Johnston rapidly scribbled a note on his paper. "Alright. Get with your leading petty officers and pass the word on this. Additionally, tonight's Plan Of the Day will also announce the news, in case there's anyone left on the ship who hasn't heard about it by now."

Jones chuckled under his breath at that remark, clearly knowing how fast news traveled through the ship's jungle drum system.

The stewards were the unofficial conductors of the The Cathedral's jungle drum orchestra. As Mendoza stood in the corner of the wardroom pantry, pretending to be busy polishing glasses and silverware, he nodded, smirked, grimaced and smiled during various parts of the XO's meeting. When all the officers had finally left the room, he picked up the empty coffee cups and full ashtrays and handed them to Reyes on the other side of the pass-thru window.

"Reyes, we're going to Sasebo!" Mendoza whispered in Tagalog. "Sushi, tempura, sukiyaki, sake, geisha girls! We're leaving today. Gonna be there for 10 days!"

Reyes' head jerked, and his eyes popped open. Smiling and humming to himself he sauntered aft along the passageway holding a tray with the palm of his upright hand as if he was a waiter in a fancy restaurant and entered the galley. Dishing out slices of meatloaf from a large pan, he couldn't contain himself any longer, he had to pass this news on to somebody. He motioned to Dorsey. "XO just had a wardroom meeting," Reyes whispered, his hand covering part of his mouth. "We're going to Japan!"

Dorsey's eyes grew wide as saucers.

"We're leaving here today," Reyes continued. "For Sasebo. We'll be there 10 days," he said with a big grin and headed back to the wardroom pantry, singing; *We can work it out, da da da da daaa.*

Dorsey immediately told one of the mess cooks who told his buddy in the deck gang who then told an electrician who told

Biagotti who told The Volt who already knew about it. Elapsed time: 2 minutes, 34 seconds.

※

Charlie Crane might have imagined himself as the ultimate authority of all navigational knowledge, but in fact it was old Chief Cunningham with his charts, tide tables and years of experience and skill with sextant and Loran who accurately calculated latitude and longitude and fixed the ship's position. The chief was one of those old souls that God had made almost as broad as he was tall, and with puffed cheeks, wide mouth and drooping jowls, along with his seniority, he had earned the crew's innate respect; and a nickname: they called him the 'Clever Pig.' Raised in a family of six females, the 50-year old chief quartermaster was of a quiet and long-suffering nature. Older than anyone else in the ship, he had been at sea more years than most of the crew had been alive, and having steamed through the Mediterranean, the Atlantic, the Indian Ocean and all corners of the Pacific, he had been there, done that, and seen it all before. With his age came experience, and with his experience came wisdom; as a result, he was of a placid countenance, and he easily and regularly acquiesced to Crane, silently accepting without protest the XO's excessive need to be recognized as the ship's navigational expert. Cunningham's philosophy was that both life and his remaining days until retirement were equally too short for him to be worrying about Charlie Crane's peculiar shortcomings. And so, it was on the third day out from Chu Lai, Cunningham's noon fix showed the Cathedral had gained another 260 miles closer to Japan. With these calculations the old chief had also determined the ship was now steaming along the north flowing conveyor belt known as the Kuroshio Current. As the ship headed northward into a 25-knot wind, classified as a 'Strong Breeze' on the Beaufort scale, the wind and current collided in a battle as old as time itself; the two opposing forces generated confused, steep waves with deep troughs and slab sides that burst against the ship's bow doors and rained down into the forward gun tub.

For the first time since departing Little Creek, the main deck and tank deck were now bare, free from the hulking LCU and the 578 tons of cement. But with the elimination of that extra weight came a price; now the ship floated higher with a higher center of gravity and she rolled with a more rapid, convulsive motion, her mast swinging through an arc of 50 degrees, much faster than many of the crew had ever experienced before. Steaming through the turbulent Gulf Stream three months earlier had nothing over the antics she was now exhibiting in the Kuroshio Current. The rolls were violent, throwing the unaware into machinery and door frames. Steaming pots of liquid slid down the galley counters and exploded against bulkheads. Equipment, thought to be thoroughly lashed down days ago, now broke loose and bowled people off their feet.

Doc Slaughter's usually quiet, do nothing routine became filled with disruption and confusion as numerous casualties staggered into the sick bay looking as if they had been in a brawl; cuts, contusions, burns, bruised ribs and black eyes were among the injuries, including Ross with a possible broken arm. With the 1st Lieutenant standing alongside the examining table, Slaughter probed the young bosun's arm, carefully feeling and prodding the radius and ulna between the wrist and elbow, trying to determine if it really was broken.

"Sir," he said to Browning. "I'm not finding anything out of the ordinary here."

"It's not broken?" Browning asked.

"Without an X-ray, sir, I can't be sure. If it is broken, it must be a stable fracture."

"A stable fracture?"

"Yes, sir, where the break lines up, and is barely out of place."

"Well, it's sure black and blue!"

"Yes, sir. Hematoma ain't pretty. He's got some severely damaged tissue here," and Slaughter ran his finger along the arm, tracing the expanding area.

"Aahhh!" Ross yelled and Slaughter pulled his hand away.

"Sorry, Ross."

"What is it, Doc, what's wrong with me?" Ross asked, his face full of apprehension.

"You've done a real number on that arm. But I don't think it's broken."

"Ross, what did you do?" Browning asked. "What happened?"

"I was coming down the ladder, sir, the one in the aft end of the tank deck. I was holding two shovels in my arms, when the sonov'a'bitch...excuse me, sir."

Browning grinned and nodded. "Go on."

"When the...the ship that is, sir...took this enormous roll. I lost my balance and it threw me into the railing. The shovels went up in the air, I fell down the ladder, and then the shovels fell on top of me...damn that hurts!" he cried as Slaughter moved the arm.

"Mister Browning, did you say we'll be arriving in Sasebo soon?" Slaughter asked.

"In 36 hours."

"We need to radio Sasebo and have the hospital standing by, sir. That would be a big help."

"Will do, Doc." Browning said, and he looked down at Ross' anguished face.

"In the meantime, I'm going to put some ice on the arm and then immobilize it. And let's keep him off duty, sir."

"Right."

"Will my arm be okay, Doc?" Ross asked.

"Yea, you're gonna be fine, Ross, just fine. Besides, this is your left arm."

"Yea, so?"

"So, it's not your drinking arm."

Throughout this mayhem, the single minded Biagotti stalked through his precious tank deck in an exceedingly bad temper, haranguing and tormenting the already exhausted deck gang into sweeping, swabbing and removing all the red dirt and cement dust collected from the beach in Chu Lai. The vile, caustic remnants were corralled into compact mounds, scooped up with shovels and unceremoniously dumped overboard.

"Take that, you filthy shit!" Mills shouted as he and Poldolski manhandled the 30-gallon trash can up to the top of the railing and poured the noxious dust over the fantail. "God, I'm glad to get rid of that stuff," Mills said waving the dust away from his face as they rested the heavy galvanized can back on the deck. "My nose has been so raw from breathing that crap, I thought it was gonna fall off."

"That might'a been an improvement," Poldolski said, but quietly under his breath so that Mills didn't hear him.

"One more can to go." Mills grimaced from the cold wind. "And that should do it."

"Damn it's cold up here!" Poldolski shivered from the strong cold wind. "I didn't know it got this cold near Japan."

"Well, you ninny, Korea is just over the horizon that'a way!" Mills pointed off the port bow. "What'd you expect?"

On the fourth day at sea Mendoza was in the wardroom preparing for the officer's lunch, methodically placing dishes, silverware, glasses and napkins on the long table, when his antennae heard Charlie Crane bragging to the captain that his latest fix indicated they had crossed the invisible boundary separating the warm waters of the South China Sea from its colder, more mysterious northern sister, the East China Sea. Mendoza's ears perked up, and by the time the senior steward's rumor mill had finished percolating that interesting bit of news throughout the ship, the crew's fantasies, already in a state of intense anticipation, transformed the approaching mythical Sasebo into a dreamy oriental Elysium; their thoughts were now filled with unlimited quantities of cheap drink, exotic food, and pearl skinned Geishas. When this information finally reached O'Toole, sitting at his cluttered desk deep down in the cramped supply office, he immediately found Rat and Smitty, and ordered them to begin spreading the word that unlimited amounts of liberty cash was now available for those who might need some additional funds; collateral was unnecessary, bad credit was not a problem, the bank was open 24 hours a day, and all of this for only a small service fee. How much of a fee was not divulged.

As the day turned to night, the ship's two V-12 diesels relentlessly clattered and throbbed in their pulsating rhythm, spinning reduction gears, shafts and propellers at full speed, pushing the ship through the increasingly colder water and more numerous banks of fog. Chief Beckers doggedly monitored the big engines, paying particular attention to the tachometers showing 744 RPMs, and the gauges reading 28-pounds of lubricating oil pressure. He rotated the switch on the pyrometer, checking each cylinder's exhaust temperature, and then lightly tapped the face of the dial showing the lube oil temperature and watched the needle jiggle a fraction of an inch. For once, he thought, all the readings were near where they should be. But being a loyal and committed proponent of Murphy's Law, Beckers also rapped the oil-stained wooden log desk with his knuckles. Looking around the engine room and breathing in the thick pervading atmosphere of diesel fuel, hydraulic fluid and hot motors, he reached into his pocket and pulled out a fresh lollipop.

"Hey, Chief," the 1st class electrician called out over the noise. "What flavor 'ya got today? Papaya?"

Beckers unwrapped the lollipop and examined it. "Passion fruit!" he yelled back and grinned with his lips tightly shut.

Down in the dimly lit aft berthing compartment Jonah shoehorned himself into his rack and inserted balls of cotton into his ears, shutting out the thrumming of the twin propeller shafts two decks below him. The red night lights gave out just enough of a gleam for him to see everything bathed in a soft crimson glow, and in the midst of these familiar surroundings he looked up toward the pipes and cables running in profusion along the overhead. Relieved that the insanity of Chu Lai was now finally hundreds of miles behind, he closed his eyes and his thoughts began spinning through multiple layers of images and memories. He visualized his mother with her bird's nest of shockingly tumbled silver hair. She was wearing her favorite long-sleeve western shirt, the faded blue checkered pattern partially hidden behind a thick white cotton apron, and she was leaning against the kitchen counter with one foot crossed over the other in that unusual way she had of standing. The afternoon light was coming through the window and it cast a warm glow on one side of her face as the other side remained in shadow, accentuating her broad brow, wide set gunmetal eyes and straight nose over a mouth that was perpetually smiling. The old hard-wood floor, the deep galvanized sink on one wall and the pitcher-shaped hand pump in the corner were all strikingly vivid. He involuntarily inhaled and held his breath as a beam of light abruptly flashed across his face; his eyes seeing the bright light glowing orange through his closed eyelids. It was Poldolski moving about the compartment in his strange shuffling gate, searching for the individuals he needed to wake for the next change of the watch. How could the past six months have gone by so quickly, Jonah thought. How was it possible to go from *McMann* in the beautiful Bay of Naples to The

Cathedral in the shitty red dust of Chu Lai? Then the Idaho ranch came back into his view. Although it was on the other side of the world and the memories seemed so long ago, he could still see every detail of the two-story white house with its wide veranda, perched on the hill at the end of that long twisty road, the outbuildings further back in the distance, the barn's weathered vertical boards standing straight and tall. The ranch was a testament to his grandfather Papa Jack's vision and persistence. Jonah knew it was Jack who had taught him the most about life, more than anyone else, certainly more than his old man, and had instilled in him the principles of discovery and purpose. Jack always emphasized his philosophy with the stem of his pipe, pointing it at Jonah as he pontificated. 'Life is what you do, not what you say you will do,' was what he said. That was the important thing. And then Jonah's thoughts shifted into another gear and the antithesis of Papa Jack entered his dream; he saw the oppressive Lieutenant Junior Grade Sanders, the Sandman, with his peculiar face, benign from one angle, malignant from the other. How can it be, he questioned the universe, that in some strange ways our dreams are able to smoothly shift from one subject to another so quickly? And then, suddenly, there was Arlene coming into focus in his mind's eye, the details of her face clear as day. He saw her funny nose and the strawberry hair and those dimples when she smiled. She always seemed impossible to approach; he never thought she would accept his invitation to go to the state fair. Was he really only 16 then? He saw the two of them on that Ferris wheel, riding high and looking down at the fairground filled with tents and caravan trucks and people walking through the midway. Arlene was sitting right next to him, her knee pressed against his leg. He could feel the electricity rush through him every time her knee touched his leg. When their seat on the Ferris wheel reached its apogee she suddenly laughed and kicked her legs high in the air and her skirt floated up her legs, exposing her thighs. Then she laughed and kicked her legs up again. But even with the big wheel turning he couldn't take his eyes off her thighs. He'd never seen a girl's thighs so close before. Then his dream shifted into a new dimension, and he saw Pattie; her wide mouth smiling, her liquid eyes staring into his, her hair bouncing as she walked in that distinctive way. How could he have been so stupid; yea, it was you Jonah, you were the one who ruined that relationship the night before you got underway from Little Creek. You ruined it, not her. The dream turned another corner, and there was 'Blue,' the Australian Blue Heeler his mother had given him for Christmas when he was 12. Jonah saw himself tying a short length of rope to his belt and the other end to the puppy's collar, and Blue followed him everywhere. Six weeks later Jonah removed the rope and the dog continued to follow him. Through the dream he clearly saw the dog's coarse blue-gray mottled coat, accented with those tawny ears, and Jonah could feel Blue's eyes looking at him, those distinctive black and orange eyes peering straight into his soul. Blue would walk alongside him down that mile-long winding dirt road until they came to the ranch gate. His mother often told the story about the ranch gate, how Papa Jack built it in 1920. She described how Jack had planted the huge 18-inch diameter white pine posts deep into the ground and then surrounded each of them with a 5-foot tall column of smooth gray granite river stones, and how he spent two days precisely carving the name *Providence* into the 10-foot long oak header board. That board must have weighed close to 300 pounds, she always emphasized. When Jonah and the dog stopped under the 12-foot high gate, he commanded Blue to sit and stay. Six hours later, when Jonah stepped out of that yellow school bus the dog was still there, alongside the gate, waiting for him. Then the dream shifted to the barn one night when his drunken father was whipping the boy with a belt. He could feel the sting of the leather on his legs and saw the red welts. Blue came out of nowhere and jumped between them, snarling and baring his canines into the old man's face. His father slowly backed away and never again confronted the boy when Blue was nearby. The dog went most everywhere with Jonah. He sat next to him in the old truck when Daniel drove them into town, to the grocery and the feed store. He would run tirelessly alongside 'Rusty,' the chestnut stock horse, as Jonah rode far out on the northern border of the ranch, checking the fence line, mending the wire for breaks and resetting downed posts. Blue eventually grew into a powerful 50-pound dynamo and became the chief cattle dog on the ranch, herding cows, nipping at their heels, barking them into submission. He was there in the heat and cold, rain and snow; there was never a coyote in sight when Blue was around. But Jonah remembered that Blue had a lazy streak. Sometimes the dog would sneak into the barn and disappear between the bales of freshly mowed hay and luxuriate in the sweet smell and dry, soft bedding. He did that on one particular cold spring night. His last night. And that night the coyotes grabbed two new-born calves out of the herd. The next morning Jonah's father found what remained of the carcasses, and he went into a rage, a rage fueled by alcohol and jealousy; rage that the dog hadn't protected the herd, and jealousy that the boy loved the dog more than him. Jonah watched the old man tying Blue to a fence post and knew what was going to happen. The boy in the dream pulled his father's arm and screamed and begged. Please don't hurt Blue, he cried. Please don't punish Blue. Jonah saw the confused black and orange eyes looking up at him, seemingly pleading, when the man shot the dog dead.

"Oh, God!" he moaned from the depths of his sleep and struggled up from the feverish hell of the dream, back into a semi-consciousness. He knew where he was now. He knew he had been dreaming. The aftermath of the dream was thick as mud in his mind, so thick he couldn't shake it. Emotion rushed through him now, surging up from his gut into his chest then into his throat, and he put his hands to his face and tried to breathe. He stayed that way for a long time. "Oh, God," he whispered. "Help me find the strength." How long can I lie here, he wondered. Another minute? Another hour? A lifetime? He held his watch up to the red light: 0515. He shook his head and achingly twisted his legs over the side of the rack, his bare feet landing on the deck. Oh, that's cold! He sat there for a moment, breathing deep, looking into space. Somehow, he found the fortitude to stand and he stepped into his trousers, slowly laced the boots tight and struggled into his jacket. Stumbling through the compartment in a daze, he twisted his way around and through the labyrinth of berths and climbed the ladder where the aroma of fresh baked buns floated through the passageway; sugar and cinnamon filled his nose.

"Hey, what you do'in?" he heard Dorsey shouting through the open galley door. Jonah turned the corner and watched as the big man from Savannah scolded his Jack of the Dust, the sailor who was in charge of the galley's storeroom. "You can't do 'dat. Was'a 'matta wit you?" Dorsey turned and saw Jonah standing in the passageway, looking through the doorway. "Well, if it ain't Jonah of the Winchester Cathedral," Dorsey said with his big wide grin. "You okay?" he asked looking closely at Jonah's weary face. "Looks like you had a rough night. Hmm, I bet 'yo could use one of these," and Dorsey picked up a large carving knife and cut through the fresh hot buns. "This'll give you a sunshine day," he said smiling, handing a bun to Jonah on the flat of the big knife.

"Thanks, Dorsey. Much obliged!"

"No problem, man, anytime. Glad to be of help to our Cathedral's gunnery department," the big cook said, and then he leaned forward and spoke in a hushed voice. "Listen, Jonah. You know, dis here Navy runs on its stomach." His eyes were wide, his face full of concerned animation. "And dat's true. But, man, I'm tell'n 'yo, I is sure pray'n every day, every day, dat when we's in the brown water, dat it's 'yo guns dat's gonna protect our ass! You know? You know what I mean?"

"Don't worry, Dorsey." Jonah said. "I've got your six," and he took a large bite out of the fresh bun, the hot sugar and cinnamon melting in his mouth. "Hmm, that's good," and he wiped the back of his knuckles across his lips. "Very good." A big smile grew along Dorsey's face.

Opening the watertight door to the weather deck, Jonah shuddered from the blast of cold, salt-filled air and quickly closed and dogged the door behind him. Zipping up his jacket he smelled the wind, the ancient wind that had traveled thousands of miles from the Mongolian steppe, sweeping down through China, over Shanghai and across the black cold water, the strong gusts rushing southward and pushing against the plodding Cathedral. Hmm, he thought, I wonder if some great Mongolian horsemen had breathed this wind before me? He turned and saw Poldolski standing the fantail watch alongside the stern anchor winch, a set of sound-powered phones on his head and the phone's cable looping toward the jack on the bulkhead.

Protected in the lee of the deck house and lighting a cigarette, Jonah also thought about his guns. Everything he needed to do had been done, either in Pearl or Subic. All his guns were now ready, all his ammunition was on board, all his gun crews were assigned and trained, and for the moment, at least, the Sandman was leaving him alone. The dreams of 30-minutes ago were gone, and now his thoughts were in that place where neither past nor future existed; he was now only in the present, with the sea racing alongside the ship, the wind in his face, the cigarette smoke blowing into nothingness. He leaned against the bulkhead and felt the vibrations and watched the wake stretching out until it was absorbed into the gray light of the early morning; gray clouds against a cold gray sky. Faintly, he heard the electric click of the

1MC being switched on by someone, probably a bosun's mate in the pilot house. He looked at his watch; 0600. He instinctively knew what was to follow as the bosun's pipe immediately pierced his solitude with its shrill trilling; an elongated piping, repeated again, tapering off to nothing.

"Now hear this, now hear this." Mills' full-throated voice boomed out from the speakers blaring through the ship and along the weather decks. "Reveille, reveille. All hands turn to. The smoking lamp is lit in all authorized spaces. Sweepers man your brooms. Reveille, reveille..."

Jonah walked to the railing and looked down at the rushing wake. He flicked the cigarette butt over the side and watched the wind take it, disappearing into the cold hissing maelstrom of the East China Sea.

※

As the ship continued northward, all those not on watch lined up in ranks on the main deck for morning quarters. They faced inboard, the toes of their shoes aligned with the longitudinal welds along the vacant deck. The Supply and Operations Divisions were on the port side, the Engineering and Deck Divisions to starboard, and as the ship rolled to starboard the 75 bodies pivoted from their ankles in order to remain upright. As the ship rolled to port, they all pivoted in the opposite direction, all the lines moving together as if they were connected by invisible, well oiled, couplings. Jonah had witnessed the phenomenon hundreds of times before, and he always thought it resembled a metronome. Port roll...sway to starboard. Starboard roll...sway to port. It was unceasing. It was fascinating to watch. And then unexpectedly the ship took a particularly heavy roll and the entire rhythm was thrown off balance; some people in the ranks stepped out of line, others put their hands forward to brace themselves against the back of the person in front of them. Then the roll resumed its former beat, and everyone regained their normal rhythm once again. Port roll...sway to starboard. Starboard roll...sway to port.

The officers were also going through this balancing act. They were lined up aft of the main hatch, facing forward, with their single rank spread out from port to starboard. Facing them was Charlie Crane with a fist-full of papers, reading out instructions for the day's routine. Positioned at a respectful distance behind and to the right of the XO, Underwood stood at a relaxed parade-rest, holding a clipboard behind the small of his back, the papers waving in the cold breeze.

"Two hours from now we'll be picking up the Sasebo pilot," Crane said, referring to his notes. "Uniform for entering port will be undress whites. However, if the weather turns colder, we may alter that to blues. Stay tuned."

Ensign Jones stood swaying in time to the ship's roll, listening to the XO, and his thoughts ran through the massive number of items on the engineering work list. And liberty. Yes, it will definitely be a busy 10 days, but surely there will be time to enjoy some of the delights Japan had to offer; hopefully plenty of good food, drink and some sightseeing.

"And a reminder to all of you..." Crane continued, "...that we will be going alongside *AJAX*, the tender, the flagship for Commander Service Group Three. Admiral Walter Patrick is known as a stickler for protocol; clean uniforms, shaved faces, spit-shined shoes and a four-oh quarterdeck watch are the order of the day. Every day. Make sure your people are in complete compliance. I don't want to see anyone out of uniform at any time." Crane looked along the line of faces in front of him. Hobson appeared very uncomfortable, his hands fidgeting and his eyes darting left and right. "Obviously you will have people involved in some heavy-duty, dirty work, and they cannot be expected to be in four-oh uniforms. So...well, just keep those people hidden and off the main deck."

Jones blinked several times and looked at the XO out of the corner of his eye, trying to stifle a laugh at that comment. Hiding people? You've got to be kidding, he thought.

"Additionally, there will be plenty of Japanese shipyard workers coming aboard. They are very professional people and are to be given the fullest respect at all times. Understood?" All the heads in the line nodded in understanding, even Browning with his piratical face. "All right. The special sea and anchor detail will be called in..." Crane looked at his watch. "In just over an hour. Any questions?" He looked at the faces standing before him. "None? Okay. Dismissed."

❧❧

Diary #106
16 May 1966
2345 Hours
Sasebo Japan.

Moored outboard of the Sumner Class destroyer USS John W. Thomason (DD-760), and the tender AJAX (AR-6), flagship of COMSERVGRU 3.

Elysium found.

Searching for the pilot boat in this morning's fog was a devilish experience. Yes, our radar had him picked out clear, but it wasn't until he was less than a hundred feet away that we finally spotted the orange and white boat looming though the vapor. How Crane and Cunningham managed to bring us to the sea buoy without incident is beyond my understanding. As we headed into the unknown, the fog was so thick only the occasional channel buoy gravely floating close alongside gave us any indication that we were still on the planet. I could hear a bell somewhere in the fog to port, and smelled what I imagined were pines, wet, saturated pines, their scent percolating through the mist. And then, suddenly, as if we had drifted through a curtain, everything around us turned green; green mountains, rushing cataracts hurrying down green slopes, a point of green land to the left, more green to the right, buildings, towers, more buildings all sitting sedately on green hillsides. And there, ahead of us in the distance, was the town of Sasebo climbing up the green mountainside with the harbor below it. The relief was palpable. Sunlight greeted us as a tug nudged us into the basin.

Within an hour of coming alongside the destroyer, Browning had stages hanging along the port side and dozens of the deck gang busily slathering the topsides with haze gray paint from the deck edge down to the waterline. With Japanese yard workers swarming through the ship, I witnessed an amazing sight, the first in my long naval career: a Japanese yardbird in boots and coveralls emerging from the engine room scuttle on the main deck; her lipstick, makeup and earrings were a shocking sight under that bright yellow hard hat.

I have a feeling that the cares, concerns and tensions of the last three months will soon drop away thanks to this ancient, mysterious, beautiful place called Japan.

Et somno ad somnum.

❦

Located at the entrance to officer's country, the ship's office was small and cramped, containing three tiny desks securely welded to the deck along the inboard longitudinal bulkhead. Overflowing file cabinets hulked along the forward bulkhead, and dozens of binders and regulation manuals rested precariously on high steel shelves. A mimeograph machine, combination safe and three chairs contributed additional disorder to the already crammed space. It was always difficult to move around the confined office, but on this particular morning with all the newly arrived official mail covering every square inch of the deck and all three of the desk tops, it had become impossible. Standing outside the Dutch door and looking into this chaos, Jonah saw Underwood and Fugete engulfed within a sea of overflowing mailbags. Boxes and envelopes of varying sizes and colors with official red stamps denoted hierarchies of classified material. Underwood sat at his desk, glancing back and forth between the registered mail and a large green log book, busily recording serial numbers and stacking the dozens of classified envelopes into the safe for later distribution. Something out of the corner of his eye made Underwood look up and he saw Jonah standing on the other side of the door.

"Looks like you got your work cut out for you," Jonah said, more of a question than a statement.

Underwood shook his head, his face betraying his bewilderment. "I've never seen so much fuken mail at one time," he said in frustration. "Now I know why we had so little mail in Subic. I think they must'a been collecting this shit for weeks before forwarding it to Sasebo."

"What you want to do today? It's Sunday, you know," Jonah said, reminding Underwood that the day being Sunday, it was holiday routine; no work.

"Yea, but Fugete and I gotta get this official mail logged in, route-stamped, and prioritized for the XO. Otherwise he's gonna blow a gasket!"

Fugete looked up from his pile of envelopes. He stared at Jonah with one eye, frowned and shook his head, obviously not happy with having his liberty cut short by all the newly arrived mail.

"When you gonna be finished?" Jonah asked.

Underwood looked at this watch. "It's 0900 now," his finger rotated around the dial. "We'll take a short break for lunch, then probably be finished by...I guess, maybe 1300."

"Okay. I'm going on the beach to see the sights. Why don't you and Brickey meet me at the EM Club at 1400."

"Sounds like a plan," and Underwood turned back to scribble in the log book. "See ya then," he said without looking up.

"Gangway! Gangway!" a voice called out and Jonah automatically moved aside as Smitty waddled up the passageway with another huge, overflowing mail bag. "More mail," Smitty said, his fat face leering through the open Dutch door.

"Oh, no! Come on, man!" Underwood stood up from his cluttered desk. "You gotta be kidding me!"

"I'm not kidding."

"Where the hell are we gonna put all this shit?" Fugete slammed a stack of envelopes onto his desk and shook his head.

"Fugete!" Underwood said loudly. "Stop being such a dumb ass complainer all the time! Just push that crap aside and make some more room!"

Fugete, growling and mumbling, pushed the dozens of cardboard boxes and manila envelopes under his desk.

"Hey," Underwood said, leaning through the open Dutch door and looking down the passageway at the back of the quickly departing Jonah. "You better make that 1500."

Jonah raised his upturned thumb as he closed the passageway door behind him.

❧❧

'Let me out'a here!' Jonah muttered to himself as he stepped off the tender's long segmented brow onto the pier. I can't believe that boot ensign looked me over that carefully. Hell, I'm not from the flagship! Who the hell does he think he is, anyway? Dumb ass, inflated ego, butter bar admiral in training is what he is! Ha, what can you say about an ensign with a face full of pimples!

He walked down the pier, stepping across railroad tracks and around oily puddles of water. Warehouses and machine shops lined the right side, the basin and the shipyard were to the left. He paused and watched a Japanese frigate getting underway, its beautifully painted sleek hull and flush deck in sharp contrast with the antique oil-burning tugboat pulling it away from the quay, the tug's tall stack puffing thick black clouds of smoke into the air. Across the harbor to the left were the dry docks, all seven of them occupied with ships undergoing repairs. Navy launches and LCVPs, yard tugs and auxiliaries made their way from and to various points in the busy harbor. Cars and trucks went up and down the pier with equipment, boxes of vegetables and large wooden crates stenciled with baffling letters and numbers. Looking up he was surprised to see the church in the distance, the same church he had seen yesterday when the ship was coming into the basin; it's tall, Gothic white steeple and two spindly towers perched on a prominent hill overlooking the harbor. Heading toward the main gate he stepped from the pier onto a sidewalk and walked past the Marines in the guard shack.

"Hey!" one of the Marines called out. "Hey, you!" he shouted.

Jonah turned and looked at the sergeant who was waving him over. Jonah pointed to himself, his eyes squinting and a perturbed look on his face.

"Yea you!" the Marine said in a loud nasal, hillbilly accent. Where's your liberty card?" The sergeant's perfectly starched Service Bravo uniform and knife-edged garrison cap looked as if he was ready for a CO's inspection. A .45 hung from a bright white guard belt around his waist. "Let's see your liberty card!"

"Who you talk'n to?" Jonah said, his blood pressure rising as he walked toward the Marine. "I'm a 2nd Class Petty Officer, you idiot! We're not required to have dumb liberty cards!" Jonah stepped right up to the Marine, crossing over the invisible dividing line of the sergeant's personal space. "Why don't you learn your regs, you dumb jarhead!" Jonah stood with his arms at his side, his body arched forward, his head jutting into the Marine's face.

"Well, I'll be damned," the Marine said, a smile suddenly lighting up his ruddy complexion. "If it ain't the famous gunner of the *USS Bushnell*!"

Jonah's head jerked back and his amazed eyes grew wide open. "Jimmie Owens?" he said in shock.

"What the hell you doing here, Wynchester?" the Marine asked shaking Jonah's hand. "Why aren't you in Key West?"

"This is unbelievable!" Jonah said pumping the Marine's hand. "Jimmie Owens? Holy Jeezum! You just about gave me a heart attack!"

The Marine stood grinning, continuing to pump Jonah's hand. "You still drinking boiler makers?"

"Hell yes, you crazy hillbilly! How the hell are you?"

"Damn good. And you?"

"I'm surprised you remembered me?" Jonah said.

"Remember you? Hell, how could anybody forget the face of the boiler maker king?"

"Ha, you were the one who always got shitfaced drinking boiler makers, not me!"

"Well, this is just amaz'n!"

"What the hell are you doing in Japan?" Jonah asked.

"Transferred here three months ago. I re-upped and they gave me the choice of duty stations. And here I am! And you?"

"We just came in yesterday," and Jonah turned and pointed down the pier. "On that shitty LST."

Owens followed Jonah's pointing hand. "Oh, you guys are outboard of the Admiral! Well, good luck with that!" he said shaking his head. "You'd better keep your nose clean with him around."

"Yea, I know. Brass hats and scrambled eggs."

"So, how long you gonna be here?" Owens asked.

"Eight more days. But never mind me, how's duty in Japan?"

"In a word? Paradise," Owens said with a big grin.

"Hey, listen, we got to get together. How 'bout showing me the town some night? When are you off duty?"

"Definitely. Let me check my..." Owens looked behind Jonah, down the pier to where a jeep was driving in their direction. "Uh, oh...you better take off. My lieutenant is coming. That guy thinks he's God's gift."

Jonah turned and immediately saw the jeep approaching. "Right," he said walking away. "Let me know when you're off duty."

"I'll get word to you," Owens shouted as he stepped back into the entrance of the guard house and straightened his uniform and guard belt.

Jonah passed through the gate and when he crossed to the other side of the street he looked back and saw Owens standing at attention, saluting the lieutenant who was jumping out of the jeep. Jonah watched the undersized officer shouting into the tall sergeant's face. Jonah couldn't hear the lieutenant's words, but his cheeks were puffed up, his neck was turning red and spittle was spraying on Owens' uniform.

"Stupid, dumb, idiot jarheads," Jonah mumbled under his breath and he walked uphill along the brick sidewalk. Dozens of motor scooters and bicycles were parked in the medium, and small appliance stores, cafes, sushi bars, restaurants and offices occupied the buildings along each side. A sign over one corner shop immediately got his attention and he crossed the street and entered the tiny cafe. Along the windows overlooking the busy street were small tables occupied by a few people reading or quietly talking and sipping coffee. Standing in front of the counter he peered up to a sign with indecipherable Hiragana characters and pictures of different types of coffee. He thought for a moment, looked down to the pretty girl in the red apron, and then back up to the sign. Pointing to the sign he smiled, ordered a small #4 and took his hot coffee to a window seat in the rear of the cafe. He watched the cars and bikes zipping by, and a small truck stopped at the curb, the driver unloading cartons and carrying them into a restaurant. The sun was struggling to break through the low cloud cover and a sunbeam suddenly came through a gap, lighting up the sidewalk just as a young Japanese woman came out of a doorway of a shop across the street. He watched her quickly stepping uphill along the red bricks, her flowered yellow dress wafting around her legs. At the intersection she stopped, turned and looked both ways before crossing the street and headed in his direction. As she ran toward him he involuntarily sucked in his breath. Looking through the window he clearly saw her face and black tousled hair and she walked by not more than three feet away. Then she disappeared around the corner. He turned in his chair, intently watching and waiting, hoping she would reappear, and suddenly realized he needed to breathe. He shook his head as if he was waving off cobwebs. God, what a day this is, he thought, swallowing the last of the coffee, and waving goodbye to the girl behind the counter, he left the shop.

The day couldn't be more perfect, Jonah thought; the bright sunlight was now filtering through the clouds, a cool breeze giving him the sensation of floating, with no cares, nowhere to go until he was to meet Underwood. He looked at his watch; plenty of time. That tall church, the one he had first seen from the ship yesterday, loomed above the surrounding buildings. Now it was just a few blocks away, and something gently prodded him in that direction. He had nothing else to do, so why not, he thought.

The stairs leading upward from the street went up and up, steeply climbing, 80 steps, and when he came to the top he was gasping for breath. God, I'm out of shape, he reflected. As he approached the tall double doors, held open with hooks from the wall, he heard the sounds of chant, lilting Gregorian Chant coming through the opening, and immediately he was transported back to his old parish church in Idaho. The sounds were unexpected, unmistakable, and all so familiar.

Veni Creator Spiritus.

Stepping into the vestibule he removed his white hat and walked up the side aisle, genuflected, and slid into a pew. He was astonished. The church was striking. Gothic, definitely Gothic architecture, but not old, certainly not more than 50 years old he guessed. He hadn't seen anything like it in, well, he couldn't remember how long; maybe a very long time ago at the cathedral in Boise. Pearl gray marble columns, easily three feet across at their base, supported the pointed arches with their richly molded ribs extending upward to the vault above the nave; he visually calculated the highest point; it must be well over 40 feet above the floor he reflected. The afternoon light coming through the expansive stained-glass windows cast a fusion of colors into the nave; red, blue, green and gold scattered across the pews and walls. He could feel the warmth of a multi-colored beam of light shining down on him. The music held him spellbound. There was a peacefulness here that he hadn't experienced in a very long time.

Imple superna gratia.

The emotions he had always felt as a boy when singing this same chant in his small church choir now rushed through him once again; the recitative passage soaring and descending, the rhythmic groups unmistakable.

Infunde amorem cordibus.

The repetitive melody floating and echoing about the expansive walls and high ceilings was mystical. He could feel the passion bubbling in him and sensed his eyes growing warm and damp. Turning around in the pew he looked behind him, up to the loft, toward the source of the chant, and he watched a choir practicing; young women singing *a cappella* while they followed the stern face and expressive hands of the choirmaster, a Japanese Dominican Nun.

Vitemus omne noxium.

He was surprised to see they were all Japanese. Well, of course they would be Japanese, he thought. But they were singing Latin. It was something he hadn't expected or thought about before; Japanese singing Latin. He looked along their faces and counted thirty-three. Except for the nun in her white and black habit, they were all dressed in casual street clothes and they all wore something to cover their hair; some had a large scarf or small handkerchief, others a veil.

Deo Patri sit gloria.

The nun suddenly clapped her hands and the chant's rhythm came to an abrupt stop. Her stern admonishment regarding some grave error had many in the choir looking down with embarrassment. She pulled a disk-shaped pitch pipe from the folds of her habit, rotated it to the correct key, raised it to her lips and blew into it. The choir simultaneously hummed the note, the nun pointed a finger to her open palm, and on her hands' down-stroke the choir began again.

Et filio qui a mortuis.

Watching the many different singers, some short and some tall, he thought about the combinations of features; round faces, long faces; large eyes, small eyes; full mouths, narrow mouths. And as he scanned the faces, row after row, he suddenly caught his breath, for there, in the uppermost row, second from the left, was the girl.

Surrexit ac Paraclito

It was the same girl in the flowered yellow dress. The same girl with the black tousled hair and remarkable eyes. The same one he had seen just 30 minutes ago through the windows of the cafe.

In saeculorum saecula.

He was astonished. It was her. She was wearing a white lace veil over her hair, and she concentrated on the book she was holding, at times looking up to the nun whose delicate hands were swimming through the air in time to the rising and falling neumes of the chant.

CHAPTER 8

ONSEN

"Can you believe that?" Jonah said as he, Underwood and Brickey slid into the back seat of the taxi. "That I ran into that Marine from Key West? I'm telling you that was one hell of a surprise...Key West is from the other side of the planet!" He looked around him at the cab's fancy upholstery and the gleaming dashboard. "Say, this is some nice taxi."

"Where you go?" the Japanese driver asked.

"We want to go to an onsen," Underwood said.

"Onsen?" the driver asked.

"Yes, a hot spring onsen, that is far out of the way."

"Far away?" the driver said.

"Yes," Underwood continued. "The best hot spring onsen, far out of the way, where no sailors go.

"No sailors?"

"Correct. A really good onsen, far away, no other sailors. And where we can get food, drinks and spend the night."

"Rooms?"

"Yes. Correct."

"Okay, you go Ryokan Tsubaki."

"Is that a hot spring onsen?"

"Hai. Yes, hot spring."

"Do they have rooms for the night?"

"Yes, rooms."

"And food? Do they serve food?"

"Yes, food. And many drink. Ryokan."

"What's ryokan?"

"Small inn; beds, food, drink, with onsen."

"Perfect. What's Tsubaki?" Underwood asked.

"Tsubaki is flower."

"A flower?"

"Means 'perfect love'."

"Hmm, perfect love, I like that," Brickey said.

"How long of a drive? How many minutes?" Underwood asked.

"Ah, maybe 15 - 20 minutes. More or less."

"More or less. Okay, thank you. Take us to Tsubaki. Arigato."

"Okay, we go." The driver pulled the shift lever down and drove the taxi away from the EM Club.

"Jeezum!" Jonah cried, looking wide eyed as they traveled up the left side of the street. "Why do they do that?"

"Do what?"

"Drive on the wrong side of the road?"

"They do that in Japan," Underwood explained, looking out the side window. "They drive on the left here."

"Damn! Yea, I saw cars doing that earlier today. But I'm telling you, it's strange. I feel as if somebody's gonna nail us head on!"

"Relax. You'll get used to it."

Jonah shook his head, looking more closely at the taxi. "Man, this car is something else, I ain't never been in a taxi this nice before. What kind'a car is this anyway?"

Underwood looked over the back of the front seat to the unfamiliar emblem on the steering wheel. "What kind of a car is this?" he asked the driver.

"What kind car?" The driver looked back at them in the rear-view mirror.

"Yea, what make, what manufacture car is this?"

"Car a Toita."

"Toita?"

"Yes, Toita."

"Hm," Underwood said with a perplexed look. "It's a Toita," he said looking at Jonah.

"Sure," Brickey said. "A Toita. Now we're experts on Japanese cars."

The cab drove through the town, always on the left side of the street, and they gradually left the busy central district behind and started uphill. They drove up a winding, tightly twisting road, thick with junipers and cedars along the sides, and they looked across steep cliffs to the mountains beyond. The late afternoon had a coolness in the air, and as they gained altitude the sun was casting long shadows from the ridge into the shockingly green valleys below.

"Smell that?" Underwood said, sniffing the air through the partially opened window.

"Hmm, smells like perfume," Brickey said.

"Yea, the air does have the scent of a perfume to it, as if the pines and junipers were mixing with spice in this high crystal air."

Jonah put his hands to his head. "Damn, my ear just popped," he said.

"We're climbing pretty good."

"I'll say!"

Houses with blue tiled roofs floated past as the cab continued steeply upwards, always upwards, going around sharp switchback turns, meeting with the occasional car going downhill in the other direction.

"You should'a seen what I saw today," Jonah said looking out the window

"What's that?" Underwood asked lighting a cigarette.

"An angel."

"Angel?"

"Yea, a Japanese angel. I was sitting in a cafe having a nice cup of coffee, much better than that stuff Dorsey brews, when this beautiful girl crosses the street, heads right at me and then walks by. I watched her through the window. She came as close as you and me."

"Sorry I missed that."

"Yea. And then about 30 minutes later I was walking up the street and decided to have a look inside this big Gothic church on the hill, and there she was again, singing in a choir."

"She's probably home with her three kids by now."

"Most likely."

The taxi continued climbing up the road, following the twists and turns, and Jonah started feeling dizzy, and a little nervous, knowing what might happen if they didn't soon come to where they were going. Now he realized why this ride was going to take 15 - 20 minutes, 'more or less' as the driver had said. He looked at his watch; 20 minutes had already gone by. It might only be eight or ten miles, but the winding road kept the speed down. The driver confidently steered the car around another curve, his right hand on the wheel, his left along the back of the seat. He obviously knows the route, Jonah thought, always going up, always going slowly uphill. They went around one extremely sharp turn, the cab slowing to a crawl in the tight switchback, then the car accelerated again. Fast, slow. Turn left, turn right. Jonah thought it was taking forever to get there. Oh, Jesus, help me, he thought, don't let me get sick.

"Tochaku shita," the driver said. "You here," and he pulled the car over to the side of the road.

"Thank God for that," Jonah inhaled. He looked at his watch. "Almost 24 minutes," he said.

As Underwood paid the driver, Jonah stepped out of the cab and stood swaying, trying to regain his equilibrium, breathing deeply of the cool, fresh air and looking slowly around him. A building with a blue tile roof was perched on the edge of a cliff, the stream below falling and rushing down through smooth river rocks polished from thousands of years of scouring water. A grouping of lilies and a small hand-carved sign were planted at the foot of a gravel path; *Ryokan - Tsubaki*, the sign read in Japanese symbols with a pink and orange camellia flower painted in the center. With their shoes crunching on the gravel surface they walked down the winding path with the thundering sounds of surprisingly strong flowing water echoing from the faces of the cliffs. Jonah felt the cool mist from the cascading water filling the air, and they opened a door leading into a small anteroom. To the left was a wall of pigeon holes, some filled with shoes, some with slippers. A tall counter was to the right and a large room beyond with tall floor to ceiling windows looking out to a remarkable view: rushing water, junipers, pines, rhododendrons and a tea house at the edge of a hot spring onsen with steam misting up from its surface.

"Yokoso." A tiny woman said, entering the ante room from a side door behind the tall counter. "Yokoso. Welcome to Tsubaki," she said with an open, polite smile, examining the sailor's uniforms as she stood behind the counter, her shoulders barely above its surface. Jonah guessed she might be in her early 50s and certainly couldn't be much more than five feet tall. "Onsen?" she asked.

"Yes, please," Underwood answered. "We'd like to have an onsen, massage, and stay the night."

She reached up to the pigeon holes and pulled out three pairs of slippers, placing them on the floor in front of the sailors. "Uwagutsu. Please remove shoes."

Underwood started untying his shoelaces. "Do you have rooms?" he asked.

"Yes, yes," the woman said, placing a paper on the counter and a pen alongside. "Rooms, onsen, massage, bar, food. Everything you find at Tsubaki," she smiled. "You sign?" she said, holding the pen toward Underwood.

"Perfect," Underwood said, and he took the pen, trying to decipher the Hiragana characters on the paper form and determine which column required what information.

The woman grinned at him. "Sign," she said pointing to the first column. "Address," she pointed to the second column. "Phone," she said pointing to the third. Underwood carefully wrote his name.

The woman watched Jonah admiring the adjacent room. "You want to look?" she said. He nodded and stepping into the large room in his slippers he felt warm sunlight coming through the remarkably tall windows. The ceiling, almost 14 feet high Jonah guessed, was built in layers. The top-most layer was of narrow boards, probably tongue and groove with the way they seemed to fit together so perfectly. Immediately below and supporting the top layer were perpendicular four by four beams stretching the width of the room. Then below and perpendicular to those beams were larger beams. And supporting the entire structure were massive beams that Jonah thought must have been at least eight inches thick and 18 inches tall. The intricate ceiling structure, window frames and built-in book case along one wall were all of the same color wood, a light blonde with a slight reddish tint, and long beautiful grain. The north facing wall was of polished river stones, and a large gray brick fireplace anchored the center. Comfortable looking overstuffed chairs rested on the pale blonde wide plank floor. The room imparted a bright, quiet, contemplative atmosphere, where in the winter Jonah imagined the snowy scene outside would be magical. Standing in the midst of this tranquil place and looking through the windows at the quick flowing stream he began to feel an unexpected peacefulness wrapping around him; the anxiety and tensions of the past several weeks beginning to fade away.

"We don't have a phone number, but our ship is in Sasebo," Underwood said to the woman.

"Yes, yes," she nodded and smiled, obviously understanding. "Navy base, Sasebo," and she wrote a group of Hiragana characters in the last column of the paper. "I show you room."

They followed her down a hallway of bright, naturally finished wood, passing room #1, and 2 and 3. Then they passed #5 and Jonah wondered where room #4 was. The woman stopped at room #6. She slid open a door made of heavy translucent paper held within a wooden frame and they stepped into a small uncluttered room with tatami mats on the wood floor and a low table in the center. "Take off slipper," the woman said. Another sliding door on the opposite wall opened to a small deck with views of cedars and the river beyond.

"This is perfect," Underwood said walking around the room in his socks, admiring the beauty and simplicity of the room's textures and colors.

"You like tea? Or drink?" the woman asked.

Underwood looked at Jonah who was nodding. "Yes," he said. "A drink would be very nice."

"I show you," she smiled and led them back up the hall to the large room and through a doorway into a bar with several small tables overlooking the river through more large windows. "Please," she said pointing to the bar stools. "Ashiko!" she called out, looking around for someone. "Ashiko!" she called again, and this time clapped her hands. The woman's pleasant demeanor was instantly replaced with a look of disapproval and she left the room.

"I think I'll take a look outside," Brickey said.

"I'll go with you you," Underwood said. "Jonah, you coming? What's the matter? You don't look so good." Underwood held the door open, looking back at Jonah staring out the windows with his back to the bar.

"That girl has my head all screwed up."

"Love at first sight?" Underwood asked as he started walking outside.

"Nah, she probably can't speak a word of English," Jonah said to Underwood's back, the door swinging closed behind him. "Besides, what would I do with a dumb Japanese girl?" and he looked up to the ceiling.

"Japanese girls are not dumb!" a female voice said behind him

&

Jonah turned and looked behind him. He was stunned. The third time in one day. It was the same young woman he had seen outside the coffee shop, the same one he had watched singing chant in the church choir. She wasn't wearing the white lace veil, but it was the same face, with the same remarkable eyes, long eyebrows, and that chin. He would recognize her anywhere, and he realized that he had just put both of his size 11 feet into his mouth.

"We're not dumb, you know!" she said, her eyes glaring at him. Her eyebrows came together, her mouth and lips were tightly closed.

"Oh, no..." Jonah mumbled, shaking his head and standing up from the bar stool. "Oh, I'm sorry. I'm very sorry. I didn't know you were there." He unconsciously held the palms of his hands up.

"Obviously." She stared at him with her arms crossed.

Jonah, realizing he had done the unthinkable, took a deep breath and thought he'd try a new tack. "I saw you singing in church today."

She didn't take the bait. "What may I get you from the bar?" she asked, all business, her large eyes carefully examining him.

"Uh," he was speechless.

"We have many liquors. What would you like?"

"Uh," he said again, completely at a loss what to say.

"Whiskey, rum, vodka, sake? Beer?" she asked, her eyes signaling impatience.

"Uh, my tall friend will have a double shot of rum, and he pointed to the empty bar stool..." he paused, thinking this isn't getting any easier. "And the other will have a rum and cola."

"And you?" she asked, her steely face continuing to show her displeasure.

Jonah stared at her, thinking she had the most intriguing face he had ever seen. "A beer, please," he said, still in shock.

"We have three brands; Kirin, Sapporo and Asahi."

"Uh, what's your favorite?" he asked in the most polite tone of voice he could come up with, attempting to speak clearly and not in his usual lazy cowboy drawl.

"I like Asahi best," she said curtly. "It is dark but not bitter. Would you like to try that?"

"Okay. Thank you."

"You're welcome."

"I saw you in church today," he said again.

She looked at him from the corner of her eyes. "Yes, I saw you too."

He was surprised, not realizing she might have seen him. "Yes...," he said, feeling a spark of excitement run through him. "You were singing chant."

"We were practicing."

"The singing was beautiful. You're very good."

"Thank you, she said," her mood softening. "I love singing chant."

"Me too," Jonah said. "I sang chant when I was in school."

"You sang chant?" she asked with a look of disbelief, her head tilted to one side.

"Yes, I did," he nodded. "For six years."

She looked as if she didn't know whether to believe him or not. "You have just arrived in Sasebo?" she asked.

He wondered how she knew they had just arrived. "Yes," he said, thinking he needed to say something more than just 'yes.' "We came in yesterday. Our ship, that is. We left Virginia, that's in the states, just over three months ago."

She looked out the tall windows. He could tell she was thinking. "Virginia," she said. "Yes," she looked back at him. "Virginia Tech. And the Chesapeake Bay?"

"Yes, exactly." Jonah was amazed with her English. And her knowledge of geography.

"I guess Japanese girls are not so dumb after all. Are they?" She stared at him with a challenging look.

"No, not at all." He gulped.

"Yes, the Chesapeake is a very long way," she said pouring rum into a shot glass.

"Yes it is, very far away," he nodded, beginning to feel relieved that she hadn't thrown the bottle at him.

"You have a funny American accent." She squinted, looking at the scar on his cheek.

"Yes." Not knowing what else to say he smiled and nodded. "I'm Jonah," he suddenly blurted out. Now why did I say that, he wondered.

"The man in the whale?" she said with a knowing look and placed the shot glass of rum on the bar in front of Underwood's vacant bar stool.

"That's me. And you must be Ashiko?" he asked. She nodded, but looked as if she wasn't happy that he knew her name. "It's nice to meet you."

She nodded again. "Your accent...you are from Virginia?"

"Ah, no," he chuckled, shaking his head. "No, I'm from Idaho."

"Idaho? Oh, yes, mountains! And cowboys. Another place far away."

"Yes," he laughed, thinking she's incredible.

"One moment please while I get your beer," and she walked through the doorway and into a back room.

Jonah took a deep breath, shaking his head as if he was trying to wake from a dream. Only I'm not dreaming, he thought.

"I chose the coldest one," she said, returning with a dark amber bottle, and she hunted through a drawer for an opener. She might be in her mid-twenties, Jonah thought, maybe 26 but not much more he guessed as he watched her move around behind the bar. He was fascinated by her face. He thought it resembled the shape of a diamond; her broad brow, resting over wide-set eyes and high cheek bones, was followed by a straight thin nose pointing to a small mouth with remarkably full lips, all tapering down toward a narrow chin. She turned her head, and her midnight black hair, looking as if it had been tousled by the wind, had a blue-purple iridescence that shimmered with changing intensity each time she moved. Her skin, and he had never seen such skin before, reminded him of his mother's face cream: an unblemished creamy alabaster. And resting in the dip between her neck and collarbone was an intriguing, small beauty mark.

"A cold Asahi," she said placing the frosted bottle and a tall wide-mouth glass onto oval bar coasters. Her obsidian-brown eyes looked straight into his.

He caught his breath and nodded. "Thank you," was all he could say.

"You are welcome. Kanpai," she said.

"Say again?"

"Kanpai. You say cheers. We say Kanpai," she smiled.

"Kanpai," he said and took a sip of the beer. "Hmm, that's good."

"I am happy you like it."

"Your English is excellent."

"Thank you. I studied at USC."

"USC?"

"In California."

USC, he thought, thinking there was only one USC in California that he knew of. "You mean Southern Cal?"

"Yes, exactly, the University of Southern California. I studied biology." She smiled.

"Biology?" he blurted out and reflected, yes, Jonah, you're the dumb one here.

"I have always been interested in the oceans. I wanted to work in oceanography. But after three years I had to leave California and come home to Japan."

"What happened?"

"My mother became ill."

"I'm sorry."

"Thank you. She is better now. She and her sister managed our ryokan. Then her sister died and my mother was left to manage it alone. Then she became ill. So, I needed to come home and help. But she is doing fine now. You met her when you arrived ."

"There's just the two of you here?"

"Oh, no. There is my mother and I, and my younger sister, with her little girl. Her husband died last year; he fell from a fishing boat and drowned." Jonah watched her as she paused for a moment, a faraway look in her eyes. "And we also have help from local women..." she said, continuing. "They come in every day; some for massage, others to clean. And to cook. And sometimes my brother comes to help, he is also a fisherman. His longline boat is in Sasebo.

"You live here...at the ryokan?"

"Oh, yes. It is normal for a small ryokan like this to have the owner live on site. This is our home."

"You own it?"

"My mother owns it."

"It's a beautiful spot."

"Yes. It has been in my family for many generations."

"But the building looks brand new," he said looking around him, amazed at the modern construction, the unique ceiling, the new doors and the triple pane windows.

"The old building, built in 1920, burned in a fire three years ago. Then we built this one."

Jonah nodded, thinking about the devastating effects of a fire. "It's very beautiful."

"Yes." The corners of her mouth turned up slightly with a faint smile.

He noticed the contrast between her sparkling teeth and her creamy skin. Her smile is hypnotizing he thought, much better than that angry pout. "Did you learn your English while at USC?"

"Some of it. Before that I went to a girl's academy, a boarding school near Nagasaki, from the time I was 10 years old. I learned most of my English there, from the Dominican nuns. My proper English, that is," and she chuckled, the first real sign that she might be getting over her anger.

"Dominicans?"

"Yes. It was a very strict place; we had to wear uniforms, tartan skirts with light blue blouses. I looked very funny. Then when I was twenty-one I went to California and a whole new world opened for me. That's where I learned to speak the real American English," and she laughed, a deep almost uncontrollable laugh, and for the first time her face lit up and her mouth broadened into a wide grin.

He was amazed at how that smile completely changed her face. "American English?" he asked.

"Oh, yes. The real American English." Her laugh was contagious and Jonah couldn't help but laugh with her. "Yes, I had three years of speaking American English with Americans; belonging to a sorority, going to football games, singing in the glee club, dating frat boys, skiing at Mammoth, weekend trips to Las Vegas." She looked wistfully out the window. "Yes, many weekend trips." She shook her head as if she was trying to come to the surface from her deep memories, and then she turned toward him and broke out in that contagious laugh again. "I even played my flute in the marching band for one year!"

"You did all that?"

She nodded, smiling with a look that revealed her past but obscured the details. "But not now. I don't get to talk to Americans often," she said wiping the surface of the bar with a small towel. "Not many come this way. You are the first in many weeks." Her smile suddenly disappeared and she became serious again as she looked toward the door opening from the outside terrace. "Your friends return," she whispered and they watched Underwood and Brickey coming through the doorway.

"Man, this is really some beautiful place," Underwood said taking his seat at the bar. "Thank you," he said holding up the glass of rum, and he took a sip. "Umm, thanks, I needed that."

"By the way," Jonah said looking at Ashiko. "This is Woody," and he pointed to Underwood. "And this is Brickey..." Then he gestured toward the Japanese girl, "...and this is Ashiko."

She nodded and smiled.

"A pleasure," Underwood said.

"We've never been to an onsen before," Jonah said. "We'd like to have the full experience; bath, massage, and also dinner. We're staying the night. What do you recommend?"

"You've not been to onsen before?" she asked in surprise.

"No." Jonah said and he, Underwood and Brickey all shook their heads. "This is our first time in Japan."

"First time. I see. Then I suggest you enjoy the hot spring first, after bathing of course."

The sailors nodded.

"Then massage, then dinner. In that order. It is always best to have massage on an empty stomach."

"Sounds good to me," Underwood said lighting another cigarette.

"So, how do we get started?" Jonah asked.

"You choose..." and she reached under the bar and placed a small card on the counter. "...from this menu. We serve kaiseki at seven o'clock. In your room."

"Kaiseki?" Jonah asked.

"Yes. Kaiseki is several different dishes made fresh. Each day our cook chooses only the freshest ingredients. These are the dishes we have today," and she checked several different ones with a pen, then held one finger up. "One moment please," and she went through the doorway behind the bar.

"Man, I'm telling you," Underwood said looking at the menu that was printed in Japanese, English and French. He took another sip of his rum. "This place is just beautiful. You should'a been outside, Jonah. You really should have. The river, the hot spring, the trees, the rhododendron, that little tea house up there. It's all just beautiful. And peaceful."

"Yea I know," Jonah said.

"You should'a come outside instead of just sitting in this room doing nothing. It's much nicer outside," Underwood pointed out the window and took another sip of rum.

"Yea, I'm sure."

"Man, I hope no other sailors ever discover this place."

"This is Natsume," Ashiko said returning to the bar with a young woman. "My sister."

The woman bowed. "Yokoso," she said smiling, a small gap showing in the middle of her upper teeth. The sailors nodded. She was young, maybe 21, Jonah thought, and very small; definitely less than five feet. He noticed her smiling, mischievous pixie face, and her black pants and white long sleeve blouse with the orange camellia embroidered on the pocket. Her long, thick black hair was bundled and tied on the top of her head. Brickey stared at her.

"Natsume will show you the bath and how to use it," Ashiko said. "And the onsen. And when you are ready, massage." She looked at her watch. "Then dinner in your room in two hours."

"Thank you," Jonah said.

"We are pleased to have you here at Tsubaki," she said smiling with a soft, open friendliness.

Jonah felt the spark of emotional electricity surge through him again.

※

Natsume led them back to their room and opened a closet filled with futons, sheets, towels and robes. She handed a freshly folded black and tan patterned robe to Underwood. "Yukata," she said. "You put on. No clothes." She gave a blue-gray yukata to Jonah, and an orange-gray one to Brickey. "You wear while you here at ryokan."

Not knowing exactly what they should do, they looked at her. "I think we should change," Underwood said.

"Hai. Yes. You change," she said waving her hands. "No clothes. Only underwear. I wait outside," she added sliding the door closed behind her.

"No clothes," Underwood repeated. "Only underwear. This is gonna be interesting," and he pulled his jumper over his head.

"You look pretty good in that," Jonah said as Underwood tied the sash on his yukata. "All you gotta do now is get your eyes fixed and you'd fit right in. You ready?"

Underwood grinned and slid the door open.

Natsume stood in the hall with her arms folded, waiting for them. "No, no, no," she cried in shock, waving her hands, looking at the sailors in their yukatas, "You wrong." She pushed them back into the room, went up to Underwood, untied the sash on his yukata, and without even thinking twice or asking permission, she pulled his robe completely open. Jonah started chuckling as he watched Underwood's eyes grow wide. "You put this first," she said pulling the right-hand section of Underwood's robe across his skinny body. "Then this," she pulled the left side over the right. "You not dead yet," she said grinning. Jonah wondered what she meant by that. "Then this," and she placed the sash against his stomach, brought the ends around his back, and then to the front again. "This go here," she said tying a half bow off to the side. "Here," she emphasized patting to her side, indicating where the bow should be placed. "Better," she said nodding and looking at Underwood with approval, making a small adjustment to the bow. Then she turned toward Jonah. "You no better," she said frowning and shaking her head. "I fix you now."

Jonah surrendered, putting his hands up in the air. "I'm ready," he said.

Jonah looked down watching her adjust his robe, feeling her surprisingly strong fingers tying the sash. She's obviously done this before, he thought. Brickey was closely watching Natsume adjust the robes, and taking her cue, he carefully rearranged his. She stepped back, looked at the the three of them and nodded in approval. "Good now," she said. "You the only smart one," she said smiling at Brickey. "Now we go to bath," and she started walking away. She turned around, "Follow!" she said impatiently, waving her hands, trying to get them to follow her.

"She's a good hand-waver," Jonah whispered as they followed Natsume down the hall. "And a good knot tier. She could teach Biagotti a thing or two."

Underwood was grinning and chuckling uncontrollably as they went through a doorway.

"Bath," she said holding a door open for them and they entered a large room with tiles covering the walls and floor. Wooden stools and buckets were neatly stacked in one corner. Along one wall was a row of faucets, and Jonah was surprised to see they were located only about three feet above the floor. Another wall of frosted windows let in the afternoon light while retaining privacy.

"You look," Natsume said tapping a sign on the wall showing a set of cartoon characters in various stages of washing. Then she turned and placed a wooden stool and a bucket in front of one of the faucets "Stool," she said sitting down. "Bucket," and she pantomimed pouring water from the bucket over her head. "Soap," she pointed to a selection of soap bottles resting on shelves at each set of faucets. "Rinse, rinse," she said holding the bucket above her head and making a circle motion over her chest and shoulders. "Onsen." She stood and opened an opaque glass door, pointing outside to the hot spring. Jonah could see mist curling up from above the thick foliage.

"I think I've got it," Underwood said examining the sign. "Look at this." Jonah and Brickey walked over to the sign and Underwood pointed. "You sit on the stool, get wet, soap up, use the wash towel, rinse off."

"Right," Jonah said.

"Then using the towel for modesty, you go out that door, walk down to the onsen, and ease into the water; you don't jump, swim or put your hair in the water. And you put the folded towel on your head, not in the water."

∽∾

They stepped onto a deck overlooking the small river gorge filled with a strikingly varied array of green plants and trees lowering down on terraces toward the river. The rushing sounds of falling water were all around them, and in the distance the mist rose up from the onsen hidden behind lush greens. The path went downhill over flat rocks and gravel, winding, twisting its way downward, past a stone lantern and cultivated shrubs. Jonah thought the variety of greens was astonishing; from dense dark blues, to yellow lime, to iridescent yellow green, all stepping downward, down towards the sounds of the cascades and the steam rising from the onsen.

The onsen was man-made, and it captured the natural hot spring flowing into it before spilling over the edges and out again.

The curving, undulating shape of the large pool and its bordering rocks looked as if the onsen had always been there, as if the ebb and flow of time had created it, and not man who had blended nature and architecture into one. The hot spring pouring into the onsen gushed through a large bamboo spout, and the water had a faint milky color originating from the minerals in the geothermal spring's ancient rock. The steam misting up from the pool's surface made the junipers and rhododendron appear to be vibrating. Jonah eased his naked body into the water, the heat surprising him, and he moved away from the bamboo spout and found a place in the pool where the temperature was not quite so hot. Looking above him, a cedar roof overhung half of the onsen, presumably to provide relief from falling rain or snow in those seasons. With his body soaking in the 98-degree water his mind began to feel as if it was floating upward with the mist, emptying out all his worry and stress. The sounds of the river rushing over the rocks below filled the entire atmosphere, creating a place where his thoughts no longer existed; the nightmares of *McMann*, the carrier fire, the captain's mast, O'Toole and Sanders, even thoughts of Pattie, were all slowly erased from his consciousness. The only things he felt now were the hot, calming water and the sounds of the river. He had never experienced such a feeling of release before. If there was a wish he could make, it would be that this moment in time would be indelibly imprinted in his mind forever.

"Have you ever felt this before? This peace?" Underwood asked from the opposite side of the onsen.

"What?" Jonah said, not being able to hear what he said over the rush of the river. "Did you say geese?"

"Have you ever felt this *peace* before?" Underwood repeated as he came closer.

"No, never. And I have to tell you, Woody, I didn't know I needed this. I didn't know just how wound up I was. Or how exhausted I was. All that stuff of the last few months, it had just piled up; I didn't understand how bad of a place I was in. Now, all this..." and he looked around him. "...all this...I can't describe it."

Underwood nodded. "I was thinking the same. It seems we get so caught up in what we're doing that we don't know there could ever be such a peaceful place."

They were lost in their thoughts. Jonah watched the hot mist rising up and up, disappearing into the sky. He thought about the remarkable number of different shades of green in the trees, how they were beyond anything he had seen. The light was now changing with the low angled evening sun, and the color casting onto the trees above him was a pale orange. A beam of sunlight hit the steaming mist rising from the onsen's surface and turned the billions of water droplets into a fiery gold.

<hr>

"I never had anybody walk on my back before," Jonah said as he tried another dish, attempting to use the awkward chopsticks. "Hmm, that's very good," he said chewing and pointing to the bowl. "Don't know what that is, but it's good."

"I was trying to guess how much Natsume weighs," Brickey said sipping his sake. "Probably less than 100 pounds, but she sure has strong hands."

"Mine..." Jonah said swallowing. "What was her name again?"

"Haruko."

"Right, Haruko. She was something else. I was lying there on my stomach, on the tatami mat, with my eyes closed. She was kneading my shoulders, when all of a sudden I felt her feet on my back. I almost jumped off the floor. But I was so relaxed I didn't move. She used her toes, her heels and the balls of her feet....man that felt good, having her walking along my back muscles and up and down my spine. She sure knew what she was doing. I think my whole body turned into jelly."

"I know what you mean...oh, now this is superb," Underwood said. "This is maguro. Tuna sushi." And he pointed with his chopsticks. "You're gonna love that."

Jonah picked up a two-inch long piece of maguro that was resting on a small block of ice, turned it around examining it, dipped it in a dark sauce and bit off a tiny piece and struggled to swallow it. "Hmm," he grimaced. "I'm not sure I understand the attraction human beings have with raw fish." His face was pinched in a look of severe uncertainty.

Underwood shook his head. "Maybe it's an acquired taste," and he chose a prawn from a bowl, looked at it closely, turned it around, and inserted the entire crustacean into his mouth.

"Oh, God! How can you do that?" Jonah said in disgust watching Underwood chew the prawn. "You're gonna eat the whole thing? Including the head? And the shell?"

"Ugh, that's awful," Brickey said, turning his head away from watching Underwood, not wanting to see him eating the prawn.

"Hmm...tastes wonderful," Underwood said chewing. Jonah could hear the crunching from across the table. "The flavor just explodes in your mouth. It has a real strong earthy taste, mixed with salt. And not only does it taste good, it's good for you too. Try it."

Jonah's face turned sour as he held the four-inch prawn with his chopsticks, examining the long antennae and the large head with its bulging eyes, the multitude of legs and the long tail.

"Well, go on!" Underwood said.

Brickey watched intently.

Jonah grimaced and closed his eyes as he slowly inserted the prawn into his wide-open mouth. He started chewing. His face turned repulsively distorted. He chewed some more, shaking his head and swallowed. He reached for the sake and took a gulp. "God...!" He gasped and took another sip of sake. "Oh, man. I can't believe I did that." He shuddered, wiping his mouth with a napkin. "Not bad tasting, but weird."

Underwood was silently laughing, silently and uncontrollably laughing, trying unsuccessfully to calm himself. "Oh, you looked funny," he said still laughing. "I thought you were going to explode. Your face was so scrunched up."

"Yea, thanks a lot," Jonah said taking another sip of sake. "It really didn't taste bad. In fact it was pretty good. But the crunching sounds..." he shook his head. "Just the thought of it!" and he leaned back from the table, chuckling. "That was something else."

"Ha ha, you had the funniest look on your face when you were swallowing that thing."

"I'm sure."

"I wish I had a camera," Brickey said.

"Okay, what's next," Jonah looked at the different bowls and the variety of foods on the table. "Now this," he said poking the items in one of the dishes. "This here is definitely beef, that I recognize for sure. Look at the marbling," and he picked up a slice of beef the size of a playing card and took a bite. "Oh, yea," he said chewing. "Now that's delicious. Hmm. Really delicious. Never tasted beef quite like that before. It's actually melting in my mouth. Brickey, have you tried this?"

"I'm about to. Did Haruko also crack your fingers?" Brickey asked.

"Yea," Jonah said. "She cracked my fingers and my toes, my ankles, my neck, just about everything...well maybe not quite everything, but almost everything," and he laughed. The combination of the hot onsen, the massage, the sake, the food, and more sake was starting to take effect. His face was getting puffy and his eyelids were partially closed. He took a deep breath. "I suddenly feel like that octopus looks," and he held up a bowl of octopus tentacles swimming in a clear sauce. "Just sort'a limp. You know what I mean?"

Underwood wasn't paying attention. Instead he picked up a spoon and tried the soup. "Oh, that's good. Very good. You need to try this soup. The one in the blue bowl."

"The blue bowl?" Brickey asked.

"Yea."

"The blue bowl," Jonah said reaching for the blue bowl. He took a cautious sip. "Hmm. Yea. That is good. I can't identify all of it...but fish...yea, fish and maybe some crab, and lots of spices."

"And seaweed," Brickey added.

"Hmm, you're right. That is good. Really good. I like that."

"All this food is quite amazing," Underwood said. "How they prepare it all, I can only guess. Some of it I understand. But the rest, I'm not sure. I know all about Italian food, from working at Mesalina's back in Bayonne, and being in Italy. But this," and he waved his hand over the table. "It's beyond anything I've ever experienced. Not only is it delicious, but the presentation...just look how it's plated. The different color bowls. The different textures of food. And everything appears as if it has been deliberately and carefully placed. Nothing is haphazard."

"Man, I'm stuffed." Brickey leaned back and put his hands on his stomach. "Really stuffed."

"What time you want to leave in the morning?" Underwood said.

"I asked Ashiko to have someone give us a wake-up at 0600," Jonah said. "She'll arrange to have a cab here at 0630. That should give us plenty of time to get back to the ship by 0700 or so."

"That'll work."

"And no breakfast. They don't start serving the full breakfast until 0800."

"After all this," Brickey moaned. "I won't need any food for days."

"Come in," Jonah said to the knock on the door.

The door slid open and Natsume's smiling face appeared, the distinctive small gap showing in her teeth. "I take plates?" she asked.

"Yes, please." Jonah stood up from the low table and stretched. "I think I'll pay the bill now, so we'll have one less thing to do in the morning."

"Can you set up our beds?" Underwood asked the tiny woman. He laid his hands along his cheek as if he was sleeping.

"Hai. Yes, beds." She bowed and looked straight at Brickey. "One moment," she said and pattered out of the room with the tray of dishes.

Jonah shuffled down the hallway in his slippers, dressed in the yukata robe, once again examining the room numbers and wondering what happened to room #4. He walked through the unoccupied main room and into the empty bar where he found Ashiko stacking glasses on shelves.

"Hello," she said turning toward him, smiling. "Did you like the kaiseki?"

"Oh, yes," he said taking a seat at the bar directly across from her. "It was the most wonderful meal I've ever had. Absolutely the best. Thank you."

"I am glad to know that. And your onsen and massage?"

"Out of this world."

She smiled and tilted her head. Jonah thought her large eyes seemed to grow even larger when she smiled. There was a moment of silence between them as they both looked at one another. Jonah felt her gaze. He sensed an emotion he hadn't felt in a long time, as if a hundred butterflies had just flown through his chest.

"I hope you will return to Tsubaki soon," she said with an expectant look, her head once again tilted in that unusual way.

"I definitely plan on it. In fact I was just thinking that I might return the night after tomorrow."

"Tuesday night?"

"Yes, that would be Tuesday. I'd like to make a reservation."

"Hmm," she said. Her obsidian-brown eyes stared at his face. She looked from his eyes to the scar on his cheek and down to his wide mouth and severe chin. "My choir is giving a recital that night. At the church. We will be singing chant. Maybe you would like to attend?"

Jonah couldn't believe she had just invited him. His pulse quickened. "A recital?"

"Yes, we will sing several selections of Gregorian Chant. Plus, some classic melodies, and opera."

"Opera?"

"That too, yes. And Sister Aloysius will accompany us on the organ. She is a famous organist from Kagoshima."

"Yes," he said nodding. "Yes, I would really like that," he smiled.

"Wonderful." Her face lit up. "And after the recital a few of my friends and I are going out, to get something to eat. Could you join me then also? And Mister Underwood and Brickey are also welcome."

She wants me to join her, he thought. "Of course, if you don't mind having someone tag along that doesn't understand Japanese."

"Ta...tag along?"

"You know, come along for the ride? Someone that's not too experienced?"

"Ah...tag along. I must remember that one." She chuckled. "But don't worry. I would translate. And most of my friends speak some English."

"What time?"

"The recital starts at seven."

"Seven?"

"Yes, is that too late?" she asked with a concerned look.

"Oh, no. Not at all."

"Good.," she smiled. "You should get there by 6:30. For a seat up front."

"Okay, 6:30."

"That way I can find you easy," she smiled again.

So, she can find me easy, he repeated silently. He felt more butterflies fly through him.

~~

Wilson and Beckers stood in the wing deck watching the Japanese shipyard workers lift the heavy supercharger up through the escape hatch from the engine room 25 feet below. The chain hoist rattled and groaned with the weight as they hoisted the bulky piece of equipment up and up, eventually pulling it through the wing door. Wilson looked around him, searching for the other yardbirds that he thought would be needed to move the supercharger through the ship and down to the tank deck. But there were only two men. And they were not very large. Four months ago in Little Creek he had watched six men, six large strong men, hoist the superchargers, one by one, up from the engine room and then move them through the compartments. Back then they had used chain hoists and a steel dolly to move them through one compartment to another. Now, on this day, the two Japanese yard workers simply tied a 25-millimeter rope from the supercharger's lifting ring to each end of a three inch diameter, six foot long pipe. Then, without hesitating, they lifted the pipe to their shoulders. The gear rose off the deck, and they started walking steadily forward, carrying the large, bulky hunk of metal evenly balanced between them. They easily stepped over shin knockers, went quickly through one compartment after another, and then down to the tank deck where a shipyard utility boat was waiting at the bow ramp.

Wilson shook his head. "It's amazing..." he said. "...the different ways different people have in accomplishing the same task; one with autocratic obstinacy, the other with expedient simplicity."

"Ha!" Beckers laughed. "Welcome to Japan!"

❧❧

Diary #107
18 May 1966
0330 Hours .... Sasebo .... Day 3.

Our latest diversion has once again struck fear into the hearts of man: the mysterious ZERO has penned another editorial. This latest piece of tomfoolery was discovered on the windows of the conn yesterday morning by one of the quartermasters who was sweeping away the shipyard's dirt. Fortunately, he had the presence of mind not to immediately erase the grease pencil ode, but instead found Chief Cunningham and reported it to him. Cunningham, who has that rare sense of humor particular to old chiefs, decided to let the poetry stand for future generations, believing it fit the definition of an artifact of historic magnitude. I quote:

> *"We have a dumb signalman named Pike,*
> *who isn't really well liked.*

> *He's so full of shit*
> *it's not hard to admit*
> *that we think he should take a long hike."*

After several people made the long pilgrimage up the ladders to pay homage to ZERO's latest work, Signalman Pike suddenly appeared and angrily rubbed it all out; a desecration of monumental proportions in my opinion. Pike, who at times takes his Master at Arms duties a little too seriously, is now stalking through the ship, his fleshy jowls and pug-shaped face peering at everyone, attempting to divine the culprit through some sort of mental polygraph. Anyone who looks the least bit suspicious is pulled aside and questioned. For my part, I hope the true identity of ZERO is not discovered, as I profoundly enjoy this type of boredom-relieving satiric comedy.

We're about to start our 3rd day here in Sasebo, and the ship is in turmoil once again. Japanese yard workers in their yellow hard hats have been swarming throughout our many spaces. Welding hoses and air hoses are everywhere; they hang from ladder railings, criss-cross through compartments and snake along passageways. The stink from burning acetylene torches and welding rods permeates the atmosphere. Yesterday's ear piercing, disturbing clamor from pneumatic hammers busting the ship's considerable rust is beginning to cause my fillings to vibrate loose. And the headache inducing fumes from fresh caustic paint being slathered on the bulkhead outside my stateroom is creating some nauseating moments. We haven't seen anything quite like this since Little Creek.

But...this is Japan, and I'm enjoying every minute of it!!! And what a great evening it was: feeling the firm earth underfoot, smelling the camphor and pine trees in the cool night air, sampling drinks at one bar after another, and enjoying delicious sushi, tempura, sukiyaki, chankonabe and miso ... and did I also say sake? ... all prepared fresh and served by a lovely, demure geisha. You couldn't ask for a better liberty port.

Here's a bit of worthy news; last evening we received a surprise message: we are going to be blessed with an addition to our humble wardroom! And what's even more interesting, this unknown quantity just happens to be a veritable, bona fide, newly commissioned ensign in the U.S. Navy Supply Corps! Seems as if we might finally have someone in that department who really knows what they're doing. In any case, I find it amusing that the Navy has such a funny sense of humor, sending us a Supply Corps "pork chopper" with the name of John Frederick Spratt.

During all the confusion of yesterday morning when Japanese yardbirds were coming and going...along with numerous enginemen, machinist mates and electricians from the tender, plus our own deck gang sweeping, swabbing and painting everywhere...Commander Service Group Three paid us a surprise visit. Apparently, the Admiral had been cruising through the harbor in his barge (a 40-foot boat used by flag officers for harbor transport) when he ordered the coxswain to lay the barge alongside our bow ramp. I happened to be nonchalantly walking through the tank deck at that moment and noticed the boat but didn't think anything of it. Suddenly two smartly dressed sailors in freshly pressed whites jumped out of the immaculate barge, held the boat tightly alongside the ramp, and a rather large, heavy man with two stars on his collar stepped from the boat onto the bow ramp. Someone must have recognized the admiral for what he was and yelled: "ATTENTION ON DECK!!!!" Those ear shattering words flew through the empty tank deck, loudly echoing from the bulkheads with enormous speed. Everyone froze at attention. One particular sailor, who shall remain anonymous, had been busily swabbing the deck with a long-handled mop. Immediately upon hearing the shouted command, he assumed the ramrod posture of attention. And then not knowing what to do with the mop, he moved it into the position of Order Arms, the business end waving and vibrating next to his head. The admiral approached at a very brisk pace, stopped, looked at the mop wielding sailor, and shook his head. The admiral continued aft; his face appeared as if he was about to chew nails. The Flag Lieutenant, trailing several paces behind, ran to catch up as the admiral went through a doorway and up to officer's country to the captain's cabin.

Mendoza later confided to me that he overheard the admiral's strong voice coming from under the thin door of the captain's cabin; the big two-star shouting something about lousy leadership, absurd lack of discipline, out of control delinquents, and if Lieutenant Kell wanted his crew to enjoy any further liberty during their stay in Sasebo, then he would just have to come over to the tender and personally retrieve the two inebriated birdbrain sailors who were caught relieving their bladders off the flagship's brow at 0135 this morning!!! Mendoza summed it up beautifully in one simple sentence: "No-bodi wod be-lebe 'dis bolsheet."

As the great Roman philosopher Lucius Annaeus Seneca once said: "Et prodigia nunquam desinet?"

※

"We're screwed," Mills whispered.

"Huh?" Poldolski said, watching the crew assembling into their ranks on the main deck for morning quarters.

"We are. We are completely screwed," Mills said out of the corner of his mouth.

"What'ya mean?" Poldolski had a serious questioning look on his face.

"Because Mendoza told me we ain't gonna have any more liberty for the rest of our stay here."

"What?"

"Cause word has it that the admiral reamed the captain out something fierce and said he would put the kibosh on all our liberty, unless the captain himself goes across to the tender and gets those two idiots out of the brig."

"Holy shit! The captain?"

"And not only that, but those two jail birds are now personage non-gratis," Mills said.

"Who?"

"Pisco and Turbe!"

"Pisco and Turbe?"

"Personage gratis."

"What?

"Which means they ain't got no names and will be treated as lepers."

"Lepers?"

"And not only that but the XO is also gonna be boiled in oil 'cause the captain ain't gonna take all the responsibility for this shit, not without someone else also having his cojones cut off," Mills added.

"Holy shit!"

"Yea, holy shit is right...those dumb sons'a'bitches, ruining our liberty."

"Wait till I get my hands on them...I'll..."

"Well, you better get in line quick cause there's a lot of other guys who are gonna be ahead of you, and by the time your turn comes around there won't be much left of those two idiots except maybe a few shoelaces and a couple of teeth."

Ultimately, it was the captain, along with Charlie Crane and Signalman Pike, who left the ship that morning, crossed over the deck of the adjacent destroyer, stepped onto the quarterdeck of the flagship, and inquired as to the whereabouts of the brig. The quarterdeck messenger guided them down a ladder to a lower deck, and then further down to another deck, and down to a third deck through a labyrinth of twists and turns, eventually arriving at the Master at Arms office.

The MA, a tall, grizzled master chief with the face of a fox, welcomed them to the brig office. "Good morn'n, sir," he said, standing up from his desk, looking at the Command At Sea insignia pinned on the Captain's shirt. "What can I do fer you t'day, sir?" he said in a lazy Ozark mountain drawl.

"I'm Lieutenant Kell..." the captain explained. "...commanding officer of *Winchester County*. This is my Executive Officer, Mister Crane. And Pike, our Master at Arms."

"Yes sir, I'm Chief Renard," he said, staring through a pair of alert, piercing eyes, looking back at the thick captain in the aviator sunglasses. The tall, skinny XO and the big signalman with the strange face stood just behind their captain.

"We're here to retrieve Seamen Pisco and Turbe," the captain said with a serious look. "They were brought in here sometime this morning."

"Oh, yes, sir," the chief said looking up to the overhead, thinking. "Seaman Pisco and Seaman Turbe," and the chief looked back at the captain. "Oh, yes, sir! You mean the brow urinators?"

The captain stared at the chief.

Crane noticed the chief shifting his tobacco chaw to the other side of his mouth.

"Yes, sir, I got 'em here. Yes, sir, raht here in my brig, sir."

Crane looked around the small compartment, at the pea green paint, the overhead covered in a confusion of electrical cables, pipes and air ducts criss-crossing in different directions. On one side of the room sat a small, gray steel desk with a typewriter, and stacks of paper and overflowing IN and OUT boxes covered most of the surface. In a corner stood a tall, dented file cabinet welded to the bulkhead, its open drawers bursting with dogged-eared papers. The cramped compartment was not what Crane expected to find in a flagship; the old peeling paint and scuffed deck were in striking contrast to the spit and polish of the ship's quarterdeck three decks above them. But what struck him more than anything else was the door in the bulkhead behind the chief's desk; he had never seen anything like it before. It was a closed and padlocked door made from one-inch wide vertical and horizontal ribbons of steel placed about three inches apart. He thought it resembled the door of a large cage. And beyond the door, a dark passageway led around a corner to somewhere; Crane didn't know where. And then he realized what was bothering him about the compartment; it wasn't the small size, it wasn't the old paint. It was the smell. There was a faint unpleasant odor emanating from something back there, in the dark, beyond the door; something of a mix between sweat, piss, puke and chlorine. He blinked his eyes, squinted and wriggled his nose.

"The admiral spoke to me, and we're here to take them off your hands," Kell said.

"The admiral spoke to you?" the chief said with a look of surprise that hovered between dumb hillbilly and sly fox. "Well, well. The admiral, you say, sir?"

"Yes, the admiral!" Kell said, putting emphasis on the word 'admiral.'

"I see," the chief rubbed his chin. "Well, if the admiral says you can have 'em, sir, well, I guess it'll be a'right for me to give 'em to ya. But they ain't very pretty, ya know. No, sir. Not what ya might describe as being ready for a captain's inspection. Ya see, sir, they got a little shitfac...uh, a little inebriated last night, sir, and they seemed to take some delight in making fools of themselves, relieving their bladders on the brow of the admiral's flagship, and doing some other unsightly things." The chief's eyebrows turned up with a knowing look. "But a few of my men, well, we took care of 'em, sir. You understand. Your boys were look'n kind'a poorly and we didn't want 'em to embarrass themselves any further, so we took care of 'em and locked 'em up. Bless their hearts."

"We'll take them now," Kell said impatiently, becoming irritated from having to stand in front of this slow moving, slow talking master chief.

"Yes, sir. No problem, sir. Glad to oblige. May I see your ID, sir?"

The captain's head jerked back and he stood frozen in place, staring at the chief.

"Yes, sir. We always ask for ID. Just to make sure nobody is aiding an abetting an escape from the brig, ya know?"

The captain slowly reached into his pocket for his wallet and held out his ID card toward the chief.

"Thank you, sir," the chief said looking up from the photo on the ID card, comparing it with the man standing in front of him. "The admiral is a stickler for protocol, ya know."

"Okay, let's go."

"We'll have some paperwork to take care of first, sir."

"Paperwork?" the captain asked in disbelief.

"Oh, yes, sir. I'm sure you don't mind. The admiral likes his paperwork, ya know, and done just right. Let me see, now, where did I put that...?" and the chief started leafing through the papers on the desk. He looked through the In-box, and then looked in the Out-box. He went through a stack of papers on the right side of the desk, and another stack on the left side of the desk, and looking into space for a moment, he finally nodded, snapped his fingers, and lifted a clipboard off the bulkhead. "Almost forgot where I put that," he said grinning, showing a large gap in his upper teeth where the cuspid and premolars were once located.

Crane glanced at the captain and could see he was becoming annoyed.

"Yes, sir, here they are. Pisco and Turbe," the chief said looking at the papers on the clipboard. "Those are some names, ain't they?" he grinned looking up at the captain. "Pisco and

Turbe. Yep, those are definitely some names," he chuckled. "Okay, sir, let me just fill out this section. Won't be but a second," he said sitting down in the beat-up chair in front of the old typewriter. The chief methodically inserted one of the forms between the typewriter's rollers, turned the platen knob, straightened the paper, and using the forefingers of each hand, started pecking the keys.

The captain inhaled and looked up to the overhead.

"Yes, sir. How did ya say your name was spelt, sir?" the chief asked.

"Kell," the captain said. "H. I. Kell."

"H. I., sir?" The chief's fingers were poised above the typewriter keys.

"Yes, H. I., as in Hotel India."

"H. I."

"Yes, Hotel India. And Kell as in Kilo Echo Lima Lima."

"Hotel Kilo Lima?" the chief asked.

"No. H. I. Kell. As in Hotel India, Kilo Echo Lima Lima."

"India Kilo?"

"No! Kilo Echo Lima Lima!"

"Uh, yes, sir, why don't ya just print it real nice and neat for me on this here piece of paper." The chief slid a sheet of paper across the desk toward the captain.

"Does anybody have a damn pen?" The captain was clearly becoming irate, and he looked from Crane to the chief.

"Oh, yes, sir." The chief handed a pen to the captain. "Feel free to use mine, sir. It's a brand new one. Even writes upside down."

The captain, trying to contain his growing anger, carefully wrote his name in large block letters and handed the paper and pen back to the chief.

"Mighty fine, sir. Mighty fine. Appreciate that." The chief pecked the letters out on the keys, adjusting the paper, nudging the carriage return, typing, rolling the platen, typing. "Ya know, I ain't never taken a typing course?" he said looking up and grinning, the missing teeth exposing tobacco juice through the gap.

The captain, with the sunglasses hiding his eyes, sucked in his breath and gave Charlie Crane a long deadly stare. The XO averted his eyes and looked down at the deck.

"Alright, sir," the chief said. "Looks like we got it all here. Let's see now, just one more minute while I check everything over to make sure. Ya know how the admiral is..." The chief carefully read through both forms, from left to right, from top down, all the way to the bottom. "Yes, sir. Looks like we got it all."

"Well, then bring'em out!" the captain said, clearly exasperated, anxious to get out of the cramped, oppressive brig.

"Yes, sir," and the chief turned to a stout, well-built 1st class bosun's mate who had been sitting in the back corner. "Pete, when you got a minute, go get Pisco and Turbe and bring'em out here."

The captain glared at the chief.

The substantial bosun's mate looked up from the magazine he was leafing through, stood slowly up from his tilted-back chair, pulled a considerably hefty key ring from his belt loop, ambled to the locked cage door, inserted the key, opened the padlock, and disappeared into the mysterious recesses of the dark passageway.

"Pete won't be but a moment, sir," the chief said smiling, his arms folded across his chest, continuing to sit behind the desk, as the captain, Crane and Pike stood before him in the small office. "Nope, won't be long now. I think your two troublemakers have just 'bout finished clean'n up their cell. We like 'em to leave the cells nice and clean for the next guest, ya know." The chief leaned back in his chair, smiling, nodding his head, looking between the captain and Crane as the sounds of jangling keys and slamming steel doors drifted out from the dark passageway. "Nice weather we're having, don't ya think, sir?" the chief said with a friendly look. "Oh, here we go," he said as the bosun's mate named 'Pete' led two bedraggled sailors into the office; their wrists were in manacles, their heads hanging down, their dirty, unshaven faces and red-rimmed eyes not wanting to look up at anyone. One of them, either Pisco or Turbe, Crane didn't know which, had an angry red road-rash bruise on his chin, the other had a flourishing black eye. Their white uniforms, clearly looking as if they had been slept in, were wrinkled, torn and splotched with grease and dried blood.

"Ya might want'a look 'em over sir..." the chief said looking at the two young sailors from the comfort of his chair. "...to make sure they are who they say they are, 'cause they don't seem to look like the pi'tures on their IDs." The chief held the ID cards up in front of each sailor. "Not quite, anyhow."

"XO?" the captain jerked his head around. "Do you recognize them?"

Crane looked at the sailors. "Uh, no sir."

The captain shook his head. "Pike, do you recognize them?"

"Yes, sir. That's Turbe." Pike pointed to the sailor on the left. "And that's Pisco."

"Alright, then let's go!"

"Sir," the chief said. "Did you bring along your corpsman? He should look 'em over, 'ya know...declare 'em fit and all."

"XO?" the captain said. "Did you notify Slaughter about this?"

"Uh, no sir," Crane said. "I didn't know we needed Slaughter."

The captain looked down at the deck and shook his head.

"Well, that's all right, sir, noth'n to be concerned about," the chief said in a subtly facetious way. "Our chief corpsman took a look at 'em just this morn'n and pronounced 'em fit as fiddles. He said they just had some hangovers, so he gave 'em some aspirin. Aw, soon enough they'll be feel'n better than a couple 'a spring chickens on a hot morning." A big grin went across the chief's face.

Crane sucked in a huge breath of malodorous air and shook his head.

"Anything else?" the captain asked with a deadly look.

"You'll have to sign for 'em, sir."

"Sign for them?"

"Yes, sir. As the admiral ordered."

The captain mumbled something under his breath, and he dashed his signature on both forms and handed them back to the chief.

The chief looked carefully at the scrawled, indecipherable signature. "Hmm," he said shaking his head. "I guess that must be your signature, sir, 'cause ya just signed it," and he looked up and smiled. "Okay, then, Pete, take off them cuffs." The big bosun unlocked the manacles and held the two sailors by their arms. "Looks like they're all yours, sir," the chief said smiling, standing up from his chair.

"Pike, take charge of them," the captain ordered, and as he started walking out of the office he turned; "Can you have someone lead us back to the quarterdeck?"

"Of course I can, sir. I bet Pete, here, would do that for you. What you say, Pete? Do you have a moment to lead Captain Kell back to the quarterdeck?

The thickset Pete looked at the chief, straightened up from leaning against the file cabinet, and without saying a word he lead them out of the office.

"Thank you for visit'n, sir!" the chief called out. "Y'all come back!"

The jungle drums started beating furiously; the news of the captain crossing over to the brig and personally retrieving Pisco and Turbe flashed through the ship at an extraordinary pace. Then the scuttlebutt overflowed onto the adjacent *USS John W Thomason*, and down into the chief's compartment, the Old Goat's Locker.

"Well, Sully, I'll tell 'ya what this is," Chief Davis was saying as he gripped a coffee mug in his hand, his thumb firmly secured along the topside edge. "What this is, is definitely one for the record books, that's what this is. That ship's captain, that Lieutenant Kell character, has sure copped it right up his fantail with that royal fuckup!"

"Yea, that may be..." his shipmate, Master Chief Sullivan said, relighting the foul-smelling end of a dead cigar. "...but it's those two birdbrain numbskull shit between the ears idiots who did all the urinating! And *they'll* be the ones receiving the evil eye at mast, and *they'll* be the ones gett'n their stripes ripped off, and *they'll* be the ones who will be confined to the ship for the next hundred years!"

"Probably. But I'll still tell 'ya what it is, Sully," Chief Davis continued, propping his feet up on a vacant chair. "What it is, is there ain't nobody's gonna remember the names of those two numbnuts who done that foul deed; but what everybody sure as hell *is* gonna remember is the name of that floating junkyard over *there*," and he nodded in the direction of the *USS Winchester County*.

And so it was, sometime during the darkness of that same night, another piece of poetic art was surreptitiously penned in that now familiar distinctive script, and signed by the mysterious *Zero*; this time onto the side of the port doghouse:

Climbing the flagship's brow so slow

> Pisco moaned he needed to go!
> Turbe cried, "Lets pee right here!"
> So they pissed out all their beer
> and signed the work Mike Angelo.

When this ode to the infamous Urinators was discovered the following morning, a large crowd quickly gathered at the scene, believing they were witness to a one of a kind masterpiece, that is until someone shouted there was another one on the starboard doghouse. The entire group then rushed to the other side as if they were looking for a clue in a treasure hunt. The ship took on an imperceptible list:

> Those idiots drank too many beers,
> and the admiral boxed our CO's ears.
> But they caught the perpetrators,
> those stupid dumb Urinators,
> and shipped them to a brig in Algiers!

CHAPTER 9

SAYONARA

"You guys are gonna love these steps," Jonah said as Underwood and Brickey followed him up the street, the 80 steep steps looming ahead of them, clinging to the side of the sheer wall going up toward the church. This time Jonah felt as if he was floating up the steps, the excitement building in him, and when he arrived at the top he felt not exhaustion, but exhilaration. Turning and looking behind him he could see Underwood and Brickey were breathing hard.

Underwood was sweating, and his face was flushed. "Damn, those steps are killers," he said gasping, leaning against a sign post. "Whoever built those things are masochists."

"What's that?" Brickey asked.

"A masochist?"

"Yea."

"People who build steps." Underwood answered.

"It sure is nice having a locker club where we can change into civvies," Jonah said, brushing dust off his boots. "And not have to worry about getting uniforms messed up."

"Yea, but that outfit of yours sure turned a lot of heads," Underwood said, pointing at Jonah's jeans, suede camel coat and black Stetson hat.

"Maybe, but my hoofs sure as hell ain't happy," Jonah looked down at his skinny-toed boots. "I just walked two miles in these things. Oww!" He lifted one of his feet off the pavement. "Now my feet are just 'bout baked; I haven't walked that far in boots since we left Little Creek!"

A densely packed crowd was gathering outside the church doors, people greeting one another, talking in quiet voices, and a young Japanese girl handed each of them a recital program as they politely nudged their way through the bustling throng. Walking up the center aisle Jonah was surprised to see how many pews were already occupied, with many more people than he imagined at this hour. Spying an empty space near the front of the church, he led them far up the aisle, and excused himself again and again as they awkwardly stepped over ankles and feet and packages in the narrow pew, eventually taking their seats in the vacant spot. The church was exactly as he had remembered it from two days ago; the tall Gothic walls and pointed arches rising up from the vault appeared even more impressive this time.

Brickey turned and gaped at the ceilings and stained-glass windows. "This is something else," he whispered, wide eyed in astonishment.

Jonah opened the program he had been holding, looking at the Hiragana characters explaining the recital's theme, the names of the choir master, the organist, the members of the choir and the selections of music; but he couldn't understand any of it. "I might as well be trying to read Greek," he quietly said to Underwood.

There was a subtle buzz of conversation throughout the church as the growing crowd, the majority of them Japanese, continued to come in, filling the main and side pews as well as the transept. A small elderly woman sitting to Jonah's right smiled, looked up at him and said something in Japanese; he smiled back and nodded. She put a finger to her lips and pointed to the sacristy on the right where a Japanese priest dressed in cassock and braided cincture was walking to the center of the chancel. The crowd immediately hushed into a respectful silence. Speaking with a microphone to the hundreds facing him, the priest welcomed those who had come to the church on this beautiful evening. He discussed the recital's program and introduced Sister Peter Mary, the choir master, and then Sister Aloysius, the visiting organist from Kagoshima. All of this was in Japanese, of course, and Jonah understood two words: 'Gregorian' and 'chant.' Then the priest repeated his address in a condensed, abbreviated English version. The two nuns bowed and took their places; Aloysius at the organ to the right, and Peter Mary at the center point of the chancel.

Peter Mary raised her hands, and on that signal the members of the choir walked in from both transepts, left and right, their lavender robes with fluted yokes and flowing sleeves seemingly levitating them across the chancel as they took their places on the steps in front of the alter; three rows of eleven each. The women had their hair pulled back and arranged in buns, exposing their brows, faces and necks, giving them a celestial, angelic look. Jonah watched them intently as they walked in, peering closely at the many faces, holding his breath, looking for Ashiko. And there she was, walking in from the left side, taking the same place during the practice of three days ago; the upper row, second from the left.

Peter Mary stood motionless before a music stand, silently appraising the choir, watching them steady into their places, waiting for the girls to find their composure. She looked at each face, making eye contact with every one of them, and all 33 pairs of eyes looked expectantly back at her. When she was satisfied they were ready, Peter Mary turned slightly to the right and with one outstretched hand, palm up, she nodded to Aloysius. The organist played a single note, a grave F minor, and then moved into the introductory passage, establishing the theme and tempo of the piece. Peter Mary followed the notes with her hands, orchestrating the organ's rise and fall, keeping the tempo's timing and pulse, climbing higher and higher, as if an audible spirit was stepping up a great staircase, going up and up to the clouds. Jonah recognized it, knew what it was immediately; he hadn't heard that musical phrase in years: *Stabot Mater Dolorosa*.

The organ paused, Peter Mary raised her arms, looked along the three rows of faces, and on her down-stroke the Soprano I group began. Three beats later the Soprano IIs joined in harmonizing, and then the Altos added the depth. A celestial melody, soaring and lilting, ascending and drifting, up and up, higher and higher, filled the church with a sound and reverberation that caused Jonah to catch his breath. He remembered his mother loved that piece; she had the LP record and played it over and over again. From his position in the pew he could clearly see the right side of Peter Mary's face, her lips distinctly mouthing the words, her eyes moving along the choir's many faces. Her expressive hands, one moment cupped, the next moment flat, conveyed the multiple signals for tempo and volume to each of the choir's three groups as the sleeves of her habit rose and floated through the air. Then, one girl, in the front row, petite and in her early twenties, sang a short, beautiful solo passage, and the entire choir joined in again. Jonah thought the girl looked familiar, but couldn't place where or when he might have seen her. She looked different, but he couldn't tell how. Then the realization hit him; yes, he knew who she was, standing there in her lavender robe, her hair pulled back in a bun; it was Natsume from the ryokan. He glanced to his left and noticed Brickey watching her intently.

In a pause between selections, Underwood leaned toward Jonah, and with his hand covering part of his mouth, whispered. "Did you know that 13th century Cistercian monks designed their church ceilings and walls to enhance the sound and modulation qualities of Gregorian Chant?"

Jonah's eyes opened wide and he looked back and whispered, "Woody, you're a walking encyclopedia."

The recital was extraordinary, the choir singing one piece after the other; chant, operatic arias, pop tunes, and more chant. The music went on and on and the audience sat spellbound as the church's walls and vaulted ceilings echoed the sound waves from one surface to another. It was a choir of angels, Jonah thought, he was mesmerized by it all, watching Peter Mary and the faces in the choir, but mostly he watched Ashiko. From where he sat in the pew, he could see her clearly in the top row, her expressive eyes following Peter Mary's hands, and occasionally he thought she might have looked at him. He never imagined that a choir could sound so majestic, or look so strikingly beautiful.

※

Ashiko concentrated intently, her black-rimmed glasses giving her a studious, professorial appearance as she drove the car up the road, the beams of the weak headlights barely penetrating into the murky fog. The small Datsun struggled uphill, its 1.0-litre motor barely pumping out 45 horsepower, and as the car crept around another sharp curve, straining to gain altitude, she downshifted into a lower gear. Jonah felt apprehension and helplessness sitting in the left front seat, the seat where he knew from experience it was he who should be driving and not Ashiko. He stared through the windshield as the wiper blades slashed across the glass from left to right, right to left, and he tried to conjure up some self-generated kinetic radar to see through the fog at the curves of the road ahead. But it was Ashiko and not Jonah, he realized, who knew the twists and turns of the mountain road, and it was Ashiko who steered the little car with practiced ease. After leaving the recital they had spent hours in the restaurant, laughing, talking, eating, drinking, communicating in 'Japanlish,' as Underwood called it, with Ashiko doing most of the translating and Natsume interjecting. Fortunately for Jonah the menu offered more than just sushi, and they all kidded him on his reluctance to try new things, especially the maguro which everyone agreed was the best in the world. And now, after all the beer and three very potent kinds of distilled Shochu, they were all more than a little tight.

In addition to Jonah and Ashiko up front, the three others were crammed into the back seat with Natsume pinned tightly between Underwood and Brickey. Even with the car lurching through the road's twists and turns Brickey was fast asleep, his mouth open, snoring softly, his head resting on Natsume's shoulder. She couldn't take her eyes off the young sailor, the pale gleam from the instrument panel providing just enough light for her to see the details of his flattop haircut and freckled face. Jonah glanced at her and noticed the look of fascination.

The car came around that familiar, tight, hairpin turn, suddenly ascending into clear sky above the fog, and Jonah knew they were almost at the ryokan, thankfully relieved to arrive in one piece. They pulled off the road onto the gravel parking area and Ashiko switched off the engine. The stillness of the night was filled with sounds from the river and fireflies danced through the air as the passengers stepped onto the gravel pathway, their shoes crunching on the uneven surface as they walked down the hill.

"I think I'm gonna call it a night," Underwood said as he entered the ryokan and took off his shoes and put on the uwagutsu. "Brickey, remember," he said pointing to the slippers. "No shoes here, only slippers." Brickey stood swaying, looking through glazed eyes at the brightly lit main room with it's tall, intricate ceiling, and the clock on the wall reading a few minutes past 1:00 AM.

"I'm done in," Brickey said somewhat unsteadily, putting on the slippers. "Good night," he said, and Jonah watched Natsume leading Underwood and the staggering Brickey down the hallway to their favorite room, number 6.

Ashiko stepped up to the level of the main floor and turned, looking down at Jonah. "Would you like to see the hotaru?" she smiled.

"The what?"

"Hotaru. The fireflies." Her head was tilted and her eyes wide.

Jonah felt that feeling of electricity, and he answered simply. "Yes."

He held the door open for her and they walked outside, sitting down on the edge of the deck with the sounds of rushing water and the mist rising from the onsen saturating their senses. At this altitude and this distance from city lights the night sky was a crystal clear inky-black, the stars in astonishing profusion, and a meteor streaked through the atmosphere.

"Nagareboshi!" she said, pointing at the shooting star. "If you see two more your wish will come true!"

The choir music and the restaurant's abundant food and alcohol had put him into an unusually calm, peaceful state. How quiet everything is here, he thought, away from the ship; no diesel smells, no screeching bosun's pipes, no banging hammers chipping paint, no hard-ass Sandman. Leaning back with his hands behind him on the deck, he breathed in the cool, fresh night air, listening to the cicadas' rising song, trilling, swelling, blending with the symphony of water falling over rocks and rushing downstream. He sensed something and turned. She was staring at him, her head tilted to the left and her expressive eyebrows arched in a longing, questioning curve. Her mouth was slightly open and her lips created a small 'O' of silent yearning. She reached over and took his hand. The electricity rushed through his chest again.

"Come with me," she whispered.

≪≫

"Reveille, guys," Jonah said, sliding open the thin wood-framed paper door. "It's 0600. Let's go."

Underwood rolled over and stared. The bags under his glassy eyes were dark and puffed. "Wha...what?" he gurgled.

"The cab will be here in 30 minutes. Let's go."

"Oh, God," Underwood said, sitting upright on his futon, rubbing his eyes, coughing. "What time did you say it was?"

"It was 0600. Now it's 0602. Time's a wast'n." He nudged Brickey's leg with his foot. "Come on Brickey. Reveille. Cab will be here in 25 minutes. Natsume is bringing coffee. Get it together."

"What are you doing up?" Underwood asked, noticing Jonah's futon hadn't been slept in.

"I never got to sleep," Jonah said, yawning and sitting in a chair. "I never came to bed." He rubbed his hands through his hair.

"Where were you?" Underwood asked, now wide-eyed.

"Not in this room," Jonah said with an irritatingly smug smile on his happy face.

"Oh, man. You didn't?"

"I ain't say'n nothing."

"I don't believe it. I just don't believe it." Underwood rapidly shook his head.

"Sorry to disappoint."

"Oh, God, what a night."

"Did you sleep okay?" Jonah asked.

"Yea, like a rock. I don't remember a thing. I just put my head down and *Wham*...I was gonzo."

"Hey, Brickey's alive," Jonah said looking at Brickey's face emerging from the folds of the blanket. "And his eyes are almost open." Brickey was looking at the ceiling through partially open eyelids, his mouth moving as if he was a cow chewing on his cud. "Whas'a matter Brickey? Bad taste in your mouth?"

"He's chewing off his hangover," Underwood said, stepping into his trousers.

"Well," and Jonah looked at his watch again. "We've got 20 minutes, so let's get a move on. Come'on Brickey. Up and at'em. The taxi will take us to the locker club. Let's move."

A knock on the door heralded Natsume, and Jonah slid the door open to reveal the diminutive girl in the hall holding a tray with a carafe of coffee; yogurt, bananas and mandarin oranges were arranged in colorful bowls next to the coffee cups. "Asa gohan," she said, her smile brightening the dim scene of tired, half-awake sailors. "Breakfast light," and she placed the tray on the low table. "We think you need today." She bent down and quickly rubbed Brickey's flattop with her knuckles then scurried out of the room, her giggle following her down the hallway.

"Ha, I think you've got an admirer there, Brickey," Underwood said, laughing.

"Umm, good," Jonah mumbled indistinctly, spooning yogurt into his mouth. "Maybe blackberry, or something similar."

"Man, you are full of vim and vigor today," Underwood said, pouring coffee into a cup. "If I didn't know better, I'd have thought you spent the night in the onsen...or something?"

Jonah choked on the yogurt, found his composure and grinned. "I'll never tell," he said as someone knocked on the door again.

"Taxi here," Natsume's voice came through the thin paper. "Taxi!"

"Okay, thank you," Underwood said at the closed door, and then turned toward Jonah. "Did we pay the bill?"

"Yea, I did last night. You guys can divvy up with me in the cab. Brickey, you ready?"

Brickey nodded, rubbed his face, took a banana from the tray and dropped it into his jacket pocket.

"Grab your gear," Jonah said picking up his overnight bag. "Vamonos!" and he slid the door open and started down the hallway.

⁂

The Cathedral's crew didn't think twice about the confusion of Japanese yardbirds or the ship's work parties crossing over the brow carrying countless crates and boxes of new equipment and spare parts; it had all become a regular occurrence since the ship arrived in Sasebo four days ago. But to an outsider, the hustle, the bustle, the mayhem, and the ear shattering noise from air hammers chipping decades of old paint into caustic clouds of dust blowing across the main deck might have brought to mind desert warfare during a violent sandstorm.

In the midst of this filth and disorder, a ten-foot square oasis of new haze gray paint had been neatly laid down on the deck near the foot of the brow, delineating the ship's inviolable quarterdeck, and a brand new, brightly varnished wooden pulpit desk, a product of the tender's carpenter shop, now sat proudly inside the perimeter. Standing alongside this new desk in his fresh whites, a .45 hanging from a guard belt on his hip, Petty Officer Wynchester manned the 0800-1200 quarterdeck watch, protecting the ship from potential enemies and unauthorized intruders. Seaman Poldolski, the watch messenger, was leaning against the desk, lazily picking red paint from his fingernails when the Officer Of the Deck appeared out of nowhere and walked up to them.

"Good morning, Mister Sanders," Poldolski said, rapidly straightening himself upright.

Sanders didn't reply, but circled around them, closely inspecting their twice-shaved faces and their uniforms, making sure the whites were white, the creases creased, the spit shined shoes shined, and their white hats were squared on their heads.

Sanders looked at Poldolski. "Your guard belt is dirty," he said. "Get a clean one. Now."

"Yes, sir." Poldolski's mouth turned down and he ran to the armory.

"Well, Wynchester," Sanders said, his hawk-shaped face watching a group of Japanese yard workers crossing the brow. "I suppose you've been enjoying the bars and fleshpots of Sasebo?"

Jonah's alarm system went to high alert. Be careful how you answer this, he thought. "Just some sukiyaki at the EM Club, sir."

"Really?" Sanders asked, looking at Jonah in disbelief.

"Yes, sir. Just a couple of sukiyaki dinners, and some sushi."

"Humph," Sanders said, looking at him suspiciously. "Well, I think I'll be going out on the town. You heard of any good places? Any interesting sights? Restaurants? Bars? Onsens?"

There's no way I'm going to answer that, Jonah thought. "Uh, no sir, nothing interesting."

Sanders stared at him for a moment as Poldolski returned with a clean, white guard belt. "Wynchester, report to me when you're off watch," Sanders said and he walked away.

"Man, that guy is one ugly hardass; I bet they never put his face on a Wheaties box!" Poldolski whispered, watching Sanders walk forward along the main deck.

"You ain't tell'n me nothing I don't already know." Jonah cocked his hat down to his right eyebrow.

"These are empty." Poldolski peered into his coffee mug, a film of dark scum sitting in the bottom.

Jonah turned and looked into the mug. "Yea, that's serious. We probably need refills."

"It's definitely indicated," Poldolski agreed.

"Well, go ahead," Jonah said. "But don't get lost. Get back her pronto." Poldolski went quickly aft with the empty mugs, coming to an abrupt halt at the galley door as Underwood came through carrying a typewriter.

"What you got there?" Jonah asked as Underwood approached the quarterdeck.

"This damn thing just packed up on me," Underwood said. "The space bar connection is broken. I've been banging on it for 11,000 miles, and it finally died."

"Well, it is an Underwood..."

"Piece of shit," Underwood repeated, ignoring Jonah's comment. "I gotta get over to the tender and get it fixed. I'm hoping they can do it while I wait, or maybe they've got a spare I can use in the meantime, because I've got a shitload of work to get done. If not, the XO is gonna go berserk."

"Have you recovered from last night?"

"Just about. But I'll tell ya one thing," Underwood said, repositioning the heavy typewriter in his arms.

"What's that?"

"Beer and Shochu don't mix."

"Thanks for the tip."

"How's Brickey doing?"

"He's hung over," Jonah said, adjusting the guard belt around his waist. "He looks like hell, but he's alive. I've got him painting the inside of the #2 gun tub."

"That'll keep him busy. But how you doing? You don't look so lively."

"I'm tired. No sleep. I think I'll skip lunch and get a couple of winks in..." and he looked at his watch. "...in about three hours. And since we've got the duty tonight, I'm gonna crash early."

"You going back to the ryokan tomorrow?"

"You bet. Ashiko has invited us on a picnic," Jonah said.

"A picnic?"

"As soon as work knocks off tomorrow I'm running to the locker club to change. You and Brickey are invited too. She and Natsume are gonna pick us up at 1630 and we're going to some island for a picnic."

"Are you sure?" Underwood asked.

Jonah nodded. "And then back to the ryokan."

"Oh, man, but I've got a shitload of stuff to get done for the XO." Underwood said.

"Well, then, meet us at the ryokan afterward."

"Okay, that'll work. I could probably be there by 2000."

"Perfect."

"I think Brickey and Natsume have developed a little attraction."

"Little? Ha!" Jonah said. "The way they were talking and looking at each other in the restaurant last night, it seemed more than just a little! She likes his haircut."

"That's funny," Underwood said. "I guess all I have to do is get a flattop and women will find me irresistible."

"YAJDEK."

Underwood laughed and started across the brow. A Japanese yard worker stood aside, allowing the tall yeoman carrying the heavy typewriter to come across first.

"Here's your coffee," Poldolski said, returning with two steaming mugs of coffee.

"Oh, man, that's awful!" Jonah grimaced from the taste of burned coffee.

"At least it's hot." Poldolski blew into the mug.

"Dorsey must'a brewed this last week! God, the stuff that comes out of that galley is ..."

"Uh, oh...!" Poldolski pointed toward the brow.

Jonah turned and looked in the direction of Poldolski's pointing finger, toward the head of the brow where a tall, thin ensign was standing at attention, saluting the quarterdeck; his immaculate khakis, cap and sparkling shoes doing little to improve the look of his strange, pale face.

"Request permission to come aboard!" the lean officer nervously bleated, holding his arm in such a rigid salute his hand was vibrating against the edge of his cap.

Jonah had never seen anyone standing at such a stiff, fixed attitude of attention before. "Permission granted," he said frowning, and returned the salute in a slow, abbreviated motion.

The ensign stepped onto the gray painted quarterdeck and stiffly saluted again. "Ensign Spratt reporting aboard for duty...with orders...to the Commanding Officer...*USS Winchester County*. SIR!"

This guy is nuts, Jonah thought. Where do they get these people? Out of comic books? He returned the salute for the second time, observing the ensign's narrow squinting eyes and the small mouth over a double chin. Jonah held out his hand for the envelope containing the ensign's orders and personnel file.

"Ensign John Frederick Spratt. S-P-R-A-T-T!" he nervously repeated, continuing to stand at attention, handing the envelope to Jonah.

"Yes, sir. Thank you, sir," Jonah said writing the name in the log book and glancing up at the tense officer. Out of the corner of his eye Jonah noticed Poldolski staring at the Spratt with a *'What The Hell??!!'* expression.

"Reporting aboard, sir!" Spratt said again.

"Yes, sir, I got it, sir," Jonah said calmly, and for the first time recognized the Supply Corps 'Oakleaf' insignia pinned on the ensign's left collar. "We've got you logged in, sir. And Poldolski here can lead you to the XO's stateroom."

"The XO's stateroom?"

"Yes, sir."

"Uh...am I rooming with the XO?"

"Probably not, sir. Are those two bags all you got, sir?" Jonah pointed to the seabag and suitcase sitting at the foot of the brow.

Spratt turned around and gasped. "Two bags? Oh, God!" His face turned red. "Oh, no! I'm missing a bag! One of my bags is missing!" He looked around him as if the missing bag might materialize. "I must have left it in the taxi!"

"Don't worry about it, sir. We'll report it. I'm sure someone will retrieve it for you. Would you like Seaman Poldolski to lead you to the XO's stateroom now?"

"What about my bags?"

"We'll get the stewards to bring them in for you, sir."

"The stewards?"

"Yes, sir."

"Are you sure?"

"Oh, yes, sir, I'm sure. Our stewards are very efficient."

"Oh, God!" and he looked around, noticing for the first time all the activity around him. "What about my missing bag?"

"You just tell the stewards, sir. They'll write out a request chit and then put out an APB."

"A what?"

"Don't worry, sir, that's just Navy lingo. The stewards' will take care of it. Anyway, you better have these with you, sir," Jonah said handing the big envelope back to the ensign. "Mister Crane might want to take a look at 'em."

"Mister Crane?"

"Yes, sir. He's the XO."

"Oh. Okay, if you're sure," Spratt said, his feeble red face looking as if it might implode.

"Yes, sir, I'm sure." Jonah turned toward Poldolski. "Excuse me; Seaman Poldolski?"

"Huh?" Poldolski's eyes narrowed in suspicion at Jonah's suddenly unexpected formal tone.

"If you have a moment, Seaman Poldolski, would you please escort Ensign Spratt to the Executive Officer's mansion...er, stateroom?"

Poldolski suddenly realized what Jonah was doing. "Absolutely, sir. It would be my pleasure," he said, trying to contain his grin, playing his part in the charade. Poldolski turned toward the ensign and bowed, motioning with his hand, mimicking a maitre d' in a restaurant. "Dis way to da XO's stateroom, sir."

"Oh, God!" Spratt said as he followed Poldolski along the main deck, walking around wooden crates and stepping over air hoses. "This is my first ship, you know."

"Is it, sir?" Poldolski said. "I would'a never guessed." Poldolski smiled and walked aft, stepping through the doorway, leading Spratt into officer's country. "I bet O'Toole is sure gonna be glad to see you, sir!"

"O'Toole?"

"Yes, sir. He's the 1st class storekeeper. And I bet, that with an officer of your experience, his job is gonna get a whole lot easier, real soon."

"Gosh, I was hoping he might be able to help me learn what I'm supposed to do!" Spratt said.

"I'm sure that won't be the case, sir. Okay, here we are," Poldolski said, stopping outside the door to the XO's stateroom. Poldolski pointed to the closed door in the brightly lit, green passageway.

"In there?" Spratt asked with a look of panic.

"Yes, sir. In there."

"What should I do?"

"Maybe try knocking, sir?"

"Knocking?"

"Yes, sir. And while you're in there with the XO, I'll get one of the stewards to bring your gear in."

"My gear?"

"Yes, sir. Your bags."

"Oh, yes. Thank you."

"No problem, sir," and Poldolski quickly vanished around the corner as Spratt raised his shaking hand up to the door.

⁂

Natsume lead them up the steep, narrow trail with little two-year-old Katsuko riding on her shoulders. Brickey followed close behind carry a bulging canvas bag. Next came Ashiko carrying a folded blanket, and Jonah brought up the rear, struggling with a large split-bamboo basket, going forever upward, stepping over wet rocks and around slippery tree roots. He had no idea what was in the basket, but it must weigh 20 pounds, he thought. The afternoon sun was warm and the exertion from climbing was making him warmer still. His jeans and long sleeve shirt did nothing to relieve the heat building up in him. Brickey and Natsume were somewhere out of sight ahead, and then Ashiko went around a bend in the trail and disappeared. When Jonah finally saw her again, she was waiting for him, sitting on a boulder, smiling with her eyebrows arched in that unique look, communicating a question, as if she was saying 'where have you been, Jonah? and what took you so long?' She grinned and laughed and started off again.

God, when is this gonna stop, he thought, continuing up and up. The black Stetson was keeping the sun off his head, but he felt he was drowning in sweat. He stopped and took off the hat, wiped his eyes with his shirt sleeve, and looked up the trail. There she was again, looking down at him, grinning. Yea, I know I'm slow, he thought. You've probably climbed this damn trail a hundred times before, and you're wearing those cute little hiking boots while I've got on these damn narrow-toed shit-kickers.

"Come on Jonah," she cried. "Don't be so slow!" and she laughed again.

He gritted his teeth and continued upward, keeping his head down, concentrating on the trail directly in front of him, struggling upward, losing his balance, grabbing at tree limbs, panting, sweating, swearing, determined not to look up again, not to look up at her grinning face. I'm gonna get up there, he thought, I'm gonna get up there, pass her on this damn trail, and beat her to wherever the hell we're going. He stepped upward, climbing, pushing himself, gasping for breath, trying to hold on to the heavy, awkward basket. The trail started to became less steep, and suddenly he found himself on level ground, bent over, his hands on his knees, gasping for breath, sweating, shaking inside, looking down at her boots. He looked up to her pants legs, then to her shirt and her face. She was silently and uncontrollably giggling, her hands covering her mouth, her stomach shaking.

"Oh, you look funny," she said between deep breaths.

And then he saw what was around them. Brickey and Natsume were looking out from the summit at sky, islands and water. From this perspective, he thought, they must be several hundred feet above sea level. An incredible view! They were on the top of a promontory and he turned around. Everywhere he looked it was sea and sky and islands; tiny islands, small islands, large islands everywhere, and with mountains in the distant background. And then he saw Ashiko's face, her exquisite face with those huge eyes, and that raven hair waving in the breeze. She was smiling that contagious smile, and he couldn't help himself; the difficult trail was below them, the exertion was past. Her face made him melt inside and he started smiling with her, uncontrollably smiling.

"My God, what a view," he said, wiping the sweat from his eyes and beginning to regain his breath.

"You like it?" she asked.

"Like it? It's incredible!"

"Worth the climb?"

"I'll say. It's beautiful. But, boy, am I ever parched."

"Parched?"

"Yea. Parched. You know, dry? Thirsty? Parched."

"Oh, yes, thirsty. Parched, a new word. I will fix that." She unfolded the tartan blanket and took one edge in her hands, snapping it high into the air, up and up, and it floated down onto the ground. Natsume spread another blanket on the ground a few feet away. "Give me the basket, please," Ashiko asked and Jonah set the beautifully made, heavily laden basket down on the blanket. "This will fix your thirst," she said opening the basket and drawing out a large thermos bottle. "To wet the whistle, as you cowboys say," she laughed, pouring liquid into a cup.

Jonah couldn't believe it. "A thermos bottle?" he said. "A gallon thermos bottle? I've just carried a gallon thermos, along with what else I don't know, from the parking area, all the way up a steep, narrow trail, over rocks and roots?" She looked at him as if she wasn't sure if he was angry or not. "This reminds me of something," he said, thinking of the time he carried that heavy pack when he and Jack were hunting in the high country.

"Reminds you?" she asked.

"I'll tell you later."

"Okay. But now you have my curiosity." She was kneeling on the blanket, removing other mysterious items from the basket.

"Umm, that's good," he said, swallowing the sweet liquid from the cup. "Very good."

"You like?"

"Yes, it's delicious. What is it?"

"Mugicha...iced barley water. I made today."

"Mu...what?"

"Mu-gi-cha...pronounce the 'G' as if it was a soft 'N.'"

"Mugicha," he said.

"Yes, good. You are learning," she said, removing several small, lacquered bamboo boxes from the basket. "We also have karaage; where you come from you cowboys probably call it *fryied chikin*," and she drew out the vowels, and she let loose with that full-throated laugh. Jonah thought her laugh was the most bewitching thing. "We also have tamagoyaki; these are small sweet omelets," she said removing the lid and placing the container on the blanket next to the karaage. "And korokke; you recognize them as potatoes. See? And inarizushi, which is rice in tofu. You say, umm, let me think. Yes, pouches. Rice in tofu pouches."

"It all looks delicious," he was salivating, looking at all the food, and suddenly he realized he was starved.

"And, for the meindisshu..." She removed small ceramic cups from a padded box and looked up at him with her head tilted, a sly look on her face. Then she held up a bottle. "Sake!" she said.

Jonah stared at the bottle with a look of shock. "You are amazing," he said shaking his head.

"Ha ha, what's even more amazing... is that you carried it all the way from the parking area!" and she laughed again.

"Yea, Jonah Wynchester, your pack horse," and he sat down on the blanket and removed his boots. "Ooh," he said kneading his toes through the socks. "That's better."

"Nurse Ashiko has the perfect medicine," she handed Jonah the cups and popped the cork on the bottle. "This is Junmai-shu..." she said pouring the sake into the cups. "...special sake made from pure koji rice." She corked the bottle and took one of the cups from Jonah. "Kanpai," she said, holding her cup.

"Kanpai," Jonah echoed and took a sip. "Hmm, that's nice. Very nice."

Natsume and Brickey, each holding one of little Katsuko's hands, started walking along the ridge trail, leaving Jonah and Ashiko in solitude.

"So, tell me, Jonah," Ashiko said, taking a bite from the karaage. "Tell me about Idaho, and about the navy; why are you in the navy?"

He looked up from the box of korokke and studied her face. Her eyes showed she was curious, he could see that, but he hated it when women asked him such questions. He could tell she was sincerely interested, but he wondered how much to reveal, how much of himself to expose to this Japanese girl, a girl that he was longing for, a girl with such an enchanting face and powerful magnetism of personality that he had utterly fallen under her spell. You've only known her six days, he thought, and now you're ready to bleed your soul out to her? Why would you do that? You may never see her again after you leave in a few days. You may never get this way again. Why expose yourself? Ignoring all common sense, he took a breath and dove straight in, head first, into the deep end of his memories, opening his past to a girl he felt a powerful thirst and hunger for. They sat on the blanket, only seeing each other and not the view around them; the islands, the sea, the sky, all disappeared. The only thing left was each other. And they ate and they talked and they drank and talked some more, and through the process she learned all about him: about the ranch, the big white house and the barn down the long dusty road, about his alcoholic father and loving mother. She listened intently as he described how his grandfather Jack had nurtured him, taught him everything, including philosophy and the finer points of life. And her face showed pain and anguish when he told her about the deaths of his two brothers, and then how his father had died, crushed under that old farm tractor. He described the excitement racing through him the morning he drove the old rusty pick-up truck away from the ranch, all the way down that narrow road to Boise, to enlist in the navy, a life he thought would be filled with excitement, but never imagined would also include pain and regret. He described the days at sea, the hours of boredom and moments of chaos and exhilaration, the magnificence of sunrise and sunset with unlimited horizons, revealed the good times and the bad, nodded in admiration about the great ships he had been aboard, and laughed and shook his head when relating the bad ones, including the ancient Cathedral. He shared his gratitude for the strong, lasting friendships he had made over the years, praising Underwood as a prime example. And he told her about Lieutenant Junior Grade Sanders, described his reptilian face and his devious nature, how he blamed others for the department's shortcomings, and related the scene of the first day he encountered the gunnery officer in Little Creek.

Their quiet spell was broken at the sound of Natsume and Brickey returning from their stroll, little Katsuko prancing between them, and the tiny little girl ran ahead and into the arms of her aunt Ashiko. Brickey picked-up the two-year-old and held her high in the air, her little squeaky voice bubbling and shrieking, laughing and giggling. He lowered her gently to the blanket and sat down next to her and she jumped onto him and grabbed his arms, holding him tight, not wanting to let go, and Brickey gently folded her into his embrace. Natsume stood to the side, watching the freckle faced, happy-go-lucky, effervescent sailor loving her child. Her eyes grew misty and a look of sweet, undisguised joy started spreading across her face.

※ ※

As the Cathedral's remaining time in Sasebo grew steadily shorter, the pace of work quickened into a chaotic tempo; noise, confusion, disruption, repairs and paint chipping completely enveloped the ship. Charlie Crane, with his ever-present Damocles sword hanging above everyone, continually pushed, prodded and threatened the crew with the loss of their liberty if the many jobs remaining were not completed by the final hour of the final afternoon alongside the tender.

Throughout this bedlam the Japanese shipyard workers somehow performed a long list of miracles, including the priority work so badly needed in the ship's engine room. Chief Beckers, who over the years had gained a keen appreciation and a seasoned eye for the abilities of different shipyards, was amazed at the efficiency and professionalism of the Japanese. For days he watched as teams of shipyard workers smoothly reassembled the newly aligned and lapped reduction gears, rebuilt the antiquated evaporators, and installed the renovated superchargers back onto the two 900 horsepower V-12 diesels. On the other side of the bulkhead, deep in the generator room, the yard workers reinstalled the rebuilt ballast tank valves with their renewed packing, gates and freshly greased hand-wheel stems.

In the galley, Dorsey witnessed the arrival of his new ice maker, a large capacity, double door, shiny stainless steel model, guaranteed, according to the Japanese operating manual, to produce at least one ton of ice per day. A sparkling brass plate affixed to its side proudly proclaimed *"Yoshida Tractor Company. Nagoya, Japan."* "It will live long," the female Japanese yard worker had said when she finished installing the new machine. "Like good Japanese tractor," and she patted the side of the big ice maker with an affectionate gesture.

"Well, dats a good thing," Dorsey commented with his head deep inside the collector bin.

"Until ship become *kamisori no ha,*" she added with a knowing look.

"Huh?" Dorsey said pulling his head out of the bin. "Until the ship becomes wha...?"

"Razor blades!" She broke out laughing, holding her stomach through her yellow coverall. She picked up her tool bag and ambled away, still laughing, her yellow hard hat tilted over to one side of her head.

The long awaited priority parts for the radio shack also arrived, allowing The Volt to breathe a sigh of relief for the first time since the ship departed Little Creek. The bespectacled radioman stood grinning from ear to ear as if it was Christmas morning, admiring the dozens of wooden crates overflowing with excelsior packing material protecting the many fragile rectifier tubes, amplifiers, oscillator crystals and detectors, all stacked along the deck in neat rows.

To Biagotti's great delight, the shipyard also rebuilt the Gray Marine engines on his two Papa Boats; those 36-foot Landing Craft Vehicle-Personnel boats. Their 225-horsepower, six-cylinder engines had seen thousands of hours of hard use over the past 20 years, and were constantly giving the enginemen severe fits attempting to deal with the problems of the ancient, recalcitrant diesels. Now the engines had new sleeves, liners, piston rings, wrist pins, gaskets, and refurbished rods and main bearings, and with a new coat of paint, they looked almost brand new.

"De're now run'n smooth as silk; even better den dey did 20 yea's ago!" Biagotti proclaimed, wallowing in new-found glory, admiring the two boats tied up alongside the ship's bow ramp. "At least more den 20 years ago!"

Mills, who was standing in the #2 boat closely examining the engine, turned and stared back at the big bosun. "Biagotti?" he said with a mistrustful look. "How could you know? How could you possibly know how those engines were running back in 1944?" Back then you were just a fat, greasy, ugly, pimple faced, snot-nosed, smelly Italian little kid, he thought of adding, that is if the screeching bosun's pipe signaling the crew's supper hadn't stopped him.

※

It was the last night, the last night in Sasebo, and it brought a mixture of sadness, expectation and fear as Jonah, Underwood and Brickey took a cab up the now familiar route, up the steep, narrow road, around the twists and turns they had become so accustomed to. Climbing higher and higher they finally came to the ryokan, the tranquil sanctuary far from the ship's constant chaos, diesel smells, and screeching bosun pipes. Now Jonah was back in the serenity of the fir and willow trees, among the pulsating sounds of falling water, the soothing mist of the onsen, and with the young Japanese woman he had come to love in a way he had never experienced before. He had become addicted to her; to her face, her delicate touch, her contagious laugh and her loving nature, and his anticipation of being with her again grew with every step he took down the gravel pathway.

Ashiko greeted him at the door in her demure way, her eyebrows up in a knowing look, communicating her pleasure at seeing him again. And Natsume, suddenly laughing when she spied Brickey, quickly walked up to him and spoke in a hushed tone. She walked them down the hall to their room where they changed into their yukatas, stored their uniforms and overnight bags in the familiar closet and then went to the bar. Ashiko served them as usual, having learned their favorite drinks; Underwood's double shot of rum, Brickey's rum and cola, and Jonah's Ashi beer. It was a weekday night and the ryokan was unusually vacant, free of other guests, and Jonah and Ashiko slipped away from the others and walked outside, down the pathway, following the edge of the undulating, rushing stream, talking and feeling the electricity passing between them. She looked up at him, at the gunmetal eyes, at the scar crossing his left cheekbone, and a look of sadness and bewilderment grew across her face.

"Are you okay?" he asked, sitting down on the bench of the tea house.

"I am sad," she said, "So very sad that you leave tomorrow, sad that I may not see you again." She gulped in a deep breath. "When I look back on these days, these few days we have had together, they now seem so short, so very short. I need to be with you, every day now, but I can't." The moisture flooding in her eyes suddenly overflowed and the tears ran down her cheeks. "You are leaving, and I am afraid you may never return."

He pulled her to him, held her close for a long time, her face on his chest, and being unable to express the thoughts flowing through his mind, he simply said, "Yes, I feel exactly the same."

"You do?" she asked, sitting up straight, her eyebrows arched, her lips slightly parted.

"Yes, but I will be back," and he turned, looked straight into her eyes and wiped the tears from her cheeks. "I promise. Whatever happens, wherever my ship goes, I'll be back. Maybe not for another month, or two, but I'll come back. Even if I have to find a way to get off the ship. I'll come back."

"You need to write me," she said. "You need to send your letters to me here at the ryokan. And I will do the same. You must give me your address, where I can write you. I need to stay connected with you."

"I will. I'll give you my address, and your mail will get to me wherever the ship is."

"Are you sure? How does my letter arrive at the ship when the ship is always moving?"

"Your letter will go to a fleet post office, in San Francisco, and they'll forward it to wherever the ship is. They'll know our schedule."

She nodded with a perplexed expression, trying to understand the incongruity of mailing a letter from Japan to San Francisco, where it would then be sent right back across the Pacific to a ship somewhere in the South China Sea; a round trip of over 10,000 miles. Whereas sending it directly south would be less than 1,800. "I think I understand," she said. "But I don't really understand," and she smiled and laughed; Jonah watched her beginning to bounce back to her usual happier self. "I think we should go back," she said, standing up. "My mother would not be pleased that I was away so long."

They walked back up the path, going uphill as the stream rushed down alongside them. They went in silence, in single file, listening to the sounds of the water, falling, gurgling.

"I think I'll pay a visit to the onsen," he said as they went through the door into the bar.

"Yes, I will see you afterward," and her unique smile that seemed to always express such anticipation and joy was back.

The bath and the onsen had become a ritual, it was now so much a part of his time at the ryokan, that he looked forward to it almost as much as he did being with Ashiko. Underwood and Brickey were already there, soaking up to their necks in the the hot milky pool. The 98-degree water, full of the earth's minerals, soothed his aching muscles and soul as nothing ever had or probably ever would he thought. He luxuriated in the pool, watching the steam float up into the trees, listening to the melody of water rushing downstream below him. His sharp-edged, turbulent thoughts of the ship and the Sandman slowly floated away in the rising mist.

He put on his yukata, making sure to fold it correctly, smiling as he thought of Natsume's instructions during their first visit, and with a happy spring to his step walked down the hallway, through the great room and into the bar with its familiar tables and chairs, where he came to a sudden stop. A rush of fiery heat ran from his gut into his chest and then into his neck and face. His whole body stiffened and his muscles retracted. There was Ashiko, at the bar, talking with a man wearing a Hawaiian shirt. The man was sitting on one of the bar stools, his back to Jonah, and Ashiko was smiling, giggling, brushing the hair from her eyes as she served the man a drink. Jonah knew from the man's back, from the shoulders, from the back of his head, knew exactly who it was. He walked up to the bar, sat down on a stool across from Ashiko, and looked square into the man's face. "Evening, Mister Sanders," he said.

◈

Sanders' head jerked up and he swiveled around in the bar stool. He was startled at Jonah's sudden appearance. "Wynchester?" the gunnery officer said, astonished. "What the hell are *you* doing here?"

Jonah sat unmoving, unflinching, staring at Sanders' peculiar, crooked face. "Same as you, Mister Sanders," he said coldly. "Just the same as you. Enjoying a little quiet time during our last night in Japan."

Jonah glanced at Ashiko. At the mention of the name "Sanders" her face had a flash of realization on it, as if she suddenly knew who this man in the Hawaiian shirt was. It was the Janus-faced man, the one Jonah had described in such detail when they were on their picnic two days ago; it was one in the same. And she saw Jonah's severe body language, his alert posture and the aggression in his eyes. She watched the hot red flush on his neck going up to his ears, and saw the piercing, unguarded hate across his face. His body was wound up tight as a spring and looked as if he was about to throw a punch at Sanders. She reflexively took a step away from the bar; "Sir, what may I get you?" she asked Jonah, trying to defuse the tension, but her voice cracked with anxiety.

Jonah turned and looked at her, confused and surprised with her strange question, but then it dawned on him: she was trying to calm him down; she understood what was happening and she was trying to change the subject and calm him down. "I'll have an Asahi," he said and turned and looked back at Sanders.

"So, Wynchester," Sanders said, his head cocked to one side, a sarcastic look on his face. "You told me you've been to the EM club, and had some sukiyaki and some sushi, but you haven't been anywhere else? You haven't even been to an onsen? Well, well, that's interesting. Really interesting."

Jonah felt the pressure rapidly building inside him. Ashiko saw his eyes dilating. He could feel himself on the edge of losing control, and a raw primeval sensation urged him to go even further. "It's none of your business," Jonah responded without thinking.

"Oh, so is that the way you want to talk to your superior officer?" Sanders calmly took a sip of his drink.

"Superior officer, my..."

"JONAH!" a loud voice called out and Jonah and Sanders both turned to see Underwood with a look of intense alarm and determination walking quickly through the doorway.

"Underwood?" Sanders said in surprise.

"Hello, Mister Sanders," Underwood said walking up to the bar and positioning himself between Sanders and Jonah. "It's nice to see you, sir." Underwood immediately recognized what was happening and he was going to try to prevent the imminent explosion. "Ma'am?" he said turning to Ashiko. "Could I please have a glass of water?"

"So, Underwood..." Sanders said. "...you're here too?" he asked, his strange eyes looking sideways at Underwood. "Well, well, the plot thickens, doesn't it? Now I know where you went every time I saw you leave the ship. How interesting. Yes, this is very interesting."

Underwood saw Jonah's grim mouth and body language, saw the volcano building inside his friend, knew the situation was going to get out of hand any second. "Ha ha," Underwood laughed, holding the glass of water. "Yes, sir. We've sure had a busy 10 days alongside the tender, haven't we?" he smiled, trying to disarm Sanders and keep Jonah quiet and in his corner. "Yes, sir, all that work, and now a pleasant evening just seeing the sites. We're pretty lucky, we just stumbled onto this place."

Sanders wasn't looking at Underwood. He didn't even seem to be hearing Underwood. Instead he was looking straight at Jonah. And Jonah was staring back at Sanders.

"Well, Mister Sanders, it's been real nice seeing you," Underwood said in a pleasant, conversational tone, putting his glass down on the bar, and he looked at his watch and tapped it with his finger. "But we've got to get going now. We've got a few other places we want to see before getting back to the ship. Right Jonah?" and he turned, looked at Jonah and motioned with his head toward the door just as Brickey came into the room. Jonah glanced at Underwood and then looked back at Sanders.

"Come on, Jonah," Underwood said trying to urge him to move off the bar stool. "We gotta go," and he reached out and gently grabbed Jonah's shoulder. Jonah violently yanked his arm away from Underwood and then stood, and slowly moved away from the bar, never taking his eyes off Sanders. "Come on, man, the cab will be here any minute..." Underwood said, reinforcing the urgency to go. "...we gotta get our stuff together."

Not understanding what was happening or what Underwood was trying to do, Brickey said, "Are we leaving already?"

"Let's go, Jonah," Underwood repeated. "You too Brickey, get your stuff, we gotta go." Jonah turned and started walking away from the bar and Underwood followed a few paces behind him.

"Have a nice evening," Sanders sneered and laughed. "I think I'll just sit here and enjoy looking at this cute Japanese bar girl."

Jonah spun around, rage glaring from his face, and he started fast walking back toward Sanders. Underwood lunged at Jonah and grabbed him in a bear-hug, the tall yeoman's arms completely engulfing the gunner.

"Brickey!" Underwood yelled, struggling with Jonah, and Brickey, finally understanding what was happening, immediately grabbed Jonah from behind. Ashiko screamed and her hands went to her face as Underwood and Brickey marched Jonah across the room and out the door to the deck.

"Let me go, dammit!" Jonah yelled.

"You're not doing this again, Jonah!" Underwood hissed inches from Jonah's face, still holding him in the bear-hug as they stood on the deck. "You're not doing it again, man!"

"Let me go!" Jonah yelled even louder, struggling against the other two.

"We might let you go Jonah, but if we do, you're not going back in there!" Underwood said in a low growl, holding tight to Jonah from the front as Brickey held him from the back.

"Let me go!" Jonah yelled again.

"Tell me you're not going back in there!" Underwood repeated. "Because if you go back in there, you damn well know what's gonna happen! You'll smash that guy's face and then you'll wind up with a fucken court martial!"

"That sonov'a'bitch!"

"Don't do it, Jonah!"

"I'll smash the fucker!"

"Jonah! If you hit him, they'll bust you all the way to Seaman Recruit! It'll be a whole lot worse than it was in Naples!"

"I'll kill him!"

"They'll send you to Portsmouth, Jonah! Portsmouth Prison, man!"

Jonah struggled, trying to break free, but he was tightly pinned inside Underwood's and Brickey's arms.

"And those fucken Marines in that prison?" Underwood continued. "Those fucken Marines will beat the shit out'a you, Jonah! They'll beat the shit out'a you with their night sticks! You want that! You want to go to Portsmouth Prison?" You want'a stand bare-ass naked in front of a bunch of jarheads? For chrissake man, get a grip! That asshole isn't worth it!"

Just then Ashiko came running through the doorway with rivulets of tears on her face, and she looked back, afraid that Sanders might be following her; he wasn't, he was still sitting at the bar, intently watching them.

She put her arms around Jonah and held him close, her face touching his, and she looked straight into the gunmetal eyes and whispered: "I ...about ...love ...Jonah. You ...most ...I've ever ..." Underwood couldn't understand all that she whispered, but he heard some of it. "Please, Jonah ...yourself ...please ...down. Woody is ...don't ...our ...a nice. Let's make ...night ...just ...us." Underwood felt the muscles in Jonah's arms slowly beginning to relax.

Jonah took a deep breath and his body seemed to deflate, his rigid stance slackening. "Let me down," he said quietly. "Let me sit on the deck." They carefully eased their grip, lowered him to the deck, and Ashiko knelt down next to him, engulfing him in her arms, rocking him slowly in a soft embrace. She held him, swaying gently, whispering to him.

Underwood looked through the windows, toward the bar, and saw Sanders still sitting there, looking intently back at them with his icy reptilian eyes and a mean looking, repulsive smugness on his face. Underwood turned toward Jonah and Ashiko in their long embrace, and when he looked back through the windows again, Sanders was walking out the door of the ryokan.

❧❧

They waited on Kotohira point, looking up the channel through the thick murky drizzle where they expected the ship to come from, watching, intently watching and waiting. Ashiko had told him she would be there, she and Natsume, waiting on the promontory where the two points of land came close to the channel, almost pinching it. And then they saw the ship, steaming slowly into view through the low banks of cloud and fog, finally heading toward them with an orange and white pilot boat following close behind. Wearing a blue rain slicker, Ashiko held a small pair of birding binoculars to her eyes, carefully scanning along the ship's deck, looking, searching for the faces she knew they must see again one more time. Her anticipation was building and the tension was causing her to shake inside. She could feel the cold mist coming down on the slicker and the heat building in her chest and along her neck and shoulders. Where is he? Where are they? The ship came closer and closer and reached the narrows opposite them, and there they were, the small almost indiscernible figures standing in the aft gun tub, just where Jonah had said they would be, waving their white hats, Jonah and Brickey waving at the two women standing next to the small cream-colored Datsun parked on the point. They were barely close enough to recognize each other, but all four of them waved and waved, and as the LST steamed past it started making its next turn in the winding channel, turning and turning, steaming away from them now, the gray truncated stern diminishing in size, slowly growing smaller and smaller until the ship disappeared back into the murk.

CHAPTER 10

COVENANT

"Brickey, tell me something," Jonah said, looking down at the strange tortoiseshell cat sitting on the armory workbench. "What you gonna call that thing?" The cat, with its yellow almost green splotches mixed into black, sat there with its face full of knowing superiority as the workbench vibrated from the propeller shafts and screws pushing the ship through the East China Sea. The cat's back was curved into a high arch and its head was leaning into Brickey's hand as he petted it behind the ears; its tail would have been pointing and vibrating straight in the air, that is if it had a tail, rather than a short, stubby protuberance with a tufted end.

"Neko," Brickey answered looking up toward Jonah.

"Who?"

"Neko, N-E-K-O," Brickey repeated. "It means 'cat' in Japanese. That's what Natsume told me."

"Neko. Well, Natsume would know, that's for sure. What you gonna feed it?"

"I bought some cat food at the shotengai, the shopping arcade before we left. But I don't think 12 cans is gonna be enough. She's eating like there's no tomorrow."

"Where you gonna keep it?"

"I was thinking here in the armory."

"Hmm, Sanders won't like that."

"Yea, probably. But she doesn't stay in one place. She was in here last night, then she disappeared right after I opened the armory this morning. Then Ross told me a little while ago he saw her in the tank deck curled up on some mooring lines. He said he walked over to her, started stroking her back, and without warning she dug her claws into his bad arm, almost slicing it off. Man, he was really pissed. His arm, you know the one he thought he broke but didn't break? Well, now it's redder than fresh hamburger. And then he told me it attacked Rat who was coming out of the DC locker."

"Couldn't happen to a nicer person."

"Yea, I know. Ross said he was gonna find the Doc and get some antiseptic."

"Oh, that will definitely get Slaughter's attention...a stray cat attacking people on the ship? Yea, that's not good."

"I was afraid of that. Anyway, after she attacked Ross she ran away, and then she reappeared here just a couple of minutes ago.

"I think you're asking for trouble, having her around, you know?"

"Yea, but ever since she came out of nowhere when we were alongside the tender, she's taken a liking to me."

"Well, it don't bother me for you to have her. Lots of people like cats. I like cats. I've been around cats all my life, barn cats anyway," and Jonah reached over to pet the cat. Neko raised her harlequin face, barred her teeth and hissed at him. He quickly retrieved his hand. "Oh, yea, now I see what Ross experienced.

Well, on second thought, there are probably some people around here who might not like cats, you know; they might want to give her a float test some dark night. I'm thinking Ross or Rat might be first on the list."

◈

A quiet, wistful, longing mood engulfed the ship as they steamed south into the waters of the East China Sea, and the crew reluctantly returned to their old cycle of work, watches and the almost forgotten passage-making routine. But their minds weren't on their jobs; their thoughts were still behind them, back in Sasebo, in the bars, in the restaurants and onsens, not wanting to acknowledge they would soon be picking up another load of cement, this time in Taiwan, and take it to that familiar, dusty, distasteful place: Chu Lai.

Early on the morning of the 4th day out, the Cathedral met a pilot boat at the Kaohsiung sea buoy, and as they entered the strange port through its narrow double breakwaters, the exotic scent of simmering food cooking over burning camphor wood fires filled the air. An old tug struggled to push the ship alongside a dilapidated pier packed with a dizzying collection of wooden oxcarts lined up in rows, all loaded with heavy pallets of bagged cement. An ancient coal-burning locomotive stood on its tracks nearby, snorting and belching acrid smoke that wafted across the ship's main deck and found its way down into the lower spaces, choking and burning the eyes and throats of all those it came in contact with.

The dozens of coolies waiting on the pier were dressed in a usual mixture of Asiatic clothing; the most commonly obvious being sandals, greasy conical hats and stained trousers rolled up to the knees. Two of the coolies leaned against their oxcart watching the ship's crew double up the mooring lines, and as the much older coolie prodded the oxen into position with his bamboo goad stick, the younger one stood with his arms crossed and a disagreeable look on his face.

"That is floating excrement!" the younger coolie said with a pinched face and he pointed to the old, slab-sided LST.

"All things old and strange are not excrement, my Younger Nephew," the older coolie quietly preached in a breathy, sing-song voice. He waved his goad stick over his head trying to disperse a swarm of flies.

"But, Esteemed Uncle, it has foul smell!" Younger Nephew replied wriggling his nose at the peculiar foreign odor wafting across from the ship's galley.

Esteemed Uncle looked up through his filmy eyes and sniffed the air. "Every man knows the smell of his own feet," he smiled, the wisdom of age triumphing over youth.

Younger Nephew frowned, looking disapprovingly at the ship's transverse bulkheads poking into the thin oil-canned hull plates. "It shall descend to the harbor's mud any moment!"

"My Younger Nephew, you will remember learned lesson..." Esteemed Uncle cautioned with a wry, knowing look, resting his sore back against the oxcart. "...that beauty is everywhere, but not everyone dares to see it."

Younger Nephew contemplated that proverb for a moment and then shook his head in disgust. "Bah! American sailors...sons of mongrels!"

Esteemed Uncle held his head upward with his eyes closed attempting to maintain his patience. "He who is kind, can never be unhappy."

"They eat raw meat and drink sugar water!" Younger Nephew declared with strong disapproving conviction.

Esteemed Uncle's mouth turned downward, his voice becoming stern as his tolerance grew thin. "The way you cut your meat, Younger Nephew, reflects your life!"

"Cut your own meat, you ancient fart!" Younger Nephew mumbled under his breath.

CRACK!!! The bamboo goad stick came flashing down on Younger Nephew's head.

"To be conscious of shame is near to fortitude," Esteemed Uncle said, smiling once again as he examined the two pieces of broken bamboo in his hands.

As soon as the ship was secured to the pier, Biagotti's deck gang had the covers off the main hatch, and the coolies began loading the pallets of cement into the ship with the help of a crane, continuously and relentlessly filling the tank deck until there was barely enough room to walk.

"I see Pike's got his police department at their posts this morning," Underwood said, lighting up a cigarette as he and Jonah leaned against the port railing watching the coolies busily loading the ship.

"Yea, he's stationed several guys down in the tank deck watch'n, keeping an eye on those coolies, making sure they don't steal nothing," Jonah explained.

"If you blink they'll rob you blind."

"Most likely."

"We're gonna miss some good Chinese food tonight," Underwood said, exhaling rancid tobacco smoke.

"After Sasebo, I'm 'fraid this would be a letdown," Jonah said. "It's just as well we're in the Starboard Watch Section and have the duty tonight, 'cause my heart really ain't interested in going ashore."

"Yea, well, I'm sure Homer will fill us in at breakfast with another one of his epic liberty stories…uh-oh…don't look now."

Jonah turned in the direction Underwood was looking and saw Pike fast-walking toward them. "Oh, shit...now what?" Jonah said under his breath and he turned away, pretending he didn't see the big signalman, hoping through some miracle he might suddenly disappear.

"Wynchester!" Pike called out, his Master At Arms badge glinting in the afternoon sun. Jonah turned to look back at Pike. "Guess what?" Pike said grinning, his pug face appearing as if he was about to announce some wonderful news.

"Whatever it is I'm sure you're gonna tell me."

"You got Shore Patrol duty tonight!"

"Oh, come on, man! You shit'n me?" Jonah said with a look of intense disgust.

"I wouldn't shit you, Wynchester. You're my favorite gunner's mate. Why would I ever shit you?"

Jonah shook his head and looked sideways at Pike. "Why me?"

"Cause you ain't got noth'n better to do, that's why. And besides, Mister Sanders thought you could use a night ashore in this beautiful liberty port; he and I made up the list."

"Oh, that's great," Jonah looked down at the deck, thinking, well of course Sanders and Pike made the list.

"You got a problem with that?"

Jonah shook his head. "I guess not, Pike. I'm always happy to help you and Mister Sanders.

Pike's eyes narrowed, as if he didn't believe Jonah. "Well that's good, Wynchester, that's good," Pike said. "Cause you're gonna meet me and Mister Sanders for instructions, in your four-oh dress whites, on the quarterdeck, at 1530. We're providing six personnel for the shore patrol, Mister Hobson's in charge, and you'll be the senior petty officer."

"Hobson? Oh, that's really great; Hobson's in charge. Thanks, Pike, you're always so kind."

"Don't mention it, ha ha. And remember: 1530," and Pike rolled away in his peculiar walk, his torso swaying one way as his bowlegs went another.

"Great..." Jonah shook his head, and he sucked in a deep breath. "...the Sandman strikes again."

Underwood dropped his cigarette over the side and they watched it floating down between the pier and the ship, its tiny stream of smoke trailing behind until it landed in the oily black water and went hissing out. "He really knows how to get under your skin, doesn't he?" he said.

Jonah continued looking down into the water. "I was think'n more along the lines of a barn door splinter under my fingernail."

⁓⁓

Jonah went down the steep brow, a white guard belt around his waist and a black and gold "SP" band around his upper arm. Mills, Homer, Ross and The Volt were milling about on the pier in the heavy atmosphere of heat and humidity, each of them wearing Shore Patrol armbands and holding serious looking, black night sticks.

"This is gonna be fun," Homer said, chewing on a wad of bubble gum. "I can't wait to bust somebody's head with this thing," and he rotated the shiny night stick and swung it downward as if he was chopping wood.

"Homer, you ain't busting *nobody* with that!" Jonah said, his black mood and lack of patience clearly showing on his sweating face. "It's for self-defense only. And even then, only as a last resort."

"Yea," Homer said grinning and brandishing the stick. "But it sure would feel nice."

"Here's the list of 'In-Bound' and 'Out-of-Bound' places," Jonah said, handing out sheets of paper. "There's a map on the back with the corresponding numbers. You're to go into every bar. Anybody caught in any of the Out-of-Bound bars must be brought to Shore Patrol headquarters immediately. Any people found drunk or disorderly are also to be brought to SP headquarters; they'll process them and return them to the ship later. The SP office is shown on the map. Mills, you and Volt will team up and cover from the SP office going north, up Haiyang Street to Baihe Street." Mills and the Volt examined their maps. "Homer, you and Ross have the southern half of Hiayang, from the SP office down to the gate. I'll go with Mister Hobson. Does that sound okay with you Mister Hobson?"

Hobson was looking intently at the map, trying to discern north from south, Haiyang Street from Baihe. He was holding the paper sideways and turned himself around in a half circle, attempting to orient the direction of the streets on the map in relation to where he was standing on the pier.

"Mister Hobson?" Jonah asked again. "Is that okay with you?" Hobson looked up, blinked twice, and rapidly nodded his head.

They walked out the seaport's gate, up Haiyang Street, and when they arrived at the Shore Patrol office they checked in with the chief in charge and then proceeded to their appointed sectors, with Hobson talking away in a monologue, a non-stop monologue about everything and nothing. Jonah listened for a while. God, I didn't know this guy was such a broken record, he thought as they walked slowly along the busy street. Unable to follow the ensign's train of thought, Jonah let himself drift into a state of mental opaqueness, blocking out the intense sunlight, the throngs of sailors, the jitneys going and coming, and Hobson's incessant droning.

The late afternoon sun bore down with an oppressive heat, and Jonah stepped through the red doorway of a bar, going from sticky humidity to the ear-piercing sounds of rock and roll music. That omnipresent devil sitting on his shoulder whispered into his ear, enticing him, prodding him: 'go on, Jonah, order a drink', it said; 'get a cold, wet beer, just one, it won't hurt you, Jonah, maybe with a shot of whiskey, you deserve it!' He stepped up to the bar and scanned the wide array of bottles along the shelf and licked his lips as the bartender watched and waited. The pallid image reflected in the bar's large mirror made him pause; a tiny thread of moral fiber bubbled up from inside, his better-self now realizing this wouldn't do, no it just wouldn't do. He shook his head and moved under the air-conditioning vent, attempting to cool down. Through the confusion of noise, sailors and bar girls, he heard that familiar E-minor electric guitar riff booming out from the juke box: *Ta da...Ta da...Te de de...Da da...De de de de*, followed by the sharp vibrations of oak drumsticks violently striking a tight snare: *Clack Clack Clack Clack*, and the dizzying beat and mysterious melody from *"Paint it Black"* followed him out the door and up the street.

Despite the presence of the Shore Patrol band on his arm and the imposing night stick in his hand, he was continually propositioned by the girls along the sidewalk, and with the sweat building on his face he began to feel hotter than the 98-degree water of the onsen. Walking through the bustling crowd, two bar girls in mini skirts suddenly ran by, giving him a glancing blow, almost knocking him off his feet.

Ta da...Ta da...Te de de...Da da...De de de de.

He thought about the cool air of the ryokan, high up on that mountain where the mist from the cascading stream once filled his senses; he pinched the sweat from his eyes. Then his thoughts shifted to Sanders and he felt his temperature rise another degree. How was it possible that Sanders had somehow managed to find the ryokan? How in the hell did the Sandman discover that place? Underwood and Brickey and I had kept it secret from everyone! Of all the damn places around Sasebo, Sanders had found us there! I can't get away from him! Jonah could feel the hot anger rising inside of him, it was the same heat that had come over him when he saw Sanders sitting at the bar, with Ashiko laughing and giggling. Did she really think Sanders was interesting? Did she like him? Why was she smiling at him? Didn't she know who Sanders was? Dammit, I had told her about him! Why the hell didn't she make the connection with the man in the Hawaiian shirt? He continued slowly along the grimy street and the evening's neon lights blinded him from every direction; he put his hand up to shield his eyes.

Ta da...Ta da...Te de de...Da da...De de de de.

I need to see Ashiko. I need to see her now. I need to be with her again. I need to get back to Sasebo. How am I going to do that? Will the ship return? When? Maybe I can get off the ship. Can I get a transfer off the ship? A transfer to Sasebo? Don't be ridiculous, there's no way you'll ever get transferred to Sasebo. But wait a minute, Owens did; a marine in Key West was transferred to Sasebo! So it is possible! But how? From the corner of his eye he noticed two boys on the opposite side of the street; one of them struck a match, the other held something in his hands and then threw it up in the air. The ear-piercing *bang-bang-bang-bang* sent him ducking and reeling as the string of firecrackers suddenly exploded in a rapid staccato of intense bright flashes, sending up a cloud of stinking smoke. He kept walking up the street with that incessant guitar riff following him, the aggressive drumbeat pounding in his head. Stepping over a gutter, he stared into the black, stinking water, and his head started swimming; his face turned white.

Ta da...Ta da...Te de de...Da da...De de de de.

Was I wrong to have given her the bracelet? She reacted so strangely. I couldn't tell if she was happy or not. The shopkeeper said it was sterling, that it was 92.5% pure. I'm not sure if that's a good thing, but the way the intricate wire band wound around itself was beautiful, and the clasp looked very secure. He remembered that last evening, with the taxi arriving. They were late, he had to go, there was no time. She looked distraught and seemed to shake inside as he kissed her goodbye and held her and kissed her again. Brickey and Underwood had yelled from the taxi, yelled for him to hurry, and he let her hands slip from his and walked away. "Wynchester!" a voice pierced through the noise and confusion. "Wynchester!" the voice yelled louder. Jonah turned in slow motion, as if he was stuck in glue, and looked toward the sound of his name. He was stunned to see someone who appeared to be Ensign Hobson standing at the entrance to a bar, the same bar, with the same thrumming, unrelenting rock beat coming through the same red doorway. Jonah was sweating profusely now, and his confused mind thought he saw Hobson transmute into a hazy, spectral figure.

Ta da...Ta da...Te de de...Da da...De de de de.

The flashing neon signs started spinning around him as if he was riding a merry-go-round. He staggered across the uneven pavement of the street into an alleyway, leaned over and vomited. For a brief moment he thought he saw Ashiko's face hovering against the brightly painted graffiti-covered wall, and then he collapsed into darkness.

✢

"What the hell's going on, Doc?" the Charlie Crane asked, standing just outside the door to the sick bay. "Why are all these people getting sick?"

Slaughter paused from checking Jonah's pulse, and looked up toward the XO. "It's not good, sir," he said sitting next to the examining table. "It's some kind'a bug," he added, and held a thermometer up to the light.

"Flu?"

"Well, sir, could be. But it's most likely some kind of intestinal bug. All the signs point to that; vomiting, diarrhea, nausea, fever; we must have picked it up in Sasebo. It's probably been incubating these last couple of days and just happened to break out when we got to Kaohsiung."

Crane shook his head in disbelief. "How many people?"

"Too many, sir. I've started to lose count," and Slaughter picked up a clipboard. "Since we departed Kaohsiung yesterday morning, we've now got, uh, 12 people sick.

"Twelve?"

"Yes, sir, so far. Let's see here...we've got..." he said looking down the list and pointing with his finger. "...two snipes, that's Tate and Gallagher. And Fugete and Holt in operations, that's four. And Brennan, he's one of the mess cooks, that makes five. Homer is six, with four more in Deck Division. And Mister Hobson."

"Hobson too?"

"And Wynchester here makes 12."

"Damn!"

"Yes, sir. And most likely more to come."

"More?"

"Oh, yes, sir. I'm sure of it. This is just the start."

"Jesus!" Crane said with a look of exasperation and caution. 'What can we do?"

"Well, I've been thinking on that, sir...and there's three things."

"What three things?"

"One is liquids."

"Liquids?"

"Yes, sir, liquids. If this is some kind of stomach bug, which I'm quite sure it is, it has to run its course. And keeping people hydrated with lots of liquids is the key. They gotta drink water,

water, water. The water keeps them hydrated, flushes out the bug, and eases the discomfort."

"Can they eat anything?"

"Only what's easy on the stomach, sir. Only what they can keep down...saltines, bread. Not much more. Dorsey must have some saltines among his stores. Oh, and bananas...I saw the mess cooks bringing several bunches aboard in Kaohsiung."

"Okay, I'll speak to Dorsey," Crane said.

"It should clear up within a few days," Slaughter explained. "But we've got to prevent others from catching it."

"How do we do that?"

"That's the second thing; we need to quarantine them."

"Quarantine?"

"Yes, sir. We need to separate the sick from the healthy. Right now we've got sick people in their bunks scattered all over the ship. I suggest getting the healthy people out of the deck division berthing compartment and turn that into a sick ward."

"The entire compartment?"

"Yes, sir. Put all the sick people in the ship into after berthing and keep them there. That would be the best place. Quarantine them from the rest of the crew. I'll need some volunteers to help."

"And the third thing?"

"We've got to disinfect the ship."

"You're kidding?"

"No, sir."

"Disinfect the ship?"

"Yes, sir. Scrub everything!"

"What do you mean scrub everything?"

"Everything, sir. Scrub every damn thing on the ship with soap, water and chlorine. And then scrub it again!"

The Puke Ward, as the aft berthing compartment was soon called, had 16 patients within an hour of receiving Crane's orders to convert it into a quarantine area. Twelve hours later there were 24 cases, including two more officers: Johnston and Jones. Every man who wasn't on watch, or wasn't retching his stomach inside out, or sitting on the seat of ease, was put to work busily scrubbing bulkheads, decks, doors, equipment, chairs, desks and the heads with soap, water and chlorine. And more chlorine. Slaughter even had the walking-wounded in after berthing cleaning that compartment along with its ugly, fetid head. And he stationed a sailor outside all the other heads in the ship to constantly clean and disinfect them. Dorsey's galley and the mess deck received a special going over; every pot, pan and piece of equipment from the overhead down to the deck was scrubbed with methodical precision. The stewards disinfected every surface of the pantry, wardroom, officer's head, bulkheads, decks and all the staterooms. And the ship's laundry machine was now working overtime attempting to wash the growing piles of stained sheets, towels and clothes stacked on the deck outside that tiny compartment. The ship had never seen such a frenzy of cleaning. By the end of the first 24 hours the Puke Ward held 29 patients.

"When do you think this is gonna stop?" Brickey asked as he and Underwood stood in the #1 gun tub, the most forward place in the ship where the sweet breeze was a far cry from the foul-smelling atmosphere below decks.

"Stop? Hell, I have no idea," Underwood said. "At this rate, maybe never. Slaughter's still got people coming into sick bay."

"I sure hope I'm not gonna catch it. I'm sleeping up here tonight. At least the air's fresh and clean. God knows I don't want to go below. I feel like I'm suffocating down there."

"The chlorine stink gives me a headache."

"Did you see the pile of stuff outside the laundry?" Brickey asked. "I was down there, walk'n toward it and I suddenly realized what was ahead of me. I stopped cold. I turned around and went the other direction. No way am I getting near that crap."

"I don't think just walking by is gonna make you sick," Underwood said. "Germs don't just jump out of a pile of laundry and attack you. If you rolled around in it for a while you might pick up some germs. But not if you just walk by. At least I don't think so."

"Well, I'm not going to take any chances, especially not after seeing what happened to Jonah. I saw him come back to the ship sicker than a dog. Puking all over. Then he started shitt'n. Oh, God...the smell! I'm not taking any chances. I'm keep'n as far away from that berthing compartment as possible."

By the end of the third day out from Kaohsiung, Doc Slaughter cautiously proclaimed victory at the Battle of Shits Creek, as the onslaught was sarcastically named. In total, 38 members of the crew had been hit with the bug in one state of severity or another, and just to make sure there were no flare-ups, Slaughter continued to have every compartment thoroughly disinfected until the morning the ship made her approach to the now familiar red dirt and swirling dust of Chu Lai.

❧❧

The ship was once again at general quarters, buttoned up tight as a drum, with the topside personnel in helmets and flak vests, and the large red hill with the white radar dome hovered in the distant haze. Sandbags were stacked on the conn and at each gun, and this time everyone knew what to expect. When the rusting boat with the smoking outboard motor came puttering out from behind the point of land, the gun crew's fingers were still hovering over the triggers, but the high state of nervous expectation experienced during their first Chu Lai beaching was now absent.

"I ain't shoot'n at noth'n unless I know for sure what I'm shoot'n at," Homer said as he and Ross stood alongside their .50 caliber machine gun, watching the small boat heading for them. "I ain't gonna risk my gun causing a friendly fire incident; no way, that's fer sure."

"Yea, well," Ross said. "What you gonna do if it's in the dead dark of night? Huh? Wet your finger and wave it in the air, as if it were some kind'a enemy detection system, or something?"

The Hawaiian shirt that greeted them last time was not to be seen this morning; instead, there were only two men in the boat and one held up a large yellow sign with the words "Follow Me" painted in bold black letters.

Well, that's a hell-of-a lot better, they're getting more organized, Underwood thought, staring out the windows of the conn at the small boat ranging alongside the ship.

Static crackled from the TBS radio and a voice filled boomed out of the speaker. Beaufort lifted the handset from its cradle and held it to his ear, listening intently. "Roger that," he said and turned toward the captain. "Captain, they say to follow them to the remaining spot at the beach. A 'T' just departed yesterday, we're to use that spot, the only vacant one. They say it's tight, but we should be able to get in there. There will be someone on the beach to guide us."

They cautiously followed the boat through the channel and into the basin where four LSTs were already on the beach unloading their cargoes. Underwood, standing on the conn with the sound powered phone, clearly saw the gap between the 3rd and 4th ship, and just as they said, a Seabee was on the beach holding a flag, directing them into the tight, narrow spot. There's no way the old man is gonna squeeze us into that hole, he thought, looking at the narrow gap and then over to the captain who was pacing back and forth on the wing of the conn. But by some miracle combination of engine orders, benevolent breeze and calm waters, the ship made its slow turn to port, steadied up on the new course, and squeezed directly in-between the two other LSTs, its bow surging gently onto the beach. "Wonders will never cease," he said quietly to himself and he coiled up the phone's cable, hung it on a hook and went down the ladder.

By the next morning the now empty ship was underway again with the remnants of red sand and caustic cement dust flowing throughout its compartments. This time she headed south along the Vietnamese coastline, well offshore and out of sight of the land, and Chief Cunningham checked off the names of the towns on the chart as they passed by: Qui Nhon, Nha-Trang, Cam Ranh Bay, Phan Rang, and Phan Thiet. On the morning of the 2nd day the cape of Vung Tau loomed off the starboard bow and the Cathedral made her way cautiously into the anchorage where dozens of freighters, tankers and other LSTs were riding on their hooks, waiting for pilots to take them up-river to Saigon. Jonah, Underwood and Homer stood on the 01-level looking out toward the anchored ships and the countless small craft skittering about, busy as waterbugs on a muddy pond. LCVPs shuttled from ship to ship and to and from the sandy beach 200 yards in the distance. One LST was on the beach, its ramp down, and a column of drab green trucks were lined up and waiting to drive through her open bow doors.

"Jeezum crowe, would you look at that!" Homer sighed with a hungry longing showing on his pockmarked face. "Bars and bikinis! What the hell is this place?"

"Sure don't look like a war zone to me!" Jonah said

"Vung Tau used to be a French resort," Underwood chimed in. "Wealthy people from Saigon would come down here to escape the heat and crowds of the city. The French called it Cap Saint Jacques. I guess it's still popular."

"Damn! Where the hell's he going?" Homer cried pointing to an olive drab 4-engine aircraft flying low with its landing gear down, and they watched it disappear behind the mountain in the foreground.

"That's a C-130," Underwood answered. "There's an airport on the other side of that mountain. That's where the base is."

"This is sure one busy place," Jonah remarked lighting a cigarette.

"Hey, Mills!" Underwood yelled to the bosun who was operating the Welin davit, lowering the port side 36-foot LCVP into the water. "What's going on?"

"We're going fishing," Mills said with a wide grin on his face.

"Come on," Underwood persisted. "Where you going in the boat?"

"Mister Johnston's got a family emergency," Mills finally explained. "He's flying back home. We're taking him to the beach."

"The beach?"

"Yea, the beach."

Jonah glanced at Underwood: he could sense the gears moving inside the yeoman's head. Their eyes met, and that familiar conspiratorial look flashed between them. Underwood looked at Jonah and moved his head to the side as if saying: 'follow me.' They walked away, leaving Homer talking to Mills.

Ten minutes later Jonah and Underwood were standing in the LCVP, .45s hanging from webbed belts on their hips as the boat motored away from the ship.

"How did you do that?" Jonah said. "How did you convince Crane to allow us to go ashore."

"Well, we had to get this classified mail to the post office ASAP," Underwood explained, patting a large leather bag sitting on the deck. "And I convinced the XO that I needed an armed escort...and who better than our esteemed gunner's mate to provide the security detail!"

"You're brilliant. The look on Sanders' face when Crane told him I was to go with you was priceless. It took everything I had not to smile."

"Yea, the XO is definitely learning his job. He's come a long way since we were in Little Creek."

"I never thought I'd hear you say that."

The landing craft motored through the anchorage, its newly rebuilt engine growling at high RPMs, pushing the boat along at 12 knots and creating its own private breeze in the middle of the warm, mill-pond water. The festive nature of the boat ride was overshadowed by reality with Poldolski standing in the cockpit with his hands on the grips of a .30 caliber machine gun. He continually looked out beyond the bow and to the sides, watching the other boats moving about in the anchorage, looking intently at seaweed and assorted garbage floating by.

"I'm glad to see you're taking your job seriously, Poldolski!" Jonah yelled over the noise of the engine.

"Anything for you Wynchester!" Poldolski yelled back, a wide grin across his face.

"Man, this is nice," Jonah yelled in Underwood's ear. "To get off the ship for awhile. And just look at this place; it's beautiful!" He lifted his head into the cooling breeze, feeling a welcome relief from the hot, sticky morning. Mills skillfully maneuvered the boat around the dozens of ships at anchor, and approaching the shore, he throttled the engine back, allowing the boat to drift forward and nudge its bow onto the beach. Mills released the brake on the ramp and it came down onto the beach with a *Thud*. They stepped off the boat, their boots sinking into the fine, soft quartz and feldspar white sand.

"Mills!" Underwood cried. "You'll be back here at 1400?" Underwood asked, and Mills made a thumbs-up sign. Underwood and Jonah each took one of Johnson's bags and the three of them trudged through the soft beach sand and up to the road where they stood looking one direction and down the other. The two-lane road traced the undulating curve of the shoreline, and scattered along its edge were dozens of beach bars with colorful signs proclaiming their names: *Bar Tijuana, Annie's Place, Blue Cloud, Starlight,* among others. All had clusters of tables, chairs and bar stools festively arranged in the sand with scores of patrons in khaki, olive drab, dungarees, plaid shorts and multi-colored bikinis milling about, drinking and laughing.

"Man, will 'ya look at that!" Jonah said, pointing to the bars. "It's not even 1000 and they're getting plastered!"

"Mister Johnson, do you know how to get to the base?" Underwood asked.

"Yea, we need to catch a ride on this beach road and go that way," and he pointed north.

"Right, and here comes our taxi." Underwood looked at the deuce-and-half Army truck heading their direction. He stepped into the road and held his thumb out, bringing the big truck to a halt. "You headed to the air base?" he asked the driver through the open window.

"Yea, hop in the back," the soldier said and they hurried around to the back, threw the bags in and climbed up to the high truck bed. The truck started off, lurching and jolting as the driver shifted through the clattering gears, and as the big 10-wheels bounced and vibrated up the road they watched the beach bars fade into the distance behind them.

"I think we need to make a stop at one of those on our way back!" Jonah yelled over the noise of the whining transmission. Underwood nodded his head with a crafty, knowing look.

"I always wanted to visit Tijuana," Jonah said, taking another sip of his beer and looking up at the *Tijuana* sign painted on the side of the beach bar. "I guess this is as close as I'll come."

"Maybe, but YAJDEK," Underwood remarked, and he laid his glass of dark rum on the table, slouched down in the chair and motioned to the Vietnamese waitress.

"Ya know, I think I could live here. Definitely live here," Jonah said waving his arm towards the dozens of beach bars and small houses sitting back from the road "Yea, just getting up late, soaking up the sun, taking long siestas, wandering over to the beach bar of the day."

"There should be a list. Sort'a the BBOD." Underwood said.

"The what?"

"The BBOD. The Beach Bar Of the Day list. You check your BBOD each morning while you're still in your rack, and you visit one beach bar a day, and the next day you visit another, and so on."

"Good idea."

"And, hell, with all these bars it'll take you at least a month before you start at the top of the list again."

"And then in the evening, there's the BROD," Jonah added.

"The BROD?"

"Yea, the Beach Restaurant Of the Day."

"The BROD. That's good. I like that. And if you eat at the BROD more than once, they punch your ticket for a freebie," Underwood laughed.

"Exactly."

"Similar to a Chinese restaurant."

"What'ya mean?" Jonah asked.

"Well, you know. In a chinkie restaurant; with two you get egg roll. Only here with two beach dinners you get a third free."

"Perfect."

The beach bar girl approached the table carrying her multi-colored tray. She had a big smile, and her bright red lipstick matched her very short red shorts. Jonah tried not to stare at the thin, white, tight tank top with the logo *Tijuana Bar* emblazoned strategically across the front.

"We need two more drinks," Underwood said looking up at her. "And we'd like two hamburgers. Two burgers all the way, loaded with everything."

"And fries," Jonah chimed in.

"Yes, and fries, please," Underwood confirmed, and he dropped several Military Payment Certificates on the table. The girl quickly picked up the small, colorful bills before they flew away in the breeze.

"How much did you give her?" Jonah asked as he watched the girl saunter away.

"A couple of bucks."

"I don't get it. Why are we getting paid in this funny money?"

"Because of the black market."

"Yea, I know. But explain it."

"If we gave them our green backs, they'd exchange them on the black market for a much higher amount of piasters...higher than the standard exchange rate. So periodically they change the MPCs for newer versions. It's supposed to eliminate the black market problem. But it's not."

Jonah looked dumbfounded and he changed the subject. "You know, Lieutenant Johnston didn't look too good today."

"I guess he's got a lot'a worries, and probably a long trip ahead of him."

"Where's he from?"

"Illinois, somewhere outside Chicago."

"That's a long way," Jonah said thinking and looking up to the cumulus clouds. "How the hell do you get from here to Chicago?"

"Maybe from here to Saigon. And then to Cubi Point. And from there probably Pearl. And then San Francisco or Los Angeles. And eventually Chicago."

"Damn, yea, that's definitely a long way. That'll take forever!"

"Probably."

"So, tell me, Woody; why are we going to Saigon tomorrow, and what happens after that? And what was that comment Mister Johnston made when we dropped him off at the air base? Something about hoping we were looking forward to the delta?"

"That's classified."

"Yea, I know. But everybody's gonna find out eventually. Maybe even tonight. So why not tell me now?"

Underwood lifted the glass to his lips and drained the last of the rum. He looked at Jonah and then turned slightly and looked around him. "More cargo," he said in a quiet voice.

"Yea, what kind'a cargo?" Jonah asked, his eyes turning into narrow slits.

"Steel I-beams, cement, ammo."

"Okay, but where to?"

Underwood's eyes scanned left and right. "Can Tho."

"Where's that?"

"Way up the Mekong Delta."

"Oh, Jeez!" Jonah said with a look of dread, and he suddenly sobered up. "Is that what Johnston was talking about when he told us to have fun on the delta?"

Underwood nodded gravely. "After loading in Saigon, we go back down the river to Vung Tau and wait for another pilot. Then it'll take us two days steaming up the Mekong to get to Can Tho. They're building a big army base there and expanding an airfield. We'll take a day to unload, and then two days back to Vung Tau. And then we'll do it again. And very likely, again and again."

◈

The pilot stumbled up the last few steps to the conn, puffing and breathing hard, and Beaufort stepped aside as the captain reached out and shook the hand of the short, sturdy Vietnamese dressed in khaki trousers and a white short-sleeve shirt; a faded green pith helmet sat firmly on his sweating head. The pilot had come aboard as the ship waited near the lower section of the Dong Nai River, and now they were slowly steaming upstream through the thick, muddy brown water toward Saigon, the banks deserted and lined with stunted mangrove trees.

They were once again at general quarters, with every hatch and scuttle closed and dogged, every gun manned, every one at their stations. Even with the morning sun barely above the horizon Beaufort was feeling the sweat building under his helmet and flak vest as he leaned against the lumpy tiers of leaking sandbags. The ship entered the mouth of the river and he watched the bizarre landscape drift by with the putrid, bare river bank the color of wet, gray clay. It had a waterlogged sheen that made it appear slippery and sticky. If you step in that stuff, he imagined, your boots would probably disappear forever. He looked out to port and then to starboard and thought he'd never seen such a depressing, ugly, miserable place; the blackened, leafless trees stretched out as far as he could see, with no relief, no green, no signs of any life, just bare, crooked limbs pointing forlornly in a forsaken Kafkaesque landscape. Three PBRs, 31-foot river patrol boats came up from behind, quickly passing the ship, their dark olive brown hulls planing across the muddy water and their crews training twin .50 caliber machine guns toward the shore. It's a relief to see some more firepower out here, he thought, and he looked to his right and saw the captain lighting a cigar.

"What the hell is wrong with all the trees!" O'Toole turned toward Underwood and whispered, his owl shaped eyes full of bewilderment as he looked out to the muddy river bank. "Why are all these trees bare?"

The trees were completely naked, only black limbs and trunks showed above the wet soil, and as far as he could see there was nothing, nothing but dark gray mud and bare trees, no green could be seen anywhere.

"Agent orange," Underwood quietly answered.

"Agent what?" O'Toole asked, again in a whisper.

"Agent Orange. It's a defoliant. A chemical. They spray it from planes. It's kills all the foliage and creates a clear field of fire, that way no VC can sneak up and try to attack us as we go up river. It's great stuff."

As they continued upstream with the pilot keeping the ship in the center of the winding channel's twists and turns, the tall, slender towers of Saigon's cathedral appeared in the distant haze far off the port bow. The ship made a turn and the famous landmark moved to the right, and then with another turn in the river, the towers moved back again.

Appearing around a bend 400 yards ahead came a haze gray MSB, a 57-foot river minesweeper towing its white paravane near the bank. The courses of the two approaching vessels brought them close alongside, passing each other starboard to starboard, and Beaufort could now clearly see the paravane with its red and black flag fluttering from a staff, the porpoise-shaped device surging through the water between the boat and the river bank, its unwieldy, razor-sharp cutting wire suspended just below the river's surface. The odd-looking, stubby minesweeper had .30

caliber machine guns bristling along her sides, and a .50 caliber gun was mounted in a round tub near her stern allowing a high, clear field of fire. Near the bow of the minesweeper a shirtless helmsman stood on the conn two levels above the main deck, casually waving his hat a them from under the shade of an awning. Then as quickly as the minesweeper appeared, it passed by, went out of sight around another bend and left the LST behind; a solitary ship steaming up the repulsive dark river to Saigon.

※

Le Boulevard Charner was long, more than a half-mile end to end; and well over 100 feet wide. Islands of palms and hundreds of flower beds graced the length of the grassy median. Cars, bicycles, cyclo pedicabs and black smoke-belching busses raced their way up the broad promenade as pedestrians dodged the traffic with smooth, practiced efficiency. Browning and Davant sat comfortably in the front seats of a pair of three-wheeled cyclos, the Vietnamese drivers pedaling from the rear and steering expertly through and around the traffic. Davant had negotiated the fare at the foot of the ship's brow, doing the talking and waving MPC script notes at the taller of the two Vietnamese, the one with passable English.

"He's obviously done this before," Davant said as their cyclos went out the gate and into the bustling afternoon traffic. "I offered him two bucks in funny money and eventually settled on five. He wanted ten, so we're under budget so far."

"Where are we going?" Browning asked, his cyclo cruising only three feet away from Davant as he gawked at the tree-lined street with its shops and restaurants. The white, brown, and yellow pedestrians were a mixed lot: bankers, bureaucrats, shop keepers, messenger boys, ladies, all moving with a purpose, all going somewhere.

"I told him we wanted the best French restaurant in Saigon," Davant said without looking up from his tourist guide book, the extended-page map flapping in the wind. "He said something about a restaurant called Saint Michel. When we get there we can take a look at that, then walk around to see if something else might be more interesting."

They cycled along the boulevard, and in the center of an intersection a white-uniformed traffic policeman standing on an elevated platform brought them to a halt, his white gloved hands signaling and waving, a whistle in his mouth blowing high pitched trilling shrieks. Browning looked around him, and on every corner there was a five-foot high enclosure made from olive drab sandbags with a canvas awning overhead, and several Vietnamese soldiers loitered about, each with .45s on their hips and M1 carbines slung on their shoulders. "Do you feel safe here?" Davant said looking up as the cyclo came to a stop. "Or do you feel somebody might take a shot at you?"

They tipped the cyclo drivers and started walking up the boulevard toward the Restaurant Saint Michel, Davant snapping photographs along the way.

"Man, take a look at that!"

Davant turned in the direction Browning was looking and saw a young Vietnamese woman dressed in a classic Ao Dai; the tight form-fitting sky-blue flowered tunic accentuating the curves of her torso as she strolled along the edge of the sidewalk. The tunic's high collar came up to her chin, and a delicate, conical palm-leaf hat secured with a silk ribbon sat well down over her long dark hair allowing only a tantalizing glimpse of her enigmatic face. As she walked purposefully along the broad boulevard in her high heels, the elegant, filmy white pants and flowing tunic gave her the illusion of floating just above the sidewalk. Forcing himself not to stare as she went by, Davant reflected that her Ao Dai might have covered everything, but it hid nothing.

The Carte Et Menus posted on the wall outside the entrance to the Restaurant San Michel read as if it had just been received from Paris: *Truffe Noire, Gratinee D'Oignons, Langoustines, Saint Michel a Cru, Cotes de Chevreuil, Rouet en Ecaille, Croquant Pamplemousse, Ecorce de Chocolat*, were only a minuscule portion of the total offering, and the odors emanating from the interior made Browning's salivary glands start to run wild. "I vote for this place," he said licking his lips. "Why bother continue looking when I think we've found it."

"Suits me," Davant said, walking from the clamor of the street into a tranquil foyer. They strained their necks and gaped up at the high arched ceiling with its large ornate wrought-iron-framed skylights streaming vast arrays of light into the long room. Circulating fans mounted on tall columns brought a faint, pleasant breeze over their heads; a great relief from the sticky heat of the noisy world outside. The immaculate tables with thick starched white table cloths and sparkling glassware, rested on a floor of fine tiles in a design of ochre-red and white lotus flowers. Great numbers of green plants and tall palms grew from immense red clay pots squatting throughout the room. An officious looking Vietnamese dressed in an impeccable tuxedo and crisp black patent leather shoes walked purposely toward them. He eyed the two Americans, immediately noticing their civilian clothes, the scuffed penny-loafers and the white socks, the wrinkled khaki trousers and buttoned-down shirts, their freshly shaved faces, and their too-close haircuts. He shook his head slightly and frowned. He had seen their type before. He knew what was coming. He dreaded even the thought of having to once again answer the repulsive questioning of *La Carte* as opposed to *Le Menu*, dealing with indecisive ordering, the lingering beyond decent propriety; two obnoxious, boisterous, slow-witted Americans taking up valuable table space, and most likely departing with too little of a tip in the end, even if the gratuity was already included in *l'addition*. After 32 years at the Restaurant Saint Michel, 16 of those as Maitre d'Hotel, the impeccable Nguyen Minh Khai was not about to lower his standards; not for anyone. Unless of course they understood the order of things, how the world turned, how the universe kept its disparate parts from falling into chaos, how things were run in *his* dining room. Holding his partially opened hand discretely in front of his cummerbund, he waited a moment for the proffered enticement. Receiving none, he brought them to a small table near the door.

Nguyen stood over them looking down with lowered eyes, a grim mouth below an impeccably trimmed thin mustache. "Aperitifs, gentlemen?" he asked in English with a French-laced-Vietnamese accent, his head turned slightly away as if there was some unpleasant odor emanating from the table.

Browning looked up. "I'll have a dry - Southern Comfort - Manhattan - on the rocks - with a twist," he said in his Texas drawl.

Davant's eyes opened with a look that communicated anticipation of a potentially interesting coming event.

"Pardon, Monsieur?" the Maitre d' asked, his eyebrows coming together.

"I'll have a dry - Southern Comfort - Manhattan - on the rocks - with a twist," Browning repeated, this time drawing out the vowels even further.

The Maitre d' drew in a deep breath, turned, looked toward the back of the room, held his hand high and loudly snapped his fingers; twice. A short, rotund *Chef de Rang* came scurrying across the tiles. Nguyen leaned over, whispered something in the man's ear, and then departed the vicinity with a condescending nose in the air.

Throughout the drinking, the ordering, the devouring of the different courses, Davant and Browning's alcohol induced glucose levels slowly rose to greater and greater heights. Their conversation grew from intriguing comments about the food, to enjoyment, to volumetric volubility. Soon they were joking away with not so oblique references to their fellow officers and the familial origins of the maitre d'hotel. Verbal caricatures of the waitstaff really got their funny bones vibrating. And finally, finishing the meal with a delicate slice of cadmium-green marzipan swimming in a sea of rich dark chocolate with a complimentary demitasse of espresso, they slouched in the chairs with their feet out in the aisle.

"'Ya know, Len," Browning said slurring his words and lighting a cigar. "This has probably been the best damn French food in the best damn Vietnamese restaurant in the worst damn armpit in the world I've ever had the opportunity to visit," and he belched. "Just look at this place! The most extraordinarily beautiful room imaginable; tall ceilings, tile floor, palm trees. It's fantastic. And then you look out the window and see the teeming, unwashed masses." He shook his head. "Yea, the waiters here and that majordomo guy might be a little stuck up with themselves, but damn, they sure know how to serve food. Did you see our waiter, holding those plates without having his thumb along the top edge? How does he do that? How does he hold the plate without having his thumb on top? Shit, if I had tried that I'd probably drop every plate in the building! Unbelievable."

"Look out," Davant whispered. "Here he comes."

"Merci messieurs," the maitre d' said approaching them and he deftly balanced a small leather folder on the very edge of the white table cloth; one half on the table, the other half hovering in thin air. "Plaisir de vous servir ici a Saint Michel." An unusual smile spread across his face as he bent in a slight bow and then walked away.

Browning picked up the *l'addition du restaurant* and sat back, his eyes wide open. "What the hell is 4,720 Piasters?" he said turning to Davant.

"How much?"

"Four thousand, seven hundred and twenty."

Davant shook his head, amazed at the number, opened his mouth as if to say something, and closed it again. "I have no idea," he finally blurted out.

Browning reached into his pants pocket and pulled out a sheet of paper, unfolded it and scanned down the typewritten words. "What's 118 divided into 4,720?" he said picking up a pen.

"Is that 118 piasters to the dollar?" Davant asked.

"Yea," and browning started scribbling on the bill. "One-hunded into 472 goes...about four and three-quarter times...uh...carry the two...yea it's about forty bucks total."

"That's not bad."

"No. Not at all. Twenty bucks each? I'd say that's pretty damn good for a multi-course gourmet French dinner with drinks. But who's counting? Ha ha ha," and they each started counting through their colorful Military Payment Certificates, laughing and counting.

They dropped heavily into the seats of the cyclos parked outside the restaurant, and continued to laugh until the humming of the chain on the sprockets and the buzz from the tires lulled them into a quiet reverie. Browning leaned his head against the vibrating frame of the awning and fell into a deep sleep, his mouth open, snoring and wheezing all the way back to the ship.

Diary #108
7 June 1966
0130 Hours ... Saigon, South Vietnam

We are here. After all these months of speculation, worry, anguish and fear of the unknown, we are here; here in the epicenter of the war Lyndon Baines Johnson defines as the ultimate struggle between democracy and communism, good and evil: we are in the Pearl of the Orient, the old French colony of rice and rubber plantations, the cross roads where East meets West, smack dab in the bullseye of what the Viet Cong consider their ultimate goal: we are in Saigon.

This sprawling city lies within the interior of the country, accessible from the sea by only one deep-water river. It swarms with people of just about every nationality, color, race and creed you can imagine: Vietnamese, Chinese, Cambodian, Laotian, French, British, Russians, Australians, Canadians, Argentinians, Germans, Swiss, Belgians, Dutch...and now Americans by the tens of thousands.

Grand boulevards with buildings of colonial period architecture, fine French restaurants, costly shops selling expensive silk blouses and diamond jewelry, all line the streets only blocks away from putrid, black canals filled with sampans teeming with people selling bananas, rice, sugarcane, hashish, opium, ammunition and contraband. Dusty, lumbering US Army Patton tanks manned by boys from Kansas and Arkansas clank through the streets alongside immaculate chauffeur-driven Peugeot's carrying rubber barons and diplomats. If the gritty sidewalks could talk they would tell us about the pedestrians hurrying to their destinations in a collection of foot-gear from army boots, to polished alligator shoes, high heels, rubber sandals, to bare feet. A glance at a street corner would reveal Buddhist monks in saffron robes standing next to Catholic priests in black cassocks; weary Methodist missionaries alongside elegant ladies with haute couture hairdos; private academy school-girls dressed in ao dais, dirty barefoot children picking pockets, and beggars, all standing next to sandbagged machine gun emplacements. The hustle and bustle is dizzying, the dozens of languages disorienting, the dichotomy of so many different people shocking. And in the midst of this semi-demi uncontrolled chaos we fill our tank deck and main deck with thousands of tons of cargo brought here by steamships from all corners of the world, cargo of which we'll take 160 miles up the Mekong River to a place called Can Tho.

The reality of our situation has now finally hit us. It has struck us with an emotional body blow so forceful that the crew cannot breathe. We are now finally confronted with the truth, the certainty that everything we've done up to this point has been child's play. Everything before now has been a drill. In 5 hours we get underway, back to Vung Tau where we'll pick up another pilot, and then steam up the unknown Mekong; the Mekong that originates with tiny drops of water from a melting glacier 18,000 feet high somewhere in Tibet, courses alongside lateral moraines and down through mountain gorges, mixes with muddy tributaries, rice paddies and human waste from riverside villages, all flowing thousands of miles downstream to greet the novitiates of our worn out Cathedral.

Last Wills & Testaments are being revised. Bags of mail are going ashore with letters to loved ones revealing the emotions of a crew on the brink. Wild stories and rumors circulate through the ship of deadly mines buried in mud, faceless swimmers attaching explosive charges to the hull, Viet Cong hiding along the river bank ready to ambush us. All these perceived nightmares have slowly infiltrated our unsuspecting subconscious. No one is immune from the trepidation, no one knows what we'll encounter, no one knows how they'll react if the nightmares materialize. Now there's a sense of overwhelming collective guilt permeating the ship, and everyone is examining their inner voice, their guide to right and wrong. Everyone is making a pledge; they're making a covenant, a Mekong Covenant; they're metaphorically kneeling within The Cathedral, promising that if we survive this coming gauntlet, if we come through unscathed, we vow to mend our ways and never sin again.

CHAPTER 11

MEKONG

The water of the Mekong was the color of a dark Stygian umber, saturated with thin viscous mud, all flowing downstream in the deeper channels at a steady 4 knots; in contrast, the shore was a shocking viridescent green, the bright emerald colors blazing and shouting. The river's mouth was well over a half-mile wide, and someone standing on one shore could barely discern a person standing on the other. Muscle-powered sampans were sculled upstream, slowly making their way close alongside the riverbank and out of the current, all going to the floating markets where they would sell their goods and buy others. Entire families squeezed into these small boats and sat in the midst of a rainbow-colored cornucopia of melons, pineapples, mangoes, durians, papaya, sapodilla and coconuts, the mound of fruit conforming to the shape of the hull as it rose from the bilge to the gunnels. Other boats with strange looking, long-shaft outboards scooted along at a much faster pace, and larger craft carried the heaviest of loads and many more passengers. All of them struggled through the brown mud-laden river, all going somewhere as fast as the strong current allowed.

At 06:30 the Cathedral weighed anchor and joined this procession in the middle of the delta artery, a watery highway without buoys or markers of any kind; if there were navigational aids, the Viet Cong would make sure they weren't around for long. Today the correct channel may be to the right, tomorrow it may be to the left, and through this constantly shifting, ever-changing aqueous thoroughfare, the Vietnamese pilot relied on his instinct and experience to conn the ship safely through the invisible channels.

Once again the ship was at general quarters, and by now everyone knew the drill: set Condition Zebra, close it down, button it up, man the 40s, the .50s and the .30s. Put on helmets and flak vests. Button shirt sleeves and stuff pants legs into socks. Jones lit off the engines in the auxiliary engine room and put all three generators on line. All stations were manned.. Everyone was at the highest level of alertness as the Cathedral pushed slowly upstream against the strong current of the great river that had traveled thousands of miles to greet them.

No one could say they had slept well; no one was able to fully relax with the engines and generators grumbling along on standby throughout the night. Those on watch remained highly vigilant for anything and everything. Reveille was sounded early, at 0500, and now everyone knew this was the real thing, this is why the ship had traveled 11,642 miles, this was what the ship was made for: carrying thousands of tons of valuable cargo into uncertain peril to an unknown shore.

Villages dotting the landscape inched slowly by, the many huts' rusting corrugated steel roofs tilting and balancing precariously on thin twisted legs stuck deep into the river's mud. From a distance the many clusters of huts resembled Lilliputian houses in a fairytale scene. Upon more closer inspection they were constructed from hundreds of individual patchwork pieces of castaway materials: corrugated steel sheets, lumber, wooden pallets, tree trunks, broken plywood, iron pipe, all ingeniously pieced together, leaning this way and that. Shirts and trousers hanging to dry in the sun waved in the breeze next to pots, pans and fishing nets as naked children played hide and seek. Small rickety ladders climbed down toward waterlilies leaning in the current. These were the rustic, exotic homes, the castles, the offices, the bedrooms and kitchens of the people of the Mekong Delta; and as Jonah thought, they were probably the homes of the Viet Cong as well. He had the feeling the curious faces of the inhabitants were looking directly back at him, examining him and his peculiar home as the ship passed by.

The sun was now beating down with an unrelenting heat and humidity. Extraordinarily massive dark gray, anvil-shaped rain clouds moved across the coconut palm groves and rice paddies, blackening out everything around them, the rain so intense it stung as it swept across the ship in 30 knots of wind. Watches were changed, the crew's dinner prepared, and the ship continued on, relentlessly going slowly upstream through the brown water.

Jonah observed it all from his GQ station at the aft 40mm, peering over the lip of the gun tub, watching the shore go by. On the conn, Charlie Crane was sitting at the base of the pelorus, behind the sandbags, holding a pair of binoculars to his chest, his helmet almost covering his eyes. Even Pike looks worried, Jonah thought, the big signalman and his odd, ugly face cowering behind the flag bags. If it gets any hotter out here, he'll probably die of stroke. He'll be holding onto a signal halyard when it hits him, and he'll slide down, down to the deck, deader than a doornail. They'll never get his fat ass down the ladder.

By 1900 that evening, having steamed only 75 miles, they anchored downstream of the village of Sa Dec, its eclectic mix of French colonial and Vietnamese architecture glowing orange in the low evening sunlight, backdropped by gray cumulus clouds hovering above a green western horizon. Several PBRs went by with their guns bristling, their frothy wakes churning and revealing the coffee color of the water. And what was an atmosphere of alertness throughout the ship, now went to an even higher level with the swiftly closing curtain of darkness; the setting sun blinked suddenly out and everything went dark, black dark. Every patch of flotsam, every coconut, every piece of bamboo floating by was illuminated by strong lights from the superstructure and main deck. The occasional WUUMPH could be heard as a stun grenade was tossed into the water to deter any swimming Viet Cong from attaching a mine to the ship. Sailors stationed along the main deck with M1 carbines carefully watched for swimmers in the water. Crews of the 40mm guns sat in the pointer and trainer seats or along the base of the gun tubs. Lights from the shore were disorienting, and small boats went up and down the river, most of them dark as the night.

Jonah rolled into his rack, fully clothed with his pants still stuffed into his socks, his boots on his feet. He stared up to the canvas of the rack above him and counted the grommets. They were spaced every 4 inches; he divided four inches into 72; multiplied by two; added the grommets along the width; times two. He couldn't sleep. He felt his brain and body were in an uncontrolled state of agitation. He visualized his arms and legs blown off, only stumps remaining. The intense fear started to overwhelm him. His heart rate increased. He felt more out of control than that day he climbed down into the generator room, into the heat and the flames. He could sense the energy being sucked out of him. A messenger came through the compartment with the beam of his flashlight sweeping back and forth, looking for the people he needed to wake for the change of the watch. Jonah knew that in a few seconds the bright light would glare into his face and a hand would grab his boot and shake it. He thought that having someone shake his foot was the worst possible way to wake up imaginable; to prevent that sudden shock, he swung his legs over the side of the rack and went up to the main deck.

The dawn was trying to break through a multitude of long horizontal clouds, the sun just beginning to glow onto the puddles of water on the deck. The heat was still ever present, but there was a slight relief, a tinge of cooler air from the strong breeze. Jonah lit a cigarette in his cupped hands and leaned against the railing, looking down into the waves of black water slapping alongside the ship.

Mills walked toward him with an M1 slung on his shoulder; he took a few steps and looked down into the water, took another few steps and looked down again. "Hey, Wynchester!" he called out. "Beautiful morning ain't it?" he said gazing out toward the growing light and the village off the port side. "You know, I think I'd like to come back here someday. Yea, come back and really take a look around." Jonah didn't acknowledge him. He didn't even see the village. His rattled brain and tired eyes just stared down into the brown water, seeing but not seeing. "Yea, I'd like to get back here and explore this place," Mills continued. "Maybe some day after the war is over," and Mills turned and looked at Jonah, seeing his face clearly for the first time in the growing light. "Man, you okay?" he asked examining Jonah's red eyes and wrinkled shirt. "You okay?"

Jonah looked up with a painful expression, and he threw the cigarette over the side. "Yea, I'm as fresh as a daisy." He walked aft to the chow line where people were laughing and joking, scraping serving spoons through lumpy scrambled eggs and burnt potatoes, picking up multiple slices of congealed bacon and barely toasted white bread, and filling mugs with ice cubes from the *Yoshida Tractor Company's* one-ton ice machine.

With the dawn, there was a visible relief; the darkness was slowly being replaced by a yellow light. What people could now see in the low light was no longer as frightening as what they couldn't see in the dark. Everyone started to breathe again. Tired eyes and faces looked out to the river, now brightening, growing hotter again, the sun now clearly above the green horizon in the east. More PBRs went by upstream and disappeared into another intense rain squall that blasted across the ship and then moved rapidly away. More heat and humidity.

There was no respite, no moment of relaxation. Before the sun was three degrees above the horizon the ship set the Special Sea & Anchor Detail, and once again proceeded upstream. The scenery went by unchanging: green shores, brown water, sampans, water buffalo, villages, always heading upstream.

※※

Twenty miles from the Cambodian border they entered a much narrower tributary of the delta and made a long sweeping turn to port, and then headed downstream for the first time, the fast moving current carrying them along for another 50 miles, finally approaching the beach at Can Tho at mid day.

For a change they made an uneventful beaching; this time into black sticky ooze perpendicular to the river's current. The engines were kept at a slow forward speed, the propellers continually pushing the ship's bow into the beach, and the stern anchor was out, preventing the stern from swinging downstream with the current. As soon as the bow ramp was down, Mills drove the green giant out of the tank deck with the first pallet of cement, soon to be followed with more cement, steel beams and the wooden crates containing the tens of thousands of rounds of ammunition. Perforated steel Marston mats had been laid down over the mud, creating an artificial surface on the shore. The green giant made its way out the bow doors with its huge 4x4 wheels rolling onto the steel matting, went effortlessly up the slope and stacked the pallets alongside the dirt road where dozens of 2-1/2-ton army trucks were impatiently waiting to carry the loads to the airfield.

"Wynchester!" Jonah turned from watching the green giant to see Sanders walking out through the bow doors; Smitty, carrying a leather mail bag, followed close behind the gunnery officer. "Get the pickup," Sanders ordered. "Drive Smith to the base post office so he can get this mail out, pronto!"

"Yes, sir! How do we get to the base?"

"Take the road that way," Sanders pointed. "It's about two miles."

"Yes, sir," and they climbed into the truck. Jonah slipped the transmission into 4-wheel drive and started up the muddy river bank, the big pick-up bouncing and jumping along the wash-board surface of the Marston mats. They turned and headed west, passing scores of Vietnamese civilians, ox-drawn carts, people on bicycles, a mother and her six children walking along the edge of the narrow dirt road, and the occasional South Vietnamese Army troops. After a mile they came to a large sign bolted to a telephone pole, and stopped to read the hand-painted red and black message:

WARNING

Attention all U.S. and free world personnel...

NO travel beyond this point

during the hours of darkness

without contacting PHONG DINH Advisor Team.

Telephone CAN THO Military 2215.

"Man, this place gives me the heebie-jeebies," Smitty said. "Can you imagine being out here at night? In the dark?:

"Not me," Jonah added.

Jonah noticed Smitty's sweating red face, the flak vest pressing down on him, his fearful eyes looking at the tall grass and a burned-out hooch alongside the road. An old Vietnamese man, his skin wrinkled and hanging from his arms, smiled at them with a toothless grin and said something they couldn't understand.

"Let's get the hell out'a here," Smitty said.

"You don't like this nice green piece of paradise?" Jonah laughed and jagged the gear shift into 1st, accelerating the big truck up the dusty ruts. Further up the road a jeep came around a bend and headed toward them with a cloud of dust flowing behind. Jonah instinctively moved his hand to his .45, his face growing immediately alert, and he brought the truck to a slow stop and looked out the window as the driver, an Army sergeant, put his hand out and halted the jeep next to them.

"How 'ya doing today?" Jonah asked in a smiling cowboy drawl.

The sergeant in the jeep examined the haze gray navy truck and the two sailors. "Where the hell you going?" he asked with a look of suspicion. A corporal sat in the passenger seat holding an M16, the barrel pointing skyward, the butt resting on the seat between his legs.

"How do we get to the post office?"

"Post office?"

"Yea, you got a post office on the base, ain't you?"

The sergeant shook his head as if he didn't believe what he was hearing. "Let me see your ID," he ordered through teeth that were clenched around a short cigar. Every word he spoke created a little cloud of smoke that rose over his head and then drifted downwind.

Jonah noticed the name 'Baum' stenciled on the soldier's freshly starched uniform shirt, and the multitude of stripes on his sleeve. Jonah wasn't familiar with army insignias, and he wasn't sure what the three stripes above a diamond and three stripes below signified, but it appeared as if the soldier must be somebody of rank; after all he was wearing that clean uniform and driving a jeep with another guy riding shotgun. Jonah reached into his tight trouser pocket, pulled out his wallet and handed the sergeant his ID through the open window.

The sergeant examined the ID, then looked up at Jonah. "What the hell is a GM-2?" he asked.

"Gunner's Mate, 2nd Class," Jonah answered. "E-5," he added, thinking that might be helpful.

"E-5?" the sergeant asked, inspecting Jonah out of the corner of his eyes.

"Right," Jonah said. "E-5."

"Humph," the sergeant mumbled, looking at the two sailors as if they were insignificant larvae. He handed the ID back to Jonah.

"So, how do we get to the post office?" Jonah asked again.

"You really need to go there?"

"Yea, we do."

"Well, then; continue on this road the way you're going for another mile or so," the sergeant pointed. "And when you come to a fork, you'll see a sign pointing to the right, to the base. Take that right fork. The main gate will be about another quarter-mile. You can't miss it."

"Thanks."

"No problem. Hey, you guys from one of those LST boats?"

"Yea, *USS Winchester County*," Jonah answered. "We just arrived at the beach."

"What's the cargo?"

"Cement, steel I-beams, lumber, some ammo."

"Any booze?"

Jonah laughed. "Ha ha. You kidding me?"

"Yea, I didn't think so," the sergeant said with a discouraged look.

"And, by the way, it ain't a *boat*," Jonah explained. "It's a *ship!*"

"Oh yea? A ship? Well, thanks for straightening me out with that unimportant detail."

"No problem." Jonah laughed.

"So, you boys be careful, 'ya hear?" the sergeant said. "Keep your eyes open. And don't get lost doing no sightseeing; if Charlie catches you, he'll cut you up into little pieces for his stew pot," the sergeant grinned and popped the clutch. The jeep bounced forward and went down the road leaving a cloud of dust blowing into the pickup.

❧❧

The deck gang worked nonstop through the night, unloading the cargo one pallet at a time, the green giant roaring through the tank deck, going out the bow doors and up the Marston mats to the road. The army trucks struggled away with full loads and then returned empty, ready for another pallet of cement or more steel beams. The pace was relentless with the sounds from the fork truck's motor echoing through the cavernous tank deck and the ship's engines rumbling and continually nudging the bow into the mud. Lights along the main deck and 01 level pierced through the night and those on guard duty with the M1s and machine guns carefully watched the beach and peered down into the black water. Tired gun crews were relieved with fresh faces; Dorsey's galley baked through the early morning hours; the sun came up in the east just as Homer had jokingly predicted, and by noon the ship had exchanged its entire cargo for a miasma of black sticky mud and white cement dust that was now tracked all through the tank deck and along the main deck. Biagotti dejectedly stared at the filth, shook his head and mumbled a long 13-syllable continuous string of cuss words.

At noon the empty ship backed off the beach with a series of smooth, deft engine and rudder orders, reeled in the stern anchor and swung her stern neatly downstream. She then went ahead on both engines with the pilot guiding them back upstream against the strong current, through the brown water, alongside the lush emerald shore, past creeping sampans and grazing water buffaloes, and by 1800 were once again anchored off Se Dec. They had survived the trip to Can Tho, unloaded the cargo, and made it back to Se Dec, all without incident. The relief throughout the ship was palpable. They were going to be okay after all.

※※

As the ship rode to her anchor, Beaufort stood his watch on the conn, leaning against the radar repeater and looking sleepily around him. There was a hint of pink sky beginning to show on the eastern horizon partially hidden by patches of ground fog, allowing just enough light for him to see the lookouts at the outboard ends of the wing. Pike was leaning against the signal lamp, smoking a cigarette. A young seaman, barely awake, had the sound powered phones. The lights on the 01 level and along the main deck shined intensely bright into the black water. All was well with the world. Beaufort yawned, took another sip of the bitter coffee, and wished he was back in that French restaurant in Saigon. He turned his wrist toward the red light and checked the time on his watch: 0520. Looking through the large green-tinted windows toward the bow of the ship he could just make out the 40mm gun crew; two were in the seats, some were standing; most were sitting on the base of the tub. They all looked very tired. A flash of intense bright light suddenly blinded him. The concussion and sound followed almost immediately.

The Cathedral shuddered.

Those on watch deep in the engine room felt the powerful shudder and instinctively grabbed anything within reach. Beckers was thrown off balance and fell to the deck plates. He looked around him in surprise, wondering what had happened. He instinctively scanned the engine control gauges on the bulkhead above him; the RPMs, temperatures, pressures, all looked normal. Then he noticed the snow, the snow falling from the overhead. But it wasn't snow; it was the asbestos cladding from the pipes overhead. Tiny flakes of asbestos were slowly falling through the air.

The crew of the forward 40mm gun were the closest to the explosion. Brickey and the others were in the tub trying to stay awake as the fog's water droplets covered them with a fine mist. Brickey leaned against the port side of the gun tub, looking into the fog and the few lights twinkling from the village. He was thinking about Natsume; her funny mouth with that gap in her teeth, her pixie face, her diminutive body, and her strong hands. And her laugh. That laugh made him smile and he shook his head as the emotion rose from his gut into his chest. As he was lost in his thoughts about Natsume he didn't notice the Viet Cong in the water floating a bomb downstream. The swimmer was heading for the bow doors, but the fog had disoriented him; 40 feet from the ship the bomb's detonator brushed against the anchor chain and an immense blaze of light flashed out as the explosion shattered the chain's 10-inch links. It also vaporized the swimmer's head and shoulders; what was left of him trailed a watery stream of blood as it sank down and down, slowly coming to rest among the ship's anchor chain, now lying along the river's muddy bottom

In the aft 40mm gun tub Jonah was lighting a cigarette when the explosion occurred. He reached out to grab the barrel of the gun and steady himself, but instead he tripped over someone sitting on the base of the tub. Struggling to stand, he looked out to starboard and heard faint, dull sounds: Phu-Phu-Phu-Phu-Phu. The sounds seemed to be coming from somewhere on the shore. Phu-Phu-Phu-Phu. Then he saw pin-pricks of light coming from the beach and heard the distinctive BING-BING-BING-BING of lead hitting steel somewhere forward of him.

On the conn, Beaufort thought someone had taken a picture of him with a giant flash bulb; his eyes saw white dots and what appeared to be sparklers flying through the air. What the hell is that, he asked himself. The sparklers were hitting the forward gun tub and along the side of the ship. They were also flying across the main deck. What's going on? Why would anyone be throwing sparklers? BING-BING-BING-BING! Something impacted into the 02 level below him, and he ducked.

Jonah now realized what he was seeing. Tracers. They were tracers coming from over there, on the beach, from that dark section along the northern shoreline. He watched, transfixed, as the tracers arced out from the blackness, their trajectory flattening out as they crossed the river, and then lowering ever so slightly before hitting the side of the ship. Then he saw tracers coming from another spot. And another. There was more than one gun. There were lots of guns on that shoreline! Then he heard rounds hitting the wooden hull of the LCVP hanging from the davits. Thud-Thud-Thud.

Beaufort was now wide awake and understood what was happening. The red night lights in the conn suddenly went out and it became pitch dark inside the small confined space. But he reached for the microphone. He knew where it was, where it must be, groping in the darkness for where it should be. His hand frantically moved along the bulkhead, searching, searching. He found it. Then he dropped it. "Dammit!" he yelled and went down on his knees, both hands now moving along the deck, feeling for the mic. He found it again and this time held it tight. He pushed the button. "NOW HEAR THIS!" he screamed uncontrollably and paused. Then somehow through the chaos he thought he'd better slow down; Beaufort, you better speak clearly or nobody's going to understand you. "Now hear this!" he repeated a little slower.

"General Quarters, General Quarters! All hands man your battle stations! This is not a drill! This is NOT a drill! General Quarters!" and he dropped the mic back onto the deck.

The crew in the forward gun tub had instantly gone to their stations with Brickey screaming. "Man the gun! Man the gun! Poldolski, shoot! Shoot over there!" and he pointed toward the flashes on the beach to starboard. BING-BING-BING-BING-BING! Rounds from the Viet Cong guns sprayed along the starboard side of the gun tub, sending splinters of lead and steel into the air. Poldolski jumped into the pointer seat, the others went to their places, and without waiting for any orders from anyone, they started shooting; shooting and loading and shooting towards the flashes of light on the northern beach. The strong lights on the main deck suddenly when out and it was dark in the tub now, the only light coming from the flashes of the firing gun as the 40mm rounds went screaming across the river, their 3,000 feet per second velocity and flat trajectory sending the projectile to the target in the blink of an eye.

In the aft gun tub, Jonah noticed something, something strange. He couldn't figure out what was happening: the southern shoreline seemed to be getting closer. But why? He didn't know the anchor chain had parted, he didn't know the ship was now drifting downwind and sideways to the current. It was then he heard Beaufort call general quarters and the forward 40mm gun started firing as he watched the beach coming closer. Now tracers were coming at them from the near shore off the port side. The VC were now firing at the ship from both shorelines. "Man the gun!" he screamed. "Man the gun! Mills, train to port, train to port!" and he frantically pushed people into their positions. "Shoot at the flashes!"

In the engine room Chief Beckers finally had the different pieces of the puzzle put together; he had felt the ship shudder, he saw the asbestos flakes falling through the air, and then he heard

Beaufort's panicky call of General Quarters. And now he could faintly hear the 40mm guns and recognized their short, quick, deep resonating, repetitive firing sequence. Boom-Boom-Boom-Boom. And then he heard the .50 calibers with their instantaneous rattling, their 500 rounds per minute rate of fire creating a continuous clatter: ChungChungChungChung. He turned from looking at the control board. "Stand by to answer all engine orders!" he yelled over the noise of idling engines, electric motors and reduction gears. "Wake up, you people!" he screamed. "Get to your stations! NOW!" and he looked up toward the repeater, the repeater for the engine order telegraph, watching for the arrow to change position, waiting for the order to come down from the bridge, the order for the engines to go from *Standby* to *Ahead*, or *Back*. He waited, impatiently waited, his left foot bouncing on the deck plates as he looked at the EOT, willing with all his might for it to move, waiting for some kind of action. But nothing happened.

Beaufort moved aside as the captain came rushing up the ladder, the big man's body bent over, his feet scrambling up the steel steps. He arrived on the conn out of breath, gasping. "What's the situation JB?" he yelled at Beaufort. BING-BING-BING! Multiple rounds impacted into the conn's large port-side window, instantly shattering it into thousands of pieces. Shards of glass flew in all directions. Beaufort instinctively leaned away. He had his back to the window and as the flak vest took most of the punishment, the back of his neck below the helmet turned red. He fell to his knees.

Jonah's 40mm gun was now incessantly pummeling the very close southern shoreline. As Mills trained the gun left and right, Ross was in the pointer seat depressing the aim-point below the horizontal; the rounds screamed out the twin barrels and instantly hit their targets. The pace was unrelenting; the four-round clips were continuously loaded into the feeders, more ammo was passed to the loaders, others lifted clips up to the tub, and runners brought more rounds from the magazine. BOOM-BOOM-BOOM-BOOM! Within this Dante-esque scene the gun's twin barrels ceaselessly fired into the beach, and with each barrel's flash, the gun crew was silhouetted for a fraction of a second, then they would be in the dark again; flash-silhouette; dark; flash-silhouette; dark. Tracers stitched all through the air with streaking stabs of light; 40mm rounds going out to the beach; more tracers from the VC's smaller caliber guns coming back to strike the ship. BING-BING-BING-BING. For a brief part of a second within this confusion and melee, Jonah's frantic mind somehow reflected on how glad he was they had sighted the gun back in Pearl; then his thought was interrupted by rounds hitting the anchor winch below him. BING-BING-BING!

Homer, standing at his .50 caliber machine gun on the port side, was only 150 feet from the beach as the ship continued drifting backward. His face was screwed up tight, his teeth were grinding, and the sweat dripped out from under his helmet as he relentlessly swept the shoreline with fire. Every muzzle flash of light on the beach instantly received an answer back from his gun. CHUNG-CHUNG-CHUNG-CHUNG! "Take that you fuckers!!!" he screamed.

Up on the conn, the captain yelled over the noise. "Are you okay, JB?"

Beaufort reached his hand to the back of his neck and felt the moisture. "I'm okay," he said looking at his hand covered in dark red, then he puked.

"Pike!" the captain yelled "Pike! Help Mister Beaufort!" Pike was crouched down behind the sandbags; his eyes were wide open in fear. He started crawling along the wing deck toward Beaufort.

The captain looked around him, at the black river, the black shoreline and the tracers coming at them from both beaches, and the tracers from the ship's guns going back out toward the shoreline. Then he got his bearings and finally noticed the ship was no longer at anchor; she was swinging in the current, the southern shore growing perilously close. "I have the conn!" he yelled. "All ahead one-third! Left full rudder!" he shouted into the voice tube.

Beckers heard the bells clang and turned to watch the pointer on the engine order telegraph swing from *Standby* to *All Ahead One-Third*. He punched a fist into his open hand. "Finally!" he yelled. "All ahead one-third!" he screamed to the enginemen at the throttles. Beckers watched the dials; he watched the RPMs climbing, the pointers on the pressure gauges moving. The engine's RPMs came up, the reduction gears were shifted, the propeller shafts started turning, the propellers spinning. His feet could feel the familiar vibration in the deck plates as the propellers started taking a bite in the water; it was a beautiful sensation he was entirely familiar with, and he smiled. "Yea, baby," he whispered, talking to the engines, cajoling the reduction gears. "Come on baby, you can do it. Come on," he whispered louder, willing the machinery into a state of smooth, perfect synchronicity. Then he felt a tremendous, violent vibration.

The captain felt the same vibration, turned and looked aft. The stern of the ship had drifted right into the tall grass of the shoreline, and watery mud was churning out from under the counter, the propellers eating into the beach, the blades bending out of shape as if they were made of soft putty. "All engines stop!" he yelled into the voice tube. The strong wind and current continued to swing the ship; as the bow turned downstream, the stern followed and the propellers oozed out of the mud into the deeper water.

With the growing sunlight the firing from the shore suddenly stopped. As quickly as the chaos started, it stopped. The pink sunlight in the east diffused into a soft yellow, and with the rising sun the Viet Cong left. They slunk back into the tall reeds and thick palm groves, they went through the rice paddies and stands of bamboo, and leaving their dead and wounded behind along the shore, they disappeared once again, back into the dark, dense green jungle.

Jonah stood in the aft gun tub, breathing deeply, looking down at the hundreds of empty 40mm brass shell casings jumbled across the deck. He also saw the gun crew, their bloodshot eyes and exhausted faces, their surprise of having come through the firefight unscathed. Everyone had survived, and they all started congratulating each other. He quickly climbed down the ladder and ran forward along the main deck, slapping Homer on the back for a job well done. Homer, with a big grin on his face, stood amongst hundreds of empty .50 caliber shells. Jonah continued running forward, smiling, feeling the elation of having survived the firefight; he couldn't wait to share his excitement with Brickey and the forward gun crew. And then he saw Doc Slaughter and several other sailors lowering a Stokes stretcher down from the forward gun tub. Doc had a grim look on his face; his mouth was turned down and his forehead was crowned with wrinkles. Holy Jesus, Jonah thought, what's going on? Oh, no, God, no, and his heart rose into his throat as he looked into the stretcher and saw Brickey; the front of his shirt was ripped open and someone had applied a battle dressing to his chest. Jonah grabbed the stretcher's handrail, and as he helped lower the Stokes, he looked down into Brickey's pale face, the blood soaking his shirt, more blood coagulating in his hair. They ran across the main deck as fast as they could carry him, the four pairs of hands, Mendoza, Poldolski, Ross and Jonah, gripping the stretcher rails with Doc running close behind. They carried Brickey over the shin knocker, hurried into the deck house with Ross yelling "Gangway! Gangway!" and went cautiously down the steep ladder into the sickbay where they gently lifted him onto the examining table.

"Ross, Poldolski!" Slaughter pointed out the door.

"Mendoza: plasma, quick," Slaughter said and he immediately went to work: he inserted a needle into Brickey's arm, took the bag of plasma from Mendoza, hung it from a hook on the overhead, connected the tube, started the drip. Then he cut off Brickey's shirt with a pair of trauma shears and Jonah saw the small hole in Brickey's chest as Slaughter replaced the battle dressing. "Doza, help me turn him...just a little," Slaughter said and they turned Brickey gently onto his side. Slaughter bent down and looked at the dressing on his back; the corpsman's mouth opened slightly and he inhaled. "Lay him back down, gently now. Put this pillow under his head, prop him up a little. And get those blankets on him."

Jonah watched Slaughter and asked simply, "Doc?"

Slaughter looked back with a knowing stare. "Talk to him."

"Brickey," Jonah said leaning over, close to the young gunner's face. "How you doing?"

"We did good, Jonah," Brickey said in a horse whisper, staring up but not seeing Jonah. "We got those bastards."

"Yea, you did, Billy," Jonah answered, trying to maintain his self-control as he looked down at Brickey. "You got 'em good. Real good."

"They never stood a chance against us." Brickey's voice was soft and scratchy, his dry mouth barely able to get the words out.

Jonah nodded, his emotion suddenly preventing him from speaking.

"You still there, Jonah?" Brickey asked, turning his head.

"Keep still, Brickey," Slaughter said, wiping blood off Brickey's face. "Don't move."

"I'm right here, Billy," Jonah struggled to answer. "I'm right here with you."

"Our guns stopped 'em cold," Brickey continued, staring toward the overhead.

"Yea they did."

"We really did a number on them."

"Yea you did."

"I don't feel so good."

"You're gonna be fine, Billy, just fine."

"Don't leave me, Jonah!" Brickey lifted a shaking hand and Jonah, tears in his eyes, took it into his and held it in a firm grip.

"I've got you, Billy. I'm right here, man."

"I want to see Natsume again."

"You will. We'll be going back to Sasebo. You'll see her real soon."

"I need to see her, and little Katsuko."

"Don't worry, you will. And when we get back, we'll go up to that nice spot, way above those islands, and have another picnic."

"And the onsen. I feel so cold right now, I want to sit in the warm onsen."

"We'll be there before you know it."

"Doc," Charlie Crane was standing in the doorway. "The chopper should be here any minute." Jonah saw the distressed look on the XO's face; he had never seen Crane look that way before.

Slaughter acknowledged the XO with a nod of his head.

"Jonah?"

"I'm right here Billy."

"You remember that great dinner we had in Naples?"

"Yea, I sure do. You drank a lot of Negroni."

"And the New Year's Eve party at The Cesspool?"

"Yea, that was some night."

"After you left *McMann* I never imagined we'd be on the same ship again."

"Yea," and Jonah's emotions now overflowed. He felt the pressure in his chest heating up, and his face turned sorrowful; his eyes glistened as he began to lose control.

"I think we got some work to do on that 40," Brickey whispered.

"Yea, we'll take care of it, Billy. Don't you worry."

"It needs some paint."

"I'm sure it does."

"And the sights will probably need aligning."

"Probably."

"You're the best, Jonah. I've never worked with anybody as good as...EEUHAAA!" and Brickey started gurgling blood from his mouth. "Jonah?" he said through the frothy blood. Slaughter immediately raised Brickey's head.

"Hang on, Billy! Hang on! I got you!" Jonah was starting to shake gripping Brickey's hand as more blood gurgled from his mouth. "Hang on Billy! Oh, God, don't let him die on me! Billy, dammit! Don't you die on me!"

They could now hear the helicopter; the Huey's engine screaming, the rotor blades thrumming in its distinctive pulsating blade slap, hovering over the main deck two levels above them.

Brickey's chest suddenly arched upward. More blood frothed from his mouth and then he slowly settled back down on the table again; quiet, not moving. Slaughter pulled a pen-sized flashlight from his shirt pocket and aimed the beam into Brickey's eyes. Then he felt the pulse, and put his stethoscope against the carotid artery and listened intently.

"Doc, the chopper's here!" Poldolski suddenly appeared in the doorway.

Jonah watched Slaughter achingly stand up from the table. The corpsman had a tired, defeated look on his face. "Don't need it now," he said quietly, and he laid the stethoscope in a drawer and gently closed it shut.

ABOUT R. D. WALL

R. D. Wall served in the U.S. Navy in the Atlantic and Pacific Fleets, including a year aboard an LST in the Mekong Delta and coastal waters of Vietnam. After the Navy he was a sports reporter, and then worked as a sailmaker and yacht broker while also involved in the design, building, equipping and sailing of one-design and large ocean racing yachts. He lives with his wife Jo, and dachshund Saltydog, among the oak and pine woods of north Florida.

You can reach him at:
    Web: www.rdwallauthor.com
    Email: author@rdwallauthor.com

Look for CHINA SEA ANTHEM, Book #3 in the Jonah Wynchester Series of Vietnam War Novels, summer of 2019.

Made in the USA
Lexington, KY
15 April 2018